Andrew Masterson is an author and journalist. *The Second Coming: The Passion of Joe Panther* is his third novel. His first, *The Last Days: The Apocryphon of Joe Panther* (1998) won the 1999 Ned Kelly Award for Best First Crime Novel and was published in the UK the same year. His second, *The Letter Girl* (1999), was shortlisted for that year's Aurealis speculative fiction award. When he is not writing, he is generally drinking Guinness.

THE
SECOND
COMING

THE PASSION OF JOE PANTHER

ANDREW MASTERSON

flamingo

An imprint of HarperCollins*Publishers*

Flamingo
An imprint of HarperCollins*Publishers*

First published in Australia in 2000
by HarperCollins*Publishers* Pty Limited
ABN 36 009 913 517
A member of the HarperCollins*Publishers* (Australia) Pty Limited Group
http://www.harpercollins.com.au

Copyright © Andrew Masterson 2000

This book is copyright.
Apart from any fair dealing for the purposes of private study, research,
criticism or review, as permitted under the Copyright Act, no part may
be reproduced by any process without written permission.
Inquiries should be addressed to the publishers.

HarperCollins*Publishers*
Level 13, 201 Elizabeth Sreet, Sydney, NSW 2000, Australia
31 View Road, Glenfield, Auckland 10, New Zealand
77–85 Fulham Palace Road, London W6 8JB, United Kingdom
Hazelton Lanes, 55 Avenue Road, Suite 2900, Toronto, Ontario M5R 3L2
and 1995 Markham Road, Scarborough, Ontario M1B 5M8, Canada
10 East 53rd Street, New York NY 10022, USA

National Library of Australia Cataloguing-in-Publication data:

Masterson, Andrew, 1961- .
    The second coming: the passion of Joe Panther.
    ISBN 0 7322 6804 4.
    1. Private investigators - Western Australia - Perth -
    Fiction. I. Title.
A823.3

Cover illustration: Adam Yazxhi
Typeset by HarperCollins in 10.5/14 Sabon
Printed in Australia by Griffin Press Pty Ltd on 70gsm Ensobelle

5 4 3 2 1   12

For Sahm, as always.
And Jane. And Alison.
And the angels of the West:
Ms Greenwood and Ms Southgate.

The city in this novel is seen through the eyes of its narrator.
Best, then, to regard it as fiction. Any resemblance to
persons living, dead or unsure is purely coincidental.

In the last days of the world false prophets and
    deceivers will abound,
sheep will be perverted and turn into wolves,
and love will turn to hate . . .

The Didache (First Century CE)

If we were, for a moment, tempted to regard these
    records
rather in the light of the nightmare ravings of a
    diseased brain,
or the crazy imaginings of some narcotised wretch of
    over-weird
humour, we should be quickly undeceived.

From the 1903 Preface to *Tortures and Torments of the Christian Martyrs*, Fr Antonio Gallonio (1591)

CHAPTER 1

I knew she was dead as soon as I woke up.

I lay still a moment, eyes open, brain yet to engage in the claustrophobic shadow of the narrow cul-de-sac. The concrete pressed against my forehead, shoulder and hip, the dust of its erosion dancing sluggishly to the cautious music of my breath.

Somewhere close by I could hear Kennedy singing 'If You Were The Only Girl In The World', almost accepting the tenuous guidance of his karaoke tape. That told me, at least, where I was, which laneway bore my unforgiving manger. The ground felt cold through the rumpled fabric of my suit. The air was warm, though, bringing to life the latent perfume of the restaurant garbage bins and the urine streaks down the flaking wall. It was still dark in the tiny right-of-way at the back of the buildings: dark and sheltered enough, at any rate, to veil its contents from the passers-by on the sun-struck street.

Mid-morning, then.

Kennedy's voice cracked. He blundered on. Had I lifted my head and peered around the brickwork I could have seen him: stood there, as always, in the mouth of the lane, the tape deck strapped to his flimsy clearance-store luggage carrier. He would be in his tired black lounge suit, his suit of many fears, hunched slightly from embarrassment, singing at the ground, looking neither at the people on the street nor his little wooden begging bowl. The acute agony of his extroversion would have been plain, the fright of his posture which made pedestrians first laugh, then drop a dollar in his bowl and hurry away, shamed by their own cruelty.

Had I lifted my head, yes, these wonders to enjoy. I did not, however. I remained immobile, eyes fixed on the woman who, if the burden of life had been still with her, would have radiated heat so close my cheek might have been warmed by her vitality. She lay, in easy sprawl, just inches from my face. Had wakefulness not come and dreams lied of comfort — as they do, as they have always done — I might have rolled on my flagstone berth and lifted my arm across her trunk with the casual certainty of a lover seeking reassurance.

I was glad I hadn't done so, all things considered.

I looked at her more closely, sorting her shape from the camouflage of shadow. Her back was towards me: a Stussy Sista muscle-top, from its label near the neck, dark blue, I fancied, gripping the curve of her spine and the crests of her shoulders. A band of tanned skin showed between the base of the tee-shirt and the waistband of her jeans, cupped out by the angle of her back, the elastic of white underpants just visible in its dale. Couldn't see her feet; nor her arms, folded or flung in front of her. The hair was blonde and short, at least at the back, square across the neck, and maybe oiled.

The main thing I could see, its focus unstable because of its proximity, was the bone handle of the knife. I assumed a blade, twice invisible because of angle and flesh, a blade large, a hunter's brutal gutting blade, buried to the hilt. Its point of entry was just above the clothing, right beneath, I thought, the fifth cervical vertebra. It would have severed the spinal cord, rent ligament and muscle, heading down through, perhaps, the brachiating nexus of the trachea. Her end must have been silent, swift, from behind, as if she knelt in futile prayer, mercy ungranted.

Kennedy finished his song, launched stammering and uncertain into 'The Moon And New York City'. Dead bodies I can handle, even first thing in the morning. Schlock Tin Pan Alley is an abomination undeserved.

I sat up, leaning back against the wall, and pulled the creased greyness of my suit here and there, checking, looking, feeling for damp. There was no blood on the fabric, and none on my hands. The killing was not my work. I'd been pretty sure it wasn't, but the confirmation was nice.

In the gloom, there seemed little blood on the ground: too little to make a sticky gleam, and far less than the crusting spread soaked across the Stussy would have suggested. Here, then, was the place of her discard, but not, it seemed, of her death. Who had lain her here, and when? Had she been dumped, silent, while I slept through the night? Or had I, oblivion come at last, lain down beside her and slumbered peaceful with the dead? Had I known her dead and sought comfort in her coldness? Had I envied her her finity?

Forever gone, what memories had played. Had I drunk a bottle of Jamesons on top of a shit-load of Emu Export? No memories there, either, but assumptions were certainly possible.

Whatever. I stood up, steadying myself against the wall, waiting for the spin to slow. She wasn't my responsibility, whoever she was. Never had been, you want to get right down to it. None of them are. I stepped over her body and walked towards the light. Yea, though I walk through the alley, I will fear no evil.

Kennedy. Now he was a problem, and not just from a tonal point of view. He would stand there at the head of the lane all day, as he always did. As the sun rose, come lunchtime, its rays would reach the nether parts and there warm and illuminate the horror it held. Kennedy would see it when he nicked down for a pee — or hear the cries of a kitchenhand finding hell in his smoke break — and wet himself with fear. The police would be summoned, and the busker, pale at the vulgarity before him, would remember that, yes, mid-morning he had seen me, walking from the shadows.

Behold, I come as a suspect.

I didn't need it. My leaving would be soon. I walked up behind him. 'Kennedy,' I said to his neck, voice low.

He stopped singing immediately. The tape continued, all jaunty strings and brass, its disconnected poverty revealed.

'Switch it off. Don't turn around.'

He bent down, did as he was told. Standing again, his shoulders tensed, his neck hunched behind his frayed black collar, as if expecting a blow.

'Do you know who I am?' I whispered.

He nodded. Twice. Fast. 'I've no money, Joe, look ...'

'How long have you been dry now, Kennedy?'

'F-four years,' he managed. 'All but.'

'I know where you live. Show's over for today. Go home and stay there, off the street.'

'But —'

It was reflex, not bravery. The smited are not brave.

'If I hear you've been out today,' I continued, quiet, sure, liturgical, 'there will come to your room an angel bearing gifts of malt and juniper: there, placed resplendent on your bed; there, your prayers and fears answered in liquid sweet and blessing. Are you a strong man, Kennedy? Can you resist the temptation of fire?'

He shuddered visibly. I am within him. I hear his cry.

'Love me,' I added, 'and I will slake your thirst.'

He grabbed his little trolley, head down, buttocks clenched, and hurried off up the street.

Thus has it always been. Offer them what they want, and they run away in fright.

I walked in the other direction, not glancing back, heading home. Another night in a laneway. Another night ended in blank accident and circumstance. Another night of trying to force an end that will not, has never, won't ever, come to restful pass.

I hate my father. I have no feelings for you. Many times have I died in your name, unbidden, wishing only for eternal night and the diligent attentions of worms and decay. Many times confounded and back.

And now, once more, I have returned.

I walk among you, your sins in my heart, your blood on my hands.

The light from the garden flooded profane into the musty fug of the hallway as the front door opened with a squeal of neglect. I closed it behind me and the shadows reclaimed, as always.

Mrs Warburton and Nessie were in the front room, the pretentiously titled drawing room. Thin, horizontal bands of light poured through the narrow gaps in the brown-stained venetians. The women seemed bound and gagged by a zealous sun, hostages long forgotten, leached of ransom.

Nessie, as always, was sitting in her wheelchair. The old woman's skinny flaking right leg was propped on a footstool. Mrs Warburton, herself at pensionable age, knelt before her, the bandages off, swabbing at the ulcer on the shin.

'You,' said my landlady, not looking up.

Nessie, until that moment possessed of a bearing insensate and boneless, twitched, and lifted her papery head a little more upright. 'You,' she echoed, making the word sound like the accusation of the whipped.

'Ladies,' I acknowledged, and kept walking along the passage.

Mrs Warburton timed herself to perfection, waiting until I had just passed the door.

'Visitor, you had,' she said. 'Didn't he, dear? Had a visitor.'

'Visitor, you had,' parroted Nessie.

This was not good news. Mine is not a house of welcome. For my head is filled with dew, and my locks with the drops of the night.

I looked back around the door. Nessie was staring at the floor, her eyes misted with cataracts. Mrs Warburton, still kneeling, looked straight up into my face. Her right hand held a twist of cottonwool, coated in something unspeakable.

'Who?' I asked.

'That woman, that friend of yours,' replied Mrs Warburton.

'The fat one,' added Nessie with a toothless sneer. 'Been up to no good, that one. You'll see.'

I relaxed a little, knowing who they meant. Enlightenment is not my gig, not since way back, so I didn't bother.

'When?'

'Little hussy, that one,' said Nessie. 'Up to no good.'

'*When*, Mrs Warburton?' My patience is boundless.

'Early, it was. Must have been nine this morning, the minx. Banging on the door. I'd not even got Nessie out of bed yet, had I, dear?'

'My tea wasn't ready,' snapped the old woman.

'Wasn't my fault, though, was it, dear? Wasn't *my* fault, your tea. Was the hussy's fault.'

'Bold as brass,' nodded Nessie. 'Missed my tea.'

'You let her in?' I asked.

Mrs Warburton made a tutting noise, and dabbed at Nessie's ulcer. The old woman didn't seem to notice.

'Let herself in, didn't she? Told her you wasn't here. She wants to know where you are, just like that. All front and no manners that one, you ask me. Well, I said it was none of my business where you were. None of hers either, I told her. Know what she did, then?'

'Tell me,' I said, as if I had an option.

'Pushed!' spat Nessie.

'Hush, dear,' said Mrs Warburton. 'Pushed right past me, she did. Just like that. Right past me, down the passage, started banging your door like there was no tomorrow. Then she shoved something under it and left, never so much as a thanks or goodbye.'

'Missed me tea,' repeated Nessie.

I have lived eternities, and felt another one might well pass before the conversation ended. My head was fogged from the trapped stillness of the air, the perfume of rot, and the slow departure of whisky. 'Any idea what she wanted?'

'Oh no,' exclaimed Mrs Warburton, scandalised. 'Well, I mean, I wouldn't, would I?'

'No, dear,' chimed Nessie. 'Oh, no.'

'I mean, really, none of my business, is it? Is it, dear, none of our business, I said?'

'None of our business,' echoed Nessie. 'Of course it's not.'

I might have smiled, had my mood been better. Instead, I threw my parting line, already knowing the response it would bring. 'Why don't you open a window, let some fresh air in?'

'Can't do *that*,' replied Mrs Warburton, dropping her soiled load and picking up nail scissors to trim the flaking necrosis from Nessie's wound. 'All that pollution. Never know what you'll catch.'

'Germs, dear,' said Nessie. 'You'd catch germs.'

I learned long ago to delegate. I left Mrs Warburton to cleanse the leper, and walked on down to the door of my room, my sanctuary, my shadowed fortress of solitude.

I arrived in Perth, the only city of any size on the west coast of Australia, a couple of years back. Don't worry about the details of the journey: it was just another trek, another pragmatic relocation in a very long line of discontinuous shifts.

Perth is the end of the world, the most isolated city on earth, surrounded by desert and scrub and unforgiving hinterland on three sides, the Indian Ocean on the fourth. For the most part it is neat, clean and prosperous: the globe's leading producer of crooked millionaires. The old call it paradise; the young, hell.

I live in its dark spaces, the parts it hides from itself. I reify its fears, and bring deliverance from suffering. I am everything it reviles, yet it calls my name a million ways. I have come. I have made my mark and left no fingerprints.

In my first days, I set about finding a place to lay my head. In my father's house there are many mansions, but somehow I have never succeeded in making a reservation. For many decades now I have favoured the obscure and the unlikely: old factories, warehouses, places inhospitable from without, empty but for the swirl of motes and the scutter of mice within. Search for me with all your heart and still I shall not be found, for my phone is unlisted, my business cash, my name but a cipher, and all referees dead.

Yet Perth is a small place as cities go, with barely a million souls inside its walls. I like to live hidden within the redundant discard of endeavours long failed, but I soon discovered that here on the rim of the world, for all its sky-scrapered ostentation, such places were few and far between. I seek the company of the poor and destitute, there to spread my love at thirty bucks a cap. There is always truth to be found among the lost; that's why no one ever listens to them. Thus, after barely a week in doorways, when my flock started to accrete, assured my presence was more than fleet, my gifts more than Borax, did I hear of the house, and of Mrs Warburton and Nessie.

The building was a large pre-war bungalow on the edge of the Northbridge entertainment district, a crumbling stucco pile in a garden of stick-dry weeds. It stood next to a car transmission place, a couple of short blocks from the railway line which borders the central business district. Mrs Warburton owned it, went the tales, and for as long as anyone could remember she had shared it with the cantankerous and severally troubled old Ness. Perhaps they were related — that was one interpretation — or perhaps simply strangers strung in mutual need. No one knew. No one ever bothered to ask.

For as long as anyone could remember, too, Mrs Warburton had rented out the back room to lodgers. My timing, for once, was good. It had recently become vacant. It was not, I discovered, a frequent occurrence. For the previous fifteen years the room had been occupied by a solitary man, a minor public servant called Jason Clitheroe. Mr Clitheroe, I read in the back copies of the local paper I found at the library, had kept himself to himself. He had neither friend nor relative to call his own. He worked in a grey partitioned office five days a week, and most nights sat quietly in his room, only going out after dark every couple of months.

He might, indeed, have continued to do so had he not been spotted one night among the shallow sand dunes of Scarborough Beach, miles from home, by an amateur ornithologist out to check some nests.

The twitcher then ran to the police station, where he told the desk sergeant that at first he thought the people he saw were simply lovers in a furtive tryst. It was, after all, the easiest way to explain why they were naked in the sand. Then he had seen the blood, seen a leg spasm, and caught the streetlight glint from something steel in a hand.

When the police raided the house and cracked open Clitheroe's door they found more than the banal detritus of a lonely man. They found eight teeth on the windowsill, three fingers in a Tupperware container, a salad crisper full of hair, an eyeball in a pickled-onion jar, two nipples in tub of margarine and a penis in the Esky. After several days, the forensics team produced some nine distinct DNA profiles, none of them the lodger's. The press dubbed the man the Marquis de Side Order. The prosecutor called him the devil incarnate.

When questioned by the police, Mrs Warburton and Nessie had both maintained they had absolutely no idea that their nice Mr Clitheroe had been stealing young lives and souvenirs.

'None of our business, was it?' Mrs Warburton had stated. 'Poke your nose in other people's business and where would you be?'

'Just goes to show,' Nessie had echoed. 'Never can tell.'

As soon as I heard the story, I knew I had found my temple. If the Antichrist could live there unrevealed for a decade and a half, a couple of years would be no problem for me. I hide in plain sight, protected by the wilful isolation of the mutually addicted, ignored as always.

I adapted. I'm good at adapting.

I turned the lock, pushed open the solid wooden door, and entered my domain. I felt no sense of homecoming, nor safety. When you've been around as long as I have, you realise that all abodes are transitory, and no sanctuary is inviolate. It contained little I would miss when the time came — as it always does — to walk away. Had the interior design been mine, I might have claimed it as my Shaker period. It was not, however. The furniture was leftover from the tenancy of the Marquis, who had evidently been a man of austere tastes as well as funny habits. The single bed had a plain, wooden bedhead, which matched pretty well the grain of the single bentwood chair, tiny escritoire and chest of drawers. The small silvered mirror and the green-stained enamel basin beneath it had both been present since the place was built.

The only things of mine in the room bore the hallmarks of a life of unasked permanence: the transient, the disposable, the ephemeral. A tiny portable television and slightly larger portable music system sat on the floor. In piles around them lay my compact discs, the flowers in my desert hum: Patti Smith, Smashing Pumpkins, Sneaker Pimps, Gang of Four, Cosmic Psychos, Palestrina, Monteverdi and others. Leaning cracked-spined against the wall were my books: the Fathers of the Church: Augustine, Tertullian, Chrysostom, and the lesser bastards they spawned. Beneath the loose floorboard in the corner, my gifts, the sacraments I offer: grams of heroin, amphetamines, some marijuana for myself.

Some people make a lot of money selling smack, I've heard. Not me. I just get by. I never took a vow of poverty. Poverty took a vow of me.

There was a folded piece of paper on the carpet, evidently slipped under the door. I picked it up, knowing its provenance.

where are you, joe? need to speak. urgent. major shit,
i think. i'm at work. ring asap (really). l.

I sighed with annoyance. The plan for the rest of the daylight hours had involved nothing more strenuous than lying on the bed, smoking a joint, and staring at the television until nightfall came and the hungry hit the streets. Now a call had come — a call I would answer, for reasons I preferred not to entertain.

As I left the house, Mrs Warburton was rebandaging the leg and tempting old Nessie with soup. Pea and ham, the one she liked.

'Not fresh, is it?' Nessie was saying, fear and suspicion in her voice. 'Not fresh?'

'Of course not, dear,' replied Mrs Warburton. 'From a can, like always.'

'Can't trust fresh,' continued Nessie. 'Never know what's been sprayed.'

As I shut the front door behind me and stepped out from beneath the brick veranda, the strengthening sun hit me like a promise of deliverance. The phone box was just around the corner. She answered on the second ring.

'It's me.'

'Where were you? I've been —'

'The pub opposite your work. Front bar. Ten minutes.'

I hung up and walked.

I was sitting at a small round table in the Brass Monkey, staring at a glass of Stella Artois and wondering whether having some breakfast first might have been a good idea, when she walked in. The sun was at her back, draping her in a luminous umber corona.

Such has been my life that regarding people through the perspective of time has been merely a recipe for certain disappointment. They all die, eventually. All of them. I must regard, it seems, only from within the safety of an endless present, an eternal moment robbed of future as I am robbed of coveted senescence. I had a beginning, an opening parenthesis of breath, but never its twin to close the aside. I am the alpha; my omega bloody miles away. Nevertheless, as I glanced up at her I couldn't help seeing her stretch over the years. She knew me from way back, and, in her way, was very special to me.

I could have cried at that thought, if tears were still an option. She will pay dearly for my affection. I know that. Nothing will stop it. See the love in my eyes, then discount it.

She used to be called Caroline. I knew her when I used to live in Melbourne. I left her to die. It had been her decision.

13

She did me a favour once, and her request for reward was an end, at last, to her wretched, smack-addicted, destitute life. I gave her five grams, one fit, and walked off to catch a train.

We met again, here, by accident, years later. 'You haven't aged at all, Joe,' she'd said.

'You have,' had been my quiet reply.

I had stared at her that day, worried that perhaps she was not who she claimed to be, but a glamour, a trap, a chimera sent to damage. The Caroline I had known had stalked Smith Street in mismatched Nike and Adidas, shiny with empty aches, hair lank and greasy, a red anger of dermatitic pain despoiling her dead-eyed face. This woman matched the basic physical description, although her frame was fuller, her posture erect, her cheeks round and free of disease. Light shone from her eyes, which no longer darted back and forth, hunting, hunted, begging for change. The hair was cropped short, shaved tight above the ears. Her clothes were of the moment: grey camo singlet, baggy-pocketed black pants and braces, shiny black Docs with bright red laces. I looked down on her as she looked up. Her breath was shallow with the surprise of reunion.

I wondered whether I should kill her. After all, she knew me from before. She knew things. If it was her. If she wasn't her, she was surely my enemy. And if she was her, she was dead already.

'Let me buy you a Jamesons, Joe,' she'd said.

It was her. I held my caution, accepted her offer.

She still drank lemonade, despite the departure years before of the hepatitis that conditioned her towards it. As we drank, she told me her tale. Within an hour of my train pulling out from the station, she said, she had been back in her flat with a fit full of ending and a mind entirely at peace. When she woke up she was in hospital, very disappointed. The perfidy of circumstance being what it is, she had chosen to OD only minutes before the real estate agent had made an unannounced visit in search of arrears.

She was offered rehab when she was strong enough. Not knowing why, she took the option. Over the following six weeks of dry screams, shakes, curses and horror, she decided that life might, just perhaps, be worth attempting again.

'You don't chase that dragon,' she told me. 'The dragon chases you. You can never kill it, just hide and hope it doesn't find you again.'

She knew that if she stayed in Melbourne she would almost certainly make her way back to the dealers, to the spit-covered balloons pried from secret places between teeth, to the tiny baggies of white, and the glinting erotic of syringes and spoons. She grabbed her dole money on her day of release, and hopped on a bus to the other side of the continent, to where she didn't know any junkies, to where the sallow faces would all appear as morbid and repugnant.

She settled, found herself a girlfriend, and put herself through computer training. In time, she found a job, working with Sappho's Sisters, a lesbian counselling service. In time, too, she decided to change her name.

'I came back from the dead,' she had explained. 'I'm not a junkie any more. I do databases and web sites. I renewed myself. It had to happen.'

Lazarette Binary sat down beside me now. She looked deeply troubled. She also looked pregnant. The latter was my fault. The former, I had a feeling, was about to become my problem.

'Gina's missing,' she said.

✝

And thus do things reduce.

Lazarette is not the only one to have changed a name. I have done so many times, countless occasions of subtle shift, linguistic lurch, perhaps five hundred, maybe more, variations on the theme of my burden. Legion are the titles of the son, each a decoy, each a mask. Rarely are they written down, and never on a cheque, a credit slip, a lease or a licence. I have walked through streets and lanes unending since my thirty-third year, innocent in the matters charged, stone guilty in others unimagined. My name protects and condemns in equal measure. I cannot harm my reputation, nor tear the oldest memories apart, though I would shout for joy to see them crumble into hatred and to scorn.

You have done this to me. My name is sometimes taken in vain, more often in vanity. That which Paul the Salesman started, you have yet to finish, yet I (the authority in this matter, not that anyone would listen) would have it end at any moment you desire. More: I would have it never so. I would have my memory purged from time: more possible, I think, than the damage done forgotten. I would have my rest begin.

Still. Not up to me. It never has been. It never was.

'I want you to be the father of the child,' Lazarette said ten months ago. 'I do not love you.'

She and her partner, she explained, were settled and adoring. For the first time in her life she felt as if she had a family. The beginnings of one, at any rate. What was needed was a child to lavish time upon: a child, she said, who would never know the parental cruelty she herself had experienced. Artificial insemination was not an option for gay couples under the law of the state. Mutually sanctioned infidelity was thus the only way.

'Why me?' I had asked, shaking inside.

'Because you'll want no part of it,' she had replied.

'Is that all?'

'No.' She said nothing more. Just then.

So I became Lazarette's back-door man. Literally. Her partner Ayzel, Laz explained, thought it best not to know the identity of the inseminator, to have no cause to look upon a stranger with envy and suspicion. So on the appointed night, determined by Lazarette's ovulatory computation, I entered through the rear door of their house. I was told that Ayzel was in the lounge room, television way up high, wilfully blind and deaf. Laz led me to the spare room, thanked me, eyes down, and pulled me to her.

The first time didn't work. We tried again fifty-two nights later. The evening was warm and humid. Afterwards we lay both naked on the bed, not touching, me smoking a Dunhill.

'You know why you?' she asked suddenly, placing her finger lightly on my arm.

'No,' I replied.

'Because I know you, Joe. I know you now, head to toe. You sold me smack for years. Most people would condemn you for that, but not me, Joe. You didn't feed my addiction; you delivered me from evil. Then you found out who murdered my friend.'

'I found out how to get enough money to blow town,' I corrected. 'Several people died. Others went mad. I avenged a death for profit, by causing many more.'

Thus has it ever been: the acres of the penetrated, intestines blue and flyblown, the unanswered cries amid the stench. They called for their mothers and for me. I never came. It wasn't my problem.

'Then,' she said, 'you gave me the means of my death. You didn't try to talk me out of it, just handed over the works. Do you believe altruism is genetic, Joe?'

'I believe altruism is a myth.' And I should know. I held the record for it, once.

'I don't. I want your genes in my child. Apart from Ayzel, you're the only person I've ever really known, dealer man. Your eyes have a dark fire in them. I want my child to have that. I know you, Joe. Sometimes I used to see you walking down the street. I used to watch. No one else ever seemed to focus on you: they'd turn away, like they were suddenly scared or something. I used to imagine you transparent, moving through the rest of us like nothing could hurt you. Sometimes I used to think you were a ghost.'

'You're not the only one,' I replied, stubbing out the smoke and sitting up.

And now Lazarette is sitting opposite, her belly swollen in the seventh month of her gestation. I looked at her, and felt once more the coldness inside me. I looked and wondered, yet again: what horror have I seeded within her? What monstrosity have I spawned? What rough beast takes form within her blameless body, what heart beats, feeding, feeding?

For she doesn't know me at all, and I will never tell her. Many times have I changed my name, but never — because I never can — my nature. I was born amid the soft odour of cow dung, a scream on a blood-soaked mattress of hay, my father, whoever he was, long gone. Yeshu, they called me. Yeshu ben Pantera. Yeshu, son of Pantera. The name shifted from the start: Yeshu, Yoshu, Joshua, Jesu, Jesus.

I died for you.

And then I awoke, three days later, scabbed on a rock in darkness, abandoned and betrayed by absence. Thus has it ever been since, these last two thousand years.

I am Joshua now, Joe for short, still thirty-three. Joe Ben Panther. I am in the most isolated city in the world, deep within parched wilderness, and my child grows inside a woman I left for dead. I think of my father, whom I have never met, and know that in hating him I must also do as he did. And soon. Perhaps the son of the son will cometh, and the mother will weep for eternity.

'Gina's missing,' Lazarette repeated.

'Gina,' I echoed, not really hearing.

'This is serious, Joe,' she prompted.

'Tell me then.' The first mouthful of beer had been awful. I took the second, and felt a homecoming.

'Gina works at the counselling service,' she explained. 'I don't think you've ever met her. She came to us about ten months ago, a year maybe. She'd not been long out of some weird religious group. Don't know what — she only mentioned it the once. Anyway, she blossomed, Joe, you know? I've seen it a couple of times before, and I guess maybe I did the same. She blossomed. Bit freaked out, but, you know, she really seemed to find herself. She comes in, does a bit of voluntary stuff around the office a couple of days a week.'

'And your point?' The beer was half gone. I glanced towards the bar, to see if it was busy. It pays to be prepared, I find.

'Last night was her birthday.' Lazarette was suddenly sombre. 'We were going to have some drinks with her at the Court Hotel, then take her out to dinner, you know? Just me, Ayz, a few of the others. She was really excited about it.

Her first birthday since she came out. Since she *got* out, I guess.'

'Let me guess,' I said, fingering the loose change in my pocket. It felt like enough. 'She never showed.'

'Right, but there's more. We waited an hour, then Ayz rang her flat from the pub. No answer. Siobhan — she works with us, too — even drove around there. No one home, she said. The front door wasn't locked. It was open a bit, apparently. Joe, it's not right. She never turned up. She hasn't been to the office all morning. Her phone's just the answering machine. Joe, it's a gut feeling, but I'm worried.'

I wasn't. I stood and walked to the bar, ordered another Stella and a lemonade. When I sat down again I stayed silent for a moment, weighing words in my mind.

'Joe?' interrupted Lazarette. 'Please try to concentrate.'

'About twenty?' I asked. 'Blonde hair, squared at the back?'

I watched the colour drain from her face. 'How do you know that?' she asked, sounding like she didn't want to hear the answer. A wise woman, Laz; always has been.

'I saw her this morning. She's dead.'

I used to earn money finding people, still breathing or not. There's no profit in reversing cause and effect.

Lazarette was staring at me, her mouth slightly open. 'How?' she managed.

'You don't know me at all, do you?' I noted.

Her eyes narrowed. 'Did you hit her up with pure or something?' she asked, suddenly ready to slash. 'She wasn't a user, Joe. She was *clean*. Did you offer her a free sample, you bastard?'

I shook my head. I am not proactive, contrary to some of the more fanciful interpretations of my past. I do not pour my spirit into empty vessels. To receive the love of the Lord, you have to ask. And pay. Thus has it always been.

'What time is it?' I asked.

Automatically, Lazarette checked her watch. ''Bout half twelve. What the hell does that have to —'

'She's in an alleyway off James Street, between the fish restaurant and the spaghetti joint. The sun should be hitting her just about now. You'll probably be able to hear the sirens from here in a minute or two.'

Lazarette stared at her lemonade. 'How, Joe?' she repeated.

I took a deep breath. 'My take? Stabbed through the back of the neck. That bit's easy. The knife's still in there. Big hunting knife, one shot. Whoever did it knew what he or she was doing. Her clothes are still on. Not much blood on the ground. She was killed somewhere else and dumped.'

'How did you find her?'

'I woke up next to her.'

Lazarette, no stranger to death, delirium or destitution, asked only: 'Was she there when you passed out?'

'I don't know.'

'Did you see anyone else?'

'I don't know.'

In the distance, the air began to dance to the counter-rhythms of ambulance and police.

'That'll be her lift,' I said.

'Why didn't you report it? No, don't bother to answer.'

I have never had a comfortable relationship with authority, from the Temple Guard and the Sanhedrin onwards. A man who smells of his raiment and whisky, a man crumpled and devoid of details: I found her, officer, dead with a knife in her back. Sit down, Mr Panther. For I am the light, and in my presence no searching is necessary. I blind the faithful to other possibilities. That was never my desire; it has always been my function.

Lazarette sobbed gently. A tear dropped from her cheek — a cheek robust with health and fluid retention — and fell into her drink. I could have said something. I could have offered words of comfort, said I didn't think she suffered, didn't think she knew what hit her. Lying isn't a sin, where no god has written the rules. It's just that sometimes it isn't all that practical. I said nothing, and lied in silence.

Laz looked across at me, her face wet. 'Help, Joe. She didn't deserve this.'

'No one ever does.'

She turned away for a moment, looking, I fancied, inside and back. 'Sometimes they do,' she whispered.

'It's a job for the police.' I heard my own hollowness, like a hymn in a cathedral.

Lazarette thumped the table: a small, impotent, furious thump. 'This town,' she began, holding something in. 'The landlord's trying to evict the centre. Said he didn't know we were a dyke shop. That's what he called it. Said it's wrong. The papers here won't take our money. They won't take ads for the centre, for other gay counselling services, for HIV/AIDS clinics, needle exchanges, the Pride March, nothing, Joe. People tried to ban Pride; some of the traders wanted it, like, at 11 pm on a fucking Monday night. Said we gave the place a bad name. None of the government ministers would endorse it. Funding's at a record low. Want to know about homophobia, Joe? Follow me and Ayz around some night. Watch us get hassled by police for kissing — just kissing, Joe — on the pavement. We don't exist. We're like another city, living in the sewers of this one. Reckon they'll find fingerprints on the knife?'

I shook my head. No sign of violence at the flat, from what I could gather: one stab, body moved and dumped. It looked like a pro job.

'Then what do you reckon?' Lazarette was almost spitting with anger. 'An unemployed dyke activist. Too much work, dealer man, unless someone puts a hand up.'

'You don't want to be in debt to me,' I said.

She paid no heed. 'Who's going to be next, Joe? That's what I wonder. What if Gina's murder wasn't personal? What if it was political? What if there's some fundamentalist crazy out there killing all the box-munchers because we're dirty godless whores or something? Who next, Joe?'

I could have stood then, and walked away. I could have. One more death committed in my name. So what? The count ages back reached orders of magnitude only dreamed of by despots. It is not up to me to atone. It never has been. I brought my gift — a love as genuine as it was misplaced — and it was long ago spit back, defiled by the screams of every half-choked heretic ripped and drawn from pubis to sternum. I find no tender mercy in forgiveness: merely a futile yearning for silence and rest, an end to the echoes of my name above the tart smell of someone else's blood.

I could have walked away. I don't know why I didn't.

'What do I get?' I asked. 'Apart from the beer you're just about to buy me.'

She leaned forward in her chair, anger mixing with shock. 'How about a better life for your son, dealer man?'

'Or daughter.'

'Son. I had an ultrasound.'

Oh mercy, I thought, what have I begun?

'It's nothing to do with me. That was the deal.'

23

.Laz shook her head. 'Okay, Joe. I know you, don't forget. How does this sit? I'm eight weeks to go, give or take. Am I right in thinking you're intending to get out of town by then?'

I nodded. There is no shame in honesty.

'And am I also right in thinking that you've got fuck-all money, and that phoney passport you paid for, back when you left Melbourne, turned out to be useless, which is why you ended up back in Australia?'

I nodded again. The passport, the small matter of two dead sweatshop owners in Denpasar, and a castrated paedophiliac priest in Manila.

'Do this,' said Lazarette, matter of fact, 'and I'll get you money.'

'How?'

'Ayzel's an engineer for one of the big building firms, and her family is rich. Leave it to me. No one will know.'

I stared at her, sightless, listening to the turbulent silence in my head. Suddenly she stood up and tossed a five-dollar note on the table. Her belly pushed hard against the fabric of her linen top, forcing out the waist of her drawstring culottes.

'Please, Joe,' she asked. 'For old time's sake.'

I want to die, I thought to myself. But that's me all over: always striving too high. Always yearning for the impossible. 'Get me everything you have on her,' I said, averting my gaze. 'Anything you can find: full name, address, last address, friends, parents, whatever that religious group was called. Meet me back here at ten tonight.'

I didn't see the expression on her face. When I eventually looked up, she was gone. I walked to the bar. It was too late for food now, anyway.

CHAPTER 2

At ten on the dot, I saw Lazarette through a beer glass darkly. She had done well, as I knew she would. She met me in the bar of the Brass Monkey, joining me at the table where I sat fresh from my ministry.

For the hours before had I walked among the multitude, cleansing the lepers, healing the sick, same old, same old. The young man Arvi had shivered in joy when I palmed the cap to his hand and folded his cash. Robert and Dropper had offered collateral, but what use have I for a Pioneer stereo? I have never driven a car, much less held a licence. They returned half an hour later, cashed up, complaining their fence had ripped them off, and bared their holy arms. As nothing to me were the sores on Julie's lips as I matched my mouth to hers and delivered unto her with my tongue.

Big Lizzy the Troll banged into a bollard as she crossed the road to meet me. She didn't seem to notice. Romano, sly Romano, asked my source; a fool intent on blessing without the intercession of the son. Every good gift and every perfect gift, I told him, cometh down from the Father of lights. Many are his names, terrible is his wrath, and secret is his stash.

'You're just another fucking businessman, Panther,' he'd replied. 'Same as all the rest.'

'Wrong,' I had responded. I fixed him with my eyes. They break through unto the Lord to gaze, and many of them perish. 'I'm a *dangerous* fucking businessman.'

He asked no more, gave freely and received, his love of me renewed.

'I got what I could, Joe,' Lazarette said when she arrived. I clinked my glass of whisky against her lemonade, said, 'Give'.

'There's a fair bit. You think you might want to write it down?'

I shook my head. Details I write to my heart. Sometimes I remember them.

Lazarette shrugged. 'Okay. She filled out a tax form when she started at the service. Full name's Gina Louise Compton. Birth certificate on the registry web site gives the parents as Ronald James Compton and Louise Astrid Fineways, address in Roleystone, up in the hills. I checked the phone book. Still there. My guess? De facto hippie couple, all natural fibres and homespun pottery. Lots like that up there.'

'Did you ring them?'

'No way. I'm not breaking the news. And that's another thing. I heard on the radio this evening the cops haven't identified her yet. They're waiting for dental records.'

'So: murdered, moved, dumped, ID taken.'

Laz nodded. 'Looks like it.'

'No one from the service told the police?'

She took a gulp from her glass, wiped her mouth, and exhaled a burden. 'No one from the service knows, Joe. I haven't told them. Jesus, I hope I'm right to trust you.'

'It's a common enough position,' I mumbled. I thought of my flock. They trusted me, though I slay them. 'What else?'

She gave her head a little shake, refocussed on the gig. 'Current address, Flat 4, 16 Marley Street, Highgate. Not far away. Moved there just before she came to us, far as I can gather. She mentioned once she used to live with a couple of people in Mount Lawley, but she had to get away. I'm thinking it was probably connected to the religious group. They work that way, from what I've read: get the cult members to shack up together.'

'Got an address?'

'Maybe. I found last year's White Pages in one of the cupboards. There's a Mount Lawley listing under Compton: 6 Noble Street. It's not in the current edition.'

My whisky was gone. I bade her wait while I bought a refill, and a stubby of Stella to chase. Returning to my seat, I fired up a Dunhill. Lazarette scowled as a cloud of smoke tumbled past her face.

'Jesus, Joe,' she snapped. 'You want the baby bloody *born* addicted?'

Chemical predeterminism, I thought. Calvin would have loved it. 'You and me, Laz. That verse was written long ago. What do you know about the religious group?'

'Fuck all. Like I said, she only mentioned it once. Said she'd escaped — was escaping — some horrible cult. Didn't go into details. Said I'd know the story.'

She would have been right there. The geometry of faith changes nothing but its numbers. Never has. Back in the second century, a mob called the Montanists threw in all their belongings and travelled to the wilderness, convinced that the New Jerusalem, me at the gates, was about to descend, just for them. It never happened. Far as I can remember, I was in Syria at the time, clad in the cloak of depression: mad Yoshu in my repentant delusions, divining augurs for alms, selling fly agaric mushrooms to shamans and charlatans both.

It's happened time and again since then, disappointment a cert, hope rising constant higher than the corpses of the slaughtered. In 2000, more than five hundred people were burnt to death in a Ugandan church. They grew tired of waiting for me, apparently. Everywhere am I beckoned, though they see me not among them.

'Parents involved, you think?'

Lazarette shook her head. 'Doubt it, not if the tree-hugger theory holds. She grows up all wholemeal, pissed off she's miles from the bright lights, diet of Joan Baez and Jackson Browne. Leaves home when she can, then does the lost-and-searching-for-meaning bit.'

'Any trouble? Ever busted?'

'No, Joe, I told you, she wasn't a user. Didn't even seem to drink much. When she first came to the service we did a bit of a ring-around — there are a few dykes in the cops, a couple who'll do favours on the QT. It's standard for us, just in case we've got a loony on the doorstep, you know. She was clean, far as we could find out.'

She closed her eyes, and took a deep breath. The swelling breasts that would soon suckle the grandson of God rose and fell in praise and sorrow beneath the fabric of her top. When she looked at me again, her eyes were not wet, but hard as tempered steel.

'What did she do to deserve this, Joe?'

I could have told her that cause has long been overrated, the just and the innocent no safer than the cruel. Thus has it always been: the young men shall die by the sword, and their sons and daughters by famine. There are scars and pocks on Lazarette's arms that will never heal. She carried the new stigmata, the five hundred wounds of Christ. I figured deep down she already knew.

'She got in someone's way,' I said instead. 'She became a threat.'

Laz stood up. 'I'm expected at home. Ayz'll be worrying. What are you going to do now?'

'Stay here till the pub shuts, then go for a walk.'

She nodded. 'Find the bastard, Joe. Make this right. And by the way, you're drinking too much.'

I necked from my glass, wiped my beard. 'Just obeying orders. Drink no longer water, but use a little wine for thy stomach's sake and thine often infirmities.'

She forced a smile. 'Who said that?'

'Bloke called Timothy,' I replied. 'He reckoned he knew me. Dead now.'

Like all of them.

There is envy in my heart.

Darkness is my secret place. I come as a thief in the night. Well, as a burglar, at least. The door to Gina's flat was locked when I arrived; closed, I presumed, by the well-meaning visitor from the counselling service the night before. It was a simple Yale, and yielded easily to the internal probing of a syringe. The door swung silently inwards; my stockinged feet touched the carpet, soft as a prayer. It was one in the morning. I feared not, for I was the first.

The walk to Highgate had taken about half an hour, the night warm, the roads almost empty. The beer I carried as a traveller expired long before I reached my destination, its death, together with the journey, bringing a lulling tiredness alleviated only by rubbing a snifter of amphetamines across my gums. Oh lord, God of my master Abraham, I pray thee, send me good speed this day.

Another fifteen minutes' grid-searching found the street and then the flats: a squat, solid red-brick set of four, two up, two down, dating from the fifties. Gina's was on the upper storey, reached by a common external staircase. No lights showed in any of the windows. I took off my shoes, and silently climbed.

Once inside, I refastened the door, checked all the curtains were closed, and risked turning on the discount-store lamp which stood on a side table next to the sofa. It took two attempts because my fingers kept slipping inside the thin disposable gloves I'd put on before entering.

The flat was small, but serviceable; spartan but neat. It bespoke of a life in which the main problem was a shortage of funds. Nothing looked new, but everything was clean and well tended. The living room, into which the front door opened, held a three-piece suite of indeterminate age and dubious taste, a kind of beige and brown weave. There was a low coffee table, a bookcase, television, small stereo next to an untidy pile of albums, and an op-shop telephone stand. The pictures on the wall were photo reproductions: a couple of high-fashion glamour shots, a Greta Garbo movie still. The albums: Indigo Girls, k.d. lang, Melissa Etheridge, Marie Wilson, *Cabaret*, bluehouse, other gender-driven choices. The books: second-hand science fiction, and a couple of feminist works — Faludi, Paglia, Greer. The serious stuff looked unread.

The bedroom contained a futon, the doona, black and red, cast over and smoothed. There was also a small chest of drawers, and a hanging rack accommodating half a dozen jackets, a couple of pairs of trousers, no dresses or skirts. The kitchen was small, with an old four-ring gas cooker and a fridge which doubled as a notice board for bills. A single plate and mug awaited washing. The bathroom was narrow, a dripping shower above the enamel bath, a tiny wall-mounted cabinet. This last revealed only the expected detritus of a solo female life. Gina was prone to thrush, apparently. Next to the box of aspirin I found a packet of diet tablets, took four and swilled them down from the basin tap.

There was no sign of the Lord, no crosses, no Bibles, no images of me twisted and agonised in the bloodshed hours before death and damning resurrection. Whatever cult had claimed young Gina's loyalty had been discarded through more than simple apostasy.

I returned to the living room, some preliminary conclusions already forming. Lazarette was probably right: Gina Compton had been a woman of comparatively sober habits, her demons under control. There was no sign of struggle, nor of blood. Perhaps she had welcomed her killer inside — a friend, a trusted face at least. Or perhaps she had been taken brutal on the road as she was heading to the pub. My instinct tended to discount the latter. There was little to support a random-killing theory: the act had been swift, the ID removed, and the dumping alley a significant tangent from any direct route she would have taken from the flat to the rendezvous point.

I knelt in front of the bookcase to take a closer look at its contents. At the left-hand end of the second shelf, wedged between the wood and an Iain M. Banks novel, I found a thin collection of what looked like brochures or folded leaflets, held together with a rubber band. Gently, I slid them out. They were four in number, entitled *You Can Win!*, *The Only Way Is Up!*, *Reaching Your Inner Goals*, and *The Road To Truth*. The front cover of each bore what appeared to be something written in Greek, above the name, 'The Transpersonal Foundation'. I had a feeling about them. I used to know Greek. My command was never as good as Paul's, but I had more than enough to deal with the necessities: can you spare some money; do you have a sister; that man over there will pay for all of this; no, I know not Chrestus. The phrase on the leaflets defeated me. I figured I might eventually nut it out. The dim light hurt my eyes, but I was able to decipher the first line of English on the topmost one: THERE IS NO GOD. I slipped the documents in the inside pocket of my suit jacket, for future reference.

The bookcase yielded nothing else of interest, but the telephone answering machine indicated three messages. I hit the play button, and hoped the volume wasn't set high.

'Hello, Gina?' began the first one, a deep female voice. 'This is Ayzel — you know, Lazarette's partner. We're just here at the Court, wondering where you've got to. Ah well, you must be on your way, I suppose.'

The second was a female voice, not young. 'Only me. Just checking you're still coming up for dinner on Sunday. Your aunt Linda called to say she might be dropping in, too, but don't let that put you off. I know she's a pain in the you-know, but she never stays long. Dad says hi.'

Mother, plainly. Little indication of parental disharmony, although I've long known to distrust such conclusions. People thought Joseph got along just fine with Mary, too, thought the cuckold of the Lord was happy to be the patsy. I thought of Ayzel then, the choice-parent of my child, a stranger to me. I thought of patterns repeating, beyond control.

Third message, male, young: 'When are you coming home, Geen? This is no way to do it. The problem is in your head. You have to confront your lack of will or your fears will win. Come home, Geen. Clem Porter says you can move up a level, half-price, accelerate your progress. We miss you, Geen, and we *know* you miss us. Come back, Geen, or no good will come of this.'

The cult, clearly. I recognised the tactics: the group-as-home, the mention of the name — cutesy, at that — four times in less than a minute. Come to think of it, I might have even invented the tactics: cast away your possessions, follow me, adopt a new persona. Now you are Simon, now you are Mark. Maybe it was me. Maybe. Too tough to remember now how much I said, and how much others said I said. My body never fails; the garden of my memory grows rampant under berry and vine.

Clem Porter. I tried to memorise the name, just in case.

I returned to the bedroom and checked the contents of the chest of drawers in the gloom. Knickers, socks, tee-shirts, shorts, a scarf. No lubes, no sex toys, no love letters, all very dull. As I turned to leave, something, a small patch of dark, caught my eye, just poking out from beneath the futon base. I picked it up, and took a moment or two to identify it. It was a pestle: a heavy, stone, grinding instrument, a solid cosh that fitted neatly in my hand. I sniffed it, finding the faint odours of pepper and basil. Not a homeware dildo, then, but a kitchen implement pressed into service as a potential weapon. She *had* been fearful of a malignant visitor in the night. Granted, the people of Perth tended to be paranoid about burglars at the best of times, but the pestle suggested an improvised, rather than prepared, weapon. She had felt someone was coming, sudden and soon.

The front door bumped gently against its jamb as someone stuck something in the lock.

A casual observation made some minutes before suddenly attained spectacular significance: there was no back door to the apartment. Neither was there anywhere to hide: no wardrobe, no space beneath the bed. My best chance, such as it was, lay with the bathroom. The tumblers of the Yale began to fall. Quickly, I walked into the narrow room and stepped into the bath. I pressed up against the wall, thus shielded by the open door. As places of concealment went, it didn't have a lot to recommend it. The pestle was in my left hand; the syringe, uncapped, in my right.

I heard the front door open and the soft sigh of a floorboard. Whoever it was, I hoped they weren't in desperate need of a leak. I started to run through some possibilities, calculating chances. A flatmate seemed unlikely for a whole host of reasons, not the least of which was that Lazarette would probably have mentioned one. A lover, perhaps? Possible. A casual lover, unaware that Gina had been missing for more than twenty-four hours, with a key and permission to drop around in the middle of the night on the off-chance? Less likely, and, anyway, I was betting against a key as the method of entry.

Just then the visitor coughed. It was an unmistakably male cough. Scratch lover, then, unless there were dark undercurrents in Gina Compton so far unrevealed. That was possible, but made for an unnecessarily complicated hypothesis. Pragmatism bade rejection.

The footsteps were gentle, and unhurried. I guessed the visitor was slowly circling the living room. The lamp was still on. Why hadn't he called out Gina's name? A burglar, then? Almost certainly not. B&E is a high-risk business, with speed the essence. There was the constant risk of being disturbed — unless, of course, you somehow knew the occupant wasn't in and wouldn't be returning. *I* knew that, hence my presence. If the visitor also knew that, then there were two big possibilities: the man in Gina Compton's living room was her killer, returned for reasons unknown; or a cop in possession of dental test results. The second possibility seemed far more likely, which immediately raised some troubling implications for yours truly, standing as I was in a murdered woman's bathtub, pestle in one hand, syringe in the other, alcohol on my breath, heroin in my underwear, and amphetamines in my pocket. Sit down, Mr Panther, just a few questions . . .

There was still one incongruity unaccounted for. The man was alone, by the sound of it. Cops never worked alone. Perhaps his partner was outside, guarding the door. Thus, even if I *did* crown the inside guy with the pestle — the idea I was working on — my escape was still not assured. I abandoned the plan, put the weapons in my pocket and opted for a different strategy. Quietly, I stepped out of the bath, and flushed the toilet. The man was turning in my direction as I came out the door, giving it my best at feigning anger, shock and surprise.

'Who the hell are you?' I demanded. 'How did you get in here? I'm calling the police.'

He smiled, just a little. If I had startled him, he did a damn good job of covering it. 'Unwise, I would think,' he said, quite calmly. 'For both of us.'

Not a cop, then — a conclusion drawn as readily from his appearance as his demeanour. We stood for a minute, at opposite ends of the living room, him between me and the front door, weighing each other up. He looked to be in his mid-fifties, to judge by the lines on his face and the grey of his temples. He was dressed immaculately in a single-breasted suit, jacket buttoned over waistcoat, shirt and silk tie, all black, all patently expensive. His shoes, also black, shone dully in the lamplight. His hands were clad in thin, tight, kid-leather gloves. His face was shadowed, eyes unclear, a thin moustache just visible.

And what would he have seen of me? A man in his early thirties, with a bearded chin and collar-length brown hair, clad in a crumpled grey suit, frayed at the cuffs and bulging at one of the pockets. A man in a faded black Beasts of Bourbon tee-shirt, disposable gloves, and black socks. A man abandoned, cast aside. An alley-and-bench man, a man addicted, a halitoid man. They look but they do not see; they listen but they do not hear.

'Let's make this easy,' he said. 'Take the television, go, and not a word shall pass my lips.' His smug smile, broader this time, revealed a regiment of startlingly white teeth.

I considered the proposal for a moment, but rejected it. I still occupied the high ground, such that it was, and it didn't take a huge leap of faith to figure that the guy was probably important to my quest — even, possibly, the end point to it. I decided to push things a bit.

'Your name,' I repeated, walking towards him. 'How dare you come in here. I'm calling the cops now.'

'Go ahead, sir. I suspect we'd both be gone by the time they arrived. What is your business here?'

I stopped walking, given how blithely the phone bluff had been called. Whatever this guy was, he was a professional at it. 'I *live* here,' I replied, as indignantly as possible.

'No you don't,' he countered. 'Gina Compton lives alone.'

'Not any more.'

'Apart from you yourself, sir, I see no evidence of your habitation.'

'I only moved in at the beginning of the week.' Then I remembered my boots, which I'd left just inside the door. I pointed to them. 'There, see?'

'And in what capacity do you live here? Where do you sleep?'

I did the indignant bit again. 'That's no business of yours.'

He gave a little bow. 'Quite so, but none, either, I think, of Gina's. Where is she, by the way?'

I tried to read his face, but couldn't see it clearly enough.

'Out.'

'Where?'

'None of your business.'

'For how long?'

'Why did you break into her — our — flat?'

I had the feeling he was enjoying himself immensely, which worried me.

'What were you doing in the bathroom, sir?'

'Taking a piss.'

'Do you always wear disposable gloves when you take a piss? Bespeaks some curious phobias, I would think. And what's that in your pocket?'

'I'm pleased to see you. Again: why did you break in?'

'Gina is a friend of mine. We belong to the same club. I'm concerned about her welfare.'

'So you break into her flat in the middle of the night?'

'We're both night owls. There are no secrets in our club.'

'What were you looking for?'

'Nothing.'

Of course I didn't believe him. The club references were obvious. I wondered whether I had the objects of his desire in my jacket pocket, whether Gina's 'horrible cult' had been the Transpersonal Foundation, whatever that was, or whether, hopelessly addicted to the pursuit of truth, she had been contemplating joining it as an antidote to whatever organisation she had recently fled. Had he entered in order to remove any evidence of a connection? I decided to chance a play.

'Clem Porter,' I said.

There was a moment's pause. He hadn't been expecting that. Name the horror, tame the beast. He was quickly back in the gig.

'At your service,' he replied, doing another little stiff-backed bow. 'How did you know?'

'Gina's mentioned you.'

He laughed then, a bitter, knowing laugh. 'Along with the other ninety-nine names of Satan, I'll bet.'

I've never met Satan, despite what the Testament maintains. I've never met God, either. These days I doubt I'd be able to tell them apart. Clem Porter was most definitely neither. He was a vain fop, a decorated dandy, full of the amorality of conceit. The time for games was at an end. I was tired, prey to the drying thirst of desire, and edgy in case the police did turn up for real. Gina was Perth born and bred, after all: it wasn't like they had to send to Lapland for her dentals. I fixed Clem Porter's eyes, still shadowed from the light, with mine. If this guy wanted to boost the stakes and serve up Biblical imagery, so be it. His call: his problem. Was I not, after all, in sport and life, the number one seed?

I felt my voice resonate way down inside, my intonation a Hammer Horror mesmer. 'And if Satan cast out Satan, he is divided against himself; how shall then his kingdom stand? Or else how can one enter into a strong woman's house, and spoil her goods, except he first bind the strong woman, and then he spoil her house?'

I have seen grown men quiver before me, women shrink into visceral fear, children scream for their mothers. Clem Porter chuckled, and threw himself down on the sofa, legs crossed, arms spread elegantly across the back.

'Matthew, if I'm not mistaken,' he smiled. 'Almost word perfect, but missing a verse, I think. I see I misjudged you, Mr ... ah?'

I remained silent, motionless, contemplating violence.

'So be it, sir,' continued Porter. 'Not bad at all. Very impressive delivery: crisp, clear, concise, a little over the top, perhaps, but that's a taste thing. Good with the eyes, good with the posture. You know, clean up the presentation — new suit, sharp and ironed, get your hair off your shoulders and trim your beard a bit — you could *have* something. You could be a *very* impressive motivator. I could help you with that, if you like.'

He was looking at me with his head cocked to the right, left eye suddenly bright and glinting, as if he'd just made me an offer I couldn't refuse. I remained impassive. Sometimes they defy me, but they all crumble in the end. All of them. I thought about how he hadn't reacted to the implications of my message. Either he didn't know what had happened to Gina, or he did but wasn't about to admit it — especially to a stranger in the house of the dead. Certainly, he didn't seem to share my anxiety about the growing likelihood of imminent cop company. Just then, he reversed the cross of his legs: a calculated gesture to regain my attention. The smile had cranked down a notch from congratulatory to sincere.

'Sir,' he said. 'I can help you realise your true potential. Haven't you always wanted to realise your true potential?'

So much has been done in the name of me, so much misery and hate in the love of me. Sometimes, even now, so deep in my anathema, I sweat awake in the night and wonder: has the peak yet been passed, or is there worse to come? When Paul the Salesman was doing his Roman schtick, so I heard, and later, among the Ophites of Origen's time, there was a tradition among some believers to swear, deeply felt, *Jesus be cursed*. Were they making a distinction between me on the earth and me risen, or did they see the horrors ahead and condemn me, realising my true potential?

'No,' I said, reaching into my pocket and pulling out the pestle. 'I want you to go.'

'Ahh,' he cooed, calm but gathering himself up from his rest. 'Violence time: the move from the rational to the irrational. An effective tactic in negotiation sometimes, sir, as I'm sure you're aware.' He was standing now, and moving towards the front door, efficient, betraying no fear. 'Your purpose here still mystifies me, but I can see that something taxes you, and now is not the time for you and I to talk business. I'll leave you, then, but my offer still stands. I'm sure you'll work out how to find me. Give my regards to Gina: make sure to tell her I was here.'

The door closed behind him. I stood still in the middle of the room, breathing hard, weapon still in my hand. Two minutes later I heard the sound of an engine in the silence of the night. I chanced a look through the window in time to see the sleek black bulk of what looked like a brand new Bentley ooze away from view. The sight of the road spurred me back to caution. Questions were forming, answers beckoning. Should the path of least resistance be the route I had to take, then perhaps the business of death and recompense could be concluded very soon. After that: money, leaving, moving, reinvention, repetition, turbulence, and, somewhere left behind me, an infant's sob in darkness.

I dropped the pestle in an armchair, pulled on my boots, killed the lamp, and shut the door behind me. Outside the night was cloudless and fresh, its effete chill foreshadowing the heat of the day. I realised I was in the wilderness, the awful, long, creeping couple of hours between the late-night hotels closing and the dawn-starters opening. I lit up a cigarette and watched its thread of smoke dance languid in the stillness of the air. A newspaper delivery van growled past, the driver glancing at the stranger on the street. I decided to walk home and have a joint with the sunrise. If sleep then failed to come, no matter: there was a six o'clock bar only two blocks up the road.

CHAPTER 3

People cry my name in hope of redemption, seep-eyed in the darkness. I am asked to intercede with my implacable father, my emanating immensity of Dadness. I am asked for the return of life and dignity, the lifting of intolerable sadness, the easing of the burdens of others. To my ears come daily the whispers of abandonment, the confidence of ritual, the wheezing groan of last-resort repentance.

All these voices in my head. All this constant clamour. Wasted breath, the lot.

A single request, cast a billion ways: make this gig better, make the next one better still. I know nothing of the afterlife, contrary to the brochures. Not a thing. Each time my violent death has come, by spike and noose, by halberd and Glock, and my brain shudders and coughs to blackness — each time, then, a spark of hope: here goes, at last, the son has rest and meets the father, the prophesies fulfil, many are the blessèd and great shall be their reward. Each time, three days, awake again, scabs hard and cracking, none the wiser, none the older. Each time the same: I am eternal in my transience. In the term *past/present*, I am the / and the / is me. In the beginning was the word. I am the punctuation of time. I mark the minutes of forever.

So I know nothing of Heaven, but I know the topography of Hell. I know its secret. I know its fear. I have the power to best it and lay low the unseen fist of Satan, my father's schizo shadow.

Hell is the place where the smack is only bicarb and the needles always blunt. Hell is where the dope is too much leaf, the speed is simply talcum and the acid bits of cardboard. Hell is where the mushrooms are only good for salads, where the ecstasy is agony and the crystal meth seems never to arrive. Hell is where the beer is light and the whisky comes from Paraguay, where the wine is grape and the cask is empty, where the smokes are just one milligram and the vend machine just busted. Hell is where you never shut your eyes, and life is unambiguous. Hell is a future full of junk mail, lotteries and new songs by the Backstreet Boys.

From such a fate do I deliver. From such horror can I spare all those who open their hearts, their wallets and their veins. For there is none without sin, but for those with the readies and the power to see, I come as saviour, deliverer of dull-eyed, heavy-lidded forgiveness.

I woke to the knock, gasping great lungfuls of air in the residual terror of a dream hard won and instantly forgotten. My breathing sounded like the endurance of martyrs.

'You all right, Mr Panther, are you?' I heard Mrs Warburton shout through the door, her tone more curious than concerned.

I fought myself down. 'Fine. Just a little anathema attack.'

I peered at the bedside clock through the curtained gloom. It was a little after seven in the morning, meaning that I'd managed barely two hours of sleep.

She knocked again.

'What is it?' I asked.

'Visitor, you got,' she said. 'Woke Nessie up. She'll be all cranky now, she will.'

Situation normal then, I thought. 'Who is it? Is it Lazarette?'

Another knock now, harder and insistent, followed by a male voice. 'Open up, Panther. Five seconds, I bust the lock.'

I didn't recognise it, but authority carries its own weight.

'Hang on,' I called, and rolled out of bed. Quickly, I threw my Beasts of Bourbon tee-shirt back on, and was halfway into my jeans when a solid blow thudded against the wood. The lock — not the sturdiest of devices — made a brief grinding shriek, followed by the creak of splinters shearing like torn teeth, and the door swung open.

'Mr *Panther*!' Mrs Warburton sounded shocked.

Next to her, in the frame, was a large man. He was, I guessed, in his mid-forties, but possessed of a heaviness around the jowls which made him look older. His skin was scarred from the departure of bad acne, and overlaid with a thin grid of burst capillaries. His hair was brown, tending to grey, and parted on the left. By the look of it, he washed it with soap. He wore a cheap grey suit over a creased off-white shirt and a skewed black tie.

Behind him, partially blocked from view, stood a woman. She was tall and also besuited, although in dark blue fabric of better quality and in receipt of better care. She was maybe in her late twenties, and wore no make-up to cover the thin spattering of freckles across her nose and cheeks. Her hair was long, black and turbulent. She was doing a poor job of concealing a smirk.

'OK, Panther,' said the man, 'put the blunt instrument away before I charge you with indecency, sit back on your bed, put your hands where I can see them and don't move.'

Now, I've been around the block once or twice during my life, and I've learned a thing or two. I've learned that a dog's rib will make a Venetian merchant part with gold if you tell him it's a relic of Saint Isidore. I've learned that a virtuous maid who forbids her neighbour sex will be burnt as a witch. And I've learned that Whitney Houston sings crap songs. Mostly, though, I've learned that throughout history there have only ever been two types of cops: those who look like cops, and those who don't.

It's only the second type that can cause major problems. This pair were clearly the first.

I zipped my fly and realised I was in no condition to be operating machinery.

'Mrs Warburton,' I said, as I sat back on the mattress, 'could I trouble you for a cup of coffee?'

'But Nessie. . .' she began, suddenly fidgeting.

'As a favour, Mrs Warburton.'

She frowned, a living counter-argument to philanthropy. Then I had an idea. 'Do this and I promise I'll take Nessie out for a spin around the block later on.'

Now the man spoke. 'Yes, Mrs Warburton. We need to speak to Mr Panther here in private for a moment. Perhaps you could make us all a cup.'

My landlady bit her lip, then nodded and walked off down the passage. It would be instant, and pissweak with it, because I'd failed miserably in trying to teach her how to use my plunger, but it would be better than nothing.

The man walked into the room, slowly, and made a show of looking around. Then he grabbed the bentwood chair, spun it expertly through one-eighty degrees, put it down, and sat so that he could lean forward onto its back, legs either side, as if he was riding it. The woman also stepped inside. She leant against the wall by the door, her arms folded, left ankle crossed in front of the right. She was tall, maybe six foot, including her hair.

Several silent seconds passed as they regarded me. I made neither move nor expression. I could wait. I'm very good at waiting. I've had a lot of practice. It's particularly easy without coffee, shower or enough sleep to speak of.

'Joe Panther,' said the man.

It didn't seem to require a response, so I didn't give one.

'That's right, isn't it?'

I thought for a moment about denying it and asserting that I was someone else — Salman Rushdie, for instance — but didn't think I had the presence of mind to pull it off. I nodded instead.

'What's your full name, Joe?'

So it was *Joe* now. 'Is this a test?' I asked.

He didn't look amused. 'These are the easy questions, Joe. Wait for the hard ones. Full name?'

I noticed he wasn't holding a notebook.

'Joshua Ben Panther.'

He snorted at that. 'Religious parents, eh?'

'My mother claimed to have God deep inside her.'

He nodded slowly. 'And where *is* your mother, Joe?'

'Dead.'

'I'm sorry,' he said perfunctorily. 'And your father?'

I shrugged. 'God knows. I never met him.'

He shrugged in return. 'Common enough story.'

'No it's not.'

'You'd be surprised.'

'No I wouldn't.'

The woman cleared her throat. 'Anxiety attacks first thing in the morning,' she said, smirking openly now. 'Sign of a guilty conscience.'

'It's a sign,' I replied, 'of being ripped from sleep stinking early by two strangers in my room. Procedure demands you have to tell me your names, I believe.'

The man reached inside his suit jacket. 'What do you do for a living, Joe?'

'I'm a friend of publicans and sinners.'

He held the wallet out towards me. 'Detective Senior Sergeant Ian Hewson. And my partner is Detective Constable Irene Chew. Homicide.'

That told me a lot. I relaxed a bit. Homicide I could handle. Drug Squad might have been a bit trickier, given the cargo beneath the floorboard. A slow wave of mental sludge washed through my head. I tried to remember the shape of the previous night, and what I'd done. Reality, memory, invention, delusion: there's little difference, you want to get right down to it. There were people, after they cut me down and left me in the cave, who swore they saw me out on foot. They did. They swore they saw me dead, bathed in divine light. They didn't. They swore it all meant something. I just swore back and walked.

So, the night before. A bit of heroin dealing, a bit of purchasing alcohol while in a state of intoxication, a tad of amphetamine consumption, some breaking and entering, a touch of theft, a modicum of threatening behaviour. Nope. No homicide there. I smiled. It felt like a smile, anyway.

'Irene,' I said, looking directly at the woman. 'Pretty name. Greek, way back. It means the peace of God.'

'Which piece?' she responded, head cocked slightly to one side.

Something heavy crashed into the door jamb, which was fortunate really, given that the three replies to her quip which had occurred to me all required the use of the word 'indivisible' and I didn't think my tongue was up to it.

Mrs Warburton grunted, realigned Nessie's wheelchair and pushed it into the room. The old woman was in a filthy pink housecoat and smelled faintly of urine. On her bony lap was balanced a tray with three chipped mugs, a sugar bowl and a small milk jug.

'You'll have to help yourself, you will,' said Mrs Warburton, sounding harried.

'You'll get no help from us, you won't,' snapped Nessie.

Hewson did a poor job of masking his distaste as he reached over and gingerly picked up the tray. Chew, out of the line of sight, didn't have to try. I watched her lips go thin, and her larynx bounce.

Hewson thanked the women, then said we'd all be fine now.

'Yes, well,' replied Mrs Warburton. 'I should hope so, I should. Got better things to do than be a char lady, you know.'

'I want my tea,' said Nessie.

'In a minute, dear,' replied her keeper, backing the chair out. 'Commode first, we'd better. You know what you're like in the morning, you do.'

Hewson put the tray on the ground between us. I grabbed a mug, sloshed in some milk and a teaspoon of sugar. The brew was far from scalding. Half of it disappeared in the first gulp. It was as frail as a hermit on bread and water, but at least now the spirit was with me, however dilute. My eyelids blinked, my mind started to hum.

Hewson sipped his, black. Chew passed.

'Now then,' I said.

Hewson looked directly into my eyes. I could see it was a strain for him, but he held it for ten seconds before finding his mug a convenient excuse to break contact.

'Where were you night before last between 6 pm and dawn?' he asked.

'Erring and straying,' I said. 'Following devices and desires. Leaving undone those things which I ought to have done.'

'And what the fuck does that mean?'

'I was drunk. Your guess is as good as mine.'

'See,' he continued. 'We'd like to know, because then we can work out how you got to where you were mid-morning.'

I put the mug to my lips and stared at him, eyes flat and unblinking, above the rim. I thought to myself: uh-oh. Then I pulled the mug back to my knees, let the silence hang.

Irene Chew suddenly propelled herself away from the wall, and walked past the bed to the window. 'Gina Louise Compton,' she said. 'Ring a bell, Joe?'

So they'd made the identification. A phone call would have sounded sometime in the vulnerable nakedness of dawn at the house of two middle-aged hippies in the hills, ending forever their tree-lined utopia. Another would be made come nine o'clock to Sappho's Sisters, telling Laz what she already knew, permitting her at last to cry and share her awful knowledge.

Would other calls be made? Certainly, yes, spreading further and further like ripples on a pond. Aunts, uncles, cousins would hear; appointments and dinners would be postponed, grief the reason; undertakers would mumble anodyne solemnities into receivers while pushing buttons on calculators; neighbours would offer tea; friends of friends would find out and wonder if they should call. In whose contact book, I wondered, would the name of Clem Porter be writ? How long before the news reached those who called her Geen? And would shock be their reaction? Geen the Has-been, I thought.

'What was that?' asked Chew.

'Never heard of her.'

'Maybe you never asked her name,' said Hewson. 'Make it easier, did it?'

'Officers.' I let the word hang while I drained my mug. 'Many are the mysteries of this world, and many, I know, are revealed to the meek, but the one I'm mainly grappling with right now is the one which concerns two detectives bursting into my room at sparrow-fart asking me about someone I've never met.'

Chew again, fast: 'How do you *know* you've never met her, if you don't who she is?'

'Good point.'

'So you admit that you *might* know her?'

I sighed, letting them both know I was finding the proceedings tiresome, but said nothing more.

'You're a heroin dealer,' said Hewson, voice flat.

Before I could answer, his mobile rang, treating all of us to a synthetic rendition of Beethoven's Fifth. 'I have to take this,' he announced, pulling his phone from his jacket pocket and disappearing through the door into the passage.

A moment of silence followed. I looked at Chew, who was standing, arms folded, near the window. She looked back at me, meeting my eyes without a blink. She was a silhouette in the morning light, shafts of fragile sun piercing the gaps in her tumbling hair.

'Well, then,' she said.

'I'm getting cold,' I stated. 'May I put my jacket on?'

It was lying crumpled on the floor.

'Of course,' she replied. 'Let me.'

Quickly, she moved two paces across the room and bent to pick it up. The action pulled the fabric of her pressed trousers momentarily tight across her buttocks, outlining a body firm, round, and, I fancied, muscular.

She took hold of it by the hem, lifted it and shook it as if trying to straighten it out. I saw too late her intention.

'You should take better care of your clothes, Joe,' she said, flapping it like a chambermaid opening out a bedsheet. A packet of Dunhills, a lighter, some loose change, a bottle top and the leaflets I had pocketed in Gina Compton's flat fell to the floor.

'What are these?' she asked of the latter, picking them up.

A brutal, nasty little thought struck me as I watched her stare at the uppermost leaflet, then bend it forwards against its rubber-band restraint to check the front covers of those behind it. Would she recognise them as items removed from the flat, and thus realise I'd been there? I doubted it, because such a conclusion implied a meticulous inventory drawn up before the murder. Gina's flat had been neat, certainly, but there was nothing in it to suggest she had entertained a fastidious habit of recording the contents of her bookcase. And even if she had, the leaflets had been squeezed in right at the end, as if hidden. Just the same, I watched her carefully as she investigated, the way her eyebrows danced in exaggerated concentration.

'The Transpersonal Foundation,' she read aloud. 'Know much about this mob, Joe?'

'Junk mail,' I replied, shaking my head. 'They were shoved in the letterbox. I must have forgotten to throw them away.'

She threw me a doubtful look. 'So if I checked with the other houses in the street, people would recognise them?'

I shrugged. 'I don't know. I don't live in the other houses.'

I could have added that multitudes claim to dwell in mine, but I didn't think it would help.

She was looking at them again. 'What's this thing in Greek? I've seen it somewhere before.'

'Probably a proverb, or a line from Homer. Very popular method of establishing importance, I understand. Quote from the ancients and you can claim to be implicit in history, a necessary outcome.'

And I should know. How often did I pull that trick, back in the early days? How often did I quote from the Pentateuch, claiming fulfilment of ancient prophesy? It was an age-old scam even then. For all the good it did me. Blood on the sand leaches down, bodies rot, weapons rust, and the screams of the dying are whipped away, cleansed by the wind. History is not the actions of men, but the memories of scribes and the contrivance of the rich.

'I don't think so,' she said. 'I don't think it's a phrase.'

She tossed the leaflets onto the bed, and appeared to dismiss them. I could see by the final glance she gave them, however, the memorising double-check, that she hadn't. I put my jacket on, thankful that for once I'd sold all the stock it had contained the day before.

Hewson walked back into the room, looking pale.

'Bad news?' asked Chew.

He shook his head, lips tight, and jerked his right thumb

back over his shoulder. 'The old woman,' he said. 'In the lounge room. On a commode.'

'Is she dead?'

'No, but whatever she had for dinner last night is.'

He sat back down on the bentwood, and stayed quiet for a few seconds, quelling his nausea. Then he stood up again, walked in front of me, and tried to tower over me.

'That call,' he said, 'was the toxicology double-check I'd requested on the remains of Gina Compton. You're done, Joe Panther.'

I raised my eyebrows. 'Meaning?'

He bitch-slapped my face. I turned the other cheek.

'These things I know about you, Joe,' he growled. 'You're a grubby little smack dealer whose name keeps cropping up in foot patrol reports, mobile reports, junkie statements, all over the shop. The only reason you're still walking around is because the Force hasn't got the resources to compile cases against pissant little street-shits like you, but the time you're on is borrowed, boy, get it? As soon as there's a bit spare — or an order from higher up — you'll have my colleagues from Drug Squad over here demanding to know your source.'

Some things never change. For centuries that was the question to end all questions: what is my source: God, man or both? They called themselves Catholics, Arians, Nestorians, Monophysites, Pelagians. They slaughtered each other by the thousand over my divinity percentage. They stormed cities, they deceived and betrayed, they slit throats in the night and knelt in the snow, humiliated, vanquished and fearful. They flayed bit by bit, placed each other beneath rocks, hung more by the hair, lumps of salt crushing their shoulders. And each who did it claimed my acquiescence in the act.

I watched sometimes. I used to watch.

And then I just kept walking. They could have asked me, of course, but no one ever did. Not that I have an answer. Which should be answer enough, come to think of it.

There are but two names which one should never utter: the name of God, and the name of your dealer. Only one of these is important. I don't know the name of God, by the way, any more than you do. You want my best guess, though, given my unique perspective? Here it is: it probably isn't Shane.

Hewson was speaking again.

'She was knifed through the back of the neck, Joe, but of course you already know that. That's what killed her, but she was dying anyway. The lab boys found a massive quantity of heroin in her bloodstream but, hey, get this, only *one* puncture mark on her entire body. That was in her neck, too, Joe. Right into the carotid. Somebody pulled her head backwards, exposing her throat, and jammed a syringe right into her.'

'Is this making you hard, Joe?' asked Chew.

I turned to reply. Hewson bitch-slapped me again. 'You were *seen*, Joe Panther. We have a *witness*.'

A cold feeling began to creep through my belly. My capacity for forgiveness is not infinite, contrary to reports.

'You were seen coming out of the alley where Gina Compton's body was dumped. That puts you on site, Joe, and we've already put heroin in your stinking hands.'

I relaxed a little. I could see where this was going. 'And what was my motive?'

He smiled. 'I don't need a motive, son. I need a result. She was nobody's wife. She was a dyke and a stirrer. No one's asking questions. I feel for her parents, that's all. They need closure, Joe, and you can provide it.'

I sighed. It has always been thus, when the bodies are cold and blue and the pious are weeping and dumbstruck. They look at the blood on the blade in their hand, and ask how the Lord could permit it. Personally, I've long preferred a more pertinent question. I asked it now. 'Unless I do what?'

'Good boy. I don't think you did it, Joe,' replied Hewson with a nasty little grin. 'Although I think you know a lot more than what you're saying. I think, to tell the truth, when Gina Compton met her maker you were nowhere near. I think you were slumped against a wall somewhere, too pissed to find your arse, never mind ram a knife through bone and cartilage in one straight shot. But, Joe ...?'

'I'll do?'

'You'll do. Get me some information, Joe. Get me something I can use. Get me a *name* and you'll never see me again. I might just tell the Drugs guys you've gone on the straight and narrow, too.' He stood up, and made a limp gesture of straightening his clothes. 'Otherwise ... well, you know.'

He turned his back on me and strode to the door. Chew walked up to me, bent from the waist and pecked me lightly on the cheek.

'Kiss it better, Joe,' she said, standing up and smirking again. 'Listen to DS Hewson and take his advice, otherwise the next lips to land on your face will belong to a tattooed multiple murderer with an engorged dick and a toothbrush shank. Pretty man like you. Think about it, Mr Panther. There are worse places to live than here.'

And then they were both gone.

I stood up at last. My clothes felt dull and gritty. I wore no underpants. The air around me smelt of stale smoke and excreted alcohol.

Woe to those who hide deep from the Lord their counsel, whose deeds are in the dark, and who say, 'Who sees us? Who knows us?' I have tarried long on this earth. But I am not to be tarried with.

✝

Many have called upon me to smite their enemy. I have never answered. Many, too, have claimed murder justified in my name.

Me, I take care of my own.

It was still only just after eight in the morning, but the bottle shop at the early opener was already doing business. I bought a bottle of gin and another of scotch, both the cheapest on the shelves. I thought about Jamesons for myself, but decided it would have been too much to carry. I bought a miniature bottle of Johnny Black instead, and necked it at the counter while I waited for my change.

Next I went to a pet shop, and bought three metres of clear plastic tubing of the sort used in aquarium aeration systems, cut into two equal lengths. At the hardware store I bought a roll of gaffer tape.

The Mogadon tablet I had taken from Mrs Warburton's bathroom cabinet was collecting lint in my pocket.

I walked into the shadows of the pubs, amusement centres and nightclubs, along pink-stained streets splashed with drying vomit like the disappointment of lovers, around crushed souvlakis and the putrid bins of snack bars. I walked without haste, a man in foul clothing with the cheap booze of promise in his hands. Shopkeepers looked away, uneasy in my presence. A derelict sitting on a bench called to me for a cigarette. I ignored him. He laid a mittened hand on my sleeve as I passed. I turned to him, glaring, and didn't release my gaze until his mumbling stopped and urine stained his trousers.

'Keep thy sorrow to thyself,' I told him, 'and bear with good courage that which hath befallen thee.'

It was too early for my flock to be about. It wouldn't be long, though, before the aches in their hearts began to gnaw, and handbags in the cafes started to go astray. I didn't care. I would be done by then.

Kennedy lived in a tiny cottage in a side street. It had belonged to his late mother, he once told me. He had been born in it, and returned to its hearth when his marriage dissolved.

I entered the garden via the back fence. The flyscreen door at the rear was unlocked, and the wooden door it shielded boasted only a simple lock, which proved no match to the probings of a fit. Once inside, I put on a pair of disposable gloves.

He was asleep on a single bed beneath a troubled sheet. He wore an off-white vest. The room itself contained only a small bedside table, on which stood a glass of water and a wind-up alarm clock. On the walls were a tacked-up poster showing a kitten in a tree above the legend 'Shit Happens!', and an old portrait of the Madonna in a vaguely Byzantine style.

'Hi, mum,' I said to it.

He woke with a start at the sound of my voice, eyes wide, and pulled the sheet up to under his chin like a Hollywood virgin. He opened his mouth to say something, but I held up my free hand and he stopped.

'Whether it be to friend or foe, talk not of other men's lives,' I said.

He started to stammer.

'I warned you.'

He stammered some more.

I held the bottles up in front of him and let them clank together. It sounded like the doleful tolling of a distant funeral. 'The angels have come.'

His face went pale.

'Joe, Joe,' he tried. 'They *forced* me. I *had* to. I have to earn a crust, Joe, you know that. I wanted to stay away like you told me, but ... but ... I've no money, Joe. I had no food for tea. I had to go back and sing, *had* to. I waited, *truly Joe*, I waited till the police car had left, really did.'

'And then they came back, and asked you questions, yes?'

As I asked this, I was crouching down, the bottles on the floor in front of me. I unscrewed the caps, and pulled the clear tubing from my jacket pocket. Kennedy's eyes opened wide, but he didn't attempt to move, except for the twitching of his feet, which I suspected was involuntary.

'They *made* me tell them, Joe. I didn't have a choice. I'd never, *never* ...'

His words dried in his throat. I had two syringes in my left hand, pulling the plungers clean out with my right.

'How much money did they give you, Judas?'

'No, Joe!' The words were a coughed explosion, immediately controlled. He continued. 'I'd never sell you out for money, Joe. *Never*! They, they ...'

I was fixing the syringes to the ends of the tubing, gaffertaping them together.

'They what?'

'They threatened to take me in, lock me up. I couldn't stand that, Joe. Look at me. I wouldn't last a day. They *terrified* me, Joe.'

Now I was doing the tricky bit: holding the other end of one of the tubes just inside the neck of the gin bottle, and surrounding it with gaffer to hold it firm and watertight.

'What was the charge?'

His eyes were locked now on the bottles. He spoke directly towards them. 'Busking without a licence.'

I couldn't help but snort with amusement. He'd sold me out to defend his right to sing Tony Bennett for pennies in public. What profit hath a man, I reflected, of all his labour which he taketh under the sun?

The tubes were sealed into both bottles now. I stood up, walked over to the bed, put my hand in my pocket and looked down upon him. I pulled out the Mogadon and held it out. 'To obey is better than sacrifice,' I said. 'Wash this down with water.'

He stared at the tablet as if it were poison. 'What is it?' he asked.

'Something to make you sleep a while.' I handed him the glass of water.

'But I don't want to sleep, Joe.'

'Yes, you do.'

He did as he was told. Blessed are the meek, because it never occurs to them to scream for help.

He would be awake for a little while yet, but he lay still as I picked up the bottles and put them down on the bedside table. I passed him the syringes, needles uppermost. 'Hold on to those, Kennedy, and don't tip them over.'

He nodded and grasped them, eager in the construct of his own fate.

It took quite a lot of gaffer to bind the scotch bottle upside down to the wall above and to the left of his head. The gin took even more, mainly because I kept getting the tape stuck to itself in the effort to lean over the bed to reach the ideal spot on the right. Eventually, however, the job was done.

Saying nothing, I took the fits from his fingers, gentle as a mother. He stared up at me, helpless, waiting, I fancied, for mercy, for the warning to be at an end, for the reprieve of the lesson well learned as he'd seen so often in the movies.

It never came. History is not the story written down. History is the silences between the sentences, the gloss of the gaps, the bits which passed before it came to pass.

He winced, but did not flinch, as I gently pushed the needles into the risen veins of his soft white forearms and sealed them with a strip of tape. The scotch tube turned the brown of drying sand, the gin one remaining clear like the thrill of a crisp spring day.

I squatted beside him to wait for his slumber.

'Four years dry, Kennedy.'

'I don't want to die, Joe,' he sobbed, looking right at my face now — a less terrifying option, I guessed, than staring at his arms in silent congress with his demons.

'Perhaps you won't.' I stroked his forehead. It was wet and cold. 'Perhaps you'll wake up and free yourself of your bonds. My guess, you won't want to.'

His eyelids started to flutter, heavily, exponentially. I stood up.

'Thou hast drunken the dregs of the cup of trembling, Kennedy,' I intoned. 'And wrung them out.'

As I closed the back door behind me and stepped into the increasing cruelty of the harsh morning sun, I thought I heard him call my name. I didn't answer.

Thus has it ever been.

CHAPTER 4

'Where you taking me?' Nessie's voice sounded not unlike the dumb screech of a Paschal lamb when it first sees the blade. 'What's this place? Don't want to go in here. Want to go home.'

We were outside the unobtrusive street-level door to Sappho's Sisters, a narrow and steep staircase presenting a considerable obstacle to our progress. The centre was in a nondescript two-storey, pre-war building on William Street, the main drag through Northbridge into town. The ground floor housed a franchise printing business. There was a table-dancing club to the right, and to the left a refurbished Rechabite Hall, its ground floor hosting a tiny barbershop and sparsely furnished internet cafe. A wide veranda provided partial cover from the aching morning heat, its usefulness decreasing as the time ticked towards noon.

I ignored the old woman's fretting and yelled up the stairs for Laz.

I am as good as my word. I keep my pledges and speak with one mind, if possibly three natures. This puts me well ahead of many of the clerics in history, which is as it should be. I had promised Mrs Warburton that I would take Nessie for a push around the block in return for that cup of coffee, and that was exactly what I was doing.

My mind was alive. I had visited the loose-lipped Kennedy and poured my spirits into him without favour nor thoughts of recompense. I long for the sleep of the just, but deliver the sleep of the just drunk. After laying him down to rest, I had returned to the house, showered, changed and slugged two cups of plunger-made Lavazza. My mind was thus as clear as my conscience. After that I'd called Laz from the phone booth, and had a brief conversation. I told her about Gina's smack attack, and to expect me in an hour or so.

It is written that with the ancient is wisdom, and in the length of days understanding. I wouldn't know. I have been thirty-three for nigh on two millennia now, and what enlightenment waits in senility must, it seems, remain always a mystery to me. Nessie was incomparably younger than I, of course, yet whatever wisdom her four-score years had brought her seemed well and truly hidden beneath a constant stream of cantankerous drivel.

Blessed are the aged, for they are good cover. I told the old lady that we were going to visit her grandchildren. As far as I knew, she didn't have any, but it would have been cruel to tell her. I put two dozen little foil wraps in her clutch purse, which she grasped to her lap, and told her they were sweeties to be given to whomsoever I suggested. She was happy to oblige — or too confused to contest the point, I couldn't really tell.

There is a furtiveness about smack dealing which can be quite depressing. I am at home in the shadows, adept at the sleight of hand, the quick flick of the tongue, the contrived accidental dropping of little bits of litter; but how much nicer it is, when circumstances permit, to step into the light and make a spectacle unto the world. Appearances deceive, I am testament to that. Not even the most hard-hearted cop in a passing divvy van would fain suspect a bewildered octogenarian in a wheelchair of supplying narcotics to the young.

Not a few junkies would rob one, however. Unless I happened to be standing right behind her.

My flock greeted me as we trundled the streets. They emerged from alleys, crow-eyed and fidgeting; pushed up from their stools in the front bars where they cradled beer for hours, sharp-eyed for unattended mobile phones; rose from the pavements where they sat gaunt with handwritten signs saying 'Homeless & Hungry'. They came in their ones and twos, and laid bare their wherewithal, which they placed in the open maw of the clutch purse and received in return a shiny sweet from a wrinkled and liver-spotted hand.

'Rot your teeth, that will,' snapped Nessie each time, by way of benediction. She might have been enjoying herself, but it was difficult to know for sure. I didn't let it bother me.

And now we were at the door. I called for Laz once more.

'Where you taking me?' hissed Nessie again. 'Is this a nursing home?'

I explained I needed to see a friend, and that it wouldn't take long. I told her she might even get a cup of tea out of the experience, which seemed to mollify her slightly. After a few minutes I heard the heavy footfalls of the mother of God on the stairs. Her face looked drawn, her eyes rimmed with red.

'I wept,' she said, even though I hadn't asked.

'It's that *fat* bitch,' snarled Nessie. 'I don't like her. Up to no good, that one.'

'And hello to you, too, Nessie,' said Laz, patronisingly.

'Don't want to talk to you,' the old lady replied, averting her eyes.

'You're not high on my A-list yourself, you crone,' came the retort.

I decided to bring the discourse back on track. 'Are you alone?'

Laz shook her head. 'Most of the women went home once the call came through about Gina. It hit them hard. I said I'd stay behind to look after the office, but really it was because I knew you might ring. Anita stayed, too, said she had work to do.'

'Anita?'

Laz's lips contorted in distaste. 'Real hardcore separatist. Self-obsessed bitch, you ask me. Took the news like she'd been told McDonald's was fast food. She'll go ape-shit when she sees a man in the building.'

I shrugged. It was no particular problem. 'So we use the cover story.'

'Dumb story, Joe.'

'It's the only one we've got. Do me a favour and grab the front of the chair.'

Laz exhaled in disgust. 'I'm pregnant, Joe. Very, in case you hadn't noticed. I'm not supposed to lift heavy weights.'

'She's not heavy. Besides, I'll be bearing all the weight from the back. You've just got to keep the front wheels off the stairs.'

She swore under her breath, but bent and assumed her burden nevertheless.

'I don't want her touching me.' Nessie scowled, and tried ineffectually to fend Laz off with a slow flick of her withered arm. We both ignored her.

The ascent began. From my position I could see quite clearly down the front of Laz's loose tee-shirt. Her breasts were swollen, inscribed with prominent blue veins, fecund and ripe with the promise of nourishment. They moved me not.

'So, again,' said Laz, puffing slightly. 'What's she?'

'I have a *name*, young lady,' interrupted Nessie.

'She's a sister.'

'You too,' said Nessie again. She rocked from side to side as we hauled her up. 'Not the cat's mother, you know.'

'Not unless the cat's mother was a complete bitch,' offered Laz, slightly louder than was strictly necessary. 'What's the story again, Joe?'

'She's a sister with some issues to resolve,' I explained. 'She thinks she wants to come out.'

'She's left it a bit bloody late, hasn't she? She's almost dead.'

'Cow,' snapped Nessie.

'She that hath clean hands shall be stronger and stronger. You place an age limit on revelation?'

'Shut it, Joe. So she's a senile sister, who are you?'

'Her carer. She can't get about by herself. Think of me as a seeing-eye dog with a beard.'

A dog, aye, I thought to myself, this time chasing after someone else's vomit. We were almost at the top now. The walls were covered in an untidy collection of blue-tacked posters exhorting the reclamation of the night, and the heretic suggestion that no means no. In the gaps between them were handwritten notices advertising spare rooms in houses, available to non-smoking, vegetarian, gay women, to share with two similar and cats called Doris Day.

'My office,' puffed Laz, 'is right across the other side of

the main room, through the door. You wheel Nessie straight through and I'll explain to Anita if she arcs up.'

'Your computer already on?'

She nodded. 'I'll join you in a sec, anyway.'

Most of Sappho's Sisters was a large open space which bore absolutely no resemblance to a temple of Aphrodite. The bare wooden floor area contained a few sofas and battered armchairs of op-shop provenance, and several cheap metal shelving units buckling beneath the weight of boxed magazines, reports and dry-looking paperbacks. On a low coffee table I could see a thick volume bearing the logo of the Equal Opportunities Commission next to copies of a glossy magazine called *Diva*. On one side of the room there was a fifties' laminated kitchen table with a tea urn and related detritus. On the other was a row of chipped desks, some of which supported computers. At one of these a woman was seated. Anita, I presumed. I could only see her from the back as I pushed Nessie, momentarily quiet, across the floor, but that back was large and broad, the neck thick, the hair crew-cut short.

She turned to look at me as I passed. I saw a hard face with pale blue eyes and a very serious steel pipe piercing her nasal septum. Mostly, however, I saw what was on her computer screen. I only saw it for a second, but that was enough. It doesn't take a whole lot of time to recognise a sadomasochistic spanking film when you see one. She opened her mouth to speak. Laz called her name in the nick of time. I continued through the door at the end, hardly bumping the chair into it at all.

Once inside I pushed Nessie as far as I could over to the left, but even so she still took up almost half of the available space.

'Want me tea,' she grizzled.

I told her to wait, and grabbed a magazine from the cluttered surface of the desk and dropped it into her lap. 'Read that,' I commanded. It was called *Wicked Wimmin*. The front cover was a grainy shot of a mohawked woman dressed in leather cowboy gear, holding a stock whip.

'Haven't got me glasses,' the old woman complained.

Just as well, I thought, and sat down before the computer. On the wall behind it, Laz had personalised her space. Sticky-taped to the surface were a cheap calendar from a local Chinese restaurant, a Peanuts cartoon strip which must have held some personal relevance, and a photograph of a tall woman in a conservative mauve two-piece suit. The woman was smiling, standing ramrod straight, with her hands clasped in front of her. She looked to be about forty years old. I realised I was looking at Ayzel. Very top end of town.

I took hold of the mouse and wrestled the cursor over to the internet toggle. The screen flashed up a home page and the modem started to make chirping noises. I sat back to wait.

Much has been written about me over the years, what I said, what I did, what I meant. I'm probably a more popular literary subject than sex, you want to get down to it. Probably more than the Spice Girls even. I can't speak to its veracity. It has nothing to do with me. I never wrote anything myself, and that's gospel.

Three of the gospels, say the scholars, drew on a single source, long since lost. They call the lost document *Q*, and think it was a collection of my sayings. Maybe I even wrote it myself. It's not true, of course. The sort of radical politics I got mixed up in back then, writing anything down was tantamount to signing your own death warrant. Not that I needed to worry, as it turned out, from any perspective. As far as I'm aware, the only Q around is a rock music magazine. Maybe I wrote that, I don't know. Maybe in my blackouts I write rock stories. Maybe I'm Paul McCartney. Maybe I shot John Lennon and stabbed George Harrison. Might as well be blamed for it. I've been blamed for everything else. Imagine there's no heaven, indeed. There isn't, as far as I can tell, but hey, what do I know? Maybe I just don't meet the entry requirements. I don't own a tie, after all.

Plenty of people, I discovered, had written about the Transpersonal Foundation. The search engine threw up 5240 hits.

I glanced over at Nessie before proceeding. The magazine was propped against her clutch purse, her head tilted to one side. Nessie tended to doze off a lot without warning. It was easily her most personable trait.

First up I triggered the Foundation's own home page. It was big and bright and very, very slick. It was also — and this did not for a moment surprise me — American. The Transpersonal program, I discovered, promised insight and breakthrough into a whole new way of living. Personal achievement and fulfilment were the dual aims, to be reached through greater confidence, prosperity, success and, to judge by the photographs, the wearing of dicky name tags.

'The Transpersonal Foundation is not a religion,' I read, although everybody in the photos looked remarkably like earnest young Mormons. The gaining of wisdom, it appeared, was a gradual process, facilitated by the taking of various courses in nebulous subjects such as 'self-expression', 'leadership', 'communication' and 'team management'. The courses were intensive and expensive both.

And I thought: He is a merchant, the balances of deceit are in his hand: he loveth to oppress.

The Transpersonal Foundation had branches in many nations, including, of course, several in Australia. The senior office bearers were listed by name. There was no mention of a Perth branch, nor of Clem Porter. This was not necessarily surprising. Perth troubles the memory of the world so rarely, it is often overlooked.

'Figured it out?'

It was Laz, squeezing her swollen bulk into the little free space left within her office.

'The computer? I know its nature these days. Trouble outside?'

'Anita's not best pleased. Anyone would think you were defiling holy ground by being here. I don't think she bought the cover story for a minute, but she's going to wear it. I'm a woman in mourning, after all.'

The sound of our voices roused Nessie. She let out a little phlegmy cough, followed by a demand for tea. I looked over my shoulder to Laz. 'Would you mind?'

'Fucking hell,' she sighed. 'I'm IT administrator here every day of the week. A man walks in, I'm the tea lady.' She turned, nevertheless, and started to heave once again through the door. 'You want one, too?'

I shook my head. 'Got any beer?'

'No, Joe,' came her disapproving reply as she walked away.

I shrugged. No matter, I could stop at a pub on the way home.

Every religion produces dissent, even when clothed in secular robes. I began punching up other sites, starting with the one called 'The *Real* History of TF'. It was written by a man claiming to be a priest and an expert on cults, so I was doubly wary. Nevertheless, it was not without illumination. The Transpersonal Foundation, I discovered, had started in the late sixties when the craze for guru-led enlightenment was at its height among the young of the United States. In those days it was called the Melchior Method, which told me a heap. Melchior was the name invented in the sixth century for one of three wise men who had allegedly attended my birth. They were Persians, Zoroastrian magi, apparently. I can't tell for sure, of course, but personally I doubt the story. I've never met a priest of any persuasion yet who couldn't find room at the inn.

Not that it mattered in this case. Hitch your wagon to things long gone, appeal to the lost knowledge of the elders, and the young will come aflock. Look and ask for the ancient paths, where the good way is. Follow the Father; venerate the dead. Or, failing that, just grab the name of some obscure old git, make it up as you go along, and claim to be acting in his wisdom.

The New Age guru in this particular case was a man who took up the cause after shoe-selling failed to make him a bomb. It was a spectacular success, according to the melancholy priest, appealing to the young middle class who wanted their enlightenment drug-free and churchless. They came in droves, and the organisation spread apace.

Then the problems began. Fearful parents began to fret, shunned by their children. Apostates began to complain of eighteen-hour rants with neither food nor opportunity to pee. Of course, they were pronounced backsliders and scorned. The shoe salesman eventually made a fast exit, followed by allegations of child abuse and tax avoidance. The organisation changed its name and modified its methods, pronouncing itself cleansed, repentant and at least twice as efficient.

The door creaked, waking Nessie again. Laz entered and handed her a mug of tea. The old woman didn't say thank you.

'Found much?'

'Tracts, gospels and commentary,' I replied.

'So what do you reckon?'

'Standard cult crap: follow me, subjugate your will, fork over your dosh and all will be fine.'

'I thought you mentioned earlier this mob wasn't religious?'

I shook my head. 'Religion has nothing to do with gods. It's about the promise of salvation by following a doctrine. Secular groups can work on mindless obedience and the pursuit of distant happiness just as well as sacred ones. Look at Amway, for instance.'

Laz forced a black chuckle. 'Had a friend once who used to sell herbal products door to door. Party plans, the lot. She had meetings with the supervisors every week. They used to sing songs and hug and punch the air, all of it. I went along once. It was like, what do you call it, a revivalist meeting — you know, when they talk in tongues.'

'Glossolalia.'

'Whatever you say, Joe.'

'What happened to your friend? Did she get rich and happy?'

'She got dead. St John's wort, nutmeg and smack, not a good mixture.'

71

I was triggering at random off the search list, pulling up people's personal sites. Many were glowing testimonials to the efficacy of TF, all weirdly similar. Others were strident condemnations from people who called themselves victims. They alleged abuse and harassment when they tried to leave the organisation, persistent phone calls in the middle of the night, demands for money, stress-related hallucinations, morbid depression, suicide attempts.

I thought of the heavy pestle by the side of Gina Compton's bed, the message on the answering machine. For religions throughout history there has been only one thing worse than an apostate, and that's an apostate left alive to talk. Had Gina been planning to go public about some nasty experiences with Clem Porter's mob? What had happened in the share house? I cursed myself for not searching the flat more thoroughly. Perhaps I would have found, hidden somewhere, something written, a rough draft of an article starting *J'accuse*.

Perhaps.

'Did Gina have her own desk here?'

'No. Catch as catch can in this place, except for this office and Lucy the manager's.'

'Was there, I don't know, a drawer that was hers, or a cupboard, somewhere she could have stashed something she didn't want at her house?'

'Like what?'

I shook my head. 'Notes, maybe. Something about this Transpersonal mob.'

'I doubt it, but I'll have a look later, if you want. Do you think she was killed because she wouldn't tell this lot what she had on them?'

I thought about that. 'Maybe, maybe not. She wasn't

tortured. It's worth a punt, though. The cops will come to the same conclusion probably by tomorrow. They'll want her papers and any personal effects she left here.'

Laz made thinking noises. 'I'll do it later today, or first thing tomorrow. Right now I don't want to, you know, go poking around a dead woman's possessions. It feels horrible, especially with Anita still in here.'

Which reminded me. I turned my attention back to Nessie, prodding her gently.

'You OK?'

'I want to go to the toilet,' she snapped, just as I'd hoped she would.

'We'll be home soon,' I said.

'No good,' she hissed, and waved her mug at me to show that it was now empty. 'Need to go *now*. Gone right through me, this tea has.'

I turned around again to look at Laz.

'No *way*, Joe,' she began, trying to back out of the room.

I raised my eyebrows imploringly. 'I can't pull an old woman's knickers down. Especially not in here. I'm sure Anita out there would go ballistic if she saw me going into the women's toilets.'

'That's all we have here, Joe.'

'Then —'

'Forget it, Joe. Yuck.'

Nessie made a strained, whimpering noise and pushed her knees together.

I shrugged. 'OK, Laz. It's your carpet.'

She growled, then grabbed the wheelchair roughly and yanked it backwards. 'You're a total bastard, Joe.'

Not without incident or protest, the pair disappeared through the door in reverse.

I gave them a minute to reach their objective, then pushed back my own chair and stood. They hadn't shut the office door when they left. Peering through, I could see the considerable bulk of Anita still bent at her work.

She was so absorbed in staring at her computer that she didn't hear my approach until I was at her side. She was no longer watching the spanking footage, with its unsteady vision and buttocks the colour of sunset. The scene now depicted a woman strung up by the wrists, naked but for a ball-gag in her mouth and stiletto heels. A man in a black hood was whipping her with a mean-looking length of knotted leather. I could see welts across her breasts and belly even through the fuzzy focus. I could see the look of fear in her eyes, too.

'Charming,' I said.

The result was predictable. Anita jumped, startled by my voice, then turned to glare at me. For a second there I saw fury in her eyes. I don't know what she saw in mine, but she blinked, and glanced down. When she looked up again, it was as if she'd drawn a veil across her vision.

'What's it to you?' Her question was sullen and challenging in equal measure.

Her tee-shirt was pale yellow, a small rainbow-flag decal at its centre. I could see a Celtic tattoo encircling her hefty right bicep, just below the sleeve. The pipe through her nose owed much to the hill tribes of Papua New Guinea.

'I've seen stuff like it before,' I said, voice neutral.

'I'll bet you have.' Her tone conveyed a hundred implications.

I nodded. 'People died. This real or fake?'

'Does it matter?'

'I don't know. Does it?'

She raised her shoulders, then dropped them, sending unpleasant little ripples down through her trunk. 'Not to me.'

'Why are you watching it?'

Her eyes narrowed. 'What are you? A cop?'

I didn't dignify the question with a response.

She let out a little sigh, figuring perhaps that the best way to get rid of me would be to humour me. I had no doubt, looking at her size and judging by her demeanour, that in other circumstances she would have tried to bat me away with no more concern than a Crusader faced with a crippled Arab; but something made her refrain. She didn't want to upset Laz, I assumed, perhaps out of compassion, or perhaps because Laz had the power to bar her from the premises.

'It's for my Masters thesis,' she muttered, then turned back to the screen and hit a couple of buttons. The tortured woman bucked and recoiled from a whiplash, forwards and backwards, three times in a row.

'I'm studying the depersonalisation and denaturing of the female form by violent erotica,' she said.

Whatever that meant. I nodded. 'Any thoughts on where the attraction lies?'

'Plenty.'

I thought of Hypatia then, don't know why. I met her once, in Alexandria, somewhere around the beginning of the fifth century. She was a pagan, an astronomer, a philosopher and, perhaps above all, a woman. Very popular was Hypatia, except with the local Christians, led by Bishop Cyril. One night she was attacked by a bunch of monks. They dragged her from her carriage and hauled her into the church of Caesareum. There they stripped her and in sight of my tortured image tore her into strips with broken tiles.

I stood outside, weeping as I listened to her screams. I could still weep in those days. When they scurried from their killing, the monks all had erections.

They made Cyril a saint.

'Some people find it a righteous turn-on,' I said.

'Don't see why,' Anita grunted. 'It's just foreplay by another name.'

Something in her reply made me momentarily doubt the wisdom of asking the question it begged. I asked it anyway. 'And what's orgasm by another name?'

She turned to look at me again. This time her pale blue eyes were still, hard and calm. 'Wham, bam, thank you ma'am,' she said. 'If I ever made a film like this, it'd be no longer than a toothpaste commercial. You finished?'

'How well did you know Gina Compton?'

Once more the grunt. She looked back at the screen. 'Had her once,' she said. 'Dud fuck.'

✝

The journey down the stairs was easy. At least it was for me. Nessie squawked each time the chair's rear wheels thumped down on a step. Lazarette followed behind, still obsessively wiping her hands.

'Are you going to need me again today?' she asked.

'I don't know. I'll ring you if I do.'

I heard her sigh. 'I'll stay here then.'

'Go home, Laz. Grieve. I'm told it can be a useful process. I can ring you there.'

'You don't have the number.'

'Give it to me, then.'

'No, Joe.'

As she said that I reached the bottom of the stairs and pushed Nessie out through the door. It was mid-afternoon and the sun scoured the pavement like the force of epiphany. Pedestrians were moderate in number, the restaurants slowly emptying as long lunches segued into early after-work drinks. I left Nessie facing the street, and turned back to look at Laz. She was biting her lower lip, distracted by something.

'Why not,' I asked.

She didn't reply for a moment. Then she said, 'Ayzel's home. Rostered day off.'

'So?'

She sighed, then sat down on the stairs as if collapsing beneath the weight of the cross.

'Ayzel doesn't know about you, Joe.' There was an awkward half-smile on her face. 'Not just about you being the father of my child ... *our* child, hers and mine. She doesn't know anything. She doesn't know you exist. I've never mentioned you, never even hinted.'

This didn't offend me. It reassured. 'So a stranger phones you up. Where's the problem?'

She tapped her hands lightly on her knees.

'Ayzel's ... not like us,' she began. 'I mean, not at all. She never had a drug problem, never did smack, never lived rough. Completely different, Joe. Good upbringing, good family. She came out to her parents when she was fifteen, and they accepted it.' Suddenly she beamed like a child. 'Did I ever tell you how I met her?'

'No.'

'I want to go home,' shrieked Nessie. 'Hot here.'

We both ignored her.

'Ever heard of the Rainbow Sash movement?' asked Laz, serious again.

I'd read about it. It was a loose congregation of Catholic laity and a few dissident priests, enjoined by their gender preferences. They were dismayed because the Church refused to recognise their right to blessings in full honesty. The Church itself maintained it wasn't persecution. They could get anything they wanted among the pews as long as they lied. Thus has it ever been.

'That's how I met her,' Laz was saying. 'The Sashers had a, a picket I suppose you'd call it, outside a church. I went along.'

This surprised me a little. 'I didn't think you gave a shit about the church.'

'I didn't. I don't. I was just ... I don't know. I was full of my new-found confidence and thought, well, you know, it would be good to lend a hand in the name of sisterhood. I went along to bolster the numbers, and, well ...' Her voice trailed off. She looked away, cheeks colouring.

'And what?'

She giggled. 'I thought I might meet a cute Christian girl. Someone different, you know? Someone without holes in her arms or screams in her dreams.'

I nodded. 'And you did.'

'Yeah, I did. Well, not so much a girl. More a woman, working on lady.' Her expression turned serious again. 'But she's different, do you see? She cares. She has ... *forgiveness* in her. I haven't hidden who I am — what I used to be — from her. Not at all. In fact, Joe, I've told her more about myself and my past and my feelings than I've ever told anybody in my life. Including you.'

She looked as if she was expecting me to congratulate her on her good fortune. My silence seemed to rankle her. 'I *mean* it, Joe. She asks and I tell her. I've told her all about smack life.'

I felt my forehead crease. 'All?'

'Except names and distinguishing features, obviously. I've told her about scoring and preparing and hitting up; about scraping for money and being sick and the rush and the nods. I've told her about how you get to the point where you tell yourself that you can't go on living with smack, but really how you're lying, because you know the truth is that you can't live without it. I can *talk* to her, Joe. Like no one else. I can, you know, tell her about things that really degraded me, and then, when I've told her, it feels like ... it feels better, somehow ... like ...'

'Absolution?' I suggested.

She considered it. 'Yeah, maybe. Like it's shit I don't have to carry around with me any more, anyway. And, Joe, I don't understand this, and I know you'll scoff, but I think the depth of her ... heart, spirit, whatever ... comes from her faith. In her own way, she's pious and loving and contemplative and, you know, deeply in love with her Lord. We don't talk about it much, but I respect her position.'

'And so you shield her from sinners.'

With an effort, she levered herself back onto her feet. She stepped over to me, looked up into my eyes, and pressed the back of her hand gently against my cheek. 'She's good and kind and decent, Joe,' she whispered. 'She believes in inherent goodness. She doesn't *deserve* to find out that someone like you exists.'

She turned and started to walk back up the stairs. 'I'll be here till six,' she called over her shoulder.

I watched her go, and thought of patterns repeating, of children denied, and parentage hidden. I thought of the unmet Ayzel, and the torments her dreams would produce.

'I'm thirsty,' crowed Nessie.

'So am I,' I said, and grabbed the chair. 'Best we do something about that.'

We stopped at a pub on the way home. I got myself a stubby of Tooheys Red and a shot of Jamesons, a small rough-gut sherry for the old woman.

'Did you enjoy your day out, Nessie?' I asked her, more to break the silence than anything.

She didn't reply.

'The fresh air must have done you good.'

Again, silence.

'You'll be ready for your dinner tonight.'

No reaction. I gave up, and stared out the window instead.

'Those sweeties,' she said suddenly.

I turned back to look at her.

'The money's in my purse.'

'I know. I'll take it out when we get home.'

Shaking slightly, she raised her glass to her lips and swallowed its contents. 'Only half of it, you will,' she said, looking straight in my face, eyes beady and sharp as a scavenger gull's.

CHAPTER 5

Even in their own house they wore the dicky ID tags. I knew them thus by name, and they were graceless in my sight.

It was dusk when I arrived at their door and knocked. The walk had taken me the best part of an hour, requiring as it did a diagonal route through Northbridge and then a trudge up the gradual incline at the top of Fitzgerald Street to Noble Street, the Mount Lawley side road in which Gina Compton's putative former cult-mates resided. Of course I hadn't remembered the address. I know my limitations and they are tighter than everyone imagines. I remembered, though, that Laz had found it, courtesy of an old telephone directory.

'So that's why I've been sitting here all afternoon, Joe,' she'd complained when I rang her to get it. 'My unborn child is brewing, my lover is at home waiting, my friend has been murdered, but my role in life today is to be your back-up hard drive.'

'I am what I am,' I'd replied. 'Eyer Asher Eyer.'

'What's that?'

Sometimes I slip. I have spoken so many tongues in my time, each as facile as the last. Language is the wrapping on the parcel of syntax, and my gift to you is but an empty box. 'Nothing,' I said. 'Name of my stockbrokers.'

She'd managed a thin laugh at that, then hung up.

I had not originally intended to visit Gina's old address until perhaps the following day, but I needed to get out of the house and it was too soon to do another delivery run.

There is something dismaying about being the object of an old woman's gloat. During the journey from the pub to the house, I had managed to persuade Nessie to drop her cut to twenty per cent. It had been a hard bargain. It's difficult to argue against silence and drool. During her flashes of lucidity, however, she had managed to make her position quite clear: either I dealt her in, or she'd talk to the police.

It was not, of course, an unassailable place from which to make a stand. According to Hewson and Chew, my economic activity had already been noted. I was being tolerated and contained, if barely. Nessie didn't know that. She did know, however, as did I, that a complaint to a uniform from a little old lady would compel action. The result would probably be more of an irritant than a felling stroke, but it was still something to be avoided. By the same token, her capacity to provide gerontological cover for me and my flock had proved rather useful. By the time I wheeled her up the garden path we had settled our bargain: henceforth, when weather, circumstances and bowels permitted, we would be a team.

'Hope she hasn't caught a cold, keeping her out like that,' Mrs Warburton had rebuked the moment we reached the door.

'That fat bitch pulled my knickers down,' Nessie whined as she was wheeled away along the passage. Mrs Warburton looked back at me over her shoulder, scowling with disapproval.

Half an hour later, the old woman had been returned, smelling slightly of something antiseptic, to the shadowed front room, where I was sitting quietly drinking a cup of coffee and contemplating a joint. Mrs Warburton instructed me haughtily, and quite unnecessarily, to keep an eye while she herself went to the kitchen to microwave some packet macaroni cheese for their tea. Nessie said nothing, appearing to have sunk once again into stupor. Had she told Mrs Warburton about the deal, I wondered. Probably not: I was pretty sure my landlady simply wouldn't have wanted to know. She considered my activities, like everything that happened outside her own insular consciousness, none of her business. I put the question to my new business partner, nevertheless. Her response might have been a wink or a muscle tic, a smile or the egestion of excess saliva. Amid such ambiguities, I find, life thrives. That's what makes it so dangerous.

I decided to have a shower, then get some air.

So now, the waning sun lost behind a bank of bulbous and pregnant storm clouds, did I stand at the strangers' threshold and bear false witness.

It was a turn-of-the-century, single-storey house, brick with a corrugated iron roof, typical of the neighbourhood. In its first incarnation it would have been the genteel expression of a sturdy, conservative middle class. These days it bore the peeling paint and scrappy garden typical of the rental jobs which surrounded the nearby university. It was a share house in an area where such arrangements were common. The house next door reeked of linseed oil, growled like a power tool and hosted a small BMW in its drive. The journey from broken-down to bijou is short indeed.

The young man who answered the door was called Iain, at least according to his name tag. I judged him to be in his mid-twenties. His shirt was white, his trousers, like his hair, black and well ordered.

Me, I was wearing my old grey suit, the dying light of the day sufficient to hide its frays and imperfections from the casual glance. It was still rather too hot to have the jacket buttoned, but I had done so anyway, figuring that if my lies were to work most of the Sonic Youth tee-shirt should remain concealed.

'Good afternoon,' I said, deep and sombre. 'My name is John Lloyd and I wonder if I might have a moment of your time on a deeply sad matter.' I was, I explained, an employee of the funeral company engaged to deal with the final interment of Gina Compton. It was my role in this solemn procedure to talk to as many of the deceased's friends and colleagues as time permitted, the better for the company orator to paint a picture of her life in the eulogy. Her suffering parents had mentioned that she had once lived at this address.

Iain nodded, reluctantly compliant with the protocols of death, and ushered me into the lounge room. It contained a two-seater sofa and four grey armchairs which looked as if they might have hailed from an office supply store. The carpet was beige, the walls dull green, unadorned by print or shelving. The over-all effect was somewhere between ascetic austerity and public service functionality. He gestured that I should take the sofa, then went off to get the others.

They gathered in less than a minute, which made me think they had been waiting just outside the room, listening, watching. It didn't bother me. Often have I been watched. Rarely have I been seen.

They were Adam and Nigel, their tags made plain, and both shared the same taste in clothes as Iain. Nigel's hair was brown, blending to ginger, and I took him to be the youngest of the three. Adam wore wire-frame spectacles and a hearing aid. They both shook my hand, then sat, completing the trinity in front of me.

'You understand, of course,' the one called Adam was saying, 'that we didn't know her very well.'

His voice betrayed the cautious and blunt pronunciation of the partly deaf. It was plainly not the one I'd heard on her answering machine, the voice pleading for her to return to the fold, the voice which called her Geen. Had death already come to her when that message was left? Or had she sat, gently shaking her head perhaps, listening to the blandishments coming down the line, before quietly walking out of the door of her flat, never to return? What had been the expression on her face: wry amusement at the folly of it all, or the sad-eyed despair of an apostate unable to escape her demons?

If I was clear on that little detail, of course, then my task would have been pretty much at its end, at least in terms of assessing the potential involvement of the geek trio whose sanctuary I had now violated. Omniscience would be nice sometimes, but not often. There are some things, after all, that even the son of God wishes not to know. The Pope's dreams, for instance. Britney Spears' IQ. Or the hopes of the poor.

So it hadn't been Adam's voice, but I didn't think it mattered. The message on the machine had been from one of the three, that was all that was germane. I couldn't mention it, of course. It had not crossed their minds to ask why my mission had to be attended to in the early evening, nor to question my source of information, nor why the sombre Mr Lloyd had failed to produce identification. They were anxious to help in any way they could, they said. The living must wait for justice, but the dead receive instant attention. Even, if Adam was to be believed, from near strangers.

'I'm sorry,' I said, affecting a slightly confused and embarrassed tone. 'I must have been misinformed. I was under the impression that Ms Compton had lived here for a while.'

'Well,' said the one named Iain, throwing a lightning glare at Adam, 'she did, but, you know, I guess she didn't really fit in. We never, you know, got close to her.'

I nodded in an understanding way, thinking: Laz found this place because the phone had been in Gina's name. I'd be willing to bet the lease was, too.

'Never mind,' I continued, giving them an ingratiating smile. 'I'm sure your impressions will still be most useful. Did she, do you think, seem a happy woman?'

The question seemed to perplex them. 'I ... guess so,' stammered Adam.

'Would you describe this as a happy house? When she was here, I mean.'

'Like I said,' replied Adam again, 'she never really fitted in. Kept herself to herself, you know?'

'All the time?'

'Well,' he said. 'Not at first. At first we all had ... ah ...'

'Common interests,' interjected Iain. I caught the warning in his tone.

'Common interests, yes, but then she, I don't know ...'

'Lost interest.' Iain again, cautious.

'Which is not uncommon,' offered Adam.

I decided to play dumb. I've had a lot of practice. 'What sort of common interests? Like sport?'

'*Intellectual* interests,' corrected Iain, offended. 'Sort of philosophy, lifestyle questions, that sort of thing.'

'I see. Are you, if you don't mind me asking, students?'

Adam nodded. 'We study a lot, yes. Like Iain said, philosophy and stuff. Psychology. Making the best use of inner strengths, learning to focus, you know.'

It was my turn to nod. 'At the university?'

Adam looked at Iain. Iain replied. 'We study privately.'

'Sort of exclusive, you know?' chipped in Adam.

'Ahh.' I smiled. 'And Gina was studying with you?'

'For a while,' conceded Adam.

'It wasn't for her, though,' said Iain. 'She lost interest and moved out.'

I tried to look as if I was digesting this latest piece of non-information, then threw in a curve ball.

'I won't take up much more of your time,' I said. 'I should thank you. Sometimes when I talk to people who weren't all that close to a deceased, they feel a need to invent things, to paint the best picture possible. All understandable, of course, but it can introduce distressing untruths into the eulogy. So thank you for your honesty. I wonder if you could shed some light on something else for me? It's a long shot, of course, but may I ask you?'

Sensing that their play-acting session was winding to a conclusion, all three relaxed visibly and accepted my compliment. Even the young Nigel — to this point still silent and wary — managed to indicate his goodwill with an effete flick of his right hand.

'I'm told that Gina was good friends with someone called Clem Porter, but I'm having trouble finding him. I wonder, did she ever mention the name to you?'

The reaction was immediate and frosty. All three shook their heads, Nigel showing momentary alarm, the others something more like anger.

'Ah well.' I shrugged. 'It was worth a try. Excuse me for asking, but I couldn't help noticing your name tags. May I ask, are you, I don't know, members of a church? Is it the Bible you study?'

Iain scoffed at that, a little more forcefully than the question required. 'There *is* no god,' he sneered.

'Well, thank you for clearing that up,' I replied. 'I'd been wondering.'

He nodded sagely, his previous displeasure gone, pleased to be of service.

'So why the name tags?' I persisted.

He slipped from confident back to defensive in a nanosecond, snapping that it was none of my business.

Adam seemed to shrink at the sound of Iain's raised voice. He tilted forward in his chair and spoke with the condescending tones of a Sunday School teacher. 'They're a kind of study aid,' he said. 'In order to find your inner potential it's important to define yourself as an individual. We wear tags to remind ourselves of our delimited reality, and the power of intelligent self-interest over flawed theories of group consciousness.'

He sat back, exhausted by his effort. I wasn't surprised. It must have taken him ages to memorise it.

The one called Nigel, so far mute, had reddened. I turned to him. 'You liked Gina, didn't you?'

Nigel nodded, blushing more. Adam smirked. Iain sneered, and looked away.

Suddenly I knew a lot. I knew that Nigel's role in the household was to do what he was told. I knew, too, that Nigel had once made a play for Gina's sweet charms, only to be rejected. Perhaps it had been his voice on the machine, his entreaties to her to rejoin the Transpersonal fold merely an excuse for trying again to attract her attention.

The quality of my mercy has been strained so long and so often that by now it is pure and inert. I decided to exercise it.

Fixing Nigel — and only Nigel — in my stare, I said, 'I suppose she might have found it difficult settling in here, three fine lads like yourselves, what with her being gay and everything.'

Nigel looked at his knees. I could see the muscles of his jaw tense and bulge. His knuckles turned pale. He was a slim man with a sunken chest and bad skin, but there was anger inside him. I glanced quickly at the others. Adam looked uncomfortable with the topic. Iain was now looking straight at Nigel, visibly enjoying his discomfit.

'Such a terrible way to go,' I continued, shaking my head sadly. 'Shot up with drugs, then stabbed through the neck.'

Nigel stood explosively, knocking his chair over backwards. His fists were clenched as he strode to the front door. He had one hand on the handle when Iain spoke. 'Nigel,' he warned. 'Sit down.'

'I need some fresh air,' responded Nigel. His tone was stubborn and defiant, but he looked only at the floor.

'Remember, Nige,' Adam contributed, 'it's all about self-control. You let life get on top of you, it crushes you.'

The statement sounded as rote as it did twee. Nigel didn't move. Iain cleared his throat, reclaiming the dominant position. I watched them closely. All three seemed to have temporarily forgotten my presence.

'Listen,' he said. 'Sit down again. No one can change the past, Nigel, you know that. No one can weep for death. It simply comes, probabilistic and random, banal and strange.

If your best friend dies, do you cry at his end or celebrate his life?'

'But...' Nigel was clearly experiencing some inner conflict. He still hadn't looked up from the floor, nor taken his hand from the door. It was plain to me, though, that he would soon do both, even if it wasn't his intention.

'Some people,' he stammered, 'they don't *deserve* to die ... not like that.'

Iain laughed then, harshly. 'Oh Nigel,' he said, 'you've still got a long way to go, haven't you? What are you up to? What is it, level three?'

Nigel nodded.

Iain continued his patronising attack. 'Level *three*. After what — two years? Sometimes I wonder if you're serious about your life, I really do. Nobody *deserves* to die, Nigel. There is no retribution, no reward. Some people die sooner, some later. It's a genes thing, a random thing, an exercise in statistical roulette, and trying to find meaning in it is about as useful as mourning the dead when they've gone. You *know* that, Nigel. You've *done* that.'

Adam, I noticed, was nodding gravely.

A silence hung for a moment, then Nigel let go of the handle and meekly crossed the room to where his chair lay. Saying nothing, looking nowhere, he set it upright and sat, fingers intertwined. Iain and Adam had watched him all the way, as if driving him with their eyes. I decided to take advantage.

'What level are *you* up to, Iain?' I asked.

'Nine,' he said proudly. A second later he looked flustered, then angry, then worried. 'What's it to you, anyway?' he challenged. 'You don't even know what we're talking about.'

I looked him square in the face. 'Gina was already dead this past year, as far as you were concerned, wasn't she? As soon as she walked out the door, she was dead to you. She found her life and lost it. For whose sake did she lose it, Iain?'

'I think you'd better go now,' he growled, standing up, eyes down, hands aquiver, terrified by his own show of courage.

Outside the night was darker than the time would have suggested. The storm clouds had swelled, pendulous, their waters starting to break. The air was warm and sticky, making my tee-shirt cling to my skin as I walked away from the house.

I knew I would have to go back there soon enough. There would have to be more questions, without the veil of subterfuge. That particular subterfuge, anyway. When I begin, I will also make an end. For the moment, though, I was content to let the aggressive Iain imagine he had repelled inquiries and quashed an in-house mutiny. He would learn in good time of his vanity.

I began the walk home at ambling pace, partly because of the heat, and partly because I am never in a hurry to see what happens next. Two blocks in I stopped at the Rosemount Hotel bottleshop and scored a 750 ml bottle of Swan lager to fuel the journey. The liveried young man behind the counter informed me that he was not allowed to crack the top on a takeaway. I suggested to him calmly that he might like to reconsider that policy and find cause for unilateral action. He did.

My mind entertained the possibilities of the day as I strolled, bottle in one hand, Dunhill in the other, oblivious to the big fat drops of rain which fell sparse and sullen around me, evaporating within seconds of hitting the concrete. Clearly there was turbulence in the tides of the affairs of the trio in the house. Clearly, too, there was an absolute prohibition on mentioning Clem Porter's name in the presence of strangers. Whatever the reason, ideology or alibi, I would discover it sooner or later. For I revealeth the deep and secret things: I knoweth what is in the darkness, and the light dwelleth with me.

I should know. I've been waiting two millennia for the bulb to blow and welcome darkness descend upon my sleep. Nothing, alas, nothing has come, but endless, empty illumination.

The streets transformed slowly from quaint suburb to the less decorative, more comforting first strands of the inner city. Manicured lawns gave way to Greek delis, dry-cleaning stores, Vietnamese restaurants, Italian butchers, and travel agents offering dust-covered promises of distant deliverance. I passed a pharmacy, a large sign on the door: NO CASH OR DRUGS OF ADDICTION KEPT ON THE PREMISES. Fair enough, I thought, but they might have done their bit for customer service and stuck another sign beneath: CASH CAN BE FOUND AT THE ATM ACROSS THE ROAD; FOR DRUGS OF ADDICTION, PLEASE GO TO JAMES STREET AND ASK FOR JOE. This world, after all, has no qualms about loudly proclaiming the other services I'm alleged to offer — salvation, forgiveness, love — with neither caveat nor caution. The only damn gig I actually turn a quid with, though, not a word. Perhaps I should pledge to tithe ten per cent of turnover to the Pentecostals, then I might get a bit of pulpit-driven plugging now and then.

For mine is the kingdom, the powder, the story. For ever and ever.

I pulled on the Swan and tried to set my thoughts in order, assess the findings of the day.

Clem Porter was obviously still right up there in the suspect stakes. Despite the emphasis within Transpersonal Foundation literature on self-responsibility, I was pretty sure that his three young acolytes rarely if ever exercised free will when it came to his affairs. They had been told never to mention his name to strangers, and they were obeying like automatons.

Here was a man who stalked in the night and moved without fear. Here was a man who when he met me in the mutual commission of crime neither flinched nor ran. Here was a man without record of life. I tried to resist the next thought, although it was about as successful as attempts by the bones of my wrists to resist the encroachments of iron. Here was a man like me. Only with more money.

I didn't like that idea.

And the young lads themselves, individually or in concert, had to be regarded as possibilities. Had Gina left voluntarily, or been ostracised by one or more of them? Iain plainly bore her antipathy. By leaving she had betrayed the principles he held dear, and perhaps, in the shallow fanaticism of group dynamics, that could not be allowed to go unpunished. There is nothing I've seen, after all, to make me assume the godless are any less passionate and vindictive than the holy. I could imagine all too easily a ritual cast to her execution.

The voice on her answering machine had been Nigel's, I was sure of that, but how coded was his message? Were the words he spoke his own? Perhaps he had wanted to entice her to return out of compassion and concern. Perhaps, too, he was made devious by desire, determined in some secret part of his mind to displace his scorned lust with dick-thickening murderous rage. Then again, perhaps the Transpersonal Foundation had nothing to do with it. Perhaps the killer had been someone else entirely: someone I knew, or someone not yet in the picture. Laz had voiced a fear of a homicidal homophobe. Gina, gay and newly out, defiantly so in her dress code and place of work, had not been raped or robbed, but she had been penetrated, front and back. Had she been killed in the end by intolerant metaphor? There are many cruel ways to die, but none so awful as by literary term.

I cut down across Russell Square, a small park at the edge of the Northbridge precinct, tossing my now empty beer bottle on the grass. A knot of homeless sat about in the rotunda in the centre of the park, some passing booze to one another, others simply waiting for something, anything, to happen. A man in grubbed overalls sat sprawled on a bench, surrounded by bulging plastic bags. He cried for his mother and God, calling them both bastards. A few teenage prostitutes patrolled the perimeter, as usual, some too young yet even to have a smack habit. A couple of them walked over to me, both short and displaying the defensive plumpness that is often a father's gift to an abused daughter. They knew me as local, as I them, so there was no hype in their greeting.

'Joe,' said the oldest one, perhaps fifteen, 'that chick murdered, down the street.'

I stared at her, finding no question to answer. Neither she nor her young companion turned away. Such is the power of children. The innocent know no fear. Innocence is not the absence of defilement, nor less the presence of love.

Innocence is the blessed state of not yet realising just how bad things can get.

Once I could have wept for them.

'She on the game?'

I shook my head. 'I don't think so, Yula.'

Yula bit gently at her lower lip. 'This is Berry, by the way. She's not been round here long. You met her?'

'Seen her around. Hi, Berry.'

I can see neither into the hearts of men nor the bones of women, and Russell Square ages the young much faster than time, but Berry looked as if she would have had no trouble recalling her thirteenth birthday. By the glint of the dark light in her eyes, I was willing to bet it had been an occasion bereft of cake and presents.

'Down from Kalgoorlie,' she said, trying unsuccessfully to make her voice sound deeper than it was.

I said nothing once more. There was nothing to say.

'But you're not sure, Joe?' Yula again.

'Sure of what?'

'If that chick was on the game?'

I thought about that. 'Not for sure, no, but I don't think so.'

'Do you know who killed her?'

'No,' I replied. 'Do you?'

For a moment her face sagged like discarded clingwrap and her eyes took on the dull sheen of sheet metal. She shook her head, and placed her hand protectively against Berry's elbow. 'No. That's the problem. Could be any of these bastards.'

Ten metres further along, at the boundary of the Square, a white Commodore pulled to a halt by the pavement. A short horn fart sounded. The car had a single occupant, large.

Yula shuddered. 'Fuck,' she said. 'Wish I was old enough to get the dole.'

Berry pulled her arm gently away. 'I'll go,' she said, the forced brightness in her voice failing to cover her fear. 'My turn. See you back here, half an hour, yeah?'

Yula and I watched then as she turned and walked over to the car, trying to swish hips barely there beneath her little frock. She put her head through the passenger window, then backed out, turned and gave Yula a thumbs-up and brave smile. As soon as she climbed inside, the car moved off, circling the park before disappearing.

Yula spat on the grass. 'Bet he wouldn't do it to his own fucking daughter.'

'Bet he would,' I replied, and walked away.

I stopped at Plaka for a shish kebab, then at the Brass Monkey for a Jamesons to wash it down, before continuing the walk to the house. Darkness had established its tenure for the night by the time I reached it, the rain for the moment stopped. The clouds were still thick, though, like a convention of medieval spirits, blocking out the moon, massing, preparing to inseminate virgins while they slept. Silently, I wished them luck in finding any.

The front room light was on, dimly visible in the cracks between the gangrenous slats of the venetian. I was sure Nessie would have long been put to bed, but clearly Mrs Warburton was still awake. She would no more leave a light on to ease my way than I would make a Jatz cracker divine.

I let myself in, intent on heading for my sanctuary with all decent haste. I glanced into the front room to acknowledge briefly her presence. She was sitting in her chair, knees together, lips pursed, arms folded.

'Evening, Mrs Warburton,' I tried.

'Visitor, you had,' she hissed.

'Laz?'

'Who?'

I sighed. 'My fat friend.'

A look of manifest hatred sprinted across her face, then she shook her head.

'Trouble, you're in,' she said.

There was a time when I tried to run with patience the race that was set before me, but that was before I discovered that my own particular race has no end. To be content to wait has no value when all that lies ahead is more waiting.

'Just tell me, Mrs Warburton. I'm very tired.'

'Don't know the meaning of the word, you don't,' she chided. 'Visitor came round about an hour back. Was that lady police officer, it was. The one here this morning.'

This was not the sort of news I wanted. I thought immediately of my stash, and of the leaflets I had removed from Gina's flat. They were the link to the Transpersonal Foundation. I wondered how valuable I would remain to the cops' inquiries if they too started peering in that direction. The Chew woman had noted them, I remembered, but good.

'The both of them?'

'Just her, it was.'

'Did she take anything?'

'None of my business if she did, is it?' rebuked Mrs Warburton.

'But you'd have noticed anyway.'

She nodded. 'Didn't take nothing, she didn't. Asked if you were in. I told her it was none of my business whether you were or you weren't. Told her I wasn't my lodger's keeper, was I? Told her you'd been out since you came in with Nessie before you left.'

'How'd she react to that?'

'Seemed confused, she did. Not much up top, that one, you ask me. Women as police, I ask you, what next?'

Lodger kills landlady if you're not careful, I thought grimly. 'What did she want?'

Mrs Warburton slowly unfolded her arms, the look on her face leaving me in no doubt that she considered such a manoeuvre grossly more than an ingrate like me deserved. She slipped her hand down the side of her chair, between the cushion and the arm into whatever ancient deposits of lint and skin flakes there resided, and pulled out a white envelope. Even from that distance I could see it bore the crest of the WA Police on its face. She handed it over. I thanked her and immediately started walking to my room.

'Here!' she cried after me. 'You going to open it, then, are you?'

'Of course,' I called back, shutting my door behind me.

I chucked it on the bed and stared at it for a minute or two. If God made trees, I pondered, then there is no envelope which can hide its contents from the mind of his son, for the Son and the Father are of natures like, indivisible and complete.

Nice theory, at any rate.

My day had been long and my feet ached from my walking. Demons shook inside me, dancing to the music of Saint Vitus. In an hour or so, I decided, I would load up and head out on another delivery run. I would be the angel flying through the midst of heaven, saying woe, woe, woe your boat, gently down the bloodstream. For the moment, though, I had some personal matters to which to attend.

A two-paper joint, thick line of speed and half of The Prodigy's *Fat of the Land* album later, I turned my attention to the envelope. Inside was the business card of DC Irene Chew, Homicide. On its reverse side was a single sentence, written in neat, cursive letters. 'Libido club, 9 pm tonight, or the lockup tomorrow morning. Your choice.'

Like free will and hell, some choice.

CHAPTER 6

The mark-up I get on my smack is not huge, but at least it's mine, which is a comfort at times. It used to gall me that I seem destined to live my endless years in a state of poverty, however poetic some of the more wholemeal congregations around the world might find that image. I mean, this has all been a lot of damn hard work, this living forever, always in the dripping shadow of atrocities for which my name provides the justification and the triumph. It gets to me after a while. In quiet moments unprepared, I crave the end of days.

A little consideration would have been nice. Not much, just a little. Imagine: just two percentage points on the back end of every crucifix, large and small, sold since they became fashionable in the fourth century, and I'd be wealthy beyond all dreams. Had I had the presence of mind, the foresight, to stitch that up during those weird few days in Emmaus after I woke up that first time, I still wouldn't be as wealthy as the churches founded in my memory, but hell, at least I wouldn't be reduced to palming powder on street corners in goddamn Western Australia.

Or maybe I might. You never know. Just as a hobby. I mean, I've done it, one way or another, dope, smack, opium, fly mushrooms, khat, peyote, cocaine, tobacco, moonshine or morphine, over centuries. That and flogging saintly relics. It's sad to admit that I don't know anything else, tradewise. Forget about the carpentry line. Joseph tried once or twice, the sap, but I'd see that look in his eye as he held his chisel and stared at me, distracted. It was the look of a man who every time he saw the son he had to claim as his own saw instead his wife violated. By the Lord God Almighty? By a filthy Roman soldier called Panthera? I've heard both stories, never met either. What do I know?

Fancied myself a teacher back in the very old days, as befitted the world's only graduate of the King Herod Childcare Method. Subsequent mass slaughter indicates it wasn't a line in which I excelled. Legion are the grovelling believers and deluded megalomaniacs who claim that I have delivered unto them revelation. I don't know how. I've never received any myself. Whatever profound procreation, mutative or miraculous, divine or DNA, that resulted in my two millennia of wandering I don't know. But it had nothing to do with teleology, and no one got sent around to check up on my progress. Is it any wonder I went truant from the true path?

So I sell salvation, biochemical forgiveness. For just a little while, I make it all go away.

I'm better at dealing, these days. It's a tough damn business to stay afloat in, even at the pissant street level at which I operate. I learned that lesson hard back in the sixteenth in Basel. I'd been doing a pretty good trade with laudanum, turning a nice penny from the sick and the slick both. I invented it, you know. Many are the things I am meant to have done, and few are those which I have. Behold: my triumphs are forgotten, my losses multiplied by millions.

It was easy, the laudanum thing, as you might expect. Water into wine; poppies into painkiller: same concept, different process. The problem was I hooked up at that time with a physician bloke called Philippus von Hohenheim, mainly because he had the cash and the cover I needed to expand the operation. Bit full of himself, but devout in his beliefs, so I thought I could trust him at least to do the thou shalt not steal bit.

Silly me. Next thing I know he's changed his name to Paracelsus and he's off up the road out of Basel, taking my formula, my stash and my cash. Made a fortune, the bastard, over the next fourteen years of travelling around the place.

It did him no good, though. One thing I learned very early on: don't shoot the loot. A dealer who uses and recommends his own merchandise is trouble waiting to happen. Paracelsus didn't twig that. By the end of his life he was a raving nutter, banging on about how Elijah was a'comin, Elijah the Alchemist, to end the world in a single act of chemical dissolution: no big bangs, no last trumps, just a quick swizzle in the cosmic test tube held above the bunsen burner of Be'elzebub and, boof, all over and God's back to the lab for another go at perfecting instant mashed potato.

So I don't use smack. Never have. I, even I, am he, and there is no god with me: I kill and I make alive; I wound and I heal. I live for ever.

I do speed when the situation demands, though, and walking up the narrow, fuggy staircase to the first-floor nightclub known as Libido I was damn glad I'd heeded the call.

The club was small, not much more than a long thin room with a bar at one end, a dance floor at the other and chairs and tables in between. The walls were painted black — flakes and scabs showing plainly when the Vari-lites spun and played across them. Its music was for the most part deep house working on shallow, its clientele late twenties trying to remember the time when they had neither mortgages nor marriages. The gender selections were casually ambivalent in a studied and deliberate kind of way. It was the sort of club that struggled by, a bolt hole for the faded aspirations of a generation painfully realising that its youthful fervour never made a difference and its taste is laughed at by the young.

I had been there before, once or twice, over the months, for one reason or another. It was an acceptable place in which to slam alcohol at three in the morning, for instance, without having to put up with the Venga Boys. The sculpted blonde door bitch with the neatly hemmed rips in her top nodded me through without asking for a cover charge. I had sold her a couple of mitsubishi ecstasy tabs once, which had come into my possession after a foolish young man attempted not to pay for the quarter ounce of dope he'd asked to buy from me. She winked as I passed. I am the good shepherd; I know my own and my own know me.

The last clock I'd seen, on the wall of the pizza parlour two doors up, indicated I was fifteen minutes early for my appointment. This was as I intended, because it gave me a little time to scope out the building. Whatever purpose DC Irene Chew had in demanding an unscheduled assignation remained, of course, unclear. I figured it was very unlikely to be a set-up that would result in a bust — after all, I was hardly going to turn up to a meeting with a known cop with my pockets full of china white — but there was no harm in checking out the escape routes, just in case.

The toilets were located behind the dance floor, down three steps and along a short corridor of brick, masonite and dusty windows covered in dustier barbed wire. The stench was throat-clutching even at so early a stage in the night. It was an extraordinary olfactory achievement, given that the club doors had been open less than an hour and the total crowd comprised perhaps a dozen dateless desperates. The fire exit doors were next to the entrance to the gents, fitted with panic bolts as required by law, and thick padlocked chains as dictated by economics. With so few people as yet in the building, the corridor was empty. It took only a minute or so fiddling about with a syringe to persuade the tumblers inside the padlocks to yield. Having achieved my aim, I set the lock to appear still fastened, put the cap back on the fit and dropped it on the ground. It was probably the first syringe deposited for the night. To judge by the harsh blue lights in the cubicles, it wouldn't be the last.

After that I returned to the main room, ordered an over-priced Stella Artois, then found myself one of the vacant curved sofas on which to sit. I put my feet up on the low table in front of me, slugged from the bottle, drew on a Dunhill and closed my eyes as the last delicious globule of mucous-mixed amphetamine slid gently down my throat. With the blast of my nostrils the waters were gathered together, the floods stood upright as a heap, and the depths were congealed in the heart of the sea.

Someone tapped my shoulder, not tenderly.

I sighed, turned my head and opened my eyes, expecting to find a large female cop in businesslike mode and no mood to argue. Instead, standing at my side was a bald-headed man in a black suit and stupid bow tie. He had a badge with a security number pinned to his chest.

'Feet off the table, bud,' he said.

I affected not hear him above the noise, and raised my eyebrows to indicate as much.

He repeated his message a bit more loudly.

I shrugged, pointed at my ear, and pulled another mouthful from the Stella.

This time, a dark look on his face, he bent towards me from the waist and bellowed at the side of my head: 'I said, buddy, get your fucking feet off the fucking table.'

If he saw my right hand moving he didn't see it in time to avoid it. My finger and thumb locked in at the sides of his windpipe, poised just hard enough to slip behind. His eyes went wide and he let out a little choking noise that carried remarkably well given the volume of the music. I fixed him with my stare. My voice must have seemed to emanate from the depths of his guts. 'Do not be haughty, Number 44,' I intoned, 'but associate with the lowly; never be conceited.'

I let go of him before the thumping in his head got too bad. He was, after all, only doing his job. He stood, manfully resisting the urge to rub at his neck and reassure himself that he still had a larynx. His eyes betrayed a swirling mixture of fear, humiliation and fury. I didn't move. I didn't take my eyes off his. I waited. I was enjoying myself.

He seemed about to speak, when suddenly something caused him to look over his shoulder. As he did so, I saw Irene Chew standing right behind him. Her lips moved. He said something which seemed to start with the word 'but' but got no further. She said something else. He turned back to me for the briefest of face-saving glares. I smiled beatifically. He stormed away, careful not to collide with Chew on his way past.

She sat down heavily next to me, kissed me dryly on the cheek, threw one long leg over the other, and shook her head. 'Can't take you anywhere, can I, Joe Panther?'

I felt I could look at her directly. This was not a chance meeting, after all. I had the feeling I was in some sort of appraisal process, so reciprocity was possible. Her hair was still black and turbulent, but the freckled face of so early that morning was gone. Even in the ever-changing light of the club, it was clear that hers was now a painted image. Her skin was coated in fine, pale make-up, her mouth violently scarlet, and her eyes lined with expertly drawn borders. It was a face-as-statement: Garbo, perhaps, Tallulah Bankhead, or the Empress Theodora. For all its studied beauty, it was not a passionate face.

She wore a different suit, this one black and cut with Swiss Army precision. Beneath her jacket, held with a single button at her solar plexus, she wore an ironed and blinding white shirt, its wide and pointy lapels overlaying those of the suit just so. Its top three buttons were undone, revealing a hint of cleavage which, while perhaps alluring to the casual glance, came a distinct second fiddle to the powerful muscles that strapped her upper ribs and collar bones. Her shoes, I noted, were also black, but high heeled, with just a touch of fetishwear about them.

'Well, Joe,' she said, extracting a cigarette from her slim black shoulder bag, all the time staring straight ahead, 'you going to buy me a drink?'

'Stoli and lime would fit the act.'

'So make it Rebel Yell and coke, plenty of ice.'

When I returned, she took the drink without thanks. I sat next to her, not too close, and drained the last of my old Stella before starting on the new. She didn't speak, so neither did I. I was determined not to show the weakness of curiosity and ask why she had summoned me.

Waiting I'm good at.

Better than her.

'So, Joe,' she began at last, her glass half-empty, cigarette gone. 'Is it a neural transmitter thing?'

'No,' I replied, 'it's a bottle of beer. They're quite common, really.'

'Humour ill becomes you, Joe.' There was not a whit of warmth in her tone. 'And it's wasted on me. Talk. It may help your future. Have you ever talked to anyone?'

'If humour doesn't work, DC Chew ... may I call you Irene, given the circumstances?'

She shook her head.

I shrugged. 'How about bafflement? What are you talking about?'

'You.'

Confusion produced defensiveness. I turned to look at her, lowered my voice, gave it a brittle edge. 'Are you wired up?'

She didn't look at me, but I could see a slow smile tilt her lips, just briefly.

She stood, turned around to face me, then lifted one leg over mine, which were stretched out again onto the table. Standing there, straddled, she looked down upon me. I met her gaze without fear.

'Feet off the table, Joe,' she said.

I did so, this time without protest.

She sat where my feet had been, knees apart. With her features like marble, and her eyes locked to mine, she put down her drink, then without artifice unbuttoned her jacket. Then she undid the three fastened buttons of her shirt, took hold of the fabric with both hands, and pulled the garment away from her. Her breasts were full and firm. Her nipples, like hermits on hilltops, were proud without need of material support. Her stomach was the shape and tint of corrugated iron in the desert. There were no wires anywhere.

I said nothing.

Calmly, she buttoned up again, and resumed her seat next to me.

'And that was not a proposition or a promise, Joe, merely proof.'

I nodded.

'So,' she said, 'neural transmitters, bipolar, multiples, what? Tell me.'

'I'd like to help,' I offered, 'but I'm afraid I'm going to need a bit of context here.'

She put her now empty glass down on the table with a measured force of irritation. 'We can do this two ways,' she said. 'You can talk to me, now, off the record, or I can report to DS Hewson tomorrow that I ran into you by accident here, now, and you forced me to expose my breasts in a crowded nightclub. Witnesses will back me up, Joe, don't you think? Our mutual friend the security thug, for one, yes? Bugger your deal with Hewson, Joe. You know it's worth shit. You want, I've got you down on sex assault, suspected psychiatric illness. I'll have you sectioned and in the bin by lunch. Think you'll talk your way out of it?'

To be honest, I thought: yes, easily, given a few days. I didn't need the hassle, though, nor the reputation. Nor maybe, given that Laz's promise of escape money was contingent on finding Gina's killer before the birth of my bastard son, could I spare the time. I attempted to look contrite.

'That doesn't work, either, Joe,' said Chew. 'I'll get us another drink, and then we talk, yes?'

'Whatever you want, Iron Balls,' I replied.

The drinks arrived. I took mine in hand and turned obligingly in on the sofa so I faced her at a forty-five degree angle. She did the same, dropping the cold bitch act.

'I think we can help each other,' she began.

'I thought that was organised this morning.'

Her face set, and her chin jutted forwards slightly. 'That was bullshit and you know it, Joe. Doesn't matter what Hewson says, after this case your gig is over in this town. Sure, if he thinks you're worth it he might be able to keep the Drug Squad off your back for a little while — but not forever, boy, you know that. Even if he does, think why. Because he *likes* you? Because he thinks you deserve a second chance? It's because he thinks you can get information useful to him. He's an ambitious bastard, Hewson. You want to be a career snout, Joe? You go ahead. Any idea how long snouts tend to last in this town?'

I thought of Kennedy. 'Pretty much,' I replied.

'Cool, then.' She paused and lit a cigarette, without offering. 'So help l'il old me instead.'

'Be your snitch instead? Why, because you showed me your tits? I'm supposed to be grateful?'

She shook her head. 'Two things, Joe. I don't want you to be my snout, not long term. I want you to be my *subject*.'

I looked again at her spiked shoes, and the severity of her suit. 'As in slave?'

'As in academic inquiry. Look, first off, I *do* want you to do all you can to help identify Gina Compton's killer. And I want that for far more reasons than Hewson ever will. Second, though, I'm not just a dumb cop.'

'I wouldn't have said that, anyway.'

'Thanks.'

'I would have said you were a dumb cop with nice tits.'

Of course I said it to see how she would react, to see if I could rile her into storming out. I had already an uncomfortable idea where the conversation was going, and if I could derail it in some way, then that was just fine with me.

It didn't work.

'Gratuitous provocation will get you nowhere, big boy,' she said. 'Not under my skin, not up my nose, and very very definitely not into my pants. I'm serious here, Panther, and I think you should listen to what I have to say. It might do us both good.'

I sighed, and necked my Stella. 'My talking you've already got. My listening costs at least another beer, with a Jamesons chaser.'

'Good idea,' she replied. 'Your shout. And I'll have a Becks with the next bourbon.'

It took a bit longer this time, the club filling up.

'So,' she said when I returned, 'I've been doing some checking up on you, Mr Joshua Ben Panther. Never been convicted, here, or Melbourne, nor overseas as far as I can tell. Arrested heaps of times. Charged once in Melbourne with assault occasioning serious injury — victim turned out to be a porn trafficker and incestuous father, delivered from your attack, as it turned out, by a federal agent in deep cover —'

The period during which I first met Laz. Caroline, as she then was. She was pretty much the only one who came out of it alive and sane, despite attempting suicide. 'Don't remind me.'

'Charges withdrawn. Flagged on databases all over the shop, especially Drug Squad Intelligence.'

'Now there's an —'

'Oxymoron, I know. Funny thing, though. All this information on you and, get this, nowhere, no date or place of birth, no identity of the mother, no name for the father. Unusual, don't you think?'

Maybe it was the dope and the speed and booze and the closeness of the club and the tone of her voice and the turn of her leg, but I was starting to feel uneasy. Back in the old days, I had no fear. If I was discovered, my identity revealed and, as it must be, automatically denied by all and sundry, all I had to worry about was the odd scourging, hanging, drawing, quartering, roasting maybe, and then slow, bloody execution. Nasty, sure, but soon enough over in the scheme of things. Three days later, as always, I'd be up and about and off somewhere else, none the wiser, none the older. Once the Enlightenment happened, though, the stakes changed. Vengeance, at least for some, gave way to intrigue. The question of who I claimed to be was replaced by the question of *why* I claimed to be who I claimed to be. These days, sprung, I would not be tortured — not in Perth, anyway, and nowhere this side of Kansas — but I was sure to be locked up, padded up, shot up and questioned by men in white coats for a very long time.

And that I would like to avoid. It is the Holy Ghost that is within me, not the Friendly Ghost. Only one of them can walk through walls, and guess who drew the short straw?

'My mother is dead and I never met my father,' I said, perhaps a little more resentfully than I intended.

'Does that bother you?'

'Not any more.'

111

'Why not?'

'I've had a lot of time to get used to it.'

She looked doubtful. 'Now here's the other weird thing about you —'

'Where is this going, DC Chew?'

'Soon enough, Joe. The other weird thing — *one* of the other weird things — about all this intelligence on you is this: you're thirty-three years old.'

'Damn strange. How old are you?'

'None of your business. You were noted as thirty-three in Melbourne, and you've said you're thirty-three here. You were in Melbourne years ago. What's wrong with this picture?'

I shrugged. I am always thirty-three. I have always been thirty-three ever since, well, I turned thirty-three. I would have it other, but some things are simply out of my control. Most things, actually, you want to get to down to it.

'They must have made a mistake in Melbourne,' I suggested.

'You invite speculation.'

'So did the Spice Girls, but I'll bet you never coerced them into buying you drinks in a nightclub.'

She laughed at that. It was short, sharp and rapidly controlled, but a laugh nevertheless. 'Might've done, given the chance. Want to know my play?'

'Want to buy me a drink first? I need to go to the toilet.'

She shook her head. 'After. You're fidgeting. My guess, you'll run as soon as I turn my back on you.'

'The thought never entered my mind,' I lied.

She crossed her legs and leant back against the sofa. Groove Armada gave way to Armand van Helden's 'The Boogie Monster'.

'You've got some sort of messiah complex, Joe. That's not speculation, by the way. I reckon that's a pretty uncontroversial assertion. The Melbourne guys noted it in detail, and there are plenty of other references here and there. Drug guys, quote, walks around quoting the Bible, quote, maybe thinks he's a preacher or something; street patrol, religious nut alky. There's more, but you know that. My play? Shit-house childhood, most of which you've blocked out, massive overcompensation for feelings of insignificance and weakness through bombastic absorption and recitation of Biblical texts, complicated by long-term substance abuse, possible manic depression or other contributory mental illness, all of which has sunk you into a life of petty criminality and violence from which you try to gain compensatory and comforting feelings of glamour, status, and supernatural powers by pretending you're a prophet.'

I realised she'd stopped talking. 'Sorry,' I said, 'what did you say?'

'You think you're bloody Jesus, Joe.'

I shook my head, and replied with quiet finality. 'I do not.'

I did not add: I *know* I'm Jesus and I would do anything not to be.

Nor: I do not want to know what I know.

Nor yet: Worse. Worse by far. I do not want to know what I still do not know.

She spoke softly now, one hand on my knee. 'Let me decide that.'

I simply stared at her. I kept my eyes dead, lest they spark and she see the fear and the anger and fury within them. These eyes which stealthily watch for the hapless took on the guise of their victims.

'Here's the deal, Joe. I'm not just a cop. I'm a cop with a degree in criminology. Now I'm a cop just starting her PhD thesis in psychology. Special subject: the link between profound delusion and criminal behaviour. Now, I don't reckon I could ever find a better case study than you, my lad. I need you, and you need me.'

'Why do I need you?'

'Because right now I'm the only person who can keep you safe and on the right side of a prison cell for a very long time. Make no mistake Joe, Hewson *will* fit you up for Gina Compton's murder if no one better comes to hand —'

'Such as the person who did it?'

'For *instance*, yes,' she responded testily. 'And if he doesn't, well, what with the Drugs Squad and the snout role, you are well and truly fucked. Sign on with me, I'll get you out of that shit-hole you live in, put you in a nice rent-free flat, line up some dole or other benefit for you, get you out of the drug trade. You let me study you, interview you, *probe* you, boy, two years max. Then, I promise, I'll fund your journey to wherever you want to go. Long as you never come back to Perth, you're home free.'

'And what's a cop's promise worth?'

'That promise,' she smiled, 'is worth exactly the same as this one: say no, and I promise I'll take you down harder and faster and longer than Hewson ever could. Clear?'

I nodded. 'Now can I have that drink?'

She reached into her shoulder bag and pulled out a twenty. 'You go,' she said. 'I'll watch you.'

I thought about bolting as I made my way to the bar past people at first reluctant to let me pass, then only too pleased once they turned to tell me to stop pushing them. By the time I'd made it to the front, however, I'd changed my mind.

114

Running now wouldn't alter a thing. I had one cop on my tail who was going to fit me up or bleed me dry, and another who was going to take me down or bang me up. I didn't like either option. I have been the object of abject fascination for millions upon millions over the centuries, but never — not since the first time, anyway — have I ever been present to witness it. If my father is God, then there is only one policy of his I've been able to deduce: never apologise, and never answer questions. I think, if we ever did meet, it would probably be the only point on which we agreed.

I picked up the drinks and pocketed the change. Walking back to the sofa I realised I still had one advantage tucked away. Neither cop knew about my arrangement with Laz. I didn't need Chew to escape, nor Hewson to keep me out of jail. All I had to do was find a killer before a baby was born.

I sat, handed over the bourbon, and downed half the Stella in one go, wishing I had more speed on hand.

'So,' said Irene.

'Can I have forty-eight hours to think about it?'

That slow smile again. She tossed her hair back with her unoccupied hand. 'You think you've got forty-eight hours of thinking time left?'

'Do I?'

She took a gulp from her glass. 'I can't protect you until you agree, Joe.'

I thought then of the start of it all, of being nailed and slashed upon a cross, calling out for the father who never came. 'No one can protect me,' I said.

'Okay. Forty-eight hours, then your ass is either mine or the collective property of the big boys in max security.'

I raised my bottle in a toast. 'Here's looking at Chew, kid.'

She didn't laugh, which really didn't surprise me. I drained the bottle, put it down on the table, then stood up. 'Gotta go,' I said. 'I'll be in touch.'

Before I could move off, she held up a hand to stop me, and emptied her glass with impressive speed. Standing up, she said she'd walk out with me. 'Tacky for a woman to be in this sort of dive alone, don't you think?'

The landing at the head of the stairs was crowded, a queue having now developed. Most of them, I noticed, as we squeezed past, were wet. My slaphead friend was nowhere to be seen.

I heard the rain before I actually saw it. It was pounding and roaring in a full force tropical downpour, sheets of huge heavy drops bouncing off the roads, turning the pavements the colour of slate, and steaming in the dull heat of the night.

'Fuck,' said Chew. 'My car's two blocks away.'

'My house is four,' I said. 'You can give me a lift.'

We started walking along the pavement, which was crowded by the bedraggled and the bedevilled both, pushing between surly groups of drunks, trying hard to use what little shelter was afforded by shop awnings and overhangs. Suddenly I felt something tugging at my sleeve, urgent, small and insistent. I turned to mete out compassion with the flat of my hand and stilled myself just in time. Young Yula had grabbed the fabric of my jacket with both hands, and was shouting at me with a voice rendered almost silent by overuse. She looked appalling: her Jebediah tee-shirt sopping wet and clinging, smeared with mud. Her face was filthy, and contorted by fear, scratches, and the unmistakable swellings of a crying child.

'Joe, *please, please, you must,*' she was screaming hoarsely. Her voice barely topped the roar of the rain, the traffic and the muffled thump of a dozen separate sound systems.

I stopped walking, sensing Chew also stop at my side. Pedestrians veered around me, unstable in the wet, colliding in the mob.

'Must what?' I asked.

'Berry never came back,' she sobbed. 'I seen the car again, but not Berry. I've looked *everywhere*. Oh god Joe, please help. I'm so *scared*.'

And then the power of speech was lost to her once more. She grabbed my sleeve again, pushed through the crowd with the driven ferocity of a rugby fullback and tried to pull me across the road, heading in the direction of Russell Square. Numb, but knowing innocence lost, I let her.

As we stumbled into the hissing traffic and the deluge I looked back. Irene Chew was following, awkward on her heels, hitching her collar against the rain.

CHAPTER 7

Desire not a multitude of unprofitable children. So many millions over so many centuries, surplus to requirements, the marked down loss-leaders of a culture more in love with life than living.

I try to help. I help where I can. For some I bring sleep and shortened years, the best I can offer. For others, my gifts are too little, too late. I have become accustomed to my inadequacies. Would that everyone else would do so, too.

'I should call this in,' shouted DC Chew.

She was perhaps five metres behind me as Yula pulled with undiminished determination through the sheltering crowds of James Street. Music spilled from the doors of clubs, sex shops and snack bars like vomit. Young men and women, groovy and gross, yelled and screeched at each other, bellowing with cupped hands across the road. The air was full of warped spectra, like ghosts and memories, as blue, yellow and pink neons refracted through the storm. I turned my head to look back over my shoulder, cannoning into someone as I did so. My new cop buddy was reaching into her shoulder bag as she strode and dodged. She pulled out a mobile phone.

I tugged against Yula's torque and halted her. The look on her young face was one of confusion. I held a hand up to her to indicate that this was but a brief and necessary pause.

'Irene!' I shouted.

She reached us in a second or two, looking offended and angry.

'Think it through, bitch,' I hissed. 'I'm not about to yell for Detective Constable Chew, not here.'

She acknowledged my point immediately, then returned her attention to the mobile. I reached out and crushed her hand against it. Our eyes locked.

'Not now and not here,' I said.

'But —'

'Shut up and listen.' I looked down and spoke forcefully to Yula. 'I need one minute. You go and stand in that doorway there. Don't move. One minute.'

She looked very scared. Nothing was making any sense to her, except within the context of dread. Glad, perhaps, to be relieved of responsibility for even a moment or two, she obeyed meekly, moving out of the rain and earshot both.

'Right.' I turned back to DC Chew. My voice sounded arid. 'This is my life, my territory, my flock and my gig. You're in my world now, and no degree in criminality —'

'Criminology.'

'Whatever, it won't help. The facts: I hardly know Yula there. Believe it or not, she doesn't use. Yet. My guess is she's maybe fifteen years old —'

Chew nodded in agreement, all professional now.

'And she sucks men's cocks to get enough damn money to survive. Lives god knows where. A squat, some pederast's hideaway, in parks, whatever. Berry, the missing one, is maybe thirteen, fourteen, down from Kalgoorlie. My feeling is that Yula's been looking after her, as best she can. Berry got into a customer's white Commodore at Russell Square several hours ago, agreeing to meet up with Yula again thirty minutes later. I saw and heard that bit — that's probably why Yula's latched on to me.'

'Also she knows you from around.'

'Bingo, and she doesn't know you, Irene Chew. If she knew you were a cop, missing friend or no, she'd be off out of here.'

Chew sighed. Her hair was now lank and heavy, rivulets and strands amplifying the contours of her face. She tried half-heartedly to wipe it. 'Tell her I don't want to hurt her, Joe.'

'She'll think you want to send her back to her parents, or to some foster home somewhere. Why do you think she's on the game, woman? At least this way she gets paid for it, and at least she's partially in control.'

'I wouldn't,' she protested. 'It's not my —'

'Like Yula cares. Listen: I've been asked for help and for once I'm going to give it. I might need help myself from other people around, and if anyone thinks I'm working with a plain-clothes dick all I'm going to get is silence. We're not in the nightclub any more. This isn't your game now, bitch, it's mine. Play it or get the fuck out of my sight.'

I could see the fury in her face quite plainly. She seemed to be having a titanic inner struggle keeping it under control. After a second or two she managed a tense nod of assent. I didn't wait for her to embellish, just took off, grabbing Yula by the hand as I passed. Suddenly she was beside us, running interference, letting the girl get through.

Russell Square was deserted because of the rain. The overhead lights which shone on its bisecting red-brick path were mournful in their bright, sparkling emptiness. The rotunda was dark. There were cars parked all around the perimeter — most, undoubtedly, belonging to visiting Northbridge punters in for the long haul. The domes of the Orthodox church nearby quivered with spray haloes.

'Right, Yula.' I had to speak loudly to top the traffic and the rain crashing into the canopies of the trees all around us. 'Tell us. Where have you looked?'

Yula said nothing, just stared mistrustfully at Chew.

'This is Irene,' I said. 'She's with me. She's cool. Now, *where*?'

'All over,' she stammered. 'I saw the car again, don't know, maybe an hour after Berry got in it. I was starting to get worried by then. Only a bit, though. I'd had a punter in the meantime and hadn't been back long.'

'Where did you see the car?'

Yula pointed to the furthest end of the Square. 'Came out the side street there, then drove down that far side. Turned off into James Street then, and that was it.'

Irene squatted down next to the girl. 'Did it stop, Yula? Did it slow down?'

'No.'

'Did you get a look at the driver?'

She shook her head.

My turn. 'Where else might Berry go, Yula? Say something happened. Say she got spooked and ran for somewhere safe. Where would she have run?'

Yula's pale grey eyes held mine for several seconds. Rain dripped from her lashes, unregarded. Then she shrugged. 'There *is* nowhere safe, Joe.'

'Where have you looked?' asked Irene.

'*Everywhere*,' squealed Yula. 'All over the park, in the alleyways there and there and there. I've been up and down

James Street lots and lots of times. You know, in case someone had got her something to eat, or the guy dropped her off further away. I was still searching when I saw Joe come out of that club. There's *nothing*. She's *nowhere*.'

'Did you check in that church?' asked the cop.

'Locked.' Yula began to shiver, whether from cold, wet or fear, I knew not. I grabbed her hand.

'Car came from the street up there, yes? Let's go look.'

The three of us trudged across the meat of the Square, stumbling and sinking into mud, tripping over discarded bottles, suffering cascades of water from overburdened tree branches. We crossed the road at the border, Chew obligingly holding her hand out to stop the traffic as Yula and I plunged on regardless. Horns blared. Rubber hissed annoyance.

The side street was a mixture of small, old cottages, dilapidated storage yards and a couple of minor warehouses. Everything was rust and twisted in the darkness. A Doberman flung itself snarling at a chain-link fence as we passed. Irene flinched, and Yula let out a tight shriek of fright. I remained silent and unblinking. On other nights, perhaps, or in other moods, I might have returned to that dog, scaled the fence and choked the life out of it, but right then I had more important things to do.

Darkness and shadows made the night as primal as a feral pig, camouflaged, silent and explosive. After every three buildings on each side of the street, a narrow right-of-way disappeared into rutted quagmires of broken weeds and discarded garbage. Stumbling frequently, we walked down each, Yula often hoarsely calling Berry's name, Chew and I silent and watchful. The detective's black suit was spattered with brown mud and shit, smeared into the fabric by the rain.

There was something large at the end of the fifth lane, a

big shadow that abruptly stopped the frail perspective of the water-filled wheel ruts leading up to it. We walked towards it, Chew having to be careful to place each foot before putting weight on it, Yula and I surging on, splashing, water to our ankles.

The object turned out to be an old black Bedford van, parked front on and filling the lane almost to the fence lines. Its windscreen was smashed and the graffiti tags across its face indicated it had been there for a while.

'Want an unprovable observation?' called Chew from just behind us.

'What you got?'

'No way to tell for sure, but my heels are telling me that the mud in these ruts sucks a lot harder than the shit in the other lanes.'

Yula and I had reached the van by now. She had ducked to its side and was edging along it, trying to get past. I started to do the same, although it was a lot more difficult for me.

'Meaning?' I called back to Chew.

'Meaning I think it's fresher.' She too had reached the van, and was also trying to push herself sideways between it and the fence.

'Meaning?' I repeated.

'Something drove down here this evening.'

I could just make out Yula ahead of me. She appeared to be nearing the back of the van. I was having trouble breathing, so tight was the squeeze.

'So,' I wheezed. 'It's a lane. Things drive down lanes.'

'Not,' puffed Chew, 'when your headlights would show that there's clearly a fucking big abandoned van you couldn't get a bicycle past, let alone a —'

Yula screamed, high pitched and terrified.

'Come on!' I yelled. 'Yula! Stay put. Don't run.'

She sounded like she was hyperventilating, drowning perhaps.

I pushed and fought against the bulk of the van, like Jonah trying to get out from under the whale. Behind me I could hear Chew grunting and swearing to herself. I heard splashes, and then rips.

She'd caught me up by the time I'd squeezed past the last bulge of the bodywork and shinned myself on the jutting exhaust pipe. As I made my first steps into the last section of the dead-end lane behind, her hand was on my shoulder, part support, part push, part pull. As she struggled out beside me with a muted cry of relief I noticed her jacket was torn, her shirt tangled and plastered against her.

Yula fell silent the moment she felt my hand touch the back of her head. She was standing bolt upright, and even in shadows relieved only by the weak throw of a distant streetlight I could see her shoulders heaving.

Chew reached into her shoulder bag and pulled out a penlight torch. She flicked it on and shone it directly in front of us. Immediately she switched it off again. I heard her make a choking sound. 'Get her out of here,' she barked.

It was too late, though. Yula had already seen it, had already looked for long enough to absorb the sight. As had I. We were both night people, at home and functioning in the dark; agile beneath the clouds when the sun has fled. When reason goes and fear steps heavy across ground unlit by stars, the young like Yula and the old like me step with it, invite it to dance. Because sometimes fear is the only friend you've got.

Berry was lying on the ground, propped up against the fence like a tossed away Cabbage Patch doll. She was still wearing her little frock, only now its centre was a mass of dark, more solid than the night which cradled her, the handle of a huge knife protruding from just beneath her ribs.

I grabbed Yula's hand. 'Come on,' I said, and started to move. As I did so, I heard an incongruous noise beneath the rain, a slight crackle and susurrus, coming from the ground at my feet. I looked down, but could see nothing in the gloom beneath the back of the Bedford. Moving my foot slightly, I heard it again.

Chew had her back turned to us. She was on her mobile, calling the murder in for real.

Quickly, I bent over, bringing my hand to my shoe and feeling around — carefully, to minimise the risk of piercing myself with a discarded fit. (I have no intention of reaping what I sow.) Amongst the rubble and squashed cans, snapped sticks and McDonald's wrappers, my fingers lighted on what felt like cellophane. It lay *on* the other shit, rather than half buried with it. Therefore it hadn't been there long. I picked it up and shoved it in my pocket without looking any more closely. The dark places of the earth are full of the habitations of cruelty.

'Let's go, Yula,' I repeated. 'Cops'll be here in a minute.'

'Your friend's a cop,' she replied, deadpan and hollow, prepared for betrayal.

'I know. That's why we've got to go.'

Chew had finished with the call. We didn't have much time. I yanked Yula towards the other side of the van.

'Wait at the head of the lane,' called Chew. 'We'll have to take statements from both of you.'

'No you won't,' I replied, pushing the girl ahead of me through the gap. 'Yula's statement can wait, and I wasn't here. White Commodore. Berry. Kalgoorlie. That's the lot.'

'Where are you going?'

I squeezed into the space, working hard. Narrow is the way which leadeth into life. I knew she wouldn't leave the scene, and reckoned we had about two minutes, tops, before the uniforms arrived to start cordoning off the area.

'I have tasted death for every man,' I called back. 'Now I want a souvlaki. Come see me tomorrow.'

She did, at 8 am. With Hewson and a back-up divvy van parked outside the house just in case I decided to do a runner. Actually, it was Hewson's mission. He had clearly pulled rank on his junior officer. By the time he arrived I was lying on my bed, clothed and showered, coffee in one hand and a battered paperback collection of early patristic writings in the other. The front door rattled as he thumped it.

'You again,' I heard Mrs Warburton say. 'Mine's a respectable house, mine is. Nessie, it's those police officers again, it is. Have you done yet?' I couldn't hear the old woman's response, but I could infer its nature from Mrs Warburton's reply. 'Well, you'll just have to wait, you will. Put the rug back over your knees and try not fidget.'

Hewson was announcing with appropriate gravitas that he needed to talk both to me and Yula.

'We know she's here, Mrs Warburton,' I could hear him declaiming. 'So why don't you bring her out before I charge you with harbouring a runaway ward of state?'

There was no way, of course, that Hewson could have known Yula's status for sure. Even her name, given her line of work, had to be regarded as suspect, but his assumption was very likely correct.

I chose that moment to make my appearance, putting down the patristics and emerging into the passage. I was still enjoying the last statement I had read, from perhaps the oldest surviving non-Biblical Christian text, *The Didache*: 'Then the Deceiver of the World will show himself, pretending to be a Son of God and doing signs and wonders, and the earth will be delivered into his hands, and he will work such wickedness as there has never been since the beginning.' Bullshit, of course. Wickedness is a constant. It is hard-wired into the world, like breathing and decay. I walked towards the front door. So then the Son of God did show himself, pretending to be a Deceiver of the World and doing lines and chunders ...

'The girl's in the kitchen,' I said.

Hewson looked even more dank and rumpled than the day before. He also looked extremely pissed off. He began to push past Mrs Warburton to get to me.

'Leaving the scene of a crime, harbouring a runaway, sexual assault on a juvenile ...'

I saw Chew squeeze up behind him, reach around and lay her hand gently on his forearm. She looked haggard. I guessed that she hadn't been to sleep since the last time I'd seen her. The complexities and grumbling logistics of murder investigation would have kept her in that foul lane for hours, especially since she had been present at the discovery of the body. Her hair looked brittle and caked, ready to crack beneath a brush or soothing hand. She'd managed to change from her wet, ripped and muddy suit, though. I concluded the squad must have kept a spare, a general purpose suit for any detective caught in such a situation. It was grey, crumpled and had something partially digested clinging to the lapel. No way would the jacket have buttoned. The arms and legs failed to reach her wrists and ankles.

Hewson looked around at her for a second, glaring, seemingly intent on saying something. Then he turned back to me and kept approaching, a look of peeved anger still evident on his face.

I wondered what story Chew had told him to explain our mutual presence at the discovery of Berry's body. Surely she hadn't mentioned anything about cutting a side deal with me for the purpose of her academic advancement. Had she mentioned the Libido club? How had she tied me in with the girls? How had she and I come to meet last night? Hewson came to a halt right in front of me, his chin and chest jutting forward as he attempted unsuccessfully to intimidate with his force of will and self-importance.

'DC Chew,' he growled, finding the name a convenient excuse to break eye contact and look around in a contemptuous manner, 'informs me that you are on the side of the angels in this one.'

'I am a little lower than the angels,' I replied, modestly.

'You're a little lower than a catfish arsehole, Panther, but my junior-ranked colleague tells me you raised the alarm on this one, helped search for the deceased and comforted the bereaved. But guess what?'

'What?'

'I think you've snowed her.' He placed the palm of his hand on my chest and shoved me backwards. I let him. Just. 'I want you back in your sty while I take a statement from the girl. Then it's your turn. Not a peep. Where did you say she was?'

'Kitchen.'

He shoved me again. 'If she tells me you laid a finger on her, Panther . . .'

The threat was left hanging as he pushed past me. It worried me not. Yula had stopped sobbing by the time I'd led her on the long walk back to the house the night before, her noises replaced by a numb silence more distressed than any cry. I'd told her she was safe, and that she should take a shower then sleep in my bed. I would sleep on the kitchen floor. I'd slept in less comfortable places, after all.

When Mrs Warburton rose at dawn for the start of her daily chores she thought I'd collapsed dead drunk and kicked me, albeit feebly, in the belly to wake me up. I must have known, even in the whirlwind from the south of my dreams, that it was she who assaulted me, for I had not smited mine enemy before opening my eyes. I had quickly explained the situation, and told her that Yula would probably be staying for a few days.

'Not a charity, you know,' had been my landlady's somewhat redundant response. Eventually she had agreed to throw some spare and threadbare bedding on the sofa in the front room — at least as soon as she finished attending to both ends of Nessie's alimentary tract. While the kettle was boiling she had entered my room and thrown Yula a green and gold striped dress pulled from somewhere in the fetid depths of her wardrobe. It might have been compassion, since Yula's own pathetic garments lay sodden and ruined on the floor. More likely she didn't want a ragged teenager on the premises when the cops turned up. She did, after all, run a respectable house.

When the girl emerged, she wasn't wearing it. She had on my Smashing Pumpkins tee-shirt — itself well long enough on her to serve as modest apparel. She seemed still withdrawn and frightened, suspicious yet nervously grateful for the weak and milkless brew Mrs Warburton placed without comment before her on the kitchen table.

I had told her to expect a visit from the police, and reminded her that because she was under eighteen she had the right to demand a responsible adult be present with her during questioning. 'I've never met a responsible adult,' had been her mumbled reply. I hadn't contradicted her.

That questioning was going on now, as I sat again on my bed, and took up *The Didache*. Very old, *The Didache*. Almost as old as me. It was written not long after my death, according to one theory, perhaps even by my brother James. I don't rate much of a mention in it, which would make sense. He was always the jealous one, James, although why I have never been able to fathom. I found him once, in a back street in Jerusalem, near the end, squatting over a cripple. His hands were on the wretch's legs and his eyes were to the sky. 'In the name of the Father,' he was hissing through clenched teeth, 'walk, you bastard, walk.'

I never understood his envy. Had I been able to lift my burden from my shoulders and lay it on my brother, then in glee and joy would I have done so. Take it, Brother James, seed of Joseph, take it and be gone. What you have I wish for; what I am given I would now pass on to thee: I yearn only for freedom and an end to endlessness.

He died, my bitter brother, millennia back. I have been jealous of him ever since.

And so I read his words as postcards from the grave. 'Keep away from every bad man, my son, and from all his kind. Never give way to anger, for anger leads to homicide.' Who had been angry at small Berry, I wondered. What bad man had invited her into his car? Had it been the same bad man so angry at Gina Compton? And then again, of Gina: are angry men that precise?

I remembered the cellophane I had found the night before, and now retrieved it from my jacket, which I'd tossed on the floor as usual. It was a fragment of something, brown and orange, shiny, one edge cutting through its text in a curve. Whatever it had contained had been baptised E-HG45. I stared at it for a moment, but no ideas came. Only fears.

I've started picking up bits of litter, I thought to myself. What next? Cigarette butts from the pavement? Would I soon become intent on plunging my arm into garbage bins and fishing around for cold KFC chips near the bottom? Would I remember if I did? The church of the Son may be built on a rock, but the boy himself stands swaying on a rope strung above a chasm.

My thoughts made me dizzy. I pushed the scrap back in my pocket to get it out of sight, then lay on my bed, letting my head clear beneath the resonant echo of my brother's ancient foreboding.

'In the last days of the world false prophets and deceivers will abound, sheep will be perverted and turn into wolves ...'

They entered maybe half an hour later. Chew was carrying a kitchen chair, Hewson grabbed the bentwood. He looked red of face and short of temper. She looked neutral and knackered, working on worried. They both sat. This time he had his notebook out.

'Account for your evening,' he demanded.

I obliged. 'Went visiting. Went to a nightclub. Found a murdered child. Came home. How about yours? Watched

Who Wants To Be A Millionaire, fell asleep sad and bitter in the armchair?'

He ignored the jibe. I caught the faintest twitch at the corner of Chew's mouth, though.

'Who'd you visit?'

'Not germane.' I still didn't know whether they'd made the link between Gina and the Transpersonal Foundation, much less the address in Mount Lawley. At this stage, I had no intention of mentioning it.

'I'll decide that.'

'On my way back from visiting I ran into Yula, who introduced me to Berry. The story starts there.'

'So you didn't know the victim?'

'Not by name.'

'Not a client of yours?'

I shook my head.

'You a client of hers?'

I made neither motion nor murmur, holding in my offence. Hewson looked up at me in the silence, trying to read my face.

'I believe him,' said Chew, softly.

Hewson chuckled mirthlessly. 'You'd believe the dead can walk.'

'They can,' I said.

'Well this one bloody can't,' he snapped. 'We got ID this morning, Panther, in case you're interested.' He flipped back a couple of pages. 'Belinda Mary Jules, aka Berry Juice, fourteen years, nine months, formerly and formally of Ochre Drive, Kalgoorlie. Father's a miner with form for aggravated assault, mother's a part-time whore in the brothels up there. Runaway. Reported missing seven weeks back.'

'And Missing Persons didn't think to ask around Northbridge? The place is a magnet for the missing.'

He bridled, as his warrant card ensured he had to. 'And the jewel in the crown of Neighbourhood Watch. I'm sure the squad fulfilled all its duties in regard to —'

I cut him off. 'And, let me guess, mummy and daddy didn't seem to give a fuck?'

'Maybe,' he conceded.

'Nobody gave a fuck except Yula out there.'

Chew spoke now. 'Who still won't give us her full name, by the way. You want to help there, Joe?'

I shook my head. She sighed.

Hewson flipped his pages forward again and took over. 'So you meet the Berry girl, then what?'

I repeated the tale of the Commodore. Then, as prompted, I said I'd returned to the house before going to the Libido nightclub.

'Why there?'

I couldn't risk looking at Chew. Hewson seemed edgy and suspicious. 'To meet someone.'

'Who?'

'Woman with big tits. She wants something from me. Nothing to do with this.'

I heard Chew's foot scrape against the floor, but remained looking directly at Hewson. I thought he was going to pursue the point for a moment, but then he changed his mind.

'So you left the club. Time?'

I shrugged.

'OK, we'll try to check. You left the club and then you found this Yula —'

'She found me.'

'Where?'

'A bit further up William Street. She saw me come out of the building, I think.'

'And she told you the other girl was missing and you helped look for her?'

I nodded. 'I try to help where I can.'

He looked at me doubtfully. 'Sure. And you met DC Chew precisely where?'

From his tone it was clear that this was the question he considered central to his investigation. The little love lost between the two partnered cops had evidently been drained away into the same muddy wheel ruts as Berry's life.

I held my hands up. 'Somewhere between there and Russell Square. My recollection comes and goes. I remember her being around at the end of James Street.'

He slapped his notebook against the back of the bentwood in frustration. 'More *detail*, Joe.'

'No idea. My brain, you know? The spirit cometh, then it goeth once more. That which seemeth clear by the moon is but the whisper of a rumour come the dawn.'

'Where's that from, shit-head? Proverbs?'

I shook my head, smiled modestly. 'I just made it up.' Still got it, boy, I thought to myself.

Hewson sighed. 'DC Chew here reckons she saw you passing while she was in Plaka shish kebabs. Reckons she went to talk to you because she was concerned for the welfare of the girl with you.'

Charming, I thought. Make me out to be a pederast. 'That'll be it then.'

Silence followed. Hewson looked at Chew. She wouldn't look at me.

'Like I said,' she said.

Hewson breathed out, wishing perhaps he could make fire with his nose. 'How you breathing, Panther? Chest constricted?'

I pulled a Dunhill from the crushed packet in my pocket and lit it. 'Same as ever. Why?'

'Two days back, a young woman in a Northbridge alley, knifed and hotshot, you seen near the body. Last night, young girl in a Northbridge alley, knifed, you seen near the body. We've not got toxicology back yet, but hey, who knows? That frame is starting to fit around you pretty snugly, boy. You got anything for us, loosen a few screws?'

'This is bullshit,' I whispered. It was a statement, not a protest. 'This is a reversal of cause and effect.'

'I've got more than enough to haul you and hold you, Panther. Easy job. Give me something, or so help me you'll do.'

'Until the next woman dies.'

He smiled. It was not a pleasant sight. 'Maybe there won't be a next woman dies. Maybe you did kill them, after all. Maybe you didn't. Maybe the guy who did, he hears we've got you banged up, he'll count his blessings and stop, or head off interstate. Maybe he'll leave you crying all alone at night for two consecutive life sentences in Heavy Town.'

I could see he wasn't joking. Gina Compton's murder had made the newspaper the day before. Page three: WOMAN SLAIN IN NORTHBRIDGE. Berry's death would make a much bigger splash — light blue touchpaper and wait for widespread parental hysteria. Dead child. Two dead females. It was odds-on that before the end of the week the police in general and Hewson's superior officer in particular would be dealing with all manner of media and talkback speculation.

They needed a result badly and even the wrong result would do.

'Joe,' said Chew, an undercurrent of pleading in her tone, 'give us something before we take it.'

It was sensible advice. I wasn't going to be much use to anyone — especially myself — locked up. I had no answers, though. Only proliferating questions. I decided to hand over one of those.

'Do you think the two deaths are related?'

Chew looked at Hewson, who stared at me, flat-eyed. 'You think they're not?'

I shrugged. 'Man looketh on the outward appearance, but the Lord looketh on the heart.'

'Another of yours?' he demanded.

I shook my head. 'Samuel.'

'Goldwyn?'

'Nup.'

'Never heard of him, then. What the fuck does it mean?'

I was serene in my reply. 'It means maybe, maybe not. The knife in Gina Compton's neck was a pretty deliberate placement.'

Chew looked thoughtful. Hewson looked as if he was barely controlling his temper.

'So what are you now, the fucking coroner?' he snapped. 'Our man likes a bit of variety, that's all. Last time hunting knife from the back; this time bloody big carving knife from the front. Just as quick, just as final.'

'Just as quick?'

'Reckon. Near as buggery, by the look of it. Knife blade hard and fast from the front, up beneath the ribs into something major. Thirty seconds, tops. Hello, girly. *Schick*. Thump. Goodbye.'

Chew's eyes were black coals of loathing. She saw me notice, and quickly smothered the moment. 'Do you think Gina Compton and Belinda Jules knew each other?'

Was the question what it appeared to be? Or had she just thrown me a lifeline? I couldn't tell. I shook my head.

Hewson, retaking the initiative, shooting a glare at Chew as he did so: 'How can you be sure there's no connection between them?'

I wasn't at all sure that there wasn't a connection between them. But I was very sure they'd never met. I decided not to make that distinction clear in my response.

'When I ran into Yula and Berry yesterday, Yula asked me about Gina. She called her "that chick", and asked me what I knew. She asked me if Gina was on the game.'

'She wasn't,' said Chew.

I looked her in the eyes at that. Hewson, too, stared at her. She looked quickly at the floor, giving nothing away but fleeting discomfit. 'According to statements.'

'My feeling, too,' I said, willing Hewson to return his attention to me. 'I told Yula not as far as I knew.'

The detective sergeant's gaze lingered for a moment on his junior, then turned reptilian to me. 'Which proves?'

'Yula didn't know her, not her name, nor anything about her. Might have seen her around, but that's all. I'd bet houses on that, if I owned any. You don't believe me, show her a photo. My overwhelming feeling is that Berry hadn't been around long enough, hadn't got brave enough, to start getting to know strangers. The only people she knew were whoever it is Yula knows.'

Hewson thought about that, tapping his pen against his notebook. 'After this,' he said to Chew, 'go back in the kitchen, get a list of friends, associates, pimps, whoever, from that girl. She's just stopped being a witness and started being an accessory. Check that list against Compton's KAs. You get a match, let me know.'

Sparks flashed in Chew's eyes. 'But sir, she won't even tell us her *own* name, never mind her ... She's traumatised and —'

'She's a teenage slut with the morals of a sewer rat, *Constable*,' he spat. 'Do it.'

She avoided my gaze, and his, just nodded.

Hewson stood, appearing momentarily satisfied with his own performance. Chew followed suit. I remained seated on the bed.

'You, Panther,' he snarled, pointing his finger directly at me. 'Not good enough. If I bang you up and you didn't kill these females, I'll still sleep peaceful at night. You're scum and the place'd be better off without you anyway.'

'Sheep will be perverted and turn into wolves,' I said.

'Whatever,' he continued. 'Twenty-four hours, Panther. Give me something concrete in twenty-four hours or you're gone.' He turned on his heel and walked out.

Chew was looking shaken, but had recovered enough composure to manage a sardonic smile. 'Still reckon you've got forty-eight hours — thirty-six now, probably — to make up your mind, Joe?' she whispered.

'DC Chew,' I began, loud enough for Hewson to hear if he was still in the passage. 'Go easy on Yula, please.' She signalled assent. I continued, now whispering. 'You owe *me*, hence. One more thing.'

'What?'

Loud again: 'Show us your tits.'

Her slap caught me hard across the left side of my jaw, forcing me to throw my hands against the bed to stay more or less upright. I didn't retaliate. I didn't take my eyes off her face, either.

She stormed out of my room. I heard her footsteps heavy on the floor, heading for the kitchen. Good, I thought to myself. Stay angry, Irene. Angry people don't think too good.

CHAPTER 8

Hewson had been gone perhaps twenty minutes. Chew was ensconced in the kitchen with Yula and the door shut when I heard Nessie's thin wail emanating from the front of the house. I ignored it, of course, partly because I was busy thinking, partly because Nessie was Mrs Warburton's responsibility, and partly because one more feeble cry of alarm after so many could hardly move me to pity.

Not so long ago, the Pope drafted a broad-ranging *mea culpa*, recording the Catholic Church's apologies for centuries of violence against Jews, non-believers, heretics and the apostate. Several senior cardinals opposed the move, feeling that it was theologically and economically dubious to say sorry to anyone about anything. The Vatican is reputed to be refusing to release a list of ten thousand people nominated as twentieth-century martyrs in my name. The organisation simply doesn't have the administrative grunt to investigate so many claims for beatification. So many shedding blood, or dying of hunger, thirst and misery, looking up to the sky with their last ragged breath and announcing that they did it all for me.

In the first weeks of 2000, a group of armed boys from Burma invaded a Thailand hospital and held seven hundred people at gunpoint. The boys were led by twelve-year-old twins, held to have divine powers by their followers. They were Christians these boys, and had lived knowing nothing but war. They wanted Thai doctors to treat their wounded comrades. They were young and silly and rash and desperate and terrified and boys. Most of them were shot dead, hands tied behind their backs.

No one put their names up as martyrs.

So much slaughter, so many deaths, still, as always. I stand here, innocent and complicit in all of them.

No one has ever apologised to *me*. Being in love, apparently, means never having to say sorry. Once I thought I was a messenger. Now I am merely an excuse. I am a cipher which no more knows its meaning than a Morse code message understands the command to drop the bomb embedded in its text. If I am a lesson, I don't know what truth I teach. I am recursive: rub away my layers, on each a promise unanswered, a plea scraped with broken fingernails on the rock of my helplessness.

Do not ask me to save you. I am the cause of this horror, sustained and entrapped by your belief. A thing becomes a thing only if it is observed and delimited. Cease to regard me and we can all die happy.

Nessie wailed again. No answering call nor footfall from Mrs Warburton. I sighed, finished packing my pockets, then made my way up the hallway to the front room. The old bitch sat, still on her commode, knees beneath a putrid blanket.

'What?' I asked, none too compassionately.

Nessie's head wobbled slowly around until her milky eyes could do their best to see me. 'That *fat* bitch,' she replied.

'She's not here,' I said.

'I know. She saw them outside and walked away again. Up to no good, that one, you ask me.'

I realised that Nessie must have been able to see through the dusty slats of the blind. Crouching down to her level and looking out I saw that Hewson's unmarked car had gone, but the divvy van was still in position, presumably to give Chew a lift when she was finished. All heart, that Hewson, I thought.

'Back soon,' I called to Nessie, and headed for the front door.

'But me doings,' cried the old woman. 'Doings done and tea time.'

I ignored her.

Outside the morning was heating up fast. The dark clouds of the previous night had blown inland, dissipated from their purge, leaving the sky a brilliant blue that hurt the eyes to look at it and promised a day hot enough to roast a saint.

I wondered for a moment whether the pair of uniforms leaning against the van had orders to prevent me leaving. They gave me the hard stare that is the stock-in-trade of the inner city patrols, but made no move towards me. I set off along the pavement at a brisk clip, figuring Laz would be heading towards her office.

I caught sight of her as I turned the corner. Lumbered as she was with fattening foetus and consequent bovine metabolism, she was in no danger of qualifying for the Olympics. I called her name. She stopped and waited, her habitual smile of greeting replaced quickly by thin-lipped concern.

'What the hell's happening, Joe?' she asked as I reached her. 'You in trouble?'

I took her by the elbow and pointed towards a half-decent coffee shop across the road. 'I'm always in trouble, but I'm still at liberty for the moment. You were looking for me?'

'No, mate,' she answered, heavy on the sarcasm, 'I thought I'd pay a spontaneous visit to that hideous old bag you live with, see if she needed her arse wiped again.'

'She does, actually. Someone will get around to it.'

We entered the cafe and found a table without difficulty. The rich pungency of coffee roast filled my nostrils. I breathed deeply, stealing its perfume. Laz had a certain look on her face. I knew better than to open the conversation while interruption was still possible, so remained silent until the waiter had taken our order — double-strength latte for me, plain mineral water for her.

'What's going on?' she asked.

I told her about Berry, and about Yula, but not about Chew. She went pale.

'So it *is* some maniac out to chop up women,' she said, not quite suppressing a shiver.

I shook my head. 'You're assuming the same person did Gina and Berry.'

'Well, look at the facts ... they were both —'

She stopped abruptly as our order arrived. I beat her on the restart.

'Cause and effect, Laz, correlation and coincidence. Listen, in the fifth century there was a mob of people over near the Danube called the Burgundians. They were about to be massacred by the Huns. Some visiting fanatic of a bishop told these poor folk that if they all converted to Christianity immediately and *feared* God — I mean, really, shit-dropping *feared* him — then they would be saved.'

143

'What's this got to do with —'

'So they did. The Huns were led by a fearsome dude called Uptar. As he charged at the head of his horde on the almost defenceless Burgundians, guess what happened?'

Laz was barely humouring me. She asked the question with hooded eyes.

'He exploded. Boof. Stomach burst open, guts everywhere, dead Uptar, Huns running away.'

'Which proves?'

'Nothing. That's my point. The Burgundians all thought that because they had contrived to be terrified of an invisible spook, their enemy had been dealt with in spectacular and gory fashion. But it was just a coincidence — weird, yes, but weird happens. Uptar, I don't know, had some horrible tumour or something and it just happened to go nova at a particularly convenient time.'

Laz gave a sad shake of her head, then sipped her drink. 'You want to get back to the subject now, Joe? You know: dead women dying here and now.'

I took a pull on my latte and fired up a Dunhill. 'What I'm saying is that I don't think the same person necessarily killed Gina Compton and Berry. There's a correlation, but not a conformity. I think it's possible that whoever killed Berry wanted her death to *look* like Gina's, that's all.'

Laz looked at the ceiling. 'So we've got *two* maniacs now? How do you know?'

'Gut feeling, plus three things. First, I think Berry died where she was stabbed, but Gina didn't. Second, Berry's corpse was a lot messier.'

Laz blanched. I didn't pause. 'And third, I'm willing to bet that they'll find no smack in her body. The hotshot didn't make the paper, remember? Just the knife.'

Laz looked thoughtful, bordering on sceptical. 'Was Berry gay?'

I shrugged. 'She was fourteen years old. Would she know?'

Laz shrugged back. 'I did. Do the cops think there are two killers?'

'Not yet. Actually, I don't know, but I don't think so.'

'They're all over the area this morning, going door to door.'

'Thanks for the warning.'

'They're asking about a white Commodore.'

'The car that picked up Berry. I saw it happen.'

Laz's eyes widened. 'You *saw* the killer?'

'I saw the car she got in. Whether it was driven by her killer, I don't know.'

'But you think so.'

I remembered Chew's observation about the mud in the laneway, how it was softer than that in the others. Commodores were heavy cars. I nodded.

Laz exhaled with deliberate force. 'White Commodore, eh? Must be fucking thousands of them in this town.'

'Which is why the streets are full of cops walking by faith, not by sight.' I swallowed the last of the latte, held up my hand to order another. Laz passed on a second mineral water, citing bladder pressure.

'Anyway,' I said. 'You came to see me, surely not just to ask these questions.'

She shook her head, entertained a worried look for a moment, then grabbed her shoulder bag from where it hung on the back of the chair and placed it on her lap. 'You remember,' she began. 'You asked me to have a poke about the office, see if Gina might have left any documents or notes there?'

'Uh-huh.'

'I did it early this morning. I don't sleep so well at the moment, and Ayzel was off to join a Sasher protest at some dawn service somewhere, so there was no reason to hang about in bed. Besides, getting there at 6.30 am was pretty much the only time I was sure of being able to move around without Anita being there.'

'Hard worker, that one.'

The look on her face conveyed her opinion without the need for words. 'Anyway, I found this lot. It was in a manila folder shoved at the bottom of a drawer in one of the communal desks.' She reached into her bag and pulled out a thin collection of primarily A4 paper. 'The folder was marked "lecture notes", but these clearly aren't.'

At first glance, I could see that some were typed, while others were handwritten. I took them from her, and spread them out roughly on the table. I recognised the nature of a couple immediately: they were downloaded testimonies of Transpersonal Foundation apostates, just like the ones I'd found on the internet. The handwritten pages were going to take a little while to decipher. There were also a couple showing typed rows of figures, some kind of bookkeeping gig. Some of the entries were circled, with hurried notes nearby.

Laz anticipated my next question. 'I've seen her handwriting before. I'd swear it's hers.'

I nodded thanks. My second latte arrived, which provided, as providence often does, a natural break in proceedings. Laz announced her intention to head off to Sappho's Sisters. I thanked her again, remained seated, and told her I might call her later.

'Sure,' she replied. 'I'll be there till six if I can stand it.'

'Have the other women returned to work there?'

She shook her head, then shrugged, then waved her hands about limply. 'Yes, no, maybe. Probably a couple will come in, but I guess they won't stay long — especially if the news of this young sex worker's death makes the radio this morning. There doesn't have to be a pattern for people to think they see one.'

I put my hand in my jacket pocket to fish out another cigarette, but during the journey my fingers became distracted. I pulled out the cellophane instead and held it up. 'Any idea what this is from?'

Laz took hold of it, peered, and handed it back. 'Don't quote me, but yeah. Looks like the wrapper from a video cassette — you know, those small ones the tourists put in their dinky little handycam things. Why?'

I put the cellophane back in my pocket. 'Wondering, that's all. Just something I picked up in the street.'

She looked concerned. 'You're getting worse, Joe.'

I made no defence. Not that she had expected one. When she started to walk off, I put a hand out and touched her.

'What?'

'How soon can you get me enough money to scram?'

'When will you need it?'

'Not long. A day or two.'

A sadness darkened her face, but briefly. She laid one hand on the potent swell of her belly, then flicked her hair as if brushing away a wish.

'I know where Ayzel keeps a couple of signed cheques, in case of emergencies. Yell when you're ready. It's going to take a bit of explaining, but she'll get over it. We've got the child to think about, she and I.'

I signalled the arrangement sounded fine, which it didn't.

✝

Mysteries are revealed to the meek, among whose number I have never counted myself. By noon, however, I felt that I had made at least some progress in decoding the contents of Gina Compton's folder. I had also downed five strong lattes and was having trouble holding the paper still enough to focus.

For this reason, I decamped from the cafe and walked in heat suffused with the mildly intoxicating odour of melting tarmac to the Fortitude Hotel. I had long been banned from the lounge bar there — something about slashing a glass across the face of a backpacking born-again, I don't remember — but the cramped gloom of the back bar, with its pool tables, old darts pennants and stringy regulars, was still traversable territory. I grabbed a can of Emu Export, and secured an empty, if sticky, table in the games room, close by the jukebox. A Guns'n'Roses song was playing at the time. I whacked in two bucks and programmed Hendrix, AC/DC and Rage Against The Machine. I needed my brain to function. I needed noise to drive it. Then I laid out Gina's papers — a dozen sheets in all — and started to work through them again.

I put the apostate testimonies to one side, figuring she'd got hold of them merely as supporting evidence to her main case. That accounted for four of the sheets. What was left were her handwritten pages, the scribbled-on bookkeeping print-outs, and a single glossy page evidently torn from a Transpersonal Foundation brochure — the Greek logo-thing was plainly visible — listing the fees for the various courses and seminars offered by the organisation.

The handwritten notes were titled, rather self-consciously, 'My Jurney'. They revealed much, apart from Gina's failure to grasp the finer points of the English language. The document was a kind of note-form chronology, detailing her involvement with the Foundation. I had the feeling that she had been intending either to use it as the basis of a much longer story, or perhaps hand it over to a journalist for much the same purpose.

She recorded how she had travelled down to the city, leaving her parental home after finishing high school. Her intention had been to enrol in a university, doing psychology (she fancied), but not before taking a year away from study in order to get some experience in the workforce. This had apparently been in accordance with her parents' wishes, who, generous and caring, had given her a couple of thousand dollars to help her 'get istablished'.

She had used the money to take a lease on the Mount Lawley house, intending to live there on her own, meeting the rent through the abundant jobs she just knew were out there somewhere. They weren't. She moved from one casual bar shift to another, never able to hold one down for long. After a few months she felt reluctantly compelled to sign on with a company which provided 'skimpies' — topless barmaids, pretty much — to pubs around the place. The company also hired out strippergrams and strippers for private parties.

The money was good, but the stress and the humiliation were awful. After several weeks she gave it away, and fell into depression and despair. She signed on for the dole for the first time in her life ('I felt so ashamed and misrabel'), sinking into a mire of daytime television and forged job applications.

Soon she was broke, morbid, and feeling hopeless. She was facing eviction, and knew she needed desperately to find some sort of help to get her life back on track. She found the

Transpersonal Foundation, she noted, through a small advert in the Sunday paper and rang the number. The first person who came to see her — 'some nurd in a name tag' — gave her a couple of glossy brochures and urged her to attend a free introductory seminar.

She did. It was given by Clem Porter.

Just what was said, and just how she ended up having coffee with him afterwards, were both unrecorded. During their conversation, however, Gina confessed that she found both the Foundation's program, as outlined, and success record, as claimed, very attractive. She very much wanted to do some of the seminars, she told Porter, but had no money at all to pay the hefty fees demanded. She didn't want to borrow any more from her parents (she added in parenthesis) because she didn't want them to know what a state she'd got herself in, and, anyway, she wasn't sure they'd approve, being vaguely Buddhist themselves.

Porter, for whatever reason, must have seen her as star material. Or, at least, potentially useful. Having ascertained her living arrangements, he suggested a contra deal. She could do the first few seminars free if she agreed to rent out her spare bedrooms to other Foundation students. She agreed.

Everything apparently went well for a while — except that she still failed to find gainful employment, no matter how much 'the sessions were improving my self-confidence'. Yet again a financial crisis loomed. She'd been cut off the dole for failing to declare a night's income she had earned working (fully clothed, she stressed) in a bar. She faced the awful prospect of not being able to meet even the quarter share of the rent she was now supposed to pay. Porter again threw her a lifeline. He offered to pay her some money — she didn't specify how much — in return for working one day a week at his office, tidying up the routine correspondence, day-to-day invoicing and the files. She'd done well at maths and accounting in school.

'That was when I started to find things out,' she wrote.

Frustratingly, that was where her notes ended. She neither specified what she discovered, nor where Porter's office was located. Clearly, though, her discoveries were related in some way to the bookkeeping print-outs she had annotated. I'd looked at these for ages in the coffee shop, and did so again now with the aid of another beer. Their specific message was opaque to me, but their nature gradually became clear enough.

There were three sheets, all bearing the same date at the top: November, the previous year. The top sheet contained four columns. The first of these comprised two or three letter entries, which I took to be initials — identifiers for specific people. The second row contained alphanumeric combinations, which correlated with those at the end of each seminar description on the brochure page. So far, thus, so good: who was doing which course. The third was also clear, showing dollar amounts which again correlated with the prices quoted in the brochure. The fourth, however, gave me a bit of trouble. It consisted of lower case letters, two or three, assigned seemingly at random: *ch, cs, cn, cc, eft.*

I twigged just as Rage Against The Machine were telling nobody in particular to get fucked, very loudly. Reading across I found an entry for GC. The last row was *cn*. GC was Gina Compton, who was paying off her debts by working. The entry *cn* might thus conceivably stand for *contra*. The others then fell into place quickly: *ch* was cheque, *cs* cash, *cc* credit card, and *eft* EFTPOS.

No worries, I thought. Just not very interesting. Then I turned to the other two sheets, which contained a similar list — only much, much longer, maybe three times the size.

I was onto my third Emu and scraping the jukebox barrel with Korn before I came to a conclusion. Every entry that had been on the first sheet was reproduced on the longer list, exactly. Above and below them, however, were perhaps another fifty entries. They were all marked *cs*. Gina had circled some of them, put question marks next to others. In notes in the margins and at the bottom she had written 'unknown', 'no record', 'no mem'ship file', and, tellingly, 'there wernt this many people at anything'.

The air in the pub was thick with seeping heat, sweat and old booze. It was my kind of place. I drained my can, crushing it at my mouth to wring out the last little drops, sat back against my chair and quietly congratulated myself.

Now I knew what Gina had feared, why she'd kept a weapon at her bedside. I knew, too, what Clem Porter had been searching for. And perhaps — just perhaps — I knew why the woman had been killed. Porter was using the Transpersonal Foundation as a laundry, keeping two sets of books, washing money, white as snow.

I bought a pie on my way out of the bar; the air outside was hotter than the oven from whence it came. I forced myself to chew its offal insides. I needed fuel. The afternoon was going to be a long one.

It was time to talk to Clem Porter. First, though, I had to find him.

And to do that, I needed to pervert a sheep.

CHAPTER 9

Truly the light is sweet, and a pleasant thing it is for the eyes to behold the sun.

Well, maybe sometimes, maybe if pleasure still held any meaning. (For what is pleasure, but the lighter steps along the path to death, a path which in my case appears infinite and wearisome?) The sun in this instance was about as sweet as caustic soda, and every bit as pleasant as drinking same. It reflected savagely off the pavement and shops and house walls as I trudged slowly up the long slow incline that led to Mount Lawley. Every parked car, every passing vehicle, caught its majesty and flashed it back, a sharp spear of white-hot glare, straight into my eyes, where it exploded into dazzling prisms through the sweat that had dripped within them.

Here, out in the open, in broad daylight, here is where reason begs forgiveness and sinks to slumber. Here in clear, clean summer heat, sterile as a bone saw, will a brain fry and start to imagine all manner of fatal fantasies. Here, where nothing is hid and shadows fall like creases on a Methodist's Sunday best, does the mind stray and imagine to itself that it can see a meaning as precise as form.

The sun shone hot and bright on Golgotha that day. High on my cross I must have been visible for miles, as the Romans intended. I must have been visible in heaven, or so I thought. There, in the bright flashes of blood loss and the illuminating zeal of a fanatic cause come to self-directed prophetic resolution, did I imagine that I knew what was going to happen. There did I mentally place a tick against all the needed symbols, retrospective and immediate, and whisper to myself through mucous-crusted swollen lips, now am I done, now is my message sent, now may I rest in father's arms.

Alas, the rest, as they say, isn't history. Not a bit of it.

I should have stayed put. I should have had a good long think. I should have remained in that tomb and waited for someone to come back to check the putrefaction. I should have had the courage of my convictions and said unto them: look, brothers, sisters, I'm still here: buggered if I know how, frankly. I think we got some thinking to do.

But no. I tried to communicate in the garden, trembling in the frightful air, then tried again and again, then fled, in horror and abandonment, messiah made deceiver, never to return. Ascended, they said. If that's the way they wanted it: I ascended across three borders in the first four months, shaking the dust off my feet, running like hell away.

It was only later that I realised I was running away from myself.

So I've never liked stink-hot afternoons.

They do, however, have one advantage. They put people at ease. With reason fled and shadowless, they tend to think that all's right with the world.

Oh dear.

There were two cars parked in the drive of the Mount

Lawley house. I could see this from my temporary position, leaning casually against the wall of a shop half a block down, drinking from a can of Coke.

The heat and the length of the walk had combined with the systemic evaporation of beer and caffeine to render my mood as cheerless as a church orphanage. The Coke was an attempt to rehydrate and revive. I wished I'd brought along some whisky to give it strength.

Or something. Anything. Let him drink, and forget his poverty, and remember his misery no more.

Two cars.

I tried to remember how many had been present when I'd made my visit in the guise of John Lloyd. I couldn't recall. I hadn't paid attention. Neither car sported an 'L' or 'P' plate. Was Nigel, the youngest of them, old enough to have qualified for his full licence? Perhaps, just, but he didn't look like the sort of petrolhead who would have gone for his plates the moment the clock clicked over on his birthday.

Or perhaps he wasn't so tender. Sometimes the young look terribly young. And sometimes their eyes look as old as the grave.

I drained the Coke and came to a conclusion: fuck knows. The house might contain anywhere between one and three people — with bets against just one. This was unfortunate, because just one was what I wanted.

I needed a plan. Half a Dunhill later, I had one. All it required was a telephone box, a taxi, and a modicum of luck.

I found the phone box just around the next corner. I couldn't see the house from it, but could be back in a decent viewing position within a few seconds of hanging up if I got a shift on. Dialling the number which Laz had provided, I found myself wondering whether they might have changed it once they took the account out of Gina Compton's name. That would knacker things, force the show to go a bit more public than I intended.

It rang. Once, twice ... I was half-expecting an answering machine, but, no, someone picked it up.

'Heh'o?'

The greenstick fracture of the syllables told me immediately who was on the line. The one with the hearing aid. God called to Adam.

My voice was almost a whisper. An urgent whisper. 'Adam, are you alone?'

'I'm ... no, Nigel's here ... Who —'

No Iain. One down. 'Then for pity's sake don't repeat anything out loud.'

'I can't hear you very well. Who are you?'

'I'll tell you when you get here. You'll thank me then.'

'What are you ... *speak up*, please ... Get where?'

Gamble time. 'Your mother's house.'

A sigh of irritation. 'Mum *knows* I can't see her unless she joins.'

Ah ha. Take the sacrament or be forever dead. It's a good trick, that one. I think I started it. 'Make an exception, Adam. She's had an accident.'

His breathing suddenly went shallow. 'What happened? Is sh —'

'Just get here.'

Hanging up, I trotted briskly back to where I could observe the house. Less than a minute had passed before the door opened and a very flustered looking young man, still wearing his name tag, strode to one of the cars. He wrenched the door open, taking two attempts to do so, jumped in and fired the engine. I couldn't quite hear it above the noise of the traffic, but I could see plumes of exhaust spew from the back as he revved.

Nigel stood in the doorway, a panicked look on his face. His arms were in front of him, palms uppermost. He was shouting something. Adam waved a dismissive hand, then started backing out, the wheels spinning as the car tried to find purchase on the loose stones of the drive. Nigel advanced two steps into the garden. The car made it onto the road, turned, and sped away. The young man remained standing, watching it disappear. His shoulders sagged, then he managed a theatrical shrug — a kind of compensatory gesture, just in case anyone had been watching — turned, and walked back into the house. I waited for the door to close.

Poor Nigel, I thought. He doesn't have a clue. Home alone, as he was.

There was always the possibility that Iain — absent, mission unknown — could turn up at any moment. It was better that he didn't, of course, but I could handle him if he did. And I had no idea where Adam's mother lived: nearby or halfway across the state. I decided, though, that I could probably count on a good half hour in which to work. Even if the woman turned out to live just in the next suburb, I was pretty sure there would be claims, counterclaims and accusations exchanged, given how dramatic and inexplicable the prodigal son's arrival was set to be.

I sighed with satisfaction. It's nice every now and then to live up to expectations. Behold, I setteth the solitary in families: I bringeth out those which are bound in chains.

Nicer still, though, to disabuse them. The rebellious dwell in a dry land.

Stage two, then.

The area being primarily residential, I decided that it would probably be quicker — and certainly less conspicuous — to return to the telephone box and ring a cab rather than try to hail one off the street. This was done. It arrived inside five minutes, piloted by an elderly, paunchy Greek man whose interest in life had long since seeped away. This was a bonus.

'What we do is this,' I explained while handing him three crumpled twenty dollar notes as a retainer. 'You park just over there, in that side street. I'm going to go into that house there to do some business. I don't know how long I'll be. Not long. Then I'll come out and join you here. Then, if I'm right, the guy I've just being doing business with will come out, get in his car and drive off. I think he's going to try to gip me on a deal, and I want to know who's in it with him.'

The cabbie folded the notes into his shirt pocket, hawked up a ball of spit and sent it flying through the open window. 'Follow that car, huh?' He switched on the meter. 'You want it, you got it. I don't see so well, you know?'

'That's what I like to hear.' I gave the car an avuncular pat on the roof, then started walking towards the house.

He probably thought it was about sex, or drugs, or some kind of weird politics. He was wrong, though. The main point I wanted to make to young Nigel was of a theological nature.

'There is no god,' I told him. Then I drove the syringe up into his nostril and straight through the side of his nose.

He went to scream, but something in his central nervous system stopped him from making the necessary facial adjustments just in time. I pushed him back inside the house, kicking the door shut behind me.

He had opened it, summoned by my polite knock, wearing a look of curious expectation. His face had just started to register my familiarity when I snaked my hand up from my pocket.

So fast had I made the puncture that there was no blood at all. I pushed him back towards the far wall of the room, knocking one of the chairs over. I kept my right hand at his face, holding the fit just so, my left grasping his neck, my own face as close as my arms would permit. The surgical steel point of the syringe protruded from his flesh like the jewellery piercing from hell. I could see it quite plainly. In his view, I imagined, it would loom large and disturbingly out of focus.

We hit the wall. I pressed my weight against him, let him cop my coffee-beer-meat-pie-cigarette-Coke breath. His eyes were wide, his breathing rapid. He kept trying to turn his face away. The slightest pressure on the fit brought it back in line.

'No god, Nigel,' I repeated, sounding very calm. 'I heard Iain tell you that. I've read that same thing in a Transpersonal Foundation leaflet. There *is* no god. Clem Porter must have told you that, too. *Blink*, boy, if the answer's yes.'

He blinked. He also whimpered.

'So you *do* know Clem Porter. What does the Transpersonal Foundation say about lying, boy?'

He said nothing. Hardly surprising really: I had a needle up his nostril and my fingers around his throat.

'No god, the Transpersonal Foundation says. Well, hey, Nigel?'

He made neither move nor gesture nor sound. I pressed a little on the fit.

'*Blink*, boy, when you're talking to me.'

He blinked several times. A tear tumbled from his left eye. The warm sting of urine filled the air.

'Good lad. Now: the Foundation is right. There *is* no god, but guess what?'

Again the blinking. Locking on his eyes, very close, I slowly pulled the needle out of his flesh. He went pale.

'I'm the next best thing. Aren't *you* a lucky boy?'

He fainted into my arms. I didn't have time for that, so I let him slip through me and crumple to the floor in a kind of almost-controlled collapse. His temple was perhaps moving a bit too fast to brake safely, but I reckoned it would only cause a little dent at most.

The knock failed to wake him, which irritated rather than dismayed me. With my foot I pushed at him until he was lying on his back. Then I went in search of the kitchen, a tap and a jug, finding all three in good order through a door and down a short passage.

When I returned I had an idea. Time was of the essence and I didn't feel like farting about with subtleties. Using the seat cushion from the fallen chair, I propped his head up so that his neck was at a forty-five degree angle. Had his eyes been open he would have been staring down the length of his body towards his feet.

Kneeling by his side, I unbuttoned his trousers, pulling them and his underpants down around his thighs, careful not to get my fingers wet. Then I did what I had to with my right hand, before pouring a trickle of water from the jug onto his slumbering face with my left.

He came to after a few seconds and began to panic. I silenced him with a holy shush and bade him in a gentle voice to focus, such that he might see the miracle.

Behold: his flaccid dick was standing upright, hanging like a drunken gymnast from the syringe through its foreskin.

His eyes rolled back in his head and consciousness fled once more. Again I anointed his face. Again his eyes fluttered open.

'Circumcision is nothing, Nigel, and uncircumcision is nothing, but keeping the commandments of God. Paul came up with that one. First letter to the Corinthians, if I recall. Brilliant move, that was: drop the entry requirement to have the flappy bit of your johnboy chopped off. Made conversions a lot easier, you see?'

He nodded, just a bit, eyes wild.

'Never thought to ask me about it, of course. Well, he couldn't. I'd done a runner years before. He and his mob were still trying to hunt me down, in case I blew the gaff on them. Put out an All Prophets Bulletin and everything.'

He didn't laugh. I wiggled the fit. He whimpered, managed: 'Don't'.

'Where's all the extra money coming from, Nigel?'

The noises he made were a little too less than human to be useful.

'The extra money Clem Porter's washing through the Foundation, Nigel. Gina knew about it. Did you?'

The word sounded like 'nuh'. I lifted the syringe, pulling his penis with it. He squealed. 'No ... no ... don't ... no money, don't know about money, Clem's never mentioned money to mmm ...'

'He's ripping you off, boy. All of you. You think I'm the bad guy? Wrong. I'm the good guy and I've got the testaments to prove it. Clem Porter's the villain here, Nigel. He's taking you for a ride. He doesn't care about you, your

161

confidence, your damn stupid delimited realities. He's using you, your friends, all your dicky name-tag-wearing nerd seminar buddies, possibly the whole Foundation idea, as a front. He just wants your money, and your loyalty to cover up whatever else he's doing.'

His eyes flashed defiance, then denial, but his mouth declined to elucidate.

'How often do you see Clem Porter, Nigel?'

He shook his head, tongue poking through pursed lips. I tugged the fit upwards, once. He bit his tongue: not hard enough to draw blood, but sufficiently to send a fresh leak of tears onto his face.

'Don't *lie*, Nigel. It's bad for the soul.'

His voice was high, his speech rapid. 'He, ah, he comes round here, maybe once a month, you know. About that. Then, you know, also, we'll see him at seminars, courses. You know, if he's taking it.'

'Why does he come round here?'

'C-c-c-coffee. Visits, you know. No reason, really.'

Sure, I thought, but let it go. 'How often do you do courses?'

'Me? Not often. Adam, Iain, they ... they do *more*. You know, they're almost always doing one. I haven't done one for months.'

'Why not? Losing faith, boy?'

'N-n-n-no. No. Not really. Need money. Adam, Iain, they have part-time jobs, so they can afford ... also, sometimes Clem lets them take, you know, *do* the beginners' courses — after the introductory — so they earn money from that.'

'And give it straight back to Porter by signing up for something else?'

'I ... I guess.'

Very neat, I thought. 'Where are the courses held?'

'All over. Anywhere. Church halls, scout halls, function rooms in hotels, you know? Clem holds that the message is the important thing. He doesn't want the, you know, Transpersonal Foundation, to have a permanent location. Says it distracts from the message.'

Not to mention making it easy to find, I could have added. 'You don't have a job, boy?'

'I'm, I'm looking.'

'So how do you afford rent?'

'My parents.'

With my left hand I flicked at his name tag. 'Do they know about this?'

His eyes widened. 'N-n-nuh. Don't tell them, please. Clem says I shouldn't even talk to them. Adam and Iain don't know I do. Please don't say anything.'

'Poor boy. Did your parents know you were in love with Gina Compton?'

He squirmed, then instinctively realised it was not the best idea to be found in a day of bad notions.

'Did she laugh at you when you tried to chat her up? Or was she kind, but firm?'

More tears.

'Did you watch while she was in the shower? Did you peek through the bathroom door like a naughty schoolboy, Nigel? Did you wank over her memory in the lonely night?'

He growled, like a kicked dog.

'And did you tell Clem Porter of your feelings, boy? Did you ask him for guidance in this tricky affair of the heart?'

His face began to crease, lower lip sticking out, preparatory to wailing. I twitched my right hand in warning. Shamed, he gathered his breath.

'He told you to go for it, didn't he, Nigel? Clem Porter told you to ... what? Assert your individuality? Meet the challenge? Overcome the hurdle?'

'Uh-huh.'

'You failed, didn't you? Just like he knew you would.'

His lips curled into a silent, impotent snarl.

It was proving to be hard work, shifting him from pitch-deep terror to wire-taut anger. I'd scared him a bit too well. But that's me: my strength is made perfect in weakness, and this guy was as weak as Budweiser.

'Oh yes, Nigel. He's taken you and your friends for a hell of a ride. He *mocks* you, boy. He knew Gina was gay, didn't he? But he never told you, did he? He let you go after her, put your delicate little heart on the line, and laughed at you when she told you to piss off, didn't he?'

His face turned scarlet. I could hear his teeth grinding as he remembered the humiliation. I kept going.

'And he shared his little joke with the others, didn't he? With Iain and Adam: told them what you thought, *how you felt*, boy, about Gina. He set you up, turned you into an object lesson — made you a fall-down comedian. This doing much for your confidence, Nigel? You self-realising yet? Did he tell you it was *your* fault she ran away?'

He'd pretty much forgotten that he was lying on his back with his genitals exposed, a stranger holding a hypodermic through his dick. His lips were curling now into a growl, and sinews were starting to rise like cables in his neck. I was getting there, moving him from terror to fury without the intervening period of reflection. I figured I'd been pretty much on the ball. I decided to push it home, lying like a bastard.

'But *he* had her, Nigel. Oh yes. He didn't tell you that, did he? All those times she used to go over to work with him. What did she tell you? That he would let her do some more courses, pay her rent for her, if she just helped out a little bit around the office? Oh, Nigel, you poor schmuck. She was polishing his *knob*, boy. He was taking her from behind, stretched over the —'

He screamed. Then he writhed on the ground, growling, fists clenched, as if some foul demon possessing him was trying to escape.

Quickly, I pulled the fit out and stood up. 'Go, Nigel,' I said. 'The wicked flee when no man pursueth. And, by the way, Jesus loves you.'

I closed the door gently behind me, and walked without hurrying to the cab.

Inside it, the air conditioning chilled like forgiveness, then like love unreturned. I settled back into the seat and lit up a Dunhill. Very soon now, I figured, Nigel would burn out of the house, full of righteous and impotent fury, and drive to wherever Clem Porter lurked. I had no interest in whatever squabble might then ensue. If either got damaged in the process, well, it could only help. My primary objective was locating the address, for later reference after dark.

'Hey,' said the cabbie. 'No smoking in the taxi.'

'You don't see so well, remember?'

He grunted. I ashed on the floor.

I'd probably ruined young Nigel. I realised that. Whatever traumas and insecurities shaped him prior to my visit were now in super deluxe form, topped with whipped self-esteem and the sheer terror that only being pierced against your will can bring. Try to rob a brave man at gunpoint and he might just attempt to talk you out of it. Do the same with a syringe, dirty or not, and his wallet will open in silence.

Nigel's fate didn't worry me. He was now just another young man fucked by Jesus. The only difference in his case: Jesus actually knew about it. And still didn't give a shit.

'Where is he, then, this friend of yours?'

Now it was my turn to shrug, never taking my eyes off the house door.

'He probably wanted to freshen up first, change his clothes maybe.'

He emerged twenty minutes later, with wet hair, swollen eyes and in mufti. Whether the switch to blue denims and a singularly bland pale brown shirt was because of the sudden onset of apostasy or because he'd urinated over his last clean Foundation ensemble was beyond my powers to know. Like most things, if you want to get really picky.

I nudged the cabbie, let him see the quarry. He turned the ignition, wound down his window and hucked up onto the road again. I decided not to ask him why he kept doing that. Besides, there was something more pressing to consider. Namely, why Nigel had just walked with purpose and determination right past the remaining car in the driveway and headed out to the pavement. The cabbie had released the handbrake. We started to move forward. I put my hand lightly on his arm, bade him wait.

Nigel was standing at the kerb of the main road now, looking left and right, plainly about to cross it. All sorts of speculation started to arise. Perhaps Clem Porter lived, or worked, locally. Perhaps Nigel didn't own the car in the drive — perhaps his was parked over the road somewhere. Perhaps he was going to see a friend, or a relative, someone just around the corner who could help him. Perhaps he was heading to the pub for a good stiff Jamesons or three to get his nerve back.

No. Scratch pub. He wasn't the pub type.

He was crossing now, running to avoid the traffic, glancing up the road into the oncoming, putting on an extra spurt to make it to the other pavement before ...

'He's gonna catch public transport,' observed the taxi driver without emotion.

A wearied groan escaped my mouth, wreathed in cigarette smoke. Slumping down in the seat, allowing myself a moment's blackness behind my eyelids, I waved a hand at the guy and issued my command, imbuing it with as much authority as the words could bear: 'Follow that bus.'

It was a long bus. This was easy to tell, especially from the rear because that was where the sign had been placed, the big sign bearing the words LONG BUS. It stopped often during its journey towards the city, and rarely got up much momentum in between. The cab driver stayed tucked in behind it, pointedly ignoring the scowls and tetchy horn-blasts of passing motorists. I could tell he wasn't happy about it, though.

'Mate,' he grumbled, after first clearing his throat. 'Your money, I know, but I know where this bus goes. City terminal. We could just meet it there.'

I shook my head. 'I don't know when this guy will get off. I might lose him.'

He tried a different tack. 'I could just drive you to the first stop in front of it and you could get on.'

Perish the thought. I could just imagine the headline: Young man goes berserk on bus — claims other passenger stuck a syringe in his dick then hurls himself through emergency exit window.

'My money. Just stay with it.'

The driver shrugged, spat, settled in.

Nigel alighted in William Street, right in the heart of Northbridge, and conveniently stood on the pavement taking deep breaths — summoning up courage, perhaps — while I got out of the cab and ducked quickly into a doorway. Something had just clicked into place. If Clem Porter's office or home was nearby, then he must know a lot more about the local geography and human tides than I had assumed.

There were plenty of anonymous buildings, or shop tops, or warehouses ripe for secret conversion around the place. He could have undercover parking somewhere, so the Bentley was never left to the tender ministrations of my flock on a fund-raising drive. Perhaps he garaged the car elsewhere, and caught public transport, like his presently overexcited disciple, who was still standing, breathing hard, trying to conquer his anxieties.

Instinctively I looked up and around, as if I expected to see Clem Porter's face staring down from a high window, or the Transpersonal Foundation symbol painted on a wall like a Christian fish in Emperor Julian the Apostate's Constantinople. Of course there was nothing, but it was interesting to speculate. What if, by pure chance, Clem Porter's place turned out to somehow have a view of the front door of Sappho's Sisters, just half a block along from where Nigel was standing? What if, by not so pure chance, Porter had watched to see when Gina Compton had left the building, persuaded her to join him for some contrived reason, and then done her over? He was a charismatic man, I knew that, and might well have been able to quell her anxieties with the promise of a quick cup of coffee just for old time's sake, no hard feelings. If he had managed to relax her sufficiently he would have had no trouble with the syringe. As Nigel had just so unobligingly demonstrated, people tend to freeze when impaled, particularly non-users.

Also the distance from the block to the James Street alleyway where she was dumped wasn't much at all. Gina Compton, deadweight, would have taken some effort to shift, but over such a short distance it wouldn't have crippled a man of Porter's size. Perhaps, too, he'd simply dropped her in the boot of the Bentley and driven round the block: in and out, returning with a conspicuous bag of McDonald's just for the sake of appearances ...

It could have worked. Yes, it could have worked.

But then why was the door of Gina's flat found ajar and unlocked when the women first went to look for her? I might have contemplated that anomaly, but Nigel was walking again, purpose and pace renewed. I hung back a couple of seconds, then started to follow, always keeping a few people in between us in case he decided to look over his shoulder. He was a dumb kid, though, and mad with anger as I'd intended. He just kept on his righteous path, neither veering nor questioning.

Except, I realised, as I saw him break into a run and suddenly disappear from sight, he wasn't going anywhere near Clem Porter's home or office. He was going full bore into Sappho's Sisters. My mind lurched and I knew: bent on purging the humiliation and horror he had just suffered at my hands, or in the past at Gina's hands, he was going to take it out on the people his fuzzing, popping mind was no doubt at that moment blaming for his pain. I started to run towards the staircase, hoping to head off the shit-storm of displacement and overcompensation I had unquestionably set in motion.

His silhouette was disappearing over the crest of the staircase as I reached the bottom. My feet sounded like Roman war drums as they landed on the steps. I tried to shout, but the intricacies of coordinating limbs, elevation, breathing and amplification fell well short of desire, producing only a choked-off barking noise. Above my own cacophony I heard a scrape, a familiar cry of alarm, a shout of warning, heavy footfalls on the floorboards, a wavering keen in a voice unknown.

Ten steps to go, three before I got a clear view.

The room came into sight just as Nigel, moving with the lightning speed and strength of the truly crazed, reached the far end of it. He scooped up an old metal desk chair and swung it hard at the fearsome bulk of Anita, who was at that point in the process of turning to acknowledge whatever it was that had just caused Laz to cry out and point. Laz was still in that position, frozen in shock. I gained the top stair. Anita was spinning wild, her meaty arms now wrapped around the back of her skull, falling forwards, knees buckling. Nigel's head twitched back and forth as if searching for something to focus on, momentarily bewildered.

I started running. Laz saw me, dropped her pose, went to speak.

Nigel suddenly realised he had a chair in his hands. He threw it away as if it were red hot, straight into Anita, who was crouched and moaning just inches from him. The chair smashed onto the top of her back and her protective forearms, then clattered across the floor. She fell to the ground with an ugly slapping noise.

Nigel swung towards Laz. 'Fucking dyke bitch!' he yelled, lashing out with his right fist, just missing her.

Laz was trying to back away, hampered by her size. Nimble she wasn't, thanks to the temple of the holy grandchild.

'Slut cow perverts!' He stepped up, swung again, caught her a glancing blow to her left cheek. She screamed — pregnancy making her more fearful than I had ever seen her — and tried again to step back.

I was almost in reach.

'You fucking killed my Gina! You took her away and then you *killed* her!'

My first punch caught him in the lower back, over his kidneys. Air blasted from his mouth like a beer bottle exploding in the sun. His spine arched, causing his head to jerk up — so I hit that, too, hard in his right ear. He staggered sideways, losing his balance. Still standing behind him, I kicked him swiftly (left leg job, not bad) just below his ribs. He made a noise which sounded as if he was trying to vomit up his own intestines, and doubled over. I raised my right fist above his head, pointing it down, middle knuckle out, then steadied for a split second, aiming for the back of his neck, right beneath his skull.

I share this moment — I caught myself thinking — with whoever paused like this only days ago above Gina Compton's neck, knife in hand.

'No, Joe!'

Laz's voice was possibly the only sound that could have cut through my blind determination at that point, just as her cry a minute before had been the only sound capable of bringing it on in the first place. I held my position, looked up at her. Nigel moaned, and collapsed to his knees, clutching his belly.

Her face was mottled red and white, betraying a nervous system unaccustomed to feeling fear after the instinctive terrier-fight reactions her long years as a junkie had instilled in her. There was a graze across her cheek, which she touched with the back of her hand and winced.

'No killing, Joe,' she said. It didn't sound like a moral position, and her eyes told me it wasn't a merciful one, just practical.

I saw her reasons, and acknowledged them. Then I reached down and grabbed a handful of sobbing Nigel's hair, pulling his head around until he was looking up into my face. 'Jesus doesn't love you any more, boy,' I whispered.

This time his scream was silent, but his actions were as loud as a Crusader army storming down Jerusalem. Scrabbling, weaving, falling once, holding himself and limping, he ran as best he could across the room, then stumbled heavily down the stairs out of sight.

A moment's silence ensued, Laz and I both staring at the door.

Then a moan — a deeper, aggrieved moan — came from my left. We both turned. Heavy, slow and deliberate, Anita was uncoiling herself from her position on the floor. She placed each palm on the ground, her forearms rising above them, and levered herself up like some obscenely sluggish lizard waking to the sun. Her head looked around, first at Laz, then at me, then at Laz again, then towards the door. There was ice in her eyes, hard and chill.

'You OK?' asked Laz, with perhaps less compassion in her tone than the circumstances might have merited.

Anita grunted in reply, gradually working her way into a standing position, still watching the door. She swayed slightly, as if groggy.

'You want an ambulance?' asked Laz. 'You might have concussion. That was a fucking har —'

The big woman held up a fleshy arm, palm out to silence her. Lurching, and accompanying each step with a deep-belly growl, she walked across the room, out of the door, and descended the stairs with a noise like a hippo on a funeral march.

'Should I . . .?'

I shook my head. 'Take care of yourself, Laz. She's big enough and ugly enough to look after her own welfare.'

She managed a guilty half-smile at that, which disappeared the moment she heard the sound of a door opening behind her. We both turned to the noise. A short, thin woman with close-cropped blonde hair and eyes as big as a giant squid's was peering out of the toilet. She was breathing hard and ready to run.

Laz exhaled, and clumsily signalled for the woman to come out. 'S'OK, Siobhan,' she said. 'All over now. This is Joe. He's on our side.'

Siobhan nodded rapidly, edged out of the door, and then sidled along the walls of the room, sticking to them even at the corners, until she reached the head of the stairs. Her tread was so light I couldn't hear her going down. I assumed she had loosed the unfamiliar cry I'd heard at the beginning.

'I have to sit down.' Laz sounded suddenly very tired.

I took her by the elbow and led her to the nearest chair. Delayed shock was about to set in.

'Go home,' I said.

She nodded. 'I'll ring Ayzel at work. She'll leave early, come get me.'

'Good.'

She looked up at me.

'Joe?'

I said nothing.

'Who was that guy? And how did you get here so quickly? And thanks, by the way.'

Who can understand his own errors? Cleanse thou me from secret faults. There was a darkness in my heart so turbulent that I could not bring myself to regard it.

'Don't thank me. He was one of Gina Compton's former flatmates. I put the fear of god into him, trying to get him to lead me somewhere.'

She seemed to consider the evidence a moment. 'How did he know where this place was?'

Then it was my turn. 'Good question. He was obsessed by Gina. I found his voice on her answering machine. Stalking is not out of the question.'

'And killing?'

'No way.'

'He crowned Anita pretty good.'

I shook my head. 'That was luck and rage. Gina's murder was calm and premeditated. Berry's, too, most likely. Plus I don't figure him for a kiddie killer.'

Then a shadow passed across her face as a sudden squall of hormones swirled through her system. Her eyes upon me entertained no patience. 'You sent him here, Joe. You razzed him up and sent him here.'

My voice stayed calm. 'I razzed him up, but I wanted him to lead me elsewhere. I had no idea he would head this way until I saw him start up the stairs.'

She didn't seem to have heard. 'God, Joe ... what if he'd hit *me* with the chair instead of Anita? What if I'd been the only one here? He could have killed the baby, Joe. *You* could have killed the baby.'

And behold, I saw a stranger looking from the eyes of a friend. There was no point in addressing the accusation.

'Ring your lover, Laz. Lock up and go home.'

She said nothing in reply. She didn't need to. There was deep anger and sad surprise on her face.

I walked away, down the stairs, and out into the early evening, the light dying a martyr's slow death.

Some ideas, I reflected, are better than others. The problem lies in telling them apart *before* you put them into action. I thrust my hand into my trouser pocket, and felt the little clingwrapped presents there within. Somewhere nearby, my flock would be shivering, dull-eyed, fingering lifted cash and waiting.

The good that I would I do not; but the evil which I would not, that I do.

The cigarette in my mouth tasted like a leper's pustule.

CHAPTER 10

I hit the front bar of the Brass Monkey with a look on my face and a silence in my throat that warned both bar staff and boozers to leave well alone. Pint of stout and a neat Jamesons, triple, repeated again, then again. Behold the mysteries and angles of three times three are mine.

I steadied myself against the bar, trying to think, trying to work things through. Nigel had just put Lazarette's unborn child in mortal danger. Lazarette and Ayzel's unborn child. My son.

I had primed him to do so: wrecked his will and set him loose. He had chosen a direction different to the one I had intended him to take. It was still, though, an outcome equally predictable given the initial conditions. I had merely chosen not to entertain it.

Sometimes I don't think so well. Never have.

Nigel was evidently more scared of Clem Porter than the women of Sappho's Sisters. Was he, however, more scared of Clem Porter than he was of me? He was pretty damn scared of me, his interrogator, his torturer. But how scared of Porter, his teacher, his saviour?

Why had Gina Compton's door been found unlocked?

How did Berry's death fit in? Porter might have had a reason to top a troublesome novitiate who knew too much, but not a fourteen-year-old runaway. Then why the similarities in location, gender and murder weapon?

What was I going to offer up to Hewson, come the morning? Or to Chew, come the afternoon? Would Laz still give me money now? Would she even ever speak to me again, her protector, inseminator, turned vicarious abuser? And, if not, how was I supposed to escape from under? As someone once said: in the midst of life, I was in Perth.

And when the fuck would that damn thick barman stop faffing with his optics and pour me my fourth whisky?

I decided not to wait, but to return later after doing a delivery round. At least helping the young feel the all-forgiving powder of the Lord inside their hearts would take my mind off present problems.

Outside the sun was giving its last shimmering blood-red bow before retiring for the night. It would have been an impressive sight had not the chasm of buildings been in the way. The air was thick with sluggish heat barely stirred by the late sea breeze, indelicately perfumed by exhaust fumes, coriander and roasting lamb. People in office gear, not long released from bondage, were heading in and out of the pubs, gasping for refreshment but anxious to reach the safety of their homes before darkness and incapacitation made them hostages to chance. The restaurants were entertaining early tables: raucous families with small children, or eager couples intent on heading to the movies or the theatre within the hour. Awkward little queues had formed at bus stops as the local day workers headed home, glad to see the back of the place other people found magnetic in its pull.

I found the young man Arvi nodding out on a bench, vomit flecking his shoes. His half-closed eyes and slurring mouth bade me welcome, but he said he didn't need my gear just then.

Robert and Dropper were sat on the pavement outside the wine cellars, passing a warm can of bourbon and cola between them. Their pupils were pinned, their grins sloppy and conversation nonsensical. Romano was nowhere to be seen, nor Sheri nor Malo nor Big Lizzy the Troll. After half an hour of walking I managed to offload just one dose, to a scrag-end called Cat, or so she said, who claimed to be a mate of Romano's, just emerged this minute from sleeping off a long night and hanging for a hit. By the look of her eyes and the sallow spread of her complexion, she didn't appear over-thrilled to have woken up at all.

To what purpose is this waste? That was the thought in my black-mood mind as I walked eyes down back towards the pub. No doubt about it: the day was a bad day getting worse by the minute. The conclusion was undeniable: someone had blown away my flock, taken their money, and spirited into the dusk. I felt violated and duped. The tabernacles of robbers prosper, and they that provoke God are secure.

I looked neither left nor right on the walk back, but inwards, only inwards.

I am not naive. I did not bring pestilence to the city, any more than I put the sun in the sky, or the blue lights in the pub toilets. I had known from my arrival that I was neither the first nor only deliverer of salvation to walk its streets. Nor were my flock the only mob which hungered, and nor were they bound to me by contract. (A foolish notion even to contemplate. No iron-clad caveat can withstand the trumpet cry of addiction.) I had figured, however, that the few other dealers in the town had the grand good sense to stay out of my way. Evidently, I had been wrong. Perhaps, I thought as I moved hunch-shouldered through the sidewalk tides, I should make an effort to assert myself and restate the gospel.

Surely they see me not as weak?

Surely they see me not as conquerable — worse, as a man of no consequence?

My spine felt suddenly cold. Surely not. I am who I am, after all. Eyer Asher Eyer. And who am I? An untidy man with gifts of tears and sleep; a bearded man who can't control himself; a lost man with more years than age; a luckless man with more smack than money; a wandering man with enemies and precious little time; an adulterous man with a son never to be seen; a weak man with questions; an old man still youthful; a youthful man too old; a puppet man; a palimpsest; a prophet gone astray.

A tired man, an idea whose time has passed.

The Brass Monkey had filled up by the time I made it back. The bar carried the wafts of cigarette smoke, long hours and inadequate deodorants. The air smelled poisoned. I floated into it like an eel finding water.

Half an hour and two more Jamesons later I'd managed to secure a spot at the bar, my elbows damp from resting on the drinks towel that topped it. My cigarette packet was half-empty, the barmaid trained to keep the whisky coming and the pint refilled from the stash of coins and notes I'd dropped next to the ashtray.

A couple of pissed idiots attempted conversation when they found themselves standing next to me to order. Each, however, quickly realised his mistake, shut up — even apologised — and walked away. That disappointed me. I was dying for some bastard to accuse me of being rude, to ask me why I was such a silent type, to demand to know why I thought him not good enough to address in reply. I was itching, really itching.

It would have been — like everything else that day — an event with unpleasant consequences. If it happened I was odds-on to be banned from the pub for a month. Again. I could have lived with that, though. They may deny me from the temple doors, yet the sacrament shall always be mine, for am I not the winepress of God?

Matchbox 20 were playing on the sound system. I wished they were there, live, in the flesh, right before me. Then I could have thrown bottles at them and brought peace back to the world.

'How could you justify that?' said a voice at my side.

'They're a crap band. I'd like to take Manic Street Preachers out with them.'

Laughter. Familiar. 'What the fuck are you on about, Joe Panther?'

I turned my head, ready for damage. The moment my eyes made it around, however, I found myself faced with the self-evident wisdom of the Commandments. Thou shalt not pick a fight with a cop unless you've already scoped an escape route.

DC Irene Chew was leaning against the bar at my side, a tumbler of iced vodka held lightly in her hands. She was wearing an immaculate two-piece black suit, the severity of which was artfully undermined by the plain but intriguingly topographic expanse of the white tee-shirt she wore beneath it. Her turbulent hair was gone. In its place she sported a very short cut, barely there, but obsessively comb-furrowed and gleaming with the dull oil of pomade.

'If a woman have long hair, it is a glory to her,' I observed.

'Bible?'

'Paul. Corinthians. Misogynous bullshit.'

She smiled. 'It got so covered in crap last night that when I finally got a break mid-afternoon today I decided it would be easier to get it cut than try for rehabilitation.'

'If thine hair offend thee, hack it off.'

'Reckon we might find a table, Joe?'

I shook my head. 'I'm fine here.'

With a sigh she accepted my position, then signalled to the barmaid for fresh drinks all round. Neither of us spoke until they had arrived.

'So,' she began, 'how *do* you justify that?'

'The Jamesons?'

'The fact that not so long ago you were in the offices of a lesbian collective, seconds away from killing the man who had been attacking the woman pregnant with your child.'

That stopped me. There are times in life when you can receive simultaneously too much and too little information.

'So tell me,' she persisted, 'was that a judgement call? Is there some semblance of conscience in you, telling right from wrong? Some weakness in your sociopathology that permits compassion when your unborn child is involved? Or did you stop just because Lazarette Binary, aka Caroline Meaghers, told you to?'

It was the first time I had ever heard Laz's former surname. It did not make me curious, except in the matter of why the cops were checking her out. Was this formal, I wondered, or one of Chew's academic extra-curricular tangents? Was it because of Laz's connection to Gina Compton? Or to me?

And was there any damn fucking way this day could get any worse?

I opted for bland. 'How did you know?'

Chew took a sip from her drink before answering. 'Siobhan is one of my informants. I just saw her. My superior officer might not be so hot for it, but you don't think you're the only one working the lesbian angle, do you?'

Siobhan, the frightened creature who had fled from the safety of the toilets when the fighting had ceased. Siobhan: had that been the name of the woman who had checked Gina's door and found it ajar? Was that what Laz had said back at the start? What did she know? What had she overheard?

'She ran and found me, yes. Made the call, set up the meet quick smart. Nervous girl, that Siobhan. She seemed to think it significant that two men were fighting in Sappho's Sisters.'

'We weren't.'

'Who was the other guy, Joe?'

My turn to pause for effect. 'Someone I might give you tomorrow.'

'What does he know?'

'Too much. Not enough.' The theme, it seemed, of today's sermon. 'It wasn't a fight, not in that sense. He went to attack whoever was in the building. I happened to see him go up there and followed him.'

Chew nodded thoughtfully, if not wholly sincerely. 'Convenient, eh? That's what I told Siobhan. You frightened her, you know. I said you might be a violent street thug, but you were *my* violent street thug.'

I bridled but decided not to react to the provocation. 'And Siobhan knew who I was?'

She shook her head. 'Not at first. Then she heard Binary call your name. She recognised it — your woman had mentioned you before, it seems.'

'She's not my woman.'

Chew leant in towards me. Her lips brushed my ear as she whispered: 'That's good, Joe, because, you know what, I think she's *gay*.'

There was a childish grin on her face as she pulled away and drained her glass.

I signalled the barmaid. Tried again. 'How did you know I'm the biological father of Laz's child?'

'I told you. Siobhan is one of my informants.'

I tried to look as if I was satisfied with the answer, but I wasn't. Lazarette had wanted secrecy in the insemination deal, and so had I. She was determined that Ayzel should not know my identity, and that therefore no one else must ever so much as guess at my role. She was certainly angry at me just at that moment, but her fury would not make her lose control and blab. If anything, it would make her more secretive — to the point perhaps where she wished she could deny my identity even to herself.

And Laz might be Laz, but she was also Caroline. And Caroline could pick a cop or a snout at a hundred metres and say nothing of consequence to either. Some survival skills are never lost, no matter how much life improves.

Thus, there was something else I didn't know. As if two thousand years of not knowing the score wasn't enough.

The drinks arrived. My Jamesons died and was born again through full immersion in my mouth. I grabbed the pint to administer the blessing, telling myself to ease up, concerned that I might crack the glass beneath my whitening knuckles.

Chew didn't seem to notice.

'You getting anywhere then, Joe Panther? Hewson's going to want his pound of flesh tomorrow. Me, too, maybe. Hope you've got a trade by then.'

Me. Always me. 'You're the cops. Where are *you* getting?'

'Through the list of usual suspects, Joe. Through due process. Through evidentiary requirements, operational protocols, correct procedures, accurate records, questions with answers, eliminations performed, leads followed up, alibis checked, statements bloody corroborated and the whole damn fucking routine box and dice, Joe Panther, while Gina Compton's body lies in the morgue waiting for her family to take it home and bury it.'

There was fire in her eyes. And there was acid in my throat.

Me. Always me. A powerful wave of resentment passed through me like an angel descending. The woman at the centre of my life was a dead one — and one whom I had never even met during the time in which she possessed the considerable conversational advantage of breathing.

'Why do you give such a shit about Gina Compton, Irene Chew?'

I thought for a moment she was going to hit me. Her elbows had shot back from the bar and joined the rest of her body, ramrod straight, square on to me, tensed and visibly quivering in anger.

'Because, Joe Panther,' she hissed. 'Because.'

And then she turned and walked out, parting the crowd like the Red Sea as she went.

That's me, I thought to myself as I stepped back up to the bar and caught the barmaid's eye, Mr Personality. How to make friends and alienate people. Oh come all ye and let me piss you off. You've got a friend in Jesus.

Irene Chew was plugged into Sappho's Sisters but good. For whatever reason, the timid Siobhan had been suborned. But there was a limit to what Siobhan could know. Then again, there was a limit to what I could know about Siobhan.

And perhaps, too, to what I could know about Lazarette Caroline Binary Meaghers.

I sculled the next Jamesons, lit one Dunhill off the butt of the other. He that is evil to himself, to whom will he be good?

The barmaid, rather nervously, informed me that I could have no more whisky unless I produced more money and stopped talking to myself in a threatening manner. I said nothing, just held onto my beer and tried to contemplate the wisdom of mugging someone round the corner. The thoughts kept getting lost inside the fog and molasses of my brain.

Then Manic Street Preachers started up on the sound system.

In despair, I threw down the rest of my pint and barged my way through the crowd to the door, out into the polyrhythmic commerce of James Street. I walked along the pavement slowly, looking neither for conflict nor custom. I told myself I was simply moving without aim, but I knew better.

Sometimes I know better.

I know this: Better is usually worse.

The alleyway was dark, a dead-end access lane that none bar the junked-out and the drunk had cause to traverse after dark. Unless, of course, they wanted to use it to dump a body.

It was deserted, as far as I could tell: no black patches in the shadows, no steaming gold arcs, neither laughter nor cries up ahead. As I walked down it, the shadows embraced me like a lover lost. At what I thought to be the right spot, I stopped, slumped back against the wall, then slid down it until I was sitting on the ground. Here, I thought, looking around at the night, was the spot where I first opened my eyes and saw a back before me.

I fiddled about in my pockets, my fingers none too agile, until I located my dope bud, cigarettes and paper. In darkness and what passed for silence I skinned up, sealing the joint shut with the last dew of saliva left in my mouth.

The glow of my inhalation suffused the air with umber. Beside me on the ground was a dark patch. Perhaps it was a remnant of Gina Compton's blood, dried and stubborn in the heat. Perhaps, too, it was an oil slick spat from a delivery truck, or the regurgitated echo of last night's thwarted love.

The dope hit my system and danced with the whisky and the pints. My vision suddenly clouded, and my head lurched leewards without moving. It would not be long now, I reflected, hoping only that my death would come before the nausea arrived.

Without meaning to, I suddenly fell sideways, coming to rest with my right elbow hard on the ground. I took another suck. Blackness flashed, and questions, half-formed, spiralled away to sickening infinity.

My elbow moved, and my shoulder met the ground, shunting a big green wheelie bin in the process. I let my head complete its weary journey, and pulled my knees in to even out the load.

The murderer rising with the light killeth the poor and needy, I thought, or tried to think. And in the night is as a thief. Then I extended my left arm, curled it around a memory, and went to sleep with the silent ghost of a total stranger.

✝

He wakeneth morning by morning, he wakeneth mine ear to hear as the learned.

In an ideal world, perhaps. In my case, he wakeneth mine ear to hear the grinding brakes of a battered white Hi-Ace van delivering fish to the side entrance of the seafood restaurant the other side of the wall. My first breath of the morning was rich with the perfume of tyre rubber, exhaust and gutted trevally.

The van driver edged past me on his way to the sliding door of his vehicle. He'd been careful not to run me over in the narrow alley. I should have been grateful, but in that waking shock of the new day my first thought was to wish that his front wheel had passed over my head. Dead, all of my problems would have melted away, resolved in the three day slumber that seems my lot when I am called to account. Nice, too, that my body would have been found in the exact same spot as the corpse of Gina Compton.

The real killer might well have breathed a sigh of relief at the news of my demise. Consumed with guilt and remorse, Panther committed suicide by hurling himself beneath a fish van at the death site. So what if it wasn't true? Most things ever said about me haven't been true, and it's never seemed to matter thus far.

Yes, indeed, the killer might have breathed easy. I would *do*, after all, as DS Hewson had so forcefully informed me. I would do, and maybe with me shouldering the burden of blame the real killer would simply stop or move elsewhere.

If a woman falls dead in Adelaide, does anybody hear? But then again, perhaps not. Hewson might be willing to let matters drop with a frame so neatly filled, but Chew? Not so. Something told me not so. I just wished something would tell me not so *why*.

'What time is it?' I asked the driver as I clambered slowly to my feet.

I'm not sure he spoke English. At least, he just looked at me, eyes wide, mute. I tapped my fingers against my wrist in the universal manner. He immediately indicated that he understood and showed me his watch. It was just before eight o'clock. I nodded thanks and started shuffling down the lane, wondering if I could make it home before the desire for coffee became unbearable.

Suddenly a shout from behind me. I turned, ready for trouble but willing it not to be. It was the van driver. He was half-smiling with his mouth, but his eyes looked desperately sad. In his hand he carried a fish. He held it out to me.

'You hungry maybe. Eat.' His pronunciation was stumbling and approximate.

I was touched. Lacking an appropriate response due to extreme caffeine deficiency, all I could do was take it by the tail, wet in my palm, nod, and walk away.

Behold, the messiah walks among you. See there, his fish, his sign.

The only problem was that the messiah was going to have to walk nigh on six blocks before he reached his house. Even so early in the morning the weather was as warm as a suckling mare's belly, and getting hotter as the minutes marched past. The pavements and walls still resonated from the sun of the day before, and the wind was from the north — a hot, dry breath that had come off the desert and blown through the flyblown Kalgoorlie dreams of Berry's miner father before reaching the stubble of my gritworn face.

The fish, in short, was in imminent danger of transubstantiation.

Around the corner, in the centre of James Street, outside the sex shop, I saw a police car parked. It was empty, its occupants presumably inside one of the early opener cafes grabbing breakfast. As I walked past the vehicle I quickly lifted up the windscreen wiper and set the trevally beneath it. Glory be, a miracle.

The sex shop had a flashing pink neon which promised 'Live Girls'. Purveyors of dead ones, of course, prefer not to advertise so openly.

I kept walking, coughing on the first Dunhill of the day.

I knew things were different the moment I let myself in through the front door of the house.

For a start, Yula was still in residence. I heard her voice as I stepped into the building, her tone calm but firm.

'No Nessie, *later*. Now do your business before Mrs Warburton comes back with your dressings.'

'Want my grandchildren.' The old woman's whinge would have done credit to an over-tired toddler.

I put my head around the door into the darkened front room. Yula was still wearing my Smashing Pumpkins tee-shirt in the manner of a smock — entirely unrevealing over her short, plump frame. Her face lit up when she saw me. The dull-eyed juvenile whore and the frightened child had both seemingly fled from her being, leaving the sharp and excited teenager.

'Joe!' she trilled, dropping Nessie's blanket back on the old woman's knees and running to give me a hug. '*There* you are! I wondered where you were but Mrs Warburton told me not worry on account of how you often don't make it home at night. Joe, have Nessie and me got something to tell *you . . . Pooh*, you stink! Have you —'

I laid a hand on her head and calmed her. 'Shut up. Let me have a coffee and then we'll talk.'

'Doings coming,' warned Nessie in a querulous voice.

'Oh shit,' whispered Yula. 'Coming, Nessie, hang on.'

I took my leave, telling Yula to meet me in the kitchen when she was done with the old one.

The kitchen itself looked like the setting for a necrophiliac's birthday party. Hanging from cupboards, draped across the table, and looping around the chairs were festoons of damp white bandage. Mrs Warburton was bent over the chipped sink, washing more of same. It was a new behaviour pattern, as far as I could recall. It was interesting to discover that Nessie's dressings weren't really dust-coloured with black spots after all.

'Mrs Warburton,' I acknowledged as I edged past her to get to the coffee plunger.

'Late, you are,' she grumbled, not looking up. 'Out all night and no mistake.'

Wrong, I thought. Out all night and plenty of mistakes.

'I see you've got Yula working.' I was trying to be pleasant. I really was.

'Can't do *everything* meself, I can't,' was the shrew-like response. 'Nice to have some help around the place, that's what it is. Not like *some* I could mention.'

'So Yula will be staying around then?'

'Long as she can pay the rent, she is.'

'And how can she do that?'

The kettle, mercifully, was struggling to the boil.

'None of my business how she does it, is it? All I know is she paid a week yesterday, she did, and that's all there is to it. Don't ask questions, me.'

Indeed, I thought. It was Mrs Warburton's most engaging trait by far. I wondered how Yula had managed to stump up some rent money so quickly. She had no source of income, as far as I knew, except working the Square. Surely she hadn't gone back on the knock so soon, with the unheard screams of Berry's last moments still ringing in her dreams, and a woman-killer on the loose? If she had, I had to credit her. She was one tough bitch. Or one stupid little girl.

I pushed the plunger down against the resistance of the coffee grounds, and tried to stop myself salivating in anticipation. Sometimes I think I'd let them crucify me again if it was the only way to get a coffee.

Only *before* I've had a cup, though.

Mrs Warburton was in no mood for idle gossip, not that she ever was. She was bent once more over the sink, making little grunting noises and exaggerated scrubbing motions.

Yula peered around the door. 'Now, Joe?'

The spirit was with me. I nodded. She walked in and sat near me at the table. Then she put her hands on the top of it. They were held together, closed.

'Please don't be angry, Joe,' she said. She opened her hands. A goodly amount of money, most of it in crumpled small denomination notes, spilled from her grasp and spread on the table.

'Yours,' she said.

I took a large gulp from my coffee. One tough bitch, all right. 'I'm not your pimp.'

She showed neither insult nor surprise. 'I didn't get that on the game, Joe. I earnt that fair and square with good honest work.'

I couldn't believe my ears. 'Doing what?'

She took a deep breath. 'Selling smack.'

There are times when the ear of the Lord hears not every prayer nor statement. There are times, too, when the Lord disbelieves his hearing. I sped up my coffee consumption, in case it helped. 'Repeat that.'

A worried look crossed her face. 'Oh, Joe, don't get mad. I won't do it any more if you say so. It was just, well, I was in your room. I'd just woken up and ...' She shot a glance over at Mrs Warburton, then dropped her voice to a whisper. 'I smelled *dope*. Well, I figured it had to be yours and it had to be in the room somewhere and, Joe, I was *gasping* because, well, you know, it's been bad, what with Berry and everything.'

'So you started searching for it.'

'Well, you weren't *around*.' Her tone was defensive. 'I couldn't *ask* you. So I followed my nose and found your stash beneath ... well, you know where it is ... and it wasn't just dope, Joe it was —'

'I know.'

Mrs Warburton's shoulders were stiff with the effort of minding her own business.

'I knew what it had to be,' Yula continued, 'because, well, everybody knows what you are.'

'No they don't.'

'What you *do*, then.'

'Some of it, perhaps.'

She hit the whisper again. 'Everybody knows you sell

gear, Joe. And, well, there I was, looking at it, and I knew Mrs Warburton wouldn't let me stay here long if I didn't, you know, give her money for rent. I thought, wouldn't it be great, but I knew you'd kill me if I did.'

I didn't contradict her. I eat the bread of wickedness, and drink the wine of violence.

She kept going. 'So I put the idea out of my head and I didn't know *what* I was going to do. Then, in the afternoon, I was sort of talking to Nessie. You know, as much as you can. And suddenly she started moaning on about wanting to go and see her grandchildren. They were all out on the street, she told me, lots of them, and they all needed her to give them the special sweeties. Well, I don't know why I thought of it, but I nicked back into your room and picked up a little foil. I showed it to her and said, like these? She got so excited she wet herself.'

Mrs Warburton fussily bundled up all the remaining bandages and took them to the hoist in the tiny weedblown backyard. I put the kettle back on for a second mug. Yula kept talking.

'So we both went out, Joe.'

'When?'

'About six.'

That explained it. My flock hadn't wanted my gifts because they'd already been given them by the young and the old. 'Go on.'

'Oh, Joe,' she wailed. 'Don't be angry. We only took thirty per cent. Nessie didn't seem happy with that, but I talked her round — just fifteen per cent each. I *needed* money, Joe, and look: we brought you back *heaps*.'

I had my back to her, filling up the plunger. 'What happens now?'

'I thought maybe we could be partners.'

'I don't want a partner.'

'Assistant, then. We'll divvy up the route. You do what you want, and Nessie and I will do the rest. It's *dead* good, Joe: a young girl and an old woman, the cops don't look twice. And, like, OK, we take a cut but I figure in the end we'll end up selling lots more over all, so you'll make *more* money, not less.'

I didn't let on as I stirred sugar into my mug, but I was way ahead of her. It was an excellent idea, long term as well as short. After all, I would be gone soon, and my flock would still be hungry. It seemed uncommonly charitable of me to be training up a Little Bo Peep this early.

'Write nothing down and don't ever rip me off.'

She cried for joyfulness. 'Oh, Joe! I won't let you down. I *promise* —'

That was when Mrs Warburton screamed in the back garden. Yula just had time to stand and I was able to turn around before the back door, already ajar, flew back violently on its hinges in a storm of shouting and the heavy thumps of Doc Martens on worn linoleum.

Yula shrieked and ran out of the room. Four uniformed cops, led by DS Hewson, barged in. I heard the front door break open at that point, and the sound of more running feet. Over the top, Chew's voice: 'Leave the others. Just Panther.'

Panther was already taken. I was by that point bent double, my nose mashed into the surface of the kitchen table, my hands held roughly at my back as some bastard racheted cuffs on way too tight.

Then Hewson's face is in my ear, his voice a low snarl. 'Right, bastard. Tell us where he is. *Now*.'

I gave the only answer I could in the circumstances. 'Where who is?'

And then I heard my voice yelling as someone yanked me back and up with the cuffs, spun me and pushed me up the hallway. I was pushed past Chew, but couldn't see her face enough in the gloom to read her. I didn't need to see Hewson's to read him, however.

'Get him down to the lockup,' he was shouting. 'Throw him in the van and if you want to take a few hard corners on the way I won't complain.'

CHAPTER 11

And on the third day, he rose.

Kennedy, that is, who turned out to be the subject unnamed in Hewson's insistent demand to me regarding the whereabouts thereof.

We were sitting in an interview room: me on one side of the table, Hewson and Chew on the other. Chew's thoughts still eluded me. My wrists remained cuffed behind me, making my position uncomfortable, unbalanced and smoke-free.

I hadn't thus far been charged, fingerprinted or mug-shotted. This was comforting.

'So, again.' Hewson's voice was quiet, laced with threat. 'Where is he? What have you done with him?'

Of course I had no idea, and of course I said as much. Truth be told, Kennedy hadn't entered my mind since that fateful morning when I poured my love inside him. Once a sinner converts, the evangelist moves on. Thus has it ever been.

'Perhaps you could give me a clue,' I suggested. 'When did you first discover your witness was missing?'

Hewson's shoulders hunched, and his right arm flexed momentarily. He didn't follow through. Instead, he let out a chuckle that was anything but amused. 'Funny guy. Very funny guy. DC Chew and I arrived at Mr Kennedy's house at approximately 8am this morning —'

I went to point out his tautology, but something in the cast of his eyes made me change my mind and keep silent my counsel.

'— in order to double-check certain points in his statement regarding the discovery of the body of Gina Compton.'

'Due process,' murmured Chew, perhaps to herself. 'Evidentiary requirements, operational protocols, correct procedures, accurate records ...'

'*Thank* you, Detective Constable.' Hewson's tone and glare made it plain that relations between the pair of them were still far from cordial. 'There being no answer to my repeated knocks on the front door, nor any attempt by Mr Kennedy to get past DC Chew waiting at the back door, we decided to force an entry.'

'On what grounds?'

'Concern for welfare.'

'Whose? His or yours?'

This time he did hit, reaching across the table and swiping at my face with an open palm. It rocked me on my seat, but I stayed upright. In the moment of silence which followed the assault, I turned my head to Chew and stared at her, calm and impenetrable. Her look in return was one of unease.

Gina Compton, I thought, holding her eyes. Suddenly I was no longer an empty vessel.

'You listening, bastard?'

I turned back to Hewson, nodded. He held his head low, like a bull.

'So do you know what we found?'

'No Kennedy, I assume.'

His handclap was slow and sarcastic. 'Give the boy a banana. He'd been there recently, though. The place stank. His bed sheets were damp with old piss, Panther. There was a fresh turd in the toilet.'

'Never been flushed with success has that man.'

'Shut it, boy. Here's what else we found: two empty booze bottles taped to the wall. Tubes ran from the bottles, Panther — tubes that ended with syringes. You know what it looked like to me?'

'Modern art?'

'Transfusion drips. Somebody shot that man up but good with cheap spirits, and I think it was *you*, Panther. It *felt* like you. It *smelt* like you.'

'Why?'

'Because it's the kind of bastard act you'd do, especially when you suspected he'd grassed on you and maybe helped me fit you up for Gina Compton's murder.'

I shook my head, playing nice. I knew that unless someone had seen me enter the house — or Kennedy had left an accusatory note — I was in the clear. I was mildly surprised to hear that he was up and about somewhere, but doubted he was about to finger me as his deliverer. I doubted, in fact, that he could remember much about my visit at all. This was in line with my policy concerning one-off beneficiaries: crash on delivery, no refunds, no receipts.

Hewson was clearly entertaining the suspicion that I had abducted the busker. Perhaps I had, but I didn't think so. Large parts of the previous night were opaque in their recollection, but I thought I was on pretty firm ground remembering that Chew had been in my company for some of the evening — thus ruling out witness kidnaps for the duration — and that I was stone-pissed and wobbly for much of the rest — thus ruling out competence.

My response was therefore glibly irritating. 'Kennedy will meet his own reward in heaven. I didn't kill Gina Compton so whatever he might have said in his statement is of no concern to me. And anyway — even if I had gone to visit him, which I didn't — there is no law against taking a man a bottle.'

'*Two* bottles, Panther. Gin and scotch.'

I shrugged. 'He must have a generous friend somewhere. Probably some eager impresario, trying to book him for Vegas.'

Now Chew spoke up, impatient and pained. 'Someone got him *pissed*, Joe. Someone took our witness and got him pissed. Whoever it was knew what they were doing. Kennedy was a recovering alcoholic.'

I made like I was taking it all in. 'It's still not against the law to buy an alcoholic a drink. In poor taste maybe, but not illegal. People do it to me all the time.'

Hewson, direct. 'And how do you think he is now?'

'Out of recovery.'

He changed tack. 'What was all that money on the table at your house this morning. Proceeds from your drug-selling yesterday?'

'No.' It's nice to be honest sometimes, I find. Good for the soul.

'I'll bet. How much smack did you sell yesterday, Panther? How many lives did you ruin?'

'I sold no heroin yesterday.' Yes, honesty was definitely good for one's demeanour — even honesty mixed in with just one tiny little baggie of a lie. And how many lives had I ruined? Well, I didn't know. I hadn't been counting. They all get to be pretty much the same after the first few centuries.

He ran his fingers through his stringy hair, doing nothing to improve its style. 'Account for your movements last night.'

I met his eyes, my gaze full of serenity. I could see he was dying to look away, but struggling hard to remain locked. My voice was a model of calm. 'Lesbian counselling service. Pub. Walk. More pub. Then asleep in an alley. *The* alley, if you want to know. There's a Chinese delivery driver who can confirm that last bit. Don't know his name, but he gave me a fish to take home.'

Hewson broke off staring at me. Chew continued to do so, her expression carefully masked.

'A fish?' Hewson seemed unusually interested in such a petty detail.

'Trevally, I believe.'

'Someone stuck a fish on a patrol car window this morning. There was some talk of it in the canteen.'

'Glory be,' I said. 'A mackerel.'

'You said it was a trevally.'

I let my eyes go hard. 'Then you know my time and direction. Nowhere near Kennedy's place.'

'I'm not interested in this morning, tough boy. We'd already found him missing by then.'

I wondered whether I should point out that anything missing is by definition resistant to the concept of being found in that state, but then I reconsidered. After all, I've been missing for two thousand years, but heaps of people claim to find me every day.

Hewson was still talking. 'Last night is more to the point. Where were you again?'

I sighed, and looked directly at Chew. I thought I saw a small spark of concern in her eyes, imagined just then her unvoiced plea: *Don't*. Alas, the ears of my deafness were not unstopped.

'Ask her,' I said, indicating Chew with my chin. 'She had an informant follow me, then tried to question me in the pub, using alcohol as an inducement.'

The look on Hewson's face would have made the storm clouds of the Final Judgement seem soft and fluffy by comparison. Chew looked shocked and betrayed — although why she had expected me to behave in any other manner was beyond me. She wanted to study me like a lab rat for two years. Was I supposed to feel grateful, to become complicit in my own degradation?

'He's taking the piss,' she said, defensively. 'It was just a chance meeting, that's all.'

Hewson didn't look like he believed her for a minute. 'A chance meeting, just like that other chance meeting the night the girl was killed?'

'It's true,' she pleaded, in a tone of voice that wouldn't have fooled even a probationary uniform two days out of the training academy.

'DC Chew,' he responded sternly, 'I will not have junior officers derailing homicide investigations in order to grandstand themselves —'

'I'm not gran —'

He held up his hand, barked: 'Ah-*uh*! Neither will I bollock them in front of suspects.' His face was an intriguing shade of pink.

'I'm not a suspect,' I threw in, just to help.

'I will therefore do it later. DC Chew, get out of this room. You are off this case. And if I have my way when you report with me to the boss's office in an hour, off this bloody squad as well.'

Chew's eyes were black as coal pits. She was looking right at him, not a whiff of fear in her carriage. 'How dare you ...'

Hewson was having none of it. This had clearly been brewing for a while. 'And how dare *you* contradict a senior officer, go behind his back, make unauthorised contact with suspects —'

I took my cue. 'I'm not —'

'Shut up!' they both snapped, neither taking eyes off each other.

Hewson continued. 'Running unrecorded informants, drinking on the job —'

She bridled at that. 'I was on my *own* time, *sir*, working on my *own time* ...'

Hewson swallowed his retort at the sound of three quick knocks on the interview-room door. It opened before anyone could answer, and a young detective in a crumpled white collared shirt peered in.

'Sorry to interrupt, DS Hewson, sir, but we thought you'd want to know this straight away.'

Hewson still didn't take his eyes off the equally furious Chew. I smiled to myself. Sowing discord is wrongly condemned in the Bible, I've always thought. As a survival strategy, it can have considerable advantages.

'What is it?' barked the DS. 'Quick, man.'

The young detective swallowed. 'There's been another murder, sir. Another knifing.'

Hewson looked up at that. Chew's face was pale. She looked nowhere. She looked worried.

Hewson just looked annoyed, as if people were dying simply to irritate him. 'Same as the others?'

The detective nodded his head. Then he shook it. 'Same MO, it looks like, sir. One difference, though. This time the victim is male.'

✝

We stood, DS Hewson and I, the sun roasting our backs, looking down from a distance of about ten metres on the bloodied remains.

I was still cuffed behind my back, a fact that bothered me only because I was gasping for a Dunhill. I knew the restraint had to be a temporary measure. No real evidence regarding the fate of Kennedy had been unearthed, and the scare tactic of having me prisoner at the lockup had demonstrably failed. (I have been grilled — once, literally — by a cacophony of inquisitors over my years, from Caiaphas to Pilate to Torquemada's mob, Brother Guazzo of the *Compendium Maleficarum* and Matthew Hopkins, the witch-finder general. Somehow a bellicose DS from west of the world didn't compare.)

Hewson had left the cuffs on me from sheer meanness of spirit. He would far preferred to have left me stewing in a cell while he went about his gruesome business, but in the explosive moment following the young cop informing him of the latest murder, confusion and paranoia had overcome his common sense. This, I felt, was fortunate. He had demanded that I come with him, because, he said, he didn't want 'you and Chew white-anting me before I have a chance to hang the bitch'. Of the silently fuming Chew he had demanded that she remain behind — given that she was no longer on the case. It then occurred to him that such a tactic would have permitted her to get to the boss before him and prepare a defence — some goody-two-shoes crap, he had blustered, about working unpaid overtime. Thus had he insisted that she too accompany him — but with me in the passenger seat, her in the back. The atmosphere in the car during the short journey had been toxic.

She stood now, Chew, some metres to our left, her gaze fixed on the body, her face unreadable.

The corpse had been discovered only an hour earlier, hidden beneath an old sheet of black plastic, hard up against a high chain-link fence which delineated the boundary between a small building site and the railway lines. It was a couple of blocks east of Northbridge, near the offices of the local Sunday newspaper, a disused indoor go-kart track and some small commuter car parks. Directly across the railway line stood the local headquarters of the St Johns Ambulance. Not that the victim was in any condition to call one.

The black plastic — according to fragmentary recollections, recorded and now relayed to Hewson by two of the uniforms tasked with door-knocking — had probably been in position at least since daybreak. A couple of nearby workers thought they remembered seeing it on their way in, but hadn't regarded it as unusual because rubbish was common in the area. Nothing else of import had yet been unearthed.

Near the body, two men in white overalls were taking photographs of skid-mark tyre tracks on cracked concrete flecked by pebbles from the railway reserve. That the victim had been driven to the spot and killed in situ was the working hypothesis.

Every few minutes an electric commuter train whispered and rocked past, the bells of the nearby level crossing tolling with blunt and inapt irony. Passengers pressed their faces to the windows, trying to work out what all the cops, whitecoats, cars and crime scene tape were about. A small blue groundsheet had been hung untidily over the fence to protect their delicate sensibilities from the gore.

The body itself was being studied by the medical examiner. The police photographer was also circling, trying not to get in the way. Technicians were combing the ground for anything useful. The black plastic had already been whisked away for testing. Two things, however, were immediately obvious to me. There was no need to point the first one out to Hewson. The second was another matter.

'Fucking big knife again,' he said, mainly to himself. 'Different wound, though. You can see that from here.'

That was the first thing. The wound was enormous, a brutal gash. Even considering the lack of visibility caused by the victim's clothes, it was pretty clear that it started somewhere near the groin and ended at the base of the sternum.

Looking up from his grisly task, the medical examiner waved to Hewson. Then he stood upright, dusted off his gloved hands in a manner incongruously cheerful, and strode in his rubber-booted feet across to us. 'Lovely day for it,' he said to Hewson. Then he looked at me. 'Who's this chap?'

Hewson dismissed my presence with a flick of his wrist. 'Helping with inquiries. What you got, Jim?'

The man called Jim regarded me momentarily as if I was pond scum, then returned his attention to the detective. 'Far too early to say much. Single fatal knife wound, as you can see. Time of death, well, that's a little fuzzy right now. Coldish night, warmish dawn. Don't know. Twenty-four hours max, but probably half that. I'll get back to you when we narrow it down.'

Hewson made a resigned grunt. 'Bottom line, Jim. Same as the other two, or what?'

Jim's chuckle was patronising. 'You *know* I don't know that. I don't even know, *strictly* speaking, if the first two are related, and won't until we get toxicology back.'

'Talking of which ...'

'Tomorrow, I'm assured.'

Hewson lunged halfway through a monosyllabic swearword before controlling himself.

'However,' continued the medical man, 'if you'd like me to *speculate* on this one ...'

I noticed Chew had edged closer, but was not attempting to take part in the discussion. Like me, she was a spectator. She turned her head every time she felt that I was watching her.

'I'd say no,' said Jim.

'Copycat?' asked Hewson.

Jim chuckled. 'Dumb copyist, if so. First, the other two victims, connected or not, were both women. This is a chap with all his bits as God intended. Second, there's some clear evidence of physical assault.'

Hewson looked surprised. 'What kind of assault?'

'Beaten up, I'd reckon. And recently, too. Bruising around the side of the head, the opposite side of the trunk and small of the back. He's got just light contusions on his right-hand knuckles, so I wouldn't think he fought back much. One lucky punch, perhaps. Looks like someone's smacked him around nicely.'

The expression on Chew's face had changed. She now looked like her brain was doing some hard yards uphill.

Suddenly she looked across at me, eyes narrowed. As imperceptibly as I could, I shook my head. She gave a single twitch of a nod in reply.

So now two of us know, I thought.

Still not Hewson, though. 'So a poor copycat? Or entirely unconnected, all similarities unintended?'

The medical examiner rubbed his chin with a gloved hand. The movement left an unsightly smear of red on his left cheek. 'So glad I never felt the urge to become a detective myself.'

Hewson looked first nauseated, then suddenly worried. 'Meaning?'

'Meaning there's a puncture mark.'

'Just one?'

'Just one, just like the young woman, but *not* like the girl. Only, there's a difference.'

'Nothing's easy, is it?'

Jim stretched up on his toes and windmilled his arms before answering. 'Single puncture mark, only one I've found so far anyway, none in the obvious places — arms, calves, you know. The left nostril, through and through.'

Hewson shook his head in disbelief. '*Right* through?'

Jim nodded.

'What can you inject like that?'

'Nothing, I'd think, but, you know I'll have —'

Hewson chanted with him: 'to wait for toxicology, I know. Are you sure it's not just a, you know, a nose piercing — for jewellery or something?'

Jim tutted doubtfully. 'Normally done with a needle gun, those things. Different marks. This is still a little swollen. My guess is it was done yesterday. Something thin and sharp was pushed through this chap's nose. The key question, I would have thought, was: did he consent to the procedure?'

Hewson glared. 'Deductions are my business, Jim. We're both agreed on that. Stupid question this, because I know you'd have already told me, but have you found anything on the body that might help with the ID?'

Jim just chuckled again, bowed slightly, and strode back to the remains.

'Shit, shit, shit, *shit*!' hissed Hewson.

I decided it was time for the second thing. 'I know who it is,' I said.

He looked stunned, then very, very angry. His voice was a whisper. 'And you've only just decided to vouchsafe this information?'

I decided to ignore his rudeness and beamed serenely. 'You didn't ask. I like to help.'

'Tell me, then. *Fast*.'

I rattled the cuffs behind me. 'Bring out the prisoners from prison, and them that sit in the darkness of the prison house.'

His next breath was part swearword, part exasperation. He walked behind me and grabbed the cuffs with little consideration for the delicacy of my feelings. In his temper he missed the keyhole a couple of times, cursing richly, giving me time to think things through a bit more.

Nigel was still wearing the same clothes he'd had on at Sappho's Sisters. One way or another, he was definitely no longer a member of the Transpersonal Foundation. One way or another, I had to find Clem Porter. I'd already tried one way. Now it was time for the other.

I brought my hands up to my face and rubbed each wrist in turn, blowing on the red constriction marks around them, trying to get the circulation working again.

'OK. Give, boy. I don't have time to fuck about.'

I looked pointedly at Chew, who was staring at Hewson and me, her expression a study in incredulity. She was too far away to hear what we were saying. All she knew was that the implacable Hewson, her nemesis, and the unpalatable Panther, her subject, were suddenly up to something.

'Let's walk a little, DS Hewson.' I tried to make my tone conspiratorial. 'He who hath ears to hear, shouldn't necessarily do so.'

He understood and nodded. I began to walk away from the crime scene, deliberately choosing a route that would take me just a tad closer to Chew. I'd thought it through now. I would have crossed my fingers if I thought it would have done anything more useful than disorder my knuckles. Hewson stuck with me, also silent, mindful of the need for discretion.

'I hope this won't take long,' I said, a little loudly. 'Only I'm supposed to be meeting someone at Caffe Sportivo at midday.'

'Think you're fucking king shit now?' snapped Hewson, still walking. 'Ordering me about.'

I hoped she understood.

I stopped once we were in the middle of the thin strip of car park. It had the added advantage of being pretty much shielded from the street by buildings. For a man like me, to be seen talking to a cop while wearing handcuffs was one thing. To be seen doing so hands-free was quite another.

'So give,' commanded Hewson, notebook out.

'His name is Nigel. I don't know his surname. He lives — lived — at 6 Noble Street, Mount Lawley. He's closely linked to Gina Compton.'

He scribbled diligently. 'How do you know all this?'

'I was going to give him to you. You asked for something and he was going to be my gift to you later today, but somebody's been and spoiled the surprise.'

Hewson shook his head, then he leant back against the low boundary fence and crossed his ankles. I wondered for a moment if he was going to waste time accusing me of the murder. I could see him thinking about it. He came to a decision. 'Everything, Panther. Everything.'

I did as I was bid. Sort of. I told him that I had discovered Gina's involvement with the Transpersonal Foundation, and the deal struck on the house. I named the other two occupants. I explained that she had mentioned nothing to her parents, nor indeed anyone outside the Foundation, which was why he didn't know already.

'The operation's run by a man named Clem Porter. Never met him. I can't find him anywhere. No record. Nothing on the web site, phone book, literature. No nothing. First contact with the organisation is always by phone. They come to you, not the other way around. I have some documentation you'll find interesting.'

'What documentation? From where?'

I ignored the second question, but ran down the contents of the manila folder.

He nodded, considering the information. 'So this Porter bloke's laundering and Gina Compton found out? At last, a motive.'

I made a non-committal grunt. Always the best response in such circumstances, I've found.

Hewson kept going. 'So why kill this lad?'

'He lost his faith.'

'Meaning?'

'I converted him to another. I turned him. I took away his

innocence. I was leading him to the light of understanding. Or your office, whichever was the closer.'

Several questions seemed to occur to Hewson at once. 'He knew about the laundry?'

I nodded.

'Because you told him?'

I nodded again.

'This Porter guy knew he knew?'

I shrugged.

'You beat him up?'

Wrath killeth the foolish man, I thought. I am no respecter of persons. 'There are two ways to convert a sinner: by persuasion or by duress,' I said. 'God makes no distinction in his love. Charge me if he files a complaint.'

'And the puncture mark?'

'No idea.' There was no point in confessing everything. We have souls — we crave mystery.

Hewson was way past booking me for assault, even if he could have proved it. 'Two victims,' he said, mostly to himself, 'both tied to the same organisation, both knowing about something illegal, both dead soon after they found out.'

Go get him, boy, I wanted to say, but wisely didn't.

A look of confusion crossed his face. 'And the other girl, the young whore? What did she know?'

I raised my hands, palms up. 'You're the cop.' Then I started to walk away.

He called after me, demanding that I make a formal statement, demanding that I hand over the documents, demanding that I obey him when he damn well gave me an order.

'I'll drop the papers round after lunch,' I called, not looking back, heading for the Court Hotel for a restorative morning drink. 'And I've written my statement on the wind. Have fun with it.'

The Court was only just around the corner. It was the inner city's main gay bar, but didn't demand a demonstration of sexual preference before admitting anyone. It had only just opened when I got there. The barman, a big man in a tight singlet, looked at me askance as I asked for a can of Emu. I didn't blame him. It was morning, after all, and I looked like shit and smelled of the lockup. What served to alert him to danger, however, also served to counsel him to peace. He gave me my drink, then retreated to the opposite end of the otherwise empty bar, from where he made no secret of watching me.

I took a slug and smiled with secret satisfaction. Before long, the Homicide Squad would be tracking down Clem Porter. Before long, large men with stale breath and poor dress sense would be grilling Iain and Adam about their deceased housemate and elusive leader. I wondered how they would take the news. I wondered whether Iain would come to rather wish there *was* a god.

The barman pushed a button on the sound system. The room was suddenly swamped by the Pet Shop Boys singing 'Getting Away With It'.

I knew Chew wouldn't tell Hewson what she knew about the bruises on Nigel's body. He wouldn't want to cut her in, and she wouldn't want to share. I wondered if she'd be up for what I had in mind later in the day.

Which reminded me.

I ducked out of the bar and into a side passage where the pub's public phone was located. I dialled Sappho's Sisters. The voice which answered wasn't Lazarette's. I asked for her.

212

'She's not in, I'm sorry.'

'Will she be in later?'

A pause, then cautious: 'I don't know. Who is this?'

I hung up.

The music had changed to Kylie Minogue's 'Breathe'. It was quite loud in the passage. I was about to walk back into the bar when something occurred to me. I turned back to the phone, lifted the receiver and listened to the dial tone.

I felt a clutch of epiphany in the pit of my stomach. Things were going to be more difficult than I had previously imagined.

Oh, sinners. Oh, reckless sinners, painted as virtuous, thy veneer just started to peel.

CHAPTER 12

Open rebuke is better than secret love. Proverbs. Probably one of the few statements the clergy and the religious gay lobby might agree upon, I reflected.

The Sasher picket Lazarette had mentioned had, for once, been outside an Anglican church, rather than the Catholic gigs that usually copped the attention. I knew this because there was a little story about it in *The Australian*, which I was idly leafing through while topping up my latte levels at Caffe Sportivo.

The Anglicans, I read, or at least a senior cleric therefrom, had echoed the Roman Catholic position regarding homosexuality as a theological no-no. It was immoral, apparently, especially when expressed in the form of Sydney Gay and Lesbian Mardi Gras. What's more, they had clear evidence that I thoroughly disapproved of the practice.

I went to the Mardi Gras once. Sold shit-loads.

I didn't find the cleric's information at all unusual. People have long claimed to know what I believed in. Depending on which dog-collared nutjob you ask, I believed in forgiving all sins, or lynching black men. I believed in rendering unto

Caesar, or tax evasion. I believed in turning the other cheek, or loading up an AK47 and letting loose for Daddy-o.

The fact that I happen to believe nothing of the sort is, of course, irrelevant. I believe nothing. Not now. Not any more. I would wish even to cease believing in myself, and would do so in the single, final blink were it not that I seem destined to be constantly awake, constantly reminded by the world of my mistakes and unintended perfidy.

I came to deliver. I remain to take the blame.

I have nothing against homosexuality, if you really want to know. I don't have any firm policy at all on sex, just as long as everyone asks nicely. I'm particularly in favour of sexual decadence, though. I can make a lot of money from sexual decadence.

The early sixteenth century was good for that. I had an in with the Vatican and Pope Alexander VI there. He used to invite all the local bigwigs round for parties, together with all the best female and male whores. The name of the game was root who thou will shall be the whole of the law. There was more mounting going on than at the Spring Racing Carnival. By the end of the night there wasn't a dry seat in the house.

I used to sell the guests opium going in, then saintly relics going out. Genuine rooster wishbone preserved undecayed from Popo Pino, one of Saint Francis of Assisi's personal flock, would I lie to you, Cardinal?

'Why'd you dob me in, shit?'

I looked up, calm and benign. A very angry-looking DC Chew was sitting down opposite me.

'She was your lover, wasn't she?'

She continued to sink until she reached the chair, the vigour of her approach suddenly gone like mist come the dawn. The muscles of her face seemed to dance beneath her skin, her expression changing by the nanosecond as if her mind couldn't quite decide which look would be the most appropriate. Finally she settled for a semblance of caved-in resignation.

'How did you know?'

'Was it serious?'

She shook her head, then nodded. 'Maybe. Casual, you know.'

'Had her once, dud fuck? Was it you who killed her?'

It was my turn to be surprised. Her right arm shot out towards me, grabbed a handful of my hair and thumped my forehead into the table top. She did it so fast that by the time neighbouring diners had turned around to see what was up, we were both back sitting in our seats, apparently looking at each other with calm regard.

'I'm still a cop and you're still pig shit, Panther,' she said, voice flat. 'Remember that. How did you know?'

I ignored the throb above my eyes. 'You knew a lot about me very early in this piece. You knew that Laz's child was mine. That puts you inside Sappho's Sisters.'

She tried for dismissive. 'Siobhan, I told you ...'

I shook my head. 'Laz hardly knows Siobhan. Not even her partner knows who the father is. But you do. Someone must have told you.'

'Laz ...'

'You're a cop. Laz would sooner saw off her own leg than mention my name in the presence of a cop.'

At least, I thought to myself, that always used to be the case.

Big Lizzy the Troll walked in and headed straight for the toilets at the back. The guy behind the bar looked worried. I caught his eye and signalled for two more lattes.

'Therefore,' I continued, 'there's a third party involved.

Someone told you. That means Laz must have told someone, and right now I'm betting it was Gina Compton. The only thing I don't know is why.'

Chew's expression had turned defensive. 'Why don't you ask her?'

'I intend to, if it becomes necessary.'

She laughed at that. 'We none of us want to know the truth, really, do we, Joe? The truth would destroy you. You think you're so special, but you're not. You're just a grubby, persistent minor crim with delusions of grandeur. Who would really protect you, Panther? Your god? He doesn't seem to have done too good a job so far, does he? I know what you are, Joe Panther. You're not a fucking messiah. You're just another of the sad horde of mentally ill this country likes to toss on the street.'

I shook my head. I will not be taunted, neither tempted. 'I am not mad, but speak forth the words of truth and soberness.'

She snorted in mockery.

I bent towards her and fixed on her eyes, very close. 'You grieve well,' I said, voice deep, visualising Gina smiling, lips parting, looking up from a pillow.

Her face collapsed.

'You could have loved her, given time and honesty.'

She nodded, then looked down at the table. My eyes burned forgiveness into the crown of her head.

'You thought you'd finally met the right one.'

Another nod, less precise this time. My light poured into her.

'You had patience. A little while longer, perhaps, and she would have come to accept that you were perfect for each other.'

Her fingers scrunched up the tablecloth. A waitress stood quiet and uncomfortable to the side of the table, lattes in her hands, unsure whether to approach. Chew's dignity crumbled beneath the ineluctable passion of my blessing.

'Then, just like that, one inattentive night, and she's gone. Murdered.'

The tears rolled freely down her cheeks. Her suppressed sobs sounded like the coughs of an infant. I reached my right hand over and rested it on her spiky hair. I let my spirit pour within her like a cleansing flood.

'Blessed shalt thou be when thou comest in, and blessed shalt thou be when thou comest out. I forgive you.'

Her head jerked back and she gasped as if orgasming. I withdrew my hand and waited. For a second she looked empty and violated, before an expression of deep offence and confusion took over.

'Did you just assault a police officer?' Her cheeks had coloured. It was a question too fragile to transform into accusation. I said nothing, meeting her eyes without blinking.

A moment passed wherein retaliatory violence was a possibility. Then she shook her head and sniffed, as if dismissing a dream. She raised her face, then imagined it tearful and snotty, so dived into her shoulder bag in search of a tissue. I signalled to the waitress to deliver the coffee.

Tough as she was, she was back in the game within a minute, although with her earlier abrasiveness gone. We were on the same side now. I had her.

'Are you still on the investigation?'

She shook her head, sniffed again. 'Temporarily suspended on Hewson's say-so. Seeing the boss tomorrow. I'll beat it.'

'I have no doubt, but now you've got some spare time on your hands?'

'I guess. Hewson's all fired up. That must have been one hell of a lead you gave him.'

I sipped the latte. Shrugged. 'Maybe. But maybe not.'

'You want to tell *me* about it?'

'Nope.'

I reached into my pocket, pulled out the section of cellophane and dropped it on the table. Chew regarded it with a look poised between bemusement and contempt.

'This is a piece of litter,' she said, 'a ripped piece of something-wrapper you probably picked up off the street.'

I was serene in my magnanimity. 'My gift to you.'

She held it up, pinched delicately between two fingers. 'What is it?'

'I found it near Berry's body. Laz told me once that when someone tries to work at Sappho's Sisters, the organisation sometimes asks a friendly dyke in the police force to do a background check on the quiet.'

She looked wary again, confused by the sudden change of tack. 'Uh-huh.'

'Are you one of those friendly dykes?'

'Joe, I'm in enough trouble as it is.'

'Do I look like a credible source of information to you? Are those background checks done on everyone, or just when someone requests?'

'Just requests, but —'

I turned over a drink coaster, and asked her for a pen. Of course she had one.

'There's the first name. Your snout-bitch Siobhan will know the surname. Can you —'

At that moment there was a commotion from the back of the coffee shop, the sound of a door slamming and a stool tipping over. Everyone turned in its direction. There was Big

Lizzy the Troll, off her face, holding her right arm, fingers down, palm outwards. A wide stream of blood cascaded from a jagged hole inside her elbow.

'Whatcha fuckin tryn a do?' she slurred, swaying towards the counter, dripping. 'Fuckin blue lights in the fuckin dunnies. Fuckin useless things. Look what they made me do, ya cunts.'

I heard several customers making unpleasant visceral noises. The barista shouted at her to leave, unwilling to move in and manhandle her out.

Then she saw me. I groaned. Big Lizzy pinned was a pain and a half.

'Hey, Joe!' she yelled, weaving towards the table. 'Look what these bastard lights made me do ...'

I stood up and turned to Chew, who was staring, transfixed. 'Make the calls, Irene, peace of god. Brass Monkey, seven tonight. Lose the high heels.'

And then was I gone, Big Lizzy stumbling out after me, yelling for a benediction I could not provide.

I walked up away from James Street. My intention had been to head home, but with the Troll in dull-eyed pursuit I changed my mind and tried instead to lose her. No junkie in his or her right mind would try to burgle the house of the Lord. It is, however, a necessary condition of *being* a junkie that one from time to time mislays one's right mind and enjoys respite in the wrong one altogether. The fewer of my flock who knew where I laid my head at night, at least nominally, the better.

So I tried to set up a diversion by ducking into the open door of the Salvation Army Fortress on William Street. A uniformed officer made to bar my way.

'This is a holy place,' he said, 'and you are a filthy drug dealer. Every night we see the wreckage of your handiwork in the alleyways and squats.'

'No you don't,' I said. 'You see your own.'

'Not this again,' he sighed.

'It's not me,' I said, 'advising the Prime Minister to veto safe injecting rooms and heroin trials. It's not me forcing kids to hit up all sorts of impure muck in the street.'

'And who is?' he asked, suffering even to address me.

'The Salvation Army. The PM's chief drugs adviser is a Sally major. Didn't you know that? I'm impressed. After all, if junkies could hit up safely with gear they trusted, then far fewer of them would die or rob or starve, and you guys wouldn't have to study war no more. Holy battles bring their own imperatives, don't they?'

It takes special forbearance and skill, I've found, to induce a Salvo to take a swing at you, but I was making definite progress in that direction. Unfortunately Big Lizzy caught up at that point and took up again her tale of woe about blue lights and big holes. The Salvo recoiled at the sight of her junkie blood.

Keeping my eyes fixed on his, I gathered her arm by the wrist and gently kissed it. 'Oh woman,' I said, wiping my mouth. 'Great is thy faith: be it unto thee even as thou wilt.'

'Fuck you on about?' slurred Big Lizzy.

'Go in there.' I indicated the Fortress with my chin. The soldier of God looked appalled. 'They'll patch you up.'

She didn't quite seem to understand, but instead looked once again at the mess of her arm, a slow frown of consternation crossing her face, cracking her toothworn mouth. 'Wish it'd stop fuckin bleeding.'

Then she sloppy-smiled as another half-notion occurred to her. She lifted the wound towards me again and, in a grotesque parody of an infant, brayed, 'Make it better for me, Uncle Joe.'

There was a time, way way back, when I might have done just that, before I came to realise that for every wound I closed, my followers would open a million more.

'He whom thou lovest is sick, Big Lizzy,' I murmured, looking away.

She grinned and swayed. 'Danny? Yeah, that's cos he hasn't had his hit yet. Gimme a deal, Joe, I'll take it to him. He'll pay you tomorrow, honest, man.'

The uniform cleared his throat as if sounding the Last Trump. 'There are people behind you trying to get *in* to be with God.'

I shook my head in sadness. 'Same as it ever was.'

He lowered his head in contrived despair. 'May the Lord have mercy on your soul.'

I bowed to him. 'And may Colonel Sanders fuck your wife.'

Lizzy followed as I walked away, worse luck. She lost momentum two blocks later, after she had trailed me past the brothels, then through the rich, spiced air around the Vietnamese food markets, all the time alternately whining for smack and bewailing her injury. In the end she slumped to her haunches, leaning back against the wall of the local mosque, a thin trickle of blood pooling at her feet, a petulant grizzle on her lips.

I continued without looking back. If sorrow does not flee, the next best thing is to leave it where it is and walk away.

My route, unplanned as it was, now took me along Brisbane Street, past the park where usually one or two of my flock could be found crouched beneath a Moreton Bay fig tree, waiting for the syringe van or the soup van, whichever came first. This time, though, the boughs sheltered naught but yesterday's rubbish and a sun-bleached sharps container.

The Fortitude Hotel held its usual contingent of arthritic bitterness. I stopped for a necessary can of beer and Jamesons chaser, contemplated lunch, then rejected the idea as an unnecessary lapse in my asceticism. Sure, I could have had a plate of the pub's curried sausages, but they were but flesh; a wind that passeth away, and cometh not again.

Outside, I hopped on a bus into the city, and then another which headed out Mount Lawley way.

I got off at the stop before Noble Street and walked in that direction just far enough to make out the house. There were two police cars in front of it — one marked, the other not. I wondered whether Hewson had drafted in a new offsider, or whether he was working solo and using uniforms to provide the necessary corroborations. I wondered if Iain and Adam were being helpful, whether they were shopping Clem Porter. I wondered how great their loyalty would be now that the man was being accused before them of as many as three brutal murders, including two uncomfortably close to home. If Hewson was any good, he'd be playing the accessory card hard and strong just about then.

Would they mention the grief counsellor who came to visit and made them cross, or the mysterious and completely untrue call about Adam's mother?

I wondered how much they knew about Nigel. I wondered specifically if he had made it back to the house between leaving Sappho's Sisters and turning up dead. Had the others been home, and what had he said to them?

I didn't think it mattered much, really. His tale of piercings and beatings would have come across as hysterical and improbable. Hewson already knew I'd roughed the lad up, and the likelihood was that the more elaborate details of my handiwork would be dismissed as diversions or embroidery on the part of his new batch of suspects.

The Lord looked upon his work, and saw it was good.

I got off the return bus close enough to home to make the journey an easy stroll. A few minutes later I arrived, intent on resting up and stocking up before heading out for the business of the evening.

There was a vase of violently red gerberas in the lounge room next to the sofa, like spatters of blood in dirt. Mrs Warburton was just rearranging them when I entered. As she turned towards me I witnessed a horrible sight. The woman was smiling.

'Present, I've got,' she beamed. 'Another bunch in the kitchen, too, you'll see.'

I didn't have to guess their provenance. The chances of Mrs W suddenly attracting a secret admirer were roughly the same as the Pope turning Hindu.

'And where *is* Yula?' I asked.

Mrs Warburton waved a hand in the air in a gesture almost whimsical. 'Out somewhere with Nessie, she is. Been out for hours, those two. They get on ever so well, they do.'

She was moving with a lightness of step I'd never seen before. It didn't last. Suddenly her face took on a cast of suspicion and greed. (Ah, I thought to myself, *there* you are.)

'You got your rent, have you?' she snapped.

I figured that Yula had probably stashed the cash from the table in my room somewhere, so the answer was yes.

However, it wasn't a subject I felt like dealing with just at that moment.

'Tomorrow morning,' I replied, and made to move off towards sanctuary.

Mrs Warburton positioned herself squarely in front of me, being brave.

'Not right, it isn't.'

'What, Mrs W?'

'Nice young girl like that, having to sleep in the living room.'

Her message was clear. She would not be disappointed, as long as she could hold her patience for a day or two more. I was not, however, about to let her know that.

'You could give her your bed,' I suggested mildly.

Some heresies are so off the wall that they do not even merit rebuttal. This was apparently one of them.

'Helps around the house, she does. More than some I could mention.'

I pushed past her, my compassion spent. 'After all I've done for you, Mrs Warburton.'

Her wheezing laugh danced on my back as I walked down the passage. 'What've you ever done for me, you lout? What?'

What indeed, what indeed? I might have said sorry, save that it would have been as hollow as a junkie's promise.

CHAPTER 13

Two hours of solitude. Door shut, big joint, three Dunhills, line of speed, television silent shining, Patti Smith's *Horses* repeating twice. Peace, peace to him that is afar off.

The album came to an end, though, just like it always does, with that lingering guitar note quavering away to silence. I opened my eyes. The late afternoon sunlight poured through the window and into my face like spew from vengeful Gaia. A woman on the screen screamed at the sight of a dishwashing machine. The speed left my system, pulling a heavy train of black tiredness behind it.

I chopped up afresh, breathed in, and headed for the world.

Behold, I come.

At the phone box I rang Sappho's Sisters. The voice which answered might have been that of Siobhan, I couldn't tell. When I asked for Laz she put me on hold for half a song (Shania Twain's 'I Feel Like A Woman', as tasteless as it was droll). Then she came back on line and informed me nervously that Ms Binary was unavailable and no, sorry, she didn't know when she'd be back.

I might have felt sad about the rift now yawning between Laz and I. I might have.

So many, though. So many sparks of friendship as the centuries roll out: the Magdalene, Saint Bridget, the grey-eyed Veronese called Catarina, the willowy Confederate widow called Marie, Hildegard of Bingen (lovely body, but prone to migraines), Jeanne d'Arc, Cameron Diaz, Judith, Salome, the whore of Babylon, Jodie Foster, Pope Joan, the Virgin Queen, the Sisters of the Poor, the Sisters of Mercy, the sisters of the night. I meet them, I see within them something sparking common with the fire in mine eyes, then they pass on into history, while I walk forwards, straight and narrow and never-ending. There is sadness in loss, but more in being left behind.

If you're prone to that sort of thing, that is. Which I'm not. Hardly ever.

At the police station I left the manila folder with the desk sergeant and asked that it be passed on to Detective Senior Sergeant Hewson immediately because he was expecting it. It was just the local station, of course, and not the city HQ where the Homicide Squad was based, but that wasn't my problem. If an organisation wants to appear ubiquitous, then it has to be prepared to deal with the consequences.

On the way to the Brass Monkey I managed to offload half a dozen deals. Two were to backpackers, another to some stringbean just in from the country, and the other three as overload to Robert and Dropper, never a pair who thought it good manners to run out.

'You should watch yourself, Joe,' grinned Dropper as he palmed me the notes.

'Why's that?'

'New bunch in town. Couple of bitches. Good gear, but.'

'I'll keep an eye.'

He looked up at me slyly, one eye a slit against the sun. 'What'd you give me if I tell the cops about them, get them out of your way?'

I studied him. As angels come dressed as devils, and sheep come in the pelts of wolves, so too can truth and fabrication live within the bosom of each other in a junkie's solemn pledge. Whatever I said next, there would be no guarantee Dropper would remember. If I forbade his testimony, still he might defy his Lord and lay bare his conscience.

'I will show you what I'll give you,' I said calmly. 'Give me your hand.'

The grin on his sallow face widened as he placed his palm in mine. He thought he was about to get a freebie — which, in a sense, he was.

'What you'll get,' I announced, as I snapped his finger, 'is nine more of those.'

I went to leave him pale and crouching, but he yelled at me through clenched teeth: 'You'll be fucking sorry you did that, Panther! I'll have the cops on *you*!'

When I turned back to admonish his impudence, Robert, wide-eyed and panicked, held up his hands in supplication. I acknowledged his actions. Blessed are the peacemakers. As I walked away, Robert was patting him on the back and whining, 'Shit man, how you going to crack car doors *now*?'

She was already at the pub when I walked in, seated at a corner table, vodka in front of her, tall glass of Stella waiting for me. She was still dressed as she had been during the day, and wasn't smiling at all.

'You realise I'm probably throwing away my career doing this,' she snapped as I sat. 'And say thanks for the bloody drink, bastard.'

'Thanks for the bloody drink, bastard,' I intoned dutifully, then drank half of it in one go.

When I put the glass down and raised again my eyes to the world she was looking right at me. 'Well? What the fuck are we doing here?'

'We're keeping our voices down for a start.'

She looked momentarily flustered, then regained control. '*Talk*, Joe.'

'What's Hewson up to?'

She snorted, then sipped from her drink before replying. 'As if you didn't know.'

'Humour me.'

'What do I fucking know? I'm off the case, remember, at least until tomorrow.'

'But still in the squad room.'

She sighed, scratched at her armpit beneath her suit jacket, and looked up at the ceiling all at once. 'Out most of the day. Had a couple of guys trying to track down something called the Transpersonal Foundation. Phoning the US and everything.'

She stopped scratching and looked back at me. 'Those leaflets I found in your jacket that time. That was that mob, wasn't it?'

I nodded.

'How did you get them?'

Some questions are best ignored. 'Did Gina ever mention it?'

Chew shook her head. 'Not that I remember.'

'She never mentioned she belonged to it, or worked for it, or that she thought they were laundering money and she was in danger?'

Chew wiped her forehead. 'We kind of kept our private lives private. We split up a while ago ...'

'Did she know you were a cop?'

She flushed. 'Not *right* away ... but, yes.'

'Then she left straight away?'

'No. She didn't seem to have any, you know, she didn't seem to *mind* ...'

'But when she left, she left suddenly?'

The crack of her glass slamming down on the table echoed around the bar. 'What's this got to *do* with anything, Panther?'

I shook my head, darted my eyes left and right, and smiled in a gesture of placation. She took the cue and stopped drawing attention to us, but I could see she wasn't happy. Neither was I, but my mood was definitely improving. My bet was it had played out like this. Gina Compton was bumping a cop, knowingly so, when she nutted out that Clem Porter had a very healthy, very secret, cash flow business. Rather than telling her lover about this, she had initiated a split. Ergo, she hadn't wanted Chew to know about it. Ergo, she'd figured out a way for Porter to buy her silence.

The question, though, was had he paid his price before she paid hers? Had she armed herself with a kitchen implement because she'd heard that Porter wanted a refund, or had he simply baulked at the price straight up? Was the pestle a bargaining chip? Or had there been another reason entirely for its presence?

I kept my counsel, changed the subject.

'Hewson.'

'Like I said, out all day. Most of it, anyway. Brought in two young guys for questioning about four o'clock. Locked them up, told another of the DCs to run up charges of obstruct police.'

So the boys weren't talking. 'Did he use them?'

'Not by the time I left. He'll use them if he wants to keep them in, but then he'd have to let them get lawyers, too.'

'Drink?'

'Do I need to be sober?'

'What do you think?'

'Vodka, please.'

When I returned from the bar, she had stolen one of my Dunhills.

'I didn't know you smoked,' I said.

She exhaled like she was purging a demon. 'Haven't for years.'

'I have that effect on people.'

Her look was as poisonous as her breath. 'Don't flatter yourself, mad man.'

I lit one myself, and made a good start on the Stella before asking her if she'd checked out the name I'd given her.

She nodded and fished out a notebook from inside her jacket. 'Easy enough given there was almost no one in my office.'

'How'd you go?'

Before she replied, she stubbed out the Dunhill, still half unsmoked, with short brutal jabs. After a moment of regarding the wreckage in silence, she grabbed the packet and lit up another.

'I sense conflict,' I observed.

'Fuck off.' She flipped open the book, although it was clear straight away that she didn't need to remind herself of its contents. 'Good and bad. Why do you want to know, anyway?'

'Tell you in a minute. Drink up and spill.'

For a second I thought we were going to get into a stupid argument. Then she sighed, shook her head and sucked the dear life out of her Dunhill. 'OK,' she began, wearily, 'the surname's Shadbolt. I got that from Siobhan. Then I hit a few problems. The address they have for her at Sappho's Sisters is care of the university department auspicing her thesis. She has a driver's licence, registered at an address in Dwellingup.'

'Where?'

'Country town. A few hours out of here to the forest.'

'Why?'

'Shut up and I'll tell you. She was born there, according to records. Folks still live there.'

'Where does *she* live?'

'That's the problem, big boy. All known addresses for her — all that I could get to, anyway — including electoral roll and driver's licence, show either the university or the parental address. She could be anywhere. Not unusual, I guess, for a student.'

'What about the university's records?'

'Thought of that. The Registrar's office had shut for the day. We can get that tomorrow, but for now, fuck knows.'

I considered this, decided against it. 'Tomorrow's too late. What kind of car does she drive?'

Chew drew a quick circle in the air with her finger. 'None registered, so either a borrowed one or a naughty one or none at all. Wouldn't be the first student not to have a vehicle. Why is this bitch so important, anyway?'

'So much for sisterly solidarity.' I drained my glass, put it down with a meaningful stare.

'I'll get you one in a minute,' she said. 'Why her?'

I chose my words carefully. 'I think she might be able to help us with our inquiries.'

She scoffed. 'That's my line. Don't shit me, Joe. Why?'

I looked directly into her eyes. 'She used to be Gina Compton's lover.'

Her reaction was immediate and dark. 'When?'

It was a question to which I did not know the answer. Therefore I did the only honest thing possible. I made one up. 'After you.'

Her head shook and her mouth formed a silent imprecation not for me. 'And you think Gina might have said something ...'

I nodded encouragement.

'Maybe about this mob, this ... what is it?'

'Transpersonal Foundation.'

'And the money laundering?'

Again, a nod.

'And whether she was scared, and who of?'

'Of whom, yes.'

She glared, shut one eye, cocked her head to one side, lowered her voice. 'Siobhan says she's as ugly as sin.'

I winked back. This was what I needed. 'Venial, mortal, deadly, original, all the charm of a tenement shit-hole.'

'And built to match, I'm told.'

'Behold now the behemoth.'

She managed a harsh chuckle at that. 'And if we find her and talk to her, we might get to the identity or whereabouts of Gina's killer faster than Hewson and his young men?'

'That's the theory,' I lied. 'Tough you don't know where she is. You could shove it right up your boss if it works.'

Chew smiled. It was an unnerving sight. She bade me wait, then headed for the bar. When she returned with the drinks, her face looked flushed.

'What I said, Joe — cheers, by the way — is that I'd not been able to find out where she lives. That's not the same as saying I don't know where she is.'

I acknowledged the distinction. 'So where is she?'

She shrugged. 'Dunno. *But*, Joe, I *do* know where she'll be in a couple of hours.'

I waited for more. It came.

'Siobhan said she'd told her she was going to the Court Hotel tonight on a cunt hunt. Her phrase, not Siobhan's.'

This was distinctly mixed news, based on assumptions I didn't want to share. I needed to find her house — preferably without her in it at the time. Clearly, though, this wasn't about to happen.

'Don't know how forthcoming she'll be in the middle of a crowded pub,' I ventured.

'And you think I'm going to come out as a cop in the beer garden? Get a grip, Joe.'

'So what do you propose?'

She grinned and upended her glass. 'Getting a grip. Come on, we've got work to do. High heels to lose, remember?'

Outside there was a knot of pedestrians waiting to cross at the lights. Among them stood three wholesome-looking women, handing out leaflets, faces alternating between deep sincerity and disapproval.

'My car's this way,' said Chew and began to head off.

I asked her to wait, telling her I was just going to pop across the street to the newsagency and pick up another packet of cigarettes.

'You could have got them in the pub,' she chided.

'Sometimes my memory's not so great. We're out now. Doesn't matter. Won't take a minute.'

The lights changed then, conveniently forestalling further squabble. As I'd hoped, the shop also sold disposable cameras. The one I bought had a flash and fitted rather well into my pocket.

I crossed back against the lights. As I reached the opposite side, one of the trio of women thrust a leaflet beneath my nose, a smile plastered across her face. The headline said JESUS CAN SAVE YOU!, especially, it turned out, if I was to attend a certain revivalist church. I thrust the paper back at her and pushed past.

'He's pissed!' I heard stage-whispered.

Two other voices joined in. 'That's right, he's *drunk*.' 'He's a *drunkard*.'

'And you, ladies,' I replied over my shoulder, gathering Chew by the elbow, 'are soliciting on street corners. I forgive you. We are one, you and I. Whoredom and wine and new wine take away the heart.'

'Blasphemer!' one of them screeched.

Someone cheered. Someone else yelled for quiet.

Chew, unamused, reversed our grip and started to haul me along the pavement. Her face had coloured. I was having far too much fun to heed my own desire for discretion.

I shouted to the sky: 'All manner of sin and blasphemy shall be forgiven unto men!'

The call, shrill and demented, came in return: 'I hope you go to hell!'

A couple of desultory jeers arose from the spectators.

I tried to turn back and finish the job face to face, but Chew kept pulling me away, her breath harsh between gritted teeth.

235

'Blasphemy against the Holy Ghost shall not be forgiven!' I bellowed.

'Fuck sake, shut *up*, you prick!' spat Chew.

'Refrain not to speak,' I began, with dignity, 'when there is — *oof, fuck.*'

With a sudden shoulder-and-hip move, she had shoved me hard, sideways into the immovable bulk of a pale green Mitsubishi Colt. It beeped and its lights flashed.

'Shut up and get in,' she commanded.

'Am I under arrest?'

'I'm not pissing about, Panther.'

The stress was plainly starting to take its toll. It's all a matter of timing, I find. I opened the passenger door. 'Can we stop at a bottle shop?'

She walked into the street, opened the driver's door, and spoke over the roof. 'There's wine,' she said, then ducked inside.

We drove without speaking through the night-lit city and across the river. I feared not, for it was obvious that the Colt was a private vehicle, devoid of two-way, and that we weren't heading to the police station. The CD in the stereo was Macy Gray, which was acceptable in my sight. After four songs, she swung off the freeway and into a maze of dull suburban streets. There wasn't much to look at, so I closed my eyes and fired up a Dunhill. Chew made no objection, but I heard her window slide down, felt the in-rush of warm evening air, like a seducer's breath.

The car pulled to a halt just as I felt the heat-bite of the filter. We were in the driveway of a modest, nondescript, single-storey house. I could see ugly grey brick veneer, conjoined with expanses of white stucco. There was a fence between the front and back gardens: neat, short, more gesture than action. Chew engaged the handbrake and switched off the engine. Macy Gray slurred into silence.

'Do you know where we are?' asked Chew, voice flat.

I shook my head. 'South somewhere. Wouldn't have a clue.'

'Keep it that way. Come on.'

She turned, opened her door and uncoiled into the night. I followed suit, rather less gracefully, scraping the crown of my head on the roof as I did.

She walked ahead of me, along a single-width slab path which ran against the front of the house. A floor-to-ceiling window, curtained, dominated the facade, revealing a dim light somewhere inside. A porch stood at the far end. From its gable swayed a single hanging basket, containing something green, fleshy and resilient. She selected a key from the bunch she had pulled from the ignition, pushed it into the lock and turned.

'My house, Panther, in case you haven't guessed.'

I made no reply.

Inside, a short hallway gave onto a large lounge room, in which a lone lamp provided determined but feeble illumination.

'You live here alone?'

'Ask that question again and I'll snap your spine.'

I doubted that she could, but not that she would do her very best to try. I inclined my head and held up my right hand to signal understanding.

'I'll be back in a minute,' she continued. 'Take a seat, try not to make it dirty and don't steal anything.'

'Why am I here?'

'Sit down, Joe.'

With that she disappeared through a door at the other end of the hall. I walked into the lounge room and sat in one of the two grey leather armchairs that complemented the sofa. The carpet was rust-coloured, reflecting thin copper threads in the beige curtains. The room also contained a low teak coffee table; a shelving unit holding television, video and stereo; a sideboard with anodyne knick-knacks; and several framed reproductions and photographs on the wall, all landscapes. I'd only had time to take in the basics before Chew returned. She had removed her shoes, revealing stockinged feet. She passed me the generous glass of red wine and the empty ashtray she'd carried in.

'Put an album on if you like,' she said, turning again. 'I'll be back out in a little while.'

I have never entertained the faith that all will be revealed in good time, but I decided that asking questions at that particular juncture would probably only delay what understanding might eventually come to pass. I signalled assent. She left. I turned my attention briefly to her small CD collection — not bad, a bit too much Petula Clark for my liking — and quickly selected Hole's *Celebrity Skin*.

As the band's half-ravaged glamour stammered into the room, I sat back in the chair, lit up, and began to wait, letting my mind wander where it would.

One of the framed photographs on the wall depicted a riot of fireworks. In the shadowed gloom of the room, its vibrant yellows and reds were about the only things that lured the attention of half-closed eyes and idling mind. Hunching forward, I peered more closely at it across the room. It only took me a moment or two to place it. It was a commercial shot of the Sydney Harbour Bridge, variations of which had been published or broadcast all around the world. It showed the bridge exploding in colour, the centrepiece of the city's New Year's Eve celebrations at the start of the year 2000. Across the face of the bridge the fireworks spelt out a single word: Eternity.

Was it a yearning, that word, or a warning? Whatever the intent, it was not a proposition of which I wished to be reminded, so I withdrew once more, closed my eyes, and listened to Courtney whinge.

Thoughts once started, though, breathe independent of the brain which bore them.

I marked the first centenary of my undeath, all those years ago, by visiting the Big Smoke. I might have been curious that week when I walked dusty and disguised through the gates and into the city of Rome. I might have been eager to check out the rumours of traders that a cult was growing in the Urb and elsewhere, based around the Jewish heretic Chrestus. Too hard to remember now the bright thoughts that refracted through my mind, a mind still unwilling to accept that neither death nor age were to be my burden. Perhaps I was hoping it had all come to naught. Perhaps, the night before, asleep on the side of the road, I had dreamed of calamity, seen catastrophe in vision, my outstretched body floating, gloating above the carnage.

Perhaps the nightmares had started by then. Can't remember.

I found the small community of Christ-followers on the outskirts of the city. There were about twenty of them in the courtyard of the house of one of the wealthy. They were all men, all dressed in plain white robes, eschewing the fabric badges of rank favoured in Rome.

And they were all gentiles, which took me by surprise. I remember wondering how gentiles in Rome came to hear the message I had tried to address to Jews in Palestine. Of course, I didn't know then about Paul, about how he had taken my ideas, adapted them, travelled with them, and won converts in my name to a philosophy I didn't recognise.

They welcomed me, a silent stranger with bowed head and hood, into their midst. They spoke in Greek, with Roman accents. I barely understood them as they stood in a circle, heads down and mumbling something I might have once said myself.

Then they handed around pieces of bread. A man gave me mine, intoning: 'Take, eat, this is my body, which was broken for you: this do in remembrance of me.'

And I recalled the words. I had slurred them, lost in despair, that last, long, strange evening. The politics had played out. The occupying forces were about to have my ass. I was prepared to be a martyr to the cause, but that didn't stop me getting all maudlin the night before.

And now came back the echo, a hundred years later. I thought I was going to vomit. 'I've already supped,' I said in stammering Aramaic, turned and walked away.

Above a comparatively quiet passage on the album I heard the sound of a throat clearing. I opened my eyes. Chew was standing in the doorway to the lounge. She was wearing a pair of tight, black kid-leather trousers, redundantly supported by wide black leather braces, which nevertheless did serve the purpose of covering the nipples of her otherwise unconstrained breasts. On her head was perched a peaked black cap.

'What do you think?' she asked.

What I found myself thinking was that the woman who stood before me was an unconventional, tall, gay, ambitious, forceful, sexually alluring, possibly unhinged cop who would find it easily within her means to make life very difficult for me — all of which added up to one huge damn pity. Before I'd had a chance to come up with anything sensible to say, though, she struck a self-effacing pose and said: 'Too "Night Porter", you reckon?'

I nodded, ignoring the begged question of too Night Porter for what. 'Too Berlin,' I agreed.

She seemed to consider this for a moment before speaking. 'Okay, so I won't try the Liza Minelli as Sally Bowles, either. Plan B. Wine's in the kitchen if you need a refill.' And then she was gone again.

I closed my eyes once more and drifted away on Courtney Love's growl.

I marked my first millennium, too.

Well, sort of. The intention was there, but what with one thing and another — a nice run of fly mushrooms in Scythia, some rich racket pickings during the more unstable regimes of Constantinople, the small problem of being executed in Venice on charges of simony — I was about 180 years late in getting to where I wanted to be.

I made it, though, in the end, after a long slow pilgrimage with my head always covered and my words kept to a minimum. I reached my sentimental objective several days after setting out on the last leg from Tiberias on the shore of Galilee. The hill where I'd given my best preach, the statement of principles which came to be known as the Sermon on the Mount, was still there, baking in the heat.

No longer, however, was it surrounded by the hard-working, the poor and pious. On this day, in what came to be known as 1187, it rang to the terrible cries of men dying and wounded, horses falling with snapped legs and whinnies of terror, and, above it all, the constant high murmur of voices beseeching my deliverance.

From where I stood to observe, I could see mounted Crusaders in white tunics and mail thundering down the slopes, slashing and jabbing at Saladin's horse-borne warriors, who swung their own weapons with murderous intent and mortifying result. At the top of the hill, men garbed as bishops prayed to me for their lives. At the base, other men with beards, dressed differently, called upon Mohammed to bring them victory. On the hill and the stony plain which surrounded it, the bodies of men lay scattered, some alone, some in drifts three or four deep. Mounds of bloodied horse flesh twitched and convulsed in agony.

The object of the slaughter, apparently (I learned this when I reached Acre), was an old crucifix held by the priests. They believed it to be the True Cross and were prepared to sacrifice thousands to keep it in Christian hands. The Moslems, of course, were equally prepared to sacrifice thousands in order to acquire the symbol of Mohammed's only serious rival.

All this for two lengths of wood, hewn no doubt by some eager merchant only years before. Perhaps it was even me. Truth to tell, I must have sold literally hundreds of True Crosses in my time: standard, miniature and economy. Some of them have even been plastic.

I have sold them by the gross. But never have I killed for one. (Okay, yeah, there was that Cardinal in Tuscany that time who tried to scurry off without paying, but I think he was all right in the end, just knocked about a bit.)

I walked away from the Mount, not then knowing the hell that awaited elsewhere in my homeland, singing softly: happy birthday to me, happy birthday to me ... There might have been tears on my cheeks, but it was probably just the sand blowing in my face.

'Well?'

I opened my eyes again. This time nothing improper was on show, merely described in cloth. She was wearing a sleeveless, strapless cocktail dress which fell in a black silk cascade from her chest to her ankles, its fall interrupted by a wide slash from pantyline to the ground. Her arms were coated in long, tight gloves which extended all the way to the arch of her biceps. Her mouth bore violent crimson lipstick.

'Too Audrey Hepburn?'

I didn't know what to say, so I said, 'You look chic.' That's what she heard, anyway.

'Too untouchable? Too goddess?'

She was being very serious when she asked these questions, the hard glint in her eyes belying the festive nature of her costume.

I nodded. 'Too expensive.'

'Good point,' she said. 'Student. I've got it now.'

Then she walked off again. I considered going to hunt for the kitchen and more red wine, but decided against it. The plonk was starting to combine uncomfortably with the beer — not to mention the dope and the speed — and I had a feeling I would not be detained for too much longer in this strange suburban interlude.

It never occurred to me to go outside and walk away. I had no idea where I was, but by the distinctly non-commercial nature of the streets I'd noticed during the journey, I knew I could think of a lot better places to be lost in.

I glanced again at the Sydney Harbour fireworks. My second millennium, some would have us think. This time I didn't do anything at all commemorative. I was working: moving smack and speed like nobody's business to the crowds gathered in the nearby city of Fremantle, the choice of substance dividing right down the centre of the pessimists and optimists.

Most people around the world decided for once that something more important than the Lord was coming. I was encouraged by that. My cult — if only for a day — had been largely replaced by reverence towards a two-number digital mistake.

The Millennium Bug didn't turn up and everybody seemed rather pleased. I couldn't understand it. Every time *I* don't turn up the skies are rent with gnashing teeth and tears and self-scourged backs in a quest for absolution, as if I am attracted to ripped flesh and tormented minds.

I am not, dear children. I am not. I have enough torment to go round.

The drums rolled to a cymbal-crashing stop.

'Right.'

This time she stood, dressed in casual wear, artfully arranged to look as if she'd taken no trouble over it at all. Her tight white tee-shirt bore the pale pink legend: PORNSTAR. The punctuation made it plain she wore no bra. The garment also had a scissored rip, stretching several inches across the top of her breasts. It was designed, I guessed, to reveal cleavage to anyone positioned correctly and of a mind to look down.

The tee-shirt itself came to a cliffhanger ending well before her olive army surplus baggy shorts began. Her midriff was as hard and rippled as I recalled. The shorts themselves she wore low on her hips, leaving a thin white border of underpants to accentuate the turn of her belly. Her calves were bare, with black Doc eight-holes beneath. Her hair had been clumped and combed with pomade.

'Yes?'

I nodded. 'Very student.'

She was all business straight away. 'Right then, let's go. Make sure you turn the CD off properly.'

I stood up and ignored the stereo completely. 'It's been a lovely fashion show, DC Chew —'

'I wasn't doing it for *your* benefit, sleazebag.'

'Of that I'm perfectly aware. Would you care perhaps to tell me just what the purpose of it all might be?'

'Can't you guess?' She had produced a shoulder bag from somewhere, into which she was busily slipping her purse, warrant card, penlight torch and handcuffs.

I nodded. 'I've got a pretty good idea, but it's not exactly standard police procedure, is it?'

She grabbed my cigarette packet from the floor and launched into mantra. 'Evidentiary requirements, operational protocols, correct procedures, accurate records, questions with answers, eliminations performed, leads followed up, alibis checked ... Blah, blah, fucking *blah*!'

The last utterance was emphasised by the flinging of the cigarette packet against the wall, scattering its contents. She was breathing through her mouth, cheeks pale, eyes wide, chest heaving. 'Someone killed my ex-lover. Someone killed my friend and I can't afford to let that be known. Well *you* know it, Joe Panther. The madman knows it and *I'm* not on duty and *I'm* not on the case and *I'm* going to fucking do something about it.'

I went to retrieve what remained of my Dunhills.

'Sorry about that,' she said, getting herself quickly under control. 'I'll buy you a new packet on the way.'

I picked up one, unbent it and checked to make sure the paper hadn't torn. My lighter, thankfully, was still where I'd left it. I picked it up and fired it. 'So you're going to the Court Hotel?'

'That's right.'

'And you'll drop me off somewhere on the way.'

'That's not so right.'

I blew smoke like revenge. 'This is *your* business, *your* lover, *your* fucking gender. What do you need me for? Anyway, I'd never get into the Court, not in the evening, dressed like this.'

She walked over to me and stood very close. 'I need you, Joe Panther.' Her breath lay on her voice like a body bag. 'And I have a very special place for you.'

I played along, feeling I didn't really have all that much choice, at least if I wanted to get back to Northbridge before dawn. 'And where is that?'

'You'll find out, but it's small and it's tight and it's warm.'

Then she scuffed her boot-heel against the floor, twirled her keys on her finger, and sashayed to the front door.

CHAPTER 14

It turned out to be the luggage space behind the rear seat of the Colt, underneath a picnic blanket. Something sharp protruded from the seat-back and poked me in the shoulder every time I moved. I was despising a day of small springs.

On the drive in she had explained the plan.

It wasn't that much of a plan, once all was said and done.

I would hide in the car. She would enter the Court and track down her quarry, armed with descriptions from me and Siobhan. She didn't think ID would be difficult. I agreed with her. Then she would allow herself to be chatted up — or do the chatting up herself if that was the way it played — and get herself invited back for a coffee. She would accept, but insist on driving her own car. This whole process, she said, might take a few hours. During which I was to remain hidden under a picnic blanket in the arse of a Mitsubishi Colt with something sharp sticking into my back.

She would then drive the target home, and go inside with her. Once that had been accomplished, she would gradually bring the conversation around to Gina Compton and see what she could find out. She was prepared to play the hard bitch, she said, if that was necessary.

Which was where I came in. Or, rather, didn't come in if it could possibly be helped. My role was to wait in the car. If she summoned me, or if I heard her shout in panic, then I was to liberate myself and make a dramatic entrance, gallant to the end in my rescue of a maiden fair.

'I know she's a big cow,' she'd told me over Macy Gray during the drive to the pub. 'Siobhan's told me about the temper on her. I just want you as back-up in case she gets cute. I'd rather not call for police assistance. I think you can see why that would be.'

I'd glanced across at her as she smoothly worked pedals, gear stick and wheel, overtaking on the freeway. Yes, I could see why.

'Because you look like a junkie slut,' I said.

'Thank you,' she replied, well pleased.

I thought it was a shit-house plan, as far as it went. I had a much better one. I decided not to share this information until such time as it became necessary.

Even then, if I could help it. And remember it.

Macy Gray was singing about how she just couldn't wait to meet me. It was a nice liaison to contemplate, but I thought it better if it didn't happen. She'd only end up disappointed.

It was getting on for 10 pm when Chew pulled the car up three blocks from the Court and ordered me to get in the back. There was no point in risking someone seeing her turn up with a passenger, she said, especially an obviously bearded male one. She had taken mercy on my soul during the journey, buying me a new packet of cigarettes and a 375ml bottle of Johnny Walker Red at a drive-through. I had attempted to bargain her up to 750ml, Johnny Black, but failed on both counts.

'Make sure you park away from a streetlight,' I said to her as I tried to find which foetal position was less uncomfortable than the others. 'The back of the car will fill with smoke from time to time.'

'I'll leave the window open a crack.' Chew was watching me in the rearview mirror. 'Have you had a pee?'

'I'll survive.' I decided that there was no such thing as a comfortable foetal position in an enclosed space, which explained, I supposed, why babies eventually struggled to be born.

Better, in their case, the devil they didn't know.

(And no, I do not harbour a foolish wish that I should never have been born from Mary's immaculate womb. My regrets and foolishness start way before then.)

'Bye, honey,' she whisper-mocked, bending down into the car from outside, before she slammed shut the driver's door.

I lay still, finding solace in the heavy darkness beneath the blanket, feeling no immediate desire to push it off. I sipped softly at the neck of the whisky bottle, like an infant at the breast, and listened to the sounds around me. Nothing was near, nothing was crisp: the music from the Court was a conveyor belt of muffled Groove Armada booms; cars and buses growled and slapped along the nearby main road; the railway gates tolled again, as insincere as ever.

Every now and then I would hear footsteps passing by: some the rapid pocking of high-heels, others the clump of boots, still others the almost silent pad of trainers. A cough, once or twice; brief fragments of conversation or laughter; once the crack of a match against a box, followed by the grateful hiss of inhalation. I'd had to light up one myself straight after, the smoke creeping from under my cover like a bad day in World War I.

Time passed like it had nothing better to do. Then, more footsteps, right outside the car, lingering this time. I remained beneath the blanket, shallowing my breath, gently replacing the cap on the bottle just in case I had to put it away. I made out two distinct pairs of feet, both too hesitant and light of tread to be Chew. They paused, walked off, returned, paused, paced, stopped.

My first thought was that someone was about to try to steal the vehicle. It would have been an inconvenient episode, but not altogether unpleasant. Bad enough you crack a car and find a Rottweiler in the back. Woe betide you find the Lamb of God.

'Just here. Yeah here. Let's do it here.' A male voice, young, whispering, tense.

'Someone will *see*.' Female, nervous.

'Bullshit someone will see. It's dark here. This car'll shield us.'

The side panel reverberated as the owner of the male voice gave it two firm taps.

Not theft, then, I concluded. Sex, perhaps? A surreptitious knee-knocker in a darkened doorway? I hoped not. The sound would do little for my temper, save that it probably wouldn't last for long.

'Aw, shit, y'reckon?'

'Come *on*, it'll be chill. I'm *hangin'*.'

Silver-tongued devil, I thought. Then I heard some other noises: a slight subvocalised complaint, the scraping of shoes against concrete, the gentle thud of two heads coming to rest against the bodywork. The action was easy enough to deduce. They were sitting next to each other on the pavement, leaning back against the Colt. I knew their intentions then, as a parent knows the wishes of a child, or the Lord knows the thoughts of sparrows.

'What if somebody comes?'

'They *won't*, man. Just hurry up and let's do it.'

For the next five minutes I listened mainly to foreground silence, counterpointed by the music from the pub. All I heard from outside the car came in disconnected moments. The brief squeak-breath of a tiny plastic bag. Scraping. The tinkle of a spoon dropped. Whispered swearwords. The scratch of a cigarette lighter. Warnings: 'careful', 'easy with it'. Some grunts through gritted teeth. More whispers: 'do me'. A murmur. A groan. A head thumping back on the metal. A sigh. A worship: 'oh god'.

Then silence for a minute or two. I was hoping they would work through their rushes quickly and stagger off somewhere. Junkies leaning against cars tend to attract cop attention.

But then, the female voice, slurred, lost, swimming back up to its own meniscus, trying to break through. 'Vince. Vince? Hey, Vince ... *Vince*! Vince, c'mon, mate, stop fucking ab ... Vince, you *bastard*, come *on*, man.'

And then came the sobs, the name repeated like a penance, the sound of movement, of pushing, body parts hitting the car. More sobs, a suppressed cry, high-pitched. The babble of a young woman not quite in the world, talking to herself, confessing, confessing, demanding guidance: 'Ohshitohshitohshit ... oh *fuck* ... oh *help* ... what to do what to do what to do what to ... '

She wailed at that point, whether intentionally or not, the high mournful keen of a Celtic widow, cutting through the muffled night like a Native American dagger through a Pilgrim.

I curled myself tighter in my foetus-pose, silently unscrewing the whisky cap again and taking the bottle to my lips. Plainly, I wasn't going anywhere for a while.

I hoped that inside the gynarchic maelstrom of the Court, DC Chew was of much the same opinion.

Footsteps arrived at a run. One person, a man by the impact noises.

'What's up? Is he hurt?'

'Oh, oh, oh, mate. He's — oh my god — he's turning blue. Vince, oh Vince. Oh, mate, please help, he's turning *blue*.'

'What's ... look at me ... what's happened?' The man spoke as if to an imbecile.

'Help, please help him. You gotta help him, *pleeease*.' More sobs.

The male voice whispered: 'Oh *shit* — I don't fucking need this.'

Your smallest wish, your tiniest curse in the night. The Lord hears.

And then he was audibly on his mobile phone. 'Ambulance, please. Yeah, there's a guy here passed out on the pavement —'

'He's turning *blue*.'

'His, ah, girlfriend thinks he might be dying. Ah, right, Northbridge. Um, far end of James Street, pretty near the corner of Stirling. Yeah, near the Court Hotel, that's right. Uh? Hang on.' A change of tone. 'Have you guys been in the pub?' Silence. 'No, don't think so. I don't think he's drunk. I think it's maybe heroin or something. Hey, look can I go now? You don't need me or anything, yeah? I mean, I don't know these people or anything like that. I just heard the girl screaming ...'

His voice was already fading into the night as he completed his excuses, leaving no sound bar the distant thump of Jamiroquai and the nearby sobbing of a smacked-out girl.

It was quite restful, except for the Jamiroquai.

Five minutes was my unchecked estimation of the time that elapsed before the growing croon of an ambulance began to fill the spaces of the night. It wasn't long before the inside of the Colt was spinning to the panic of red and blue lights, like cheap acid at a high school disco.

I lay very still and listened to the unflustered preparation of equipment, the forced cordiality of the two ambos, the scrape and snap of cases being opened, plastic being ripped.

'How long's he been like this? What's his name, love? And yours?'

Silence. Brief.

'Just your first name, that'll be all right. Just need something to call you by, eh?'

The girl, meek, shrill: 'His name's Vince. I'm Sandy.'

'Vince. You did right to call us, Sandy. Has Vince had any drugs this evening? Has he, Sandy? See, I think he has. I think he's had some heroin. The cops aren't here, Sandy, and this is important: has he had some smack? You've both had smack, yeah? Yeah. OK.'

'How long ago did you hit up, Sandy?'

'Got a pulse. Has he OD'd before, Sandy? Yes? How many times, Sandy? How many times has Vince OD'd before? Just the once, yeah?'

'Bullshit,' one of them whispered under his breath.

'OK, Sandy. Now Vince is very sick. We're going to give him a needle and that should do the trick, okay. But then, listen to m—, no *listen* to me: no more smack for him tonight. Or you. Get him home. He's gonna be pretty crook for a little while and then you should —'

The sermon was interrupted by a deep-lung gasp that sounded like Lazarus returning from death. Which it was, in a sense. While one ambo had been talking to the quietly blubbing Sandy, the other must have shot Vince full of Narcan. Wonderful stuff, Narcan: one shot and all the demons in your veins just flee. It's the pharmacological equivalent of scepticism.

And just like the sudden revelation of the material world, not all its recipients are wholly grateful.

I could hear Vince moaning, coughing a little, clawing his way back to consciousness, trying to ask what happened.

'You OD'd, Vince,' explained one of the ambos. 'You turned blue and passed out. You might have been dead if Sandy here hadn't raised the alarm. You've had a very lucky escape, Vince. Next time, you know, next time we might not be able to get here so fast, or maybe no one will see you —'

Vince interrupted with a groan of despair. 'Where's me *hit*, man?'

Sandy's voice: 'You were *dying*, Vince. They had to.'

A wail of petulant disappointment. 'Aw, *fuck*, mate. Me hit. Aw, fucking *shit*, man.'

An angry fist hit the car.

'Well, Bob,' came an ambo voice, fecund with sad expectations met, 'our work here is done. Let's go. Bye, Vince. Reckon we'll see you again soon.'

There was no reply from Vince, and only indistinct whispers from Sandy. An engine roared, and suddenly my world was plunged once again into blessed blackness.

I listened as Sandy gently cooed, trying to console her boy from the depth of her own fear and fast returning smacked-out lethargy. Vince, though, sounded utterly despondent, his words constant variations on the same theme, whispered like prayer. 'I'll never get any more tonight. Never find any more tonight. Never find those women again.'

'We maybe *might*, Vince,' hushed Sandy, not sounding like she believed herself. 'I mean, how far can they *get* with a wheelchair?'

It was more than I could bear. I am not, as many might hold, completely devoid of compassion. When thou makest a feast, call the poor, the maimed, the lame, the blind: And thou shalt be blessed.

I said that. Apparently.

Carefully, in the dark, I shuffled from beneath my blanket and wound the side window down a mite. I could see the tops of their heads below me. 'Pssssst!' I hissed.

They both jumped like I'd shoved cattle prods up their fundaments.

I whispered again, imbuing my words with serene authority. 'Be not afraid.'

'Wha' the fuck?' By the sound of it, Vince wasn't quite wholly back in the game.

Sandy stood up and went to peer in the window.

'Turn away,' I warned. She did.

'Come to me, Vince,' I commanded.

Quivering, he did as he was told, levering himself up and around onto his knees before the window, the glass opaque to his unbelieving eyes. I pulled a baggie from my pocket and held it out to him through the crack. Dumbly, dimly, he tried to snatch it. I closed my palm over it easily.

'Your lucky day, Vince,' I said. 'I'm having a resurrection sale. For you, just twenty bucks.'

'I haven't got —'

'He that findeth his life shall lose it; and he that loseth his life for my sake shall find it.'

I began to withdraw my hand. Immediately he called to Sandy, pleading. A brief quarrel ensued. After half a minute, Sandy handed him two tens. He handed them to me. I let him take the deal.

'Go in peace,' I said. 'For to him that is joined to all the living there is hope: for a living dog is better than a dead lion.'

I don't think he understood me, nor even cared. Without a thank you, he staggered off, Sandy weaving behind, this time no doubt to look for a more private place in which to taste my love.

What is your life? It is even a vapour, that appeareth for a little time, and then vanisheth away.

Satisfied, I shoved the two grubby notes into my pocket and curled back beneath the blanket. The whisky scoured my throat like the love of the Logos. I watched the smoke from my Dunhill ascend like the souls of the forgiven, collecting in lazy spirals against the roof of the car before suddenly finding the angel of deliverance and slipping at speed in a fine thin trail out the window and away to heaven. In the distance, a song, a thumping devotion: 'God is a DJ'.

'And here it is — the great green beast!'

The announcement and the rich laughter which accompanied it clearly fell from the disguised and duplicitous mouth of Detective Constable Irene Chew, temporarily suspended from the Homicide Squad, currently engaged in an act of unauthorised entrapment. A second laugh, slightly deeper and sounding more polite than spontaneous, echoed her call. Two sets of strong, ordered footsteps began to slap against the road, growing louder at each pace.

It was a lame way to refer to a dinky little car, but served well enough to warn me of their approach. Quickly, I stubbed out the Dunhill against the wheel arch, screwed the top back on the scotch, and curled myself tight beneath the blanket. I realised that the inside light would come on when Chew opened the door. I should have thought of that earlier and disabled it, but, hey, contrary to widespread opinion, I'm not perfect. I held my breath and hoped that Anita would be too enamoured by the visible charms of Chew to bother looking into the back of the vehicle.

Assuming, of course, that the detective had made the ID correctly and hadn't just wasted a couple of hours chatting up the wrong bull dyke entirely.

The car suddenly beeped twice as Chew used the remote to trigger the locks. The noise made me jump. I just hoped in my blindness that the woman was demonstrating the good sense to show off from a distance.

This was apparently the case. The footsteps continued to grow louder, their impacts diverging now as two people walked to their assigned doors.

'Jesus fuck, look at this.' The voice was undoubtedly Anita's, undoubtedly disgusted, and undoubtedly just outside the window.

I wondered if she'd seen something, some dim twitch through the glass, some muscular spasm of which I was not aware. I get the shakes sometimes. If she were to open the door, reach in and pull away my shroud, what then? What pandemonium would unleash, what opportunities be lost?

'What's the matter?' Chew's voice, sounding concerned.

'It's nothing,' Anita snapped. 'Just a fucking syringe here on the pavement, that's all. Nearly bloody trod on it. Jeez, they shit me, junkies. I just wish they'd all get fucking AIDS and die.'

Chew laughed nervously at the remark, then made a banal comment about the lack of sharps bins around the town and a weak joke about not wanting any kind of pricks in her herself.

'Too right, sister,' replied Anita, and pulled open the passenger door as if she was trying to deprive it of its hinges.

Chew got in. I listened as they settled themselves, as seatbelts whirred and clicked into place, as lips touched, made sucking noises, and formed a polite 'Mmmm ...' at the conclusion.

I could smell booze-breath coming from Chew's side of the car. Nothing from Anita's.

'Right, then.' Chew, all business again. 'Where to?'

'Christ, woman, what have you had in this car? It stinks in here. It smells like something died.'

I should be so lucky, I thought.

'Long story,' said Chew, no doubt trying to think of one. 'Boring. Did shopping the other day, got distracted, left it in the back of the car in the sun and everything perishable did. Can't get the smell out. Tried everything.' I heard the playful slap of palm against thigh. Chew again: 'So, come on, *where*? I want to take you on the ride of your life.'

Oh, puh-*leeze*, I thought. Give it a rest.

Anita, however, seemed to respond to such blandishment, and gave an address just to the west of the CBD. Chew fired the engine. The car lurched forward and Macy Gray croaked into the night once more.

Her voice died after bare seconds.

'What's the matter?' asked Chew.

'Can't stand that bitch. Too soft by half.'

Chew let out a nervous chuckle. 'My apologies. What would you prefer?'

'Ani DiFranco.'

'No can do, sorry. She sounds too much like she's talking to her therapist for my liking.'

'That's because she doesn't give a shit who's listening to her or not. I like that in a woman.'

'Sorry? What did you say?'

'Was that a joke?' The substitution of tone in Anita's voice, from banter to defensive challenge, had been sudden and sharp.

Chew evidently picked up on it, because she made a couple of quick, reassuring I-was-joking statements and then pointedly changed the subject, asking whether she should stop at a bottle shop and pick up some wine, maybe, on the way.

Yes, I thought.

'No,' said Anita. 'I've got everything we'll need at home.'

Bitch, I thought.

After that, the pair fell into a silence that was mutual, if not wholly relaxed. I decided to chance a look. Carefully, I edged my head out from underneath the blanket, looked up and forward. The back seat was in the way, so I had to slowly lever myself up onto one elbow to get a better view. Heads and shoulders were the best I could manage. Chew looked tense, working on jumpy. Anita, even from behind, looked plain scary. She was wider than the seat, and didn't appear to be wearing a top, but I was sure that wasn't the case. Her hair, like Chew's, glistened with oil. There was coarse stubble on the creases at the back of her neck, which ended before the wide expanse of her bare upper back and shoulders. I assumed that she was wearing some kind of boob tube or bustiere arrangement — an oddly feminine choice in one sense, perhaps, but I could see the reason why. In a military line across the top of her back there were ten thin, conical steel points sticking out about an inch proud of her flesh. I'd seen the sort of thing before — it's a piercing technique using implanted magnets and detachable ornamentation — but never one so hardcore.

This woman, I thought to myself, has a real thing about pain.

'I don't normally let anyone come home with me, you know,' she said suddenly to Chew. 'You're privileged.'

'And so are you,' came the reply, a little too fast. 'I don't normally go home with strangers.'

Or drive around with Jesus in my hatchback, she might have added, but didn't.

Anita turned to look at her at that point. The expression on her face was cold and serious. I saw the muscles of her shoulders twitch, and ten steel spikes jump as one to attention.

I couldn't tell if Chew noticed. She was driving, looking forwards at the road. At that moment she made a routine rearview mirror check, in which she must have seen my eyes staring back at her. I raised my eyebrows in warning, but she made no move to acknowledge. Instead, she stomped on the brake, causing the little car to lurch to a halt. Straight away she accelerated again.

'What was that about?' asked Anita.

'Sorry,' said Chew. 'I thought I saw a dog crossing the road, but it was nothing, I guess. I must be tired.'

I lay still and silent, once more beneath the blanket, and dabbed the lapel of my jacket against my nose. There was blood oozing from it, thanks to its sudden and unplanned collision with the seat-back. I didn't mind too much. Without the shedding of blood, there is no forgiveness of sins.

I closed my eyes, made no more move to observe, and waited in obscurity for the car to slow down and stop.

In the meantime, I forgave myself in advance.

CHAPTER 15

An angel came unto me. It took my outstretched hand, its shining eminence above, its golden arm of salvation below, and lifted me from the field of battle, pulling me up and away from the twisted carnage in which I lay bleeding.

'Son of God?' it asked, in a voice sweeter than manna.

'How did you know?' I replied.

'Wake up, for fuck's sake,' the angel hissed. My hand fell and cracked against the floor of the car.

I opened my eyes, not to salvation, but to the word PORNSTAR below and a shadowed cop's face above, very close to mine.

'Stay awake, you shit,' she said impatiently. 'You never know.'

'Too right.'

'Too right what? Too right you'll stay awake?'

'Too right I never know. Where's the behemoth?'

'Inside her house. We got here a couple of minutes ago. I said I had to come back out because I'd left my purse in the car. I wanted to check you were still with us. Bloody good job I did. You were snoring, Joe.'

I pinched my nose. A clot of dried blood came away in my fingers. 'No I wasn't,' I replied. 'Has she said anything yet?'

'I haven't raised the question. I'd better go before she gets suspicious. She only wants me for my body, that's obvious, but I'm going to try to get what information I can from her before I have to tell her I'm a nice girl who doesn't bonk on first dates. I think it'll be all right, but listen out, eh?'

'Don't strain anything.'

Her voice hardened. 'It's her knowledge I hope to take, Panther, not her weight. And by the way, were you dealing smack out of my car while I was in the hotel?'

I could not tell a lie, so I remained silent. She took that as an affirmative.

'You've got some disgusting habits, Joe Panther,' she spat, backing out.

'It's not a habit,' I corrected, sadly. 'It's a calling.'

The door shut and silence once more descended.

A few seconds later I heard the echoing thud of a house door closing. I waited, still and curled, for another five minutes, then decided it was time to make the first cautious move.

Carefully I propped myself up from the floor and peered out of the window. The car was in what at first appeared to be a narrow cul-de-sac. A second look, however, revealed it as a courtyard, a mutual driveway access for a line of five small single storey units set at right angles to the road.

The one directly in front of me was lit from the outside by a single authentic reproduction coachlight, its beam illuminating a plain white facade, a tiny gravel path, two ornamental trees in pots, and a rectangular parking bay which held a vehicle covered by a sun-protector tarpaulin.

Squinting, I could just make out a narrow side gate, the same size as the dividing fences — maybe six foot.

The front window of the unit was curtained and lit from within. A shadow passed across it from time to time. After a few more minutes, I wound down the back window. Muffled by glass and cloth, I could hear the faint but insistent assertions of Ani DiFranco and, every now and then, what sounded like laughter. I wondered what Hewson might think of Chew's interrogation technique.

I wondered, too, how he had treated Iain and Adam, and whether they were back at their house, or locked, tiny and scared, inside a barred room in the dubious company of several drunks, two recidivist housebreakers and a mentally ill wife-basher. I presumed their current sleeping arrangements depended on whether Hewson had managed to extract from them an address for Clem Porter. If so, I wondered what else he had discovered that I should know about.

I thought I had it all worked out, but I knew not to trust those thoughts. I thought I had it all worked out in Jerusalem, too, and look where that got me.

Slowly, painfully, I opened the car door and slithered out, one limb at a time. I almost cried out with the cramping pain, but managed to hold my tongue. Once outside, I stood up and stretched, willing the blood to flow and the nerves to cease their restless fretting. I had no idea of the time, but the coolness of the air told me it was very late. It also told me that I was well overdue for a leak. I looked around and noted the absence of lights in all the other units. Sleep, sleep, good neighbours, I bade in silence. Perhaps you entertain angels unawares. Perhaps the Son of Man slashes on a car tyre in your courtyard.

I brought forth the waters abundantly.

Then I crept stealthily in the night, past the Colt and softly across the handkerchief garden to where the tarpaulin-covered car was parked. It was not the only car in the units so covered, the method of protecting paintwork being common enough when no roof was available to do so. I wondered, though, how precious the paint on Anita's car would turn out to be.

Crouching at the back of the vehicle, I gently worked at the drawstring arrangement that sealed the cover underneath the chassis. It took a minute or so to work it loose, then to lift the corner up and back gently.

The car was white. A bit more lifting and pulling and fiddling found its rear badge. It said: COMMODORE.

I congratulated myself for having just confirmed that Anita drove the single most common make, model, and colour of car in the country. I wondered what more I might find, should I pull the veil from its body and check out its interior. The front passenger seat, for instance. I decided, however, that there was a limit to the understanding I needed. If the upholstery had a story to tell, it could tell it to someone who cared.

For the sake of form, I quickly pulled the tarp back to its original position. Then I ducked around the other side of the car, crouched down in the darkness between it and the side fence, and tried to work out what to do next.

Ani DiFranco was still moaning on. I heard a peal of laughter. Chew. Nervous, too high-pitched.

Out of sight between the vehicle and the fence, I pulled the Dunhills from my pocket and lit one. As I put the pack back my finger brushed against something small. I grabbed hold of it and pulled it out. Must be my lucky night, I decided.

I was holding the last of a foil of speed, which I'd forgotten all about.

Just what I needed.

There was too much breeze and too little time to warrant chopping up and making a nice line of it all, so I simply peeled back the wrapping, plunged in my finger and rubbed coarse grains across my gums.

I must have done it a bit too forcefully the second time. My finger came away smeared with red. No matter. I'd just accidentally punched an express route through to my bloodstream, but I figured a bit of high-speed commuting would be all to the good.

A spark started snapping across a synapse somewhere in the front of my brain, like one of those gas-igniter guns you find in kitchens. There wasn't enough fuel built up to trigger a flame yet, but it would come. I was sure of that.

On bended knees on the oil-stained concrete, I sucked in the Dunhill, watching its tip flare like the holy flame of Saint Brigid, then die down like the first thrill of baptism. Here is my fatality, I thought; smoke this in remembrance of me. Two more drags, then I stubbed it and tossed it.

The music stopped as I stood up to head for the side gate. I froze, eyes on the front curtain, waiting for a twitch, listening for a shout. A minute passed, like a wound healing. Then Cher started singing. I breathed out at last. Cher. This woman is one sick puppy, I thought.

It was only a few paces until I reached the wooden side gate. Gently and slowly, I tested it, lifting it against and with its hinges. It was locked. Through a square gap halfway up it was possible to reach through and slip the catch — except that the catch had, of course, been secured with a big, ugly padlock. I thought about climbing over the top, but rejected the idea. The available space was narrow, the planks all ended in points. The potential for falling was just too great, especially since my balance tends to go without warning sometimes.

I am nothing, however, if not patient. I pulled a fit from my pocket, uncapped it. Holding it between my fingers, I reached through into the black behind the gate. It was awkward, having to work the syringe essentially backwards and blind, but Cher had bellowed through just two songs before I felt something give and heard the satisfying *schnick* of the mechanism popping free.

The gate didn't squeak as it opened, which was a blessing. I made my way up a narrow path, feeling the rough texture of the wall against my left shoulder, the splintering coarseness of the fence brushing my right. If Anita uses this route, I mused, odds-on she walks down sideways. My foot stubbed something large and softly echoing. My hands identified it as a plastic wheelie bin. With an effort, I squeezed past.

The back garden was dimly lit by the half-moon and a streetlight. It was very small, and seemed to contain nothing bar concrete slabs and a clothesline. White underwear and singlets, one peg apiece, hung like Klansmen brought to justice. I could still hear Cher, but only when I held my breath.

The rear entrance boasted a security flyscreen in front of a sturdy wooden door. Neither presented a problem, although the flyscreen tended to clang and rattle if I worried the fit inside its lock too strongly. I was concerned the noise might disturb some dog in a neighbouring yard, thus setting up a clamour to be investigated. If any ears heard my violation, however, they kept their silence.

The back door neither scraped nor creaked as it opened inwards, which was handy. Slowly, quietly, I closed it behind me, then stood for a couple of minutes, waiting for my eyes to grow accustomed to the gloom.

Cher was wishing she could turn back time. How often had I wished exactly the same thing? Pointless, of course. What's done is done: the dead have decayed: the living wake in fright, still believing.

The surroundings began to harden in my sight, gaining form, filling the universe. The back door gave directly on to a small kitchen. I could identify cupboards, the stove, fridge, a little table with a single chair. There were two plain white doors, both closed, set in the right-hand wall, and another, also closed, directly in front of me. A thin glow came from beneath this last: clearly through there lay the front of the house: the lounge room, a bedroom, probably. What else?

In a momentary dip in Cher's verse, disconnected phrases.

'...don't see that we can't discuss ...' Chew. Controlled.

'...better things, sister, to ...' Anita. Determined.

Of the other two doors, one had to lead to the bathroom, and maybe a laundry. The other was a mystery. Before tackling it, however, I tiptoed the few steps to the fridge, and carefully pulled open the door, seeking nourishment. The inside light came on, throwing out enough to indicate the linoleum on the floor was a kind of baroque-patterned brown and hadn't been cleaned for a while. The shelves held the usual bits and bobs of crusty cheese and wilted lettuce, chocolate biscuits and peanut butter. There was also a dozen bottles of Red Bull. It wasn't the domestic brand, but the real stuff from Thailand: little brown-glass cough-mixture bottles full of liquid which tasted unpleasant but fired your brain up like a jolt of electricity. They could be found tucked away in some of the local Asian grocery stores, an open secret amongst the ravers. There was no alcohol at all in the fridge, which was a bitter disappointment. Not for her, the blood of my new testament. Not for her, the remission of sins.

I grabbed one of the Red Bulls, cracked it and sculled. The woman is a speed freak, I concluded; a non-boozing, pain-loving, body-piercing speed freak. That meant her physical bulk had to be more muscle than fat. I put the top back on the empty, replaced it on the shelf and grabbed another.

'... couldn't we talk about this later?' Anita. Peeved.

She goeth after her straight away, as an ox goeth to the slaughter.

'... so much better if ...' Chew. Dissembling.

Abstain from fleshly lusts, which war against the soul.

I replaced the second empty bottle, gently closed the fridge, and turned to the door least likely to conceal a toilet. I opened it carefully, but again it was silent. One step inside, I closed it again. Darkness hugged me to its bosom like a prodigal returned.

Cher finished. I made neither sound nor move.

'... not into monogamy ...' Anita. Justifying.

'... ever with another ... another, you know, activist?' Chew. Directing.

More music. Took me a minute to place it. Me'shell Ndegeocello: strong bass, strong voice, strong tattoos. The woman had some taste after all.

She also had a shit-load of video cassettes. I could just make them out in the dull, filtered moonlight squeezing through the flyscreen-covered window at the other end of the room: rows of them, stacks of them, on shelves, on the

269

desk, on the floor, their cases, for the most part, ghostly and white.

The room itself was tiny, too small to fit even a single bed inside, the sort of leftover alcove often termed a 'study' or 'den' by real estate agents. It contained a desk, on which sat a small television topped by a couple of rectangular black boxes. These I assumed to be video players accommodating different formats. The cassette cases were of two distinct sizes: big, normal ones, and smaller, dinky ones. There was also, I came to see, a rack containing what looked like CDs, although I guessed that they too held pictorial images of some sort. There didn't seem to be any playback mechanism for them. I assumed they required a computer. A three-shelf bookcase stood wedged against one wall. There was an office chair in front of the television, but it didn't look as if there would be enough room to swivel it without hitting something.

'... possible that we have mutual friends ...' Chew. Exploring.

'... a lot of questions, don't you?' Anita. Resisting.

The light was nowhere near enough to make things out clearly. I decided to take a risk, and grabbed a handful of vids from the nearest stack. These I laid side by side at the base of the door, trying to make sure the gap between it and the floor was completely covered. Then I switched on the light.

The room was the nerve centre of Anita's academic work. The absence of a computer, I decided, was probably the sole reason she spent any time at Sappho's Sisters.

I checked the book spines first. It was a mixed collection, but the unifying theme was apparent. There were copies of feminist works, old and new: Faludi, Greer, Dworkin, a torn copy of Valerie Solanas's *Scum Manifesto*. These were interspersed by a couple of history books on feminist themes; I noted one called *Goddesses, Whores, Wives and Slaves: Women in Classical Antiquity*, by Sarah B Pomeroy. Then there were the sex books: *The Prehistory of Sex* by Timothy Taylor, and a number of perhaps less disinterested works with names like *Leatherfaeries, Fetish Life* and *Hard Bodies*. On the bottom shelf, what looked like scholarly examinations of violent erotica were stashed in next to textual and pictorial examples of the genre, ranging from Marquis de Sade classics to studies of Pasolini's films to books with titles such as *Die, Slut!*, *The Body of Woman* and *Snuff!*.

'...don't see why we can't before ...' Anita. Persuading.

'...nothing. It's just I like to know who I'm going to bed with ...' Chew. Peacekeeping.

'I thought we were ...'

Me'shell Ndegeocello's backing singers soared, drowning the rest.

I sat down in the desk chair and studied the spines of the vids. Most of the larger cases were neatly labelled, some with print-out text which indicated their provenance as residents of a university audio-visual collection, others with handwritten notes detailing when they were taped off television. The selection was impressive: Charles Gatehead piercing docos, Pasolini films, Russ Meyer flicks, *Vampirella*, *Lolita* (both versions), a whole slew of titles which, from the salacious puns of their titles, I assumed to be unrepentant violent porn. What else, for instance, would *The Blair Bitch Project* or *Nine-and-half weeks (tied up and ass fucked)* possibly turn out to be?

'...is this, you know, a game, sister?' Anita. Deeply ambiguous.

'...it was just a simple question. Look...' Chew. Defensive.

The smaller video-cassette cases were unlabelled. I recognised the maker's mark and number on the spine, though.

I fired up the television, mute on, flicked on the smaller of the playback machines, and shoved in a cassette chosen at random.

'...OK, I *knew* her, all right?' Anita. Challenging.

'...I didn't *mean* to...' Chew. Placating.

'I don't want to ...'

The music reasserted its dominance.

The tape resolved from snow to image. Black. Wobbly. Obviously handheld. A pinky sheen: something across the very bottom of the screen, moving with the camera. Blotchy lights: red, white, smearing unfocussed as the camera moved. A doorway, unstable, passing to the right: more lights inside. Mostly, dark things. A woman looms from somewhere, passes, distorted, giving a self-conscious child-wave, blowing a kiss. She was wearing, what, a bra top, maybe, black lipstick maybe. I had the impression of long fingernails. More movement, still the sheen. Lights flare and bend like Dali's clocks. Moving down a corridor? Walking, definitely. I hit fast-forward: the image jerked and spat, lights spitting past. Suddenly, the screen is much brighter, glaring out. The image dips and spins, zooms in and out as whoever is holding the camera fights to get focus and exposure under control. I brought the tape back to normal speed. Now there are several people in shot. A party, maybe? The people belong to both genders, but there is a similarity between them which divergent genitalia can not obscure. They are dressed, to greater or lesser extents, in studded black leather: straps, crotch pouches, caps, wristbands, collars. They are gathered in a huddle, the two closest to the camera showing bare backs and strapped-apart buttocks to the screen. A couple of the others look around, acknowledge the camera, mouthing 'Hi'. One of them taps the two in front. They look around, move to the side.

Still that pink sheen at the base of the screen. I stared, worked it out. It was skin: the camera was being held at such an angle — on the shoulder, probably — that its field of vision didn't quite exclude the operator. Skin. Bare skin. Where? Top of the trunk, somewhere.

'...no, I haven't been lying to you. I ...' Chew. Losing ground.

'...shut up and show me ...' Anita. Gaining confidence.

The people in front of the camera move aside, revealing the object of everyone's attention. On a vertical rack, a woman hangs, wrists crossed and tied above her head. She has a ball-gag in her mouth. Her eyes are wide, very scared. Maybe she was a willing participant at first; not now. She moves her head from side to side, but her own upper arms restrict the movement. The camera starts to pan down her body, revealing her to be naked except for a spiked collar, red high-heeled shoes, and ropes around her ankles. The pan also reveals more of the camera operator: I see a thick, meaty thigh moving briefly into the frame and out again. A momentary firming of the pink, still unclear. And something black, something hooded and round and black. The camera pans back up the woman's body, which seems to be straining against its bonds, then down again. As the shot changes, the black thing re-enters the frame. I paused the image, stared. Unmistakable: the head of a penis, big, but black like rubber. A condom, maybe.

I fired the image again. It continued its slow, lascivious journey up the woman's trunk, too close now to be in focus. Then, once again, the face, the wide eyes, the mouth distended by the ball-gag.

The camera jumps when the first slap comes, failing to capture much of the violent spasm the hand engenders in the woman's almost immobile face. The focus is better for the second one, coming in from the left. The woman looks as if she is trying not to vomit behind the gag.

I hit the stop button, then the eject.

'...make you forget *all* your ...' Anita. Seducing.

'... I'm not sure I'm ready ...' Chew. Playing weak.

'... give you *nothing* to regret ...'

I grabbed a second cassette, then a third and fourth. With each I hit fast-forward, then opened up the image at random. Always the same: the pink haze at the bottom, the occasional glimpse of big black rubber-covered cock. Corridors. Passageways. Parties. Leather folk, willing and not so. Men and women as submissive victims, but mostly women. Alone sometimes; with spectators close by at others. The camera operator slapped, whipped, paddled, spanked, fist-fucked, mounted from behind with that big black weapon. Sometimes there was blood. Once, a young woman bent naked over a wooden horse, not moving, red and welted, the camera panning down to eyes more dead than alive, her mouth hanging open, drool unregarded.

'Maybe I'd better be ...' Chew. Giving up.

One more tape. Fast-forward. Random stop. Play. Same frame, but this time no pink sheen. The sheen was, what, fuzzy green or something, too close to resolve.

'Wait there. I promise ...' Anita. Moving.

The screen. The view: the top of a steering wheel,

darkness, lights sliding up a windscreen, lurching sideways as the vehicle turns, revealing ... nothing. Blackness. Fuzz. Then again: same view, different street, perhaps, too difficult to tell. A pan sideways, lights sliding past another window, something familiar, there.

Nearby: footsteps, a door closing. Not the front or back doors. Wrong echo.

I kept looking. Another stop and start. Same view. A lean in, not a zoom. Door opening, camera wobbling, door closing. Door opening again. Closing. Not a home movie like the others, I decided, but a rehearsal for something else.

More footsteps, muffled by extra walls.

Then, there, a quick glimpse of accidentally perfect focus through the car door during the third attempt. A lurid pink neon sign: LIVE GIRLS. I knew that sign, had passed it a thousand times on James Street. The camera operator must have twigged, too, because the car door was pushed open further, and the sign brought in to fill the whole screen, shaking slightly, flashing endlessly: LIVE GIRLS, LIVE GIRLS, LIVE GIRLS ...

I hit stop and clambered out of the chair. Me'shell Ndegeocello was still playing, but I could no longer hear the sound of conversation, even with my ear pressed to the inside of the study door. Had they moved to the bedroom? Or had one of them gone to the toilet? I didn't think so, because the footsteps I'd heard didn't sound like they were anywhere near the back of the house, but it was impossible to be sure. Perhaps there was a second toilet up the front, an en suite. Perhaps they were just having a quiet moment.

It would have been useful to know, but not essential. I grabbed one of the smaller cassettes and stuffed it in my pocket alongside my cigarettes, realising as I did so that I hadn't had a smoke since entering the house.

Perhaps there was hope for me yet.

Slowly and silently, I switched off the light, kicked the video cassettes on the floor to one side, and then opened the door. There was no sign of life, and the door connecting the front and back halves of the unit was still closed, light glowing dimly from beneath.

I opened it, scarcely breathing. Me'shell Ndegeocello grew louder. I could see a short, wide passageway, front door at the other end. A wide archway to my left, closed wooden door to the right. Still no one speaking. Left: lounge; right: bedroom, I decided. Edging down the passageway, back against the wall, my Docs sunk softly into cheap, cream carpet.

Taking a final breath, and flexing my fingers in case I needed to use them, I peered around the archway.

'Light dawns for the righteous, and joy for the upright of heart,' I whispered.

Chew was sitting by herself, still fully clothed, on a three-seater sofa. Her legs were crossed, arms uneasily at her sides, fingers tapping. Her shoulder bag was on the floor at her feet. She had been staring at the wall, lost in thought. When she heard my voice she jumped like a mink meeting its maker, but managed in a split second to downgrade a scream to a little squeak of surprise.

I entered the room, standing tall, hands now in my jacket pockets.

Her hiss was like that of an angry cobra. 'What the fucking hell are you doing in here, you demented ... You're supposed to be ... Just get the fuck out of —'

'Getting anywhere?' I whispered back.

She pouted, angry and disappointed both. 'She's a fucking animal. I've got her to admit knowing Gina — I said she was an old friend of mine — tried a couple of times to get her to gossip about the murder, but every time I try to talk about anything that might yield something useful she just changes the subject and tries to get her hand up my shorts.'

'Women are such beasts, aren't they?'

'Hasn't even offered me a drink.'

'She hasn't got any. I checked the fridge.'

She puffed her chest out, outraged at my effrontery. Then she realised what she was doing and sat back again. 'How long have you been ... ?'

'Where is she?'

She groaned, bent forward, picked up her bag. 'Changing into something more comfortable, she said. No kidding: that's what she said. I hate to think. Ah, *shit*. Seeing you're here, it's blown anyway. Maybe we should go, pass the lead on to Hewson, play by the ... '

She noticed I was standing still, shaking my head.

'What, Joe?'

I pulled the cassette out of my pocket and handed it over. She gave it a brief glance, noting, perhaps, that there was no writing on it. With a look in equal parts puzzled and pissed off, she held it out to me.

'So it's a video cassette. What's on it?'

I shrugged. 'You should never treat signs from the Lord lightly.'

For a second she continued to look puzzled and angry, then she peered again at the cassette and a light started to dawn on her face. When she looked up at me again, her expression was one of determination mixed in with just a skerrick of fear.

'The wrapper ...' she said to herself.

Then came the unmistakable sound of the bedroom door opening. I held my finger up to my mouth, staring Chew directly in the eyes, before clambering over her and throwing myself to the floor behind the sofa. It was the only possible spot, and not a great source of reassurance. I didn't mind, however, because I didn't intend to stay there very long.

Footsteps. Chew gasped.

'Any questions you've still got after this, sweet sister, I'll be happy to answer them.'

Anita's voice dripped with lust, but with something else also. There was a bravado in it, a chemical bravado. I knew that she'd hyped herself up, was in the habit of hyping herself up. I didn't know what, of course, but I could take a shrewd guess. It had to be something that worked quickly: cocaine, maybe, speed, ice, PCP, crystal meth, MDMA. Whatever — Red Bull alone it wasn't.

The sofa bulged as Chew pushed back against it. 'What the *fuck* are you doing?' She sounded panicked, losing control.

The sound of Anita moving, heavy, slow, inexorable. 'You'll love it, sister. They always love it.'

Her breathing sounded like a martyr stretched in the sun, harsh and full of devotion.

Chew, back in the game, pulling serious: 'Back off! I'm a pol— *urgh*!'

The ugly sound of a very large body thumping down on another drowned out the final plaintive notes of Me'shell Ndegeocello. The sofa slid back hard, almost crushing me against the wall. I could hear shallow breathing, teeth-grit recitations of 'no', springs squeaking, feet hitting the ground, and always, always above, the grating, growling tide of Anita's breath.

PCP, I decided. Time for work.

I pulled out the disposable camera from my pocket and grasped it ready in my left hand. Then I stood up and looked down on creation. 'Smile!' I cried.

Anita, trying to straddle on top, feet still on the ground for leverage, looked up. Chew, resisting, pressed back on the sofa, also looked up, but upside down. Their chins were almost touching. The flash made both of them recoil and blink.

My protection is in place, I thought to myself with a small sense of accomplishment. Then I punched Anita in the face as hard as I could.

My knuckles throbbed from the impact, but the force of the blow was enough only to cause her to move back a step or two, quickly rub her cheek and automatically check the integrity of her nasal piercing. Maybe, indeed, the punch hadn't even done that. Maybe she'd moved back simply out of surprise at finding an uninvited, oddly familiar man with a camera behind her sofa while she was trying to date-rape a woman she'd picked up in the pub.

Whatever the real cause of her discomfit, she took only a second to recover from it. She stood up straight, arms out in front of her, muscles flexed, and roared in anger. She could have easily passed for an all-in wrestler, especially given her costume.

She was wearing her film-making gear. The ten points across her back stood to shiny attention. Her massive torso was covered only by a criss-cross of three-inch-wide black leather straps, each fixed with two parallel rows of square studs, over and under her breasts. Her nipples were pierced by tiny Celtic swords. Around her hips she wore a pair of tight, black, leather shorts, over which was strapped an eye-wateringly large, very erect, very thick, black rubber dildo.

It wasn't a toy of loveplay; it was an instrument of torture. Her legs were bare, the powerful, thick muscles of her thighs ridged with sinew and movement as she leant forward now and surged towards Chew and I.

The brief check to her attack had been enough, however. Chew threw herself from a sitting position and grabbed the big woman around the waist, pushing her backwards, grunting as the dildo hit her in the stomach. I vaulted over the sofa, kicking off from the back of it, and dived towards Anita's upper body, shoulder first. Between us we had too much force and momentum for her to resist. In a fearful clatter and thump of falling bodies, she toppled backwards onto the floor, with Chew and I each hitting her with our full weight. Chew yelped as the strap-on again dug into her. I landed with Anita's monstrous, gnarled, steel-lined nipple in my eye. It felt like I'd been punched in a bar brawl.

The woman let out a roar and started to flail wildly with her thick, muscular arms. She smelled of sweat, secrets and sex denied. I struggled to bring my left leg up onto the mound of her chest and dig my knee into her sternum. I positioned my right hand around her throat, just managing to get my fingers either side of her neck, then grabbed my wrist with my left hand to strengthen the grip.

Anita bucked and roared. I could feel her beginning to slip loose, building momentum to roll sideways, tipping me off. If that happened, the whole of creation would groaneth and travaileth in pain.

'DC Chew,' I said through gritted teeth. 'You want to do something police-like now?'

'I'm on it,' I heard.

I risked a look behind me. Chew had one arm pressing down across the tops of Anita's struggling thighs. With the other she was pulling her bag towards her. She hooked it in, then reached inside and pulled out her handcuffs. 'Ready?' she asked, pushed for breath.

I nodded. 'Right hand on three.'

'One two three.'

On her count I pressed down hard against Anita's throat while at the same time lifting my legs as if playing leapfrog. My weight on landing winded her. My knees came down firmly across her biceps. She gasped and ceased to struggle for a moment — enough for Chew to lunge forward and snap a cuff on her right wrist.

'Now!' she called.

Letting go of her throat with one hand, I grabbed the cuffed arm and hurled myself sideways, pulling it with me. Chew was ready to lend assistance, shoving hard at Anita's rising shoulder. With a roar of angry despair, the big woman rolled over onto her front. Chew quickly grabbed the still-flailing left arm and cuffed it to the right behind the back. In my haste to get out of the way, I slipped and reflexively thrust both arms out in front of me to break my fall. My palms landed on Anita's shoulders, spikes jabbing into both, drawing blood.

Chew and I stood up, looked at each other in silence, puffing, and then down at our handiwork. Anita lay trussed and quiet on her stomach like an elephant seal at rest, her lunar buttocks forced up into the air by the unbending will of the dildo trapped beneath.

'Hoist on her own petard,' said the detective, managing a weak smile.

Anita groaned, then flexed her arms against the restraint of the cuffs. They held, but it was unnerving to watch for a second.

Suddenly, Chew was all business. She picked up her bag, walked over to Anita and pushed her firmly in one thick shoulder with the sole of her boot. 'Roll over, bitch. No means no. Nobody ever told you that?'

She pushed again, harder this time. Anita bucked and rolled, collapsing across the axis of her own inertia and landing heavily on her back, wincing momentarily as her bulk began to crush her wrists. Her eyes were under control within a second: cold, blue and defiant. The dildo sprang up into the air, like Caligula's jack-in-the-box.

'No,' continued Chew, reaching into her bag. 'Don't suppose they did. Don't suppose you ever gave them a chance. Now, as I was about to say before you jumped me ...' She bent low and held out her warrant card. 'Sweet li'l Irene from the Court Hotel is in fact big bad Detective Constable Chew from the Homicide Squad, and I've got a few questions to ask you, dearie-sweetums.'

Anita's eyes clouded briefly, but then cleared, chilled as a mountain spring. With her chin she indicated towards me. 'And him?'

Chew stood upright again. '*That*, my girl, is a mentally ill man by the name of Joshua Ben Panther. He needs a lot of help. I very strongly advise you not to make him upset.'

Anita glared at me. Her message was, paradoxically, pointed and blunt: 'I know who you know.'

'Yes,' I agreed, 'but you should know who I *don't* know.'

That seemed to confuse her. I decided that was a good thing. It had confused me as well.

'Right then, Joe,' said Chew. 'I believe you have something to show us.'

CHAPTER 16

We hauled Anita to her feet and harried her to the study. She used her bulk and intransigence to make the journey as difficult as possible. Chew pushed from behind, one hand lifting the cuffs, the other cupped around the back of the neck. I pulled from the front, left hand grasping the nexus of the chest straps, right pulling on the dildo.

Chew commented that I showed the beginnings of a technique which, duly perfected, might win me many friends at the Court. I declined to respond.

We forced her down into the desk chair, Chew reworking the cuffs so that her arms were trapped behind the back. I threw on the first tape I'd seen, just to give Chew the idea. After a minute or two I stopped it, then replaced it with the car-driving tape, to give her the other idea. I watched the colour drain from her cheeks as the possibility of what we might find somewhere on the remaining cassettes rose in her mind.

'Jesus,' she said to herself.

'Research for my thesis,' Anita stated, calm.

'Back in a mo,' was my contribution, before I ducked out to the kitchen and grabbed four bottles of Red Bull.

Bringing them back to the office, I clanged them down noisily on the desk. I twisted the caps off two, handed one to Chew, kept the other.

'Can you believe it?' I asked. 'Not a drop of booze in the house. Plenty of these, though. Pity, eh? You know how I get on speed-drinks.'

She didn't, but played along. 'And you're bleeding already.' She pointed to the stigmata on my hands. 'There'll be no stopping you, will there?'

I rubbed the back of my neck, then my forehead, smearing blood across it. I made my voice contrite and helpless. 'I fear not.'

Chew shook her head, then bent low to Anita's ear, playing the same routine that she had first played with me.

'Kiss it better, Anita. Joe here, mad, is an ugly sight, you know. Nothing stops him once he gets started. Doesn't have to fear the law, you see. He goes off his head and damages you, he's so psycho it's the Mental Health Act he has to worry about, not the Criminal Code. Nothing I can do to control him, once he gets started. Look at him, Anita. He look like a man with nothing left to live for to you?'

I grimaced obligingly, thinking: neither of you knows the half of it. My voice was deep and resonant. 'The land is full of bloody crimes, and the city is full of violence.'

Chew again, her lips almost brushing Anita's skin. 'Which tapes, bitch? Quickly.'

Anita's expression was truculent and offended. 'Don't know what you're talking about.'

'Gina Compton, Belinda Jules, Nigel Ferris. Which tapes?'

'Gina was a dud fuck. Never heard of the others.' Eyes defiant.

Chew slapped her hard across the face. 'Didn't you even ask their *names*, you monster?'

I reached over, laid a calming hand on Chew's shoulder. When I withdrew it there was red on the whiteness of her tee-shirt. She didn't notice. I picked up a stack of the cassettes.

'Find yourself a piece of wall to lean against,' I said. 'Let us watch and be sober.'

It was a harrowing journey, even with liberal use of the fast-forward function. There were many more bondage scenes, grubby and ill-focussed. We found two more car-driving tapes. In each she seemed to be trying to perfect her technique, rehearse her scenario. Sometimes we turned the volume up. The bondage scenes usually revealed a sonic background of strangely appropriate music. I recognised Nine Inch Nails, Ministry, Wagner. The car tapes were calibrated only by the arid sound of controlled, committed breathing. The first fresh one we found contained more disconnected sequences of driving at night, turning, stopping, the door opening and closing. The same green sheen was present at the base. A shirt, I decided. In the second, the pink was visible again. She had tried it driving around in battle dress. The car and the vision slowed, the passenger window winding down. Big Lizzy the Troll appeared suddenly, fuzzy, resolving into her heavy-lidded, familiar self — working the beat at Brisbane Street, I assumed. She leaned in, giving Anita a goodly glimpse of leathery, freckled cleavage, her words distorted: 'Up for it?' Then the gradual change of expression on her face as she realised what she was looking at, what manner of punter she was addressing. Harsh instructions from the other side of the lens: 'Get in. I'll pay what you ask.' A hand appearing at the bottom of the screen, heading for the door handle, frame shaking. Big Lizzy backing away fast, palms up. 'No fucking way, fuck off ...' An angry and sudden cut to snow, snapping a swearword in half.

An hour, four cigarettes and two more Red Bulls later, we found another. This time she had got it down pat. No camera, no costume at the pick-up point. This could be assumed, because the tape opened with the focus firmly on small Berry, cowering against the inside of the passenger door of the moving car, mumbling and whimpering, incomprehensible and scared. The pink sheen was in shot. Anita must have stripped down to business after the pick-up, keeping her victim locked in. The child's cheeks were tear-stained.

Then the vision was through the windscreen, its fractured night-light images slurring like a drunkard's anecdote. Things were clear enough, however. The ghostly hulk of the abandoned Bedford van loomed in the bumping illumination of the headlights.

'Oh god,' whispered Chew to herself.

Anita said nothing. Her eyes were fixed on the screen, her face a mask.

There were no surprises in what followed. The tiny and intimidated teenager was pushed forward, roughly, between the van and the fence, the journey lit by a single travelling spotlight which must have been part of the camera. The space behind the van. The mewling and hysterical pleading. The fat hand thumping against the thin chest, pushing Berry back up against the fence. The harsh instruction not to move. The shaky attempt to fix a close-up on the wide-eyed, trembling and filthy face. The sudden distortion of terror, the silent terminal shock as the knife hit home.

Chew gagged.

'No longer than a toothpaste commercial,' I said into the silence.

Anita turned to look at me. Her eyes were full of hate.

Chew regarded her, then whipped her face away to mine, suddenly freaking. 'Get that fucking dick off her, Joe. Get it *off*. I can't bear to look at it. *Now*, Joe, get the fucking thing out of my sight.'

I did as I was bid, and knelt down behind the odoured bulk of the murderess. The dildo appeared to be held in place by means of leather straps which went around her waist and between her legs, buckling together just above her arse.

'I'm a student film-maker,' she said, deadpan.

'And, what?' Chew's voice sounded like gravel. 'Murder is art?'

Anita's response was a snort which turned into a cough. Her body jerked and quivered. My fingers lost hold of the buckle. My nose caught the odours of dried sweat and scorn.

'*Murder*,' she echoed, 'is politics. Filming it is art.'

Chew turned her head away. I looked at her from around the pale, doughy form of the dyke-beast. She seemed trapped, unsure where to put her gaze, eyes darting restless between the suspect and the screen. I regained a grip on the buckle and its strap, tugging it hard to try to release the pin. Anita made a guttural noise when the leather bit her skin. It was a noise like pleasure.

The sound tripped Chew's wire, big time. Slowly, she repositioned herself, turning so that she stood directly in front of Anita, feet apart, hands on hips, shoulders back. Then she bent smoothly from the waist, spine straight, until her face was right where she wanted it to be.

'Listen, bitch,' she growled. She was so close to Anita's nose she could have licked it had she wanted to. Whether it was the proximity or the intimidation I don't know, but something made the behemoth shunt herself suddenly backwards against the chair. The strap slipped from my fingers again.

'There's just you, me and the madman here,' Chew said, 'so nothing you say right now is going to end up anywhere. But know this: you're gone, slag, you're gone. Now, right at this point I don't give a fuck how you're intending to plead or what kind of psycho defence you intend to mount. Right now this is personal. Right now I want the answers to two questions.'

I caught hold of the strap and pulled again. The pin was proving stubborn. Anita arched her back in response, pulling against the cuffs. She moaned again.

'Question one,' said Chew. 'Why did you kill that girl?'

I gave the strap another go, twisting it against her skin in an effort to release it. As I did so, I heard her exhale. I leaned back on my knees and looked around. Chew's stare drilled into her face, but Anita was gazing directly at the rent in the detective's tight tee-shirt. She began to speak, voice quiet and breathy. She rocked her weight back and forth on the chair as she did so.

'I make student films. I'm a student of reality. Reality isn't and television is. I take the wretched and uplift them. I take beginners and make them stars. I put unsuspecting people on the spot and say, "Die, you're on candid camera". I make documentaries, slices of life, flies on the wall, warts and all. I reposition youth to serve more grown-up needs. I contain harsh language, violence, sex scenes and adult concepts. I am a multitude. I'm a late-night infomercial, call me now. I push the boundaries of expression. I defend free speech. I am an argument for censorship and a cry for civil liberties.'

I pulled hard at the strap, twisting it back against itself. The buckle pinched her skin, making it welt. She rocked faster, spoke louder.

'I'm an avenger, a vigilante, a hero to the poor. I'm a right-wing death squad. I'm the White Hand, the Red Brigade, the Black Death. I make adverts for products not yet invented. I make my choices and they make theirs. I appropriate. I collage. I montage. I simulate. I pastiche. I empty acts of meaning and fill them up anew. I hate little bitches and spotty boys who hit me. I love great art and reportage. I don't believe an artist can record without creating. I am both my subject and my object. I am genius unacknowledged. I am bold and I am beautiful. I'm just a girl who can't say no. I am a product of my time. I don't have to be wrong; I don't have to be right: I have only to be postmodern and sponsored ...'

It took a while, but I finally managed after several sharp tugs to loose the pin from its hole in the strap. The leather fell slack. I let go of it. 'All yours,' I said to Chew.

'I am out for justice,' continued Anita, her breathing now deep and repetitive. 'I am out for applause. I am a self-made woman and an icon to my sex. I am validated by my actions and I don't need your approval to affirm —'

Chew grabbed the dildo by its hideous shaft and pulled hard, ripping the straps and the buckles out from under Anita's thighs. I watched the tips of the leather and the point of the pin flick up from the impetus, and sting at her skin before scraping away beneath her.

Anita howled, perhaps in fury, perhaps in climax: 'I'm an *angel*!'

Then she slumped, gasping for breath, spent.

I stood up behind her, just as Chew landed the head of the dildo right into the side of her face. Anita's head rocked under the impact. I remembered the trussed-up woman in the first S&M home movie, and the look of shock and betrayal she had shown. I couldn't see Anita's face from where I was, but, judging by the unaltered mask of contempt on Chew's, I guessed she was being nowhere near as expressive.

'Second question,' said the detective, calm and standing upright again.

'Take the cuffs off me, babe.'

Chew ignored her. 'Why'd you kill my lover?'

I wondered if Anita knew who she meant, other than by the obvious process of elimination. I wondered whether Gina had lain with her head on a pillow in this very house and giggled as she confided that her girlfriend — one of them, anyway — was a cop. I wondered how Anita had reacted: was she even now fulfilling the fantasy the thought had engendered? I wondered whether Chew was imagining the betrayal.

'You going to give me an answer, bitch?'

Anita pulled against her cuffs, pushing her head towards Chew, looking up at her, chin jutting out. 'Yes,' she said.

The room was silent for a minute, the women locked in a staring contest.

Neither blinked.

'Well?' asked Chew.

'Suck my cock, ho,' replied Anita.

The detective turned away, cheeks colouring and arms trembling. 'Joe.' She sounded as if her tongue was coated in something viscous. 'Let's keep searching.'

The promise of a fine day was filtering through the room's single small window by the time we found the tape containing Nigel's death. I'd had no doubt it would turn up, which was the main reason I'd hung around, fighting off increasingly passionate cravings for beer, for whisky, for something other than Dunhills to smoke. It was marginally more sophisticated than the Berry tape. Anita was a fast learner, filmwise. This time there was an establishing shot. A brief exterior of the Noble Street house, at dusk it looked like. The cut to Nigel in the car, excited and frightened both, revealed night.

She had followed him home somehow, marked his house, then waited somewhere until conditions were right, like anthrax awakening to spring rain. Nigel had therefore probably been able to relate his extremely bad day before he went out into an even worse night. He had spoken of me, no doubt, and my questions. To whom did he speak? And who else got to hear?

There were only three tapes left. Chew sped through them, becoming increasingly agitated, incrementally less professional. The dildo was still in her hand, knuckles white against its blackness. At the conclusion of the last I announced that I was going for a pee and another Red Bull. I did neither. Instead, I walked through the kitchen, out the back door, down the side of the unit and into the world. As I made the circuit I heard the dull sound of thick rubber hitting flesh, and Chew shouting, furious and fearful both: 'Where is it? Where's Gina? Where's Gina's tape? I want to see Gina ...'

She weepeth sore in the night, and her tears are on her cheeks: among all her lovers she hath none to comfort her.

The house was silent when I arrived, with no one yet awake. I padded along the passage, entered my sanctuary, rolled up a joint and lay, staring at the ceiling, knowing nothing above. Sleep came with the roach still winking its final goodnight in the ashtray.

My slumber was black and still and featureless for once, surrendering me up to the melancholia of waking only when the sun was sagging like a wheezing geriatric, finished for the day. I lay still on first awakening, calculating the passage of the hours by the light, idly watching motes of dust spiralling in the thermals of the last few rays to bend through the window. Through the wall I could hear the unhurried clatter of dishes being stacked on the draining board: Mrs Warburton, making herself busy. No indication of other voices, other movement. I concluded that Yula and Nessie must be out, fulfilling their considerable work ethics.

Grabbing the remote from its spot on the floor, I switched on the little TV at the foot of the bed. While an asinine quiz show ground its unstimulating way to a conclusion, I rolled up a quick single-paper number and fired it. A coffee would have been nice, but then so would eternal salvation, divine forgiveness and the sleep of the just, and you can't have everything.

I *could* have a coffee, of course, coffee being both the product and cause of free will. But acquiring it would have meant movement, and I wasn't quite ready for that. Besides, I wanted to catch the evening news, coming up at the end of the quiz show.

Chew must have moved fast. Just how she had explained the manner in which she made her deductions, the bizarre fashion of her dress, or the semi-naked and bruised condition of the suspect were unknown to me. That she had, however, was obvious, since she was standing visible, wearing the awkward stand-by suit again, behind Hewson who appeared in the formal talk role on the story which topped the news bulletin.

'Police today made a breakthrough in the Northbridge serial murder case,' the newsreader announced, 'with the arrest of a suspect in West Perth early this morning. Anita Ellen Shadbolt, twenty-nine, is tonight in custody after being charged with the knife murders of Belinda Jules, fourteen, and Nigel Ferris, twenty. Police sources also admitted that Shadbolt, a university researcher, is the prime suspect in the murder of Gina Louise Compton, the first body found. Officer in charge of the investigation, Detective Senior Sergeant Ian Hewson, said the breakthrough came when ...'

My attention began to wander. I'd heard all I needed to hear. I wondered if Hewson or Chew would try to get back in contact. Neither, surely, would be stupid enough to try to take a statement from me, given that the testimony of a man of my standing was very unlikely to be considered credible in a court of law — an irony which had long ceased to amuse me.

I heard a knock at the front door. I also heard Mrs Warburton swear to herself, put something down on the draining board, and begin a long, slow walk up the corridor to answer it.

It was possible that Hewson would try to follow through on his threats to either turn me or turn me in, now that he had no need to frame me. The thought wasn't too disturbing. He would be busy for days now with Anita, collating the evidence discovered so far, and directing the hunt for something to tie her to the first killing. By the time he got around to picking up where he left off, I would be gone.

I could hear Mrs Warburton clomping back down the corridor.

And Chew? Well, a visit from her to thank me for all my help would have been nice, but I figured that was about as likely as the Archangel Gabriel descending to open a dry-cleaning store. It was odds-on, though, that I was no longer the target of her academic ambitions. Anita Shadbolt would make a far more fascinating case study, and one in which she could legitimately claim a vested interest. Also, the big bull dyke was hardly going to be in a position to piss off halfway through the research.

Besides, Chew was no dumb bunny. She would know damn well that I was in possession of a lovely snapshot of her in a very compromising position with a giant, naked, gay killer wearing a strap-on appendage and not much else. The precise circumstances of its composition were not important. What *was* important, from her point of view, was that no one else in the police force ever got to see it. I was pretty sure she could foresee the exact circumstances in which such a regrettable revelation might come to pass.

I exhaled a plume of smoke from the joint with greater than usual satisfaction. For once, I felt in front of the game.

Mrs Warburton knocked on my door. 'Visitor, you got. That fat bitch.'

'Tell her to come in, would you, please?'

Her tut sounded like a rib cracking. 'Not your servant, I'm not. Anyway, already told her that. Says she won't enter the house, she won't.' Her voice began to fade as she drifted back to the kitchen. 'Stuck-up hussy, you ask me ...'

With a weariness that hadn't been apparent a minute before, I rolled off the bed, stood up and made a token effort at straightening the clothes I had now been wearing for two days. As I walked down the passage I could see her at the open front door: a bulbous silhouette, ripe, standing strong with her feet slightly apart and her hands on her hips. I swear, I could almost hear the beating of two hearts, and beneath the sweet reassurance of her own breath, the guarded growl of something which knew what lay ahead and was determined to best it.

In my last two steps, I feared for her.

She met my gaze like it was a tax demand. 'I suppose you'll want your money now.'

There was neither warmth nor gratitude in her voice. My inadvertent endangerment of her foetus had scarred our friendship in a way that heroin never could. Days ago, perhaps, she would have been silently sorry to see me go. Now, she couldn't wait to be shot of me.

'What do you mean?' I asked.

Her scowl was immediate. 'Oh, don't piss about, Joe. It's all over the news. Been all over the radio and the wire service web sites since lunch. Anita's been arrested for the murders. Can't say that surprises me, looking back at it now. There's been no mention of your name anywhere, of course, but that's hardly unusual. I asked you to find out who killed Gina and now you've done that, so I've come to pay you, as arranged.'

I made to speak. She held up a hand, stern.

'No, Joe. Don't talk. We're through talking. You nearly killed my son. Even if you didn't have anything to do with Anita's arrest, I still want to give you money. You're too unstable, Joe. It's all got to you — your beliefs, the booze, the drugs. I used to think you were one of a kind, but now I reckon you're just another psychotic who should probably be locked up. I don't want you around: for my sake, for Ayzel's, for the child's.'

She reached into the pocket of the Thai fishing pants that were tied loosely around the swollen promise of her belly, pulling out a folded cheque and pen. 'You got a figure in mind or do you trust me?' she asked.

I looked for a moment and thought. I thought about taking the cheque — made out to cash, of course — and being on a plane within twenty-four hours. Darwin sounded like a good idea. I'd heard there were some people there who, given the right incentive, could supply a nice-looking passport and even a passage out on a container ship. Like the mystery of the Kabbala, all I needed to do was say a number and I was free. I didn't, however. Perhaps it was from a neurotic desire to finish things, or some vestigial sense of justice, but I doubted so. Perhaps it was from a lingering wish to do something for the son I would never see, and who would never even know of my existence. Perhaps. I didn't want to analyse things much. I didn't want to have to face the question: Am I doing this because I love he who is yet to come? Or because I fear him? Or perhaps it was simply because I was hanging for a coffee, a shower and several large Jamesons, not necessarily in that order, and that my disordered mind was trapped in a synaptic gridlock until the lights started working again.

Whatever the reason, invited now to speak, I did so. 'Put that away, Lazarette. I haven't earned it yet.'

'I said I don't care about that. The crisis is over and it's time for you to —'

'Anita didn't kill Gina.'

That stopped her. For a second. 'But the news is saying *she* —'

'She's been charged with the murder of Berry off the Square, and Nigel — he was the guy who attacked you, by the way.'

The news produced no whit of reaction in a pair of eyes softened by pregnancy and love, but only after being fired flint-hard in the kiln of her previous life.

'Which means —' she began.

I decided I didn't have the time. I needed coffee. 'Which means I haven't earned your money yet.'

'But —'

'You'll hear from me.'

I closed the door in her face, turned and headed for the bathroom.

Caffeined up, cleansed and clothed, I was seated in the kitchen by the time I heard a key in the front door and the awkward tangle of feet and wheels entering. Mrs Warburton, in the front room staring at the television, greeted Yula and Nessie with uncharacteristic enthusiasm, inviting the younger to shunt the older over to her for matters of hygiene and gossip.

'Your grandchildren, Nessie, how are they?' I heard her ask.

'Profitable,' came the creaking reply. 'I have profitable grandchildren.'

Her multitude of years, I mused, had at last brought her wisdom.

Yula's footsteps down the corridor were light and quick. Her face, when she looked around the edge of the door, was radiant and flushed with confidence.

'Come in,' I said.

She entered with a stride firm enough to demonstrate her new spirit, yet diffident still to show me I remained the boss. She was no longer wearing my Smashing Pumpkins tee-shirt. Instead, she sported a purple and red top featuring the Japanese pictograms currently fashionable in the clubs, above a pair of bright blue cargo pants and chunky lace-up shoes. The sunglasses she held in her hand looked like Ray-Bans. Everything looked new.

So few days before, her wretchedness had been boundless. Now her age was clearer than the noonday; she shone forth, she was as the morning.

'Good day at the office?' I asked.

She laughed like a mountain spring, reached into the baggy knee-pocket of her pants and pulled out a neat wad of notes. She handed them over, giving me a daughter's peck on the cheek as she did so. 'Your cut for today,' she chirped. 'I put yesterday's in the stash hole, seeing you weren't around. Hey, is it true they've caught the bastard who killed Berry?'

I confirmed. 'Bastardess, though.'

Her eyebrows scaled her forehead. For all her rapid adjustment, she still had much to learn. 'A *woman*?'

'Yep. Homicide isn't gender specific.'

'Guess not.' She sat down at the table, brushed one young hand through her hair. 'I'm glad someone got caught. I hadn't known Berry for long, you know. It's awful what happened to her and I miss her sometimes, I *do*, but ... '

She ground to silence, looking as if she were about to admit to heresy. I used my eyes to say: proceed.

'But ... well, it all seems so long ago, Joe. I know it wasn't, only a few days, but it feels like it was a *lifetime*. Me then and me now, well.' She grasped the hem of her top in the fingers of each hand, pinkies extended, tipped her head as if she was curtsying. Suddenly she looked very young and gawky. 'Whoever I was last week, Joe, I'm not now.'

No, I thought. Last week you were a juvenile prostitute. Now you're a juvenile drug dealer. It was definite progress, of a sort. I try to rescue those who are being taken away to death, even if I can't hold back those who are stumbling to the slaughter.

'You've adapted well,' I said.

She made a theatrical shiver. 'The thing that gets me is that I almost got into that car, took that punter. Only reason I didn't, really, was because I was talking to you. Jesus, you saved my life, Joe.'

I lowered my eyes, mock-penitent. 'An accident. It won't happen again.'

She pealed with laughter, shaking her head, blushing slightly. 'You're such a *dag*,' she said, grinning. Then, suddenly, all business. 'OK, I'd better make sure Nessie's done bowel stuff. I want to do another run before she falls asleep for the night and it really slows things up if she has to take a crap while we're out. Tried to take her into a pub for a pee yesterday and they wouldn't let me in. Reckoned I was too young.'

I smiled with her. 'Youth is relative.'

'Not one of *my* relatives, Joe.' She stood up and started walking back down the passage. 'Can't wait to get rid of it. Roll on adulthood, I say.'

Perhaps she was right. Eternal youth would get terribly frustrating after a time. Not too mention costly, all that Clearasil.

Not that I would know, of course. Eternal early middle age, though. I'm a full bottle on that one.

CHAPTER 17

Who can number the sand of the sea, and the drops of rain, and the days of eternity? Not I, not I, my children. I have found it best over the centuries to try not to contemplate immensity, and to regard infinity as the deathly form of life: there, inevitable, but far too depressing to consider. In the wilful denial of forever can the peace of the moment be found.

Or perhaps not. Perhaps such comfort is but a mirror, smoked and frosted by fire and wind. Perhaps in the sacrifice of evanescence lies the glimpse of judgement: the point where time and matter coalesce into singularity, and I am at an end precisely because I never began.

And perhaps my mind is prey to phantoms bred of lack of food, abundant booze, caffeine, dope and enough speedy stuff to fuel a university philosophy exam.

After Yula and Nessie left for their mid-evening delivery run, I waited half an hour before heading outside myself. In part I did so because I didn't want Yula to think I was following her, in some way keeping an eye. Contrary to what you may have heard, I do not watch over the world. In part, too, I did it because I knew that at some point soon I would have to confront unpleasant matters, and that the first step that night onto the pavement outside might set the train of poor providence in motion.

Yet most of the reason I delayed was because I just couldn't seem to get my shit together to stand up. So long had it been since food of any real description had come my way that my stomach felt clenched and repentant, like a cave-dwelling hermit in a winter squall. Food seemed like a temptation, a barrier to the purity of the mystery faith set up and worshipped in my mind by the congregation of intoxicants there assembled.

I knew the nature of the spirit that moved within me, and was not afraid because it wasn't the first time it had happened. I knew, though, that if metabolic apostasy was not to cast me low beyond rescue, I had to take the sacrament of souvlaki fast. Weak at the knees and befuddled of vision, after all, I would be useful to no one. Right then, as always, I heard a billion voices whispered in request, a cacophony of obligation falling upon my ears. Time was, so long ago, that I would have cried tormented at the thought of such piety and pity going unrewarded. Time was, back at the start, I dreamt of nothing more than the just alleviation of the suffering of my brethren through the intercession of my absent dad.

So many ages have passed since then, so many people slain in the name of the cross of me.

And still my father reveals not his mystery, nor even his name to his long-forgotten son. I hear your voices. I do. I hear your prayers in the night, your muttered pleas, your frantic, single bargain: spare me this pain, and I will give you my love so tender. Ask not what you want of me, but rather what I want of you: your silence; your disregard; your longed for, impossible disproof.

The earth swayed beneath my feet. The firmament was hostile. I made it, however, out of the door and into a night long and full of tossing till the dawn.

I turned the corner and walked along William Street, heading for the Plaka on James. The road heaved and sighed as knots of cars united by the traffic lights cruised by and passed ahead. Some turned here or there into Northbridge back roads. The rest continued on, over the bridge, into the chasms of the city just beyond. The lights of skyscrapers seemed to erupt like molten fountains, setting hard in a moment, thrusting towards heaven as if salvation could be won by nothing more than money and phallic likeness. Better by far, I thought, the buildings around me: low and old and modest, lit by the lights of passion and sex. Show me the mighty temple and the neon-lit lap-dancing club. Ask me into which I would rather enter to spread my impotent love and you will know the answer in your heart. Some things never change.

There were people on the sidewalks, of course. They spilled from the restaurants, sated, perhaps, or full and baying now for the later delights of the nightclubs. They stood in undecided groups, looking askance as the poor and the homeless pushed past with eyes on the ground, minds on vacation. Some sat outside the cafes, chatting, smoking, holding forth, while others stalked in fleshly lust with eyes like hunters and the instincts of prey.

And in amongst them, I noticed, my flock, its numbers growing thanks to the evangelist Yula and the miracle of Nessie's clutch purse. Every few yards I saw the faithful: sitting hunch-kneed against shop fronts, heavy-lidded and dull; arguing, slurred and hoarse with celibate lovers; waiting gaunt in dark places; leaning back in banged-up cars, blood like dew on their soft-flesh arms; standing, swaying, lost; eyes closed on benches, arms folded to puff out biceps, all camouflage and gesture; walking backwards in front of well-dressed couples, begging bus fare, grinning, cadaverous; lying alone in derelict gardens, wondering sad where it all went wrong.

Come to me my children, take the sacrament from my disciples.

By the time I turned into James Street, past the pungent temptation of the Brass Monkey, cigarettes had banished hunger once again. I knew in my head that sustenance was craved, but my heart was full of the wonder of creation, my eyes bedazzled by the demons which sprang unbidden from the coloured lights and flashes. They were, I could feel, all around me in the air, lithe bodies wrapped in cloaks of neon gas, brushing past my face, these incubi and succubi, rubbing smooth and willing devil-breasts across my cheek, dabbing the sweat from my brow in flirtatious flight, whispering adoration.

I knew them to be there, my demons, but bade them quiet. No others could see them. My cover was holding. I opened my eyes and beheld a vision. As one, all the diners and the clubbers and red-light johnnies faded in the air, wavering a moment before passing to invisibility, leaving only a street full of those in the thrall of my gifts. As far as I could see, bathed and blessed in the pink and blue signs flashing LIVE GIRLS, LIVE GIRLS, LIVE GIRLS, sat, stood and swayed the congregation, the multitude.

Oh, I thought to myself, how fast the message spreads, how great the love I give. As one then, it seemed to me, did they turn to regard their saviour. As one did they manage a sloppy grin of greeting, a head-bob of respect. And then, as one, as one and all, did their voices unite (though their lips did not move) into the devoted chorus and chant of the blessèd and forgiven: *Chasin', chasin', chasin'* ...

'I-iiiifff *you* were the only boy in the worl', nnn I-iiii ws th'only girrr ... ah, fuck it.'

I looked around at the sound of this discordant voice and beheld a dead man walking in defiance of my will. From out of the rancid alleyway between the pub and a throbbing nightclub lurched Kennedy. He was dressed as before in his single frayed black suit, although now it was coated and caked with foulness. He walked with his knees bent, his arms held out to facilitate at least a little balance. In his right hand he grasped a half-empty bottle of rot-gut port, the mark of which was plainly visible crusted in the corners of his mouth. His face was covered in stubble, interspersed with angry cuts where he might have tried to shave. His skin looked dry and flaky, his eyes framed in wet black shadows, the pupils wide, the whites cracked by capillaries.

He didn't see me as he swayed from his resting place and straight into the middle of the road. There he looked up at the vertiginous heights of the night sky, howled, and executed a clumsy, staggering pirouette, arms wide, bottle at a dangerous angle.

'Mooooooonnn rivahh,' he bayed, 'wider than a mile, I'm crossin' you in style, some —'

A car right behind him sounded an impatient horn blast. Kennedy spun at the sound, almost toppling over. Then he bent from the waist towards the windscreen and hoisted his bottle aloft for emphasis.

'Fug you,' he announced, suddenly formal. 'Fug you, sir. I ... say ... *fug* ... you, *pal*!'

With an imprecation muffled by prudently sealed windows, the driver steered the vehicle around the wavering drunk and drove off with an offended roar of acceleration. Kennedy watched it go, a momentary look of confusion on his face. Then he seemed to remember something.

'And fug your mother, too, basser!' he yelled, before his decaying equilibrium bade him lurch sideways and complete his journey across the road. There he collided with me, standing, watching, entertaining demons and regarding my flock.

'Kennedy,' I said.

'Ohgoodjesusfuckmedead,' he exclaimed, without a trace of trepidation. 'You're fuggin' *alive*. Drink?'

I took the proffered bottle and upended it into my mouth. There was a furry deposit around the glass, but it revolted me not. These lips have kissed the sores of the plague. A pisshead's port doesn't rate.

I handed it back. He grabbed it like a babe offered a teat, swallowed, then took a step back, grinning with yellow teeth. 'As I live an' fuggin' *breathe*, it's Joe Panther. The fuggin' man himself.'

'Meaning?'

'Meaning, my son, it's a fuggin' *miracle*.' He threw his arms up to the sky, lost his balance, and had to concentrate a moment before he recovered it. '*That's* what it is: a fuggin', genuine, real gone *miracle*. Fuggin' dead bloke. Gone. *Foof*! Here he is. Talkin' to him.'

I tried to stare him into servility. It used to be easy, but his eyes refused to focus long enough to get the message. 'Is there something you want to tell me?' I asked.

He guffawed at that, then made hacking noises in the back of his throat. 'I'll tell you — *you*, that is, no one else — a story, yeah?'

'I'm all ears.'

305

He swayed a bit, trying to remember something. Then he took a big pull on his bottle, followed by a deep breath.

'I bow to you,' he announced, nearly toppling over in the attempt. 'I *bow* to you, Joe Panther: my wossit, my rescuer-thing-buddy, my fuggin' bloody *saviour*. Bow to you. I had a dream, you see ...'

'A dream?'

'Full on fuggin' *dream*, son, and guess what? You were in it. You — cop this — you fuggin' came to me *in my dream*, Joe Panther. How good is that?'

'Kennedy —'

'No bullshit, Joe. There I was, asleep ... or maybe *dreamin'* I was asleep, you know? Asleep, anyway. And you come up in my dream and — guess what — I was fuggin' *terrified* of you, I don't mind sayin'. Terrified. In the dream, yunnerstan. And you came to me and, you know, you reached your hands out to me and took my hands and took them and — clear as fuggin' day, it was — you ... where was I?'

'I took your hands.'

He clapped me heavily on the shoulder. I forbore punching him.

'Fuggin' *right* you did, Joe Panther. Here: you took my arms and you poured *your fuggin' blood inna me*. There. Foof. Blood. From you. To me. All your fuggin' blood. Fuggin' amazin'.'

'Then what happened?'

'You *died*, son. That was what was so great. You *died* for Kennedy, mate. You took all my, you know, *sins*, and washed them away with your blood. You fuggin', what you call it, *resolved* me ... That it? Resolved, absolved? Dissolved? ... Whatever. You fuggin' did that in my dream and then you died and took my sins away.'

'And you survived.'

The insides of his eyelids were red and inflamed when he opened them wide.

'Sur*vived*? I was fuggin' *reborn*, son. Born a-fuggin-gain! Look at me, man! Before, I was fuggin' scared of everything. Not now. Now I know no fuggin' fear!' He roared, then, until the coughing stopped him. 'I am one big bad fuggin' *mother*fugger and I owe it all to you, Joe Panther.'

I inclined my head in a show of modesty. It seemed the most sensible thing to do at the time. 'You're too kind.'

His weathered, filthy face suddenly changed from inane congratulatory grin to furious scowl.

'Fug off,' he snapped. 'Wasn't *really* you. You think it was really fuggin' *you*, y'basser? Was a fuggin' *dream*. Nothin' a do with you at all.'

'How do you know, Kennedy?'

He threw his arms out in dramatic display, nearly punching a passing parking inspector in the process. His tone turned dogmatic.

'Cos if it was *really* fuggin' you, you'd be fuggin' *dead*, wooncha? Or there'd be some kind of *sign*, some fuggin' great hole in you where your blood come out into me. Look.' With much difficulty, he rolled up one grubby sleeve to reveal an angry bruise and scab on the underside of his forearm. 'See? Like that. There'd be a fuggin' *mark* on you if it was *really* you, but it wasn't, see? Was a dream. *Foof*. Sleep. Dream. Born again.'

'Like this?' I asked, and calmly held out to him my hands, palms upwards. On each, swollen and red, was the stigmata caused by Anita Shadbolt's shoulder spikes.

'Reach hither thy finger,' I said, 'and behold my hands.

Yet a little while, and the world seeth me no more; but ye see me: because I live, ye shall live also.'

And he did, leaning in looking very perplexed, gently prodding my palm with a single cracked and black-nailed finger. His eyebrows danced a can-can before he looked up at me again. Our eyes met just for a second before his slid away like a paraplegic on a snow slope.

'Well, *fug* me,' he exclaimed, then shook his head in bewilderment.

'Do you doubt?' I asked.

He attempted dignity, failing miserably. 'I do *not* doubt ...' His eyes rolled to the heavens as he tried to collect his thoughts. He sighed, shrugged, swigged deep from his bottle. '...that this is all far too fuggin' weird for *me,* pal.'

And then he turned and staggered away, weaving through the invisible innocents and the crouching chorus of my flock, singing Celine Dion's theme song from *Titanic*.

I watched him go, feeling nothing whatsoever. If a man die, shall he live again? Or is it simply that life hath no more dominion over him?

Perhaps I might have considered such matters at length over a beer or a whisky. Perhaps I might have skinned a number and let my mind go awander into themes and variations. Perhaps, too, I might have remembered to eat.

Perhaps. But it was not to be.

Kennedy had just staggered far enough away to be lost to sight — and hence to thought — when I became aware of something huge and cold and smooth beside me. I turned, more curious than concerned. A large, dark Bentley had stopped next to me, purring like a lion, seeking whom it may devour. Its windows were mirrors, darkly.

The front passenger door was pushed open. I looked into the void. Behind the steering wheel sat Clem Porter. In his hand was a mean-looking pistol, pointed straight at my belly.

'Get in,' he said.

I was not afraid. I did as I was bid.

Inside, the vehicle smelled of cigar smoke and expensive furniture polish.

'Look at the floor,' he commanded.

I did so.

Then did divine light spring from my mind, exploding in a fountain of red forgiveness, pulled around the naked body of an angel, who cast cloth aside, took my head in her arms, pressed my face between the perfumed breasts of dreaming and bade me sleep so still.

CHAPTER 18

I am in the thick darkness, but God is nowhere to be found. It is silent down here, but I know that I am neither alone nor serene. Here, then a moment, somewhere, I sense turbulence above. Behind, perhaps. Pain. Yes, there is pain. It swells and it breathes. It watches me and waits, patient.

And I am nowhere that I know. Somewhere in this blackness — flickering now, dry lightning across the horizons of my sleep — there is noise. There is, what, a dull roar. Traffic perhaps, far away.

And what language does the traffic speak? The lightning flashes prompt long-forgotten words, phrases, muddles of syllables. I am in Rome again, and I am hearing the chant: *agapé, agapé, agapé* ... A man in a white tunic is saying to me slowly, praise God and eat the meat with gladness and singleness of heart. He is talking to me in a Greek long not spoken, and he uses the names for love. Yet I do not hear his Hellenism, but rather see it, flashing bright and blinding, scant echoes of memories recalled, perhaps, or the ragged cues of wishes unfulfilled. There is an alphabet chaotic in my head. I used to know it once, so long ago.

And now I am aware of myself. I am self-aware. I am sat,

slouched, my left elbow hard upon the wooden arm of an upright chair. Is this Passover, and am I a patriarch? Must I teach my son the orthodoxy? (And do I recall? Did I really as a child sit at table opposite Joseph, exchanging the calls and responses of the Haggadah, sipping kosher wine and tasting bitter herbs? Does the tip of my tongue flinch in recollection, or is that too a sentiment invented in my darkness, a mere and random function of some neural attempt at context?)

The light is brighter now. There is a phrase in Greek before me, its individual shapes familiar some, strange others, its meaning a holy mystery. I see it now before me, black against white. Here: hold my hand and pray with me, let my vision be before you. Here. My gift. My mystery:

$$\Delta x \, \Delta p > h/4\pi.$$

A half-word, a half-phrase, of two natures, neither one nor the other, like a man and a god, a messiah and a water-cracker. With thick lips glued by dried saliva, made arid by the long departure of alcohol, I attempt to speak its name out loud and tame it.

'Duxduphup ...' I try again, just the first half, certainties only: 'Dud.'

'A word, Mr Panther, that in the idiom of New Zealand could be construed to mean the absence or end of life. But then again, unnecessary, since the words "New Zealand" already signify same.'

I recognised the voice, and with its entry into my mind, context and history began to form. Memory resumed its chronography: I had witnessed the obeisance of the flock, then the resurrection of Kennedy. Then Clem Porter had pulled up in his big Bentley, pointed a gun at me and — this thought began to filter now — cracked me on the back of the head with it and rendered me unconscious.

And with that revelation the pain began afresh, deep and throbbing at the top of my neck, amplifying the boom of the bloodflow through my brain. Reflexively, I lifted my hand to rub my wound. Interesting, I thought: I do not appear to be restrained. Hand touched swollen flesh.

'*Jesus*!' I snapped.

'So you tell yourself, I've heard.'

The sound of his voice again prompted sense to triumph over sensitivity. I ceased exploring my injury, and concentrated instead on opening my eyes. Of course they had been fluttering. That must have been what gave him his cue to speak. And through their intermittent function I must have perceived and played with the Greek letters which were facing me. I forced my eyes to open and focus, and there they were: black on white, neatly printed inside a large framed expanse upon a smooth and plastered wall.

The wall glowed golden in sunlight refracted. Between it and me was a substantial oval wooden dining table, lustrous in its veneer. Opposite me, arranged elegantly in an antique high-backed dining chair, was Clem Porter, eyes alight, snub-nosed handgun pointed straight at me.

'Good afternoon,' he said, all business. 'The name of God, the chemical formula for sodium chlorate, the equation for Heisenberg's Uncertainty Principle. Some things were simply not designed to be pronounced.'

Thinking now, I knew of what he spoke, but my face was evidently not up to the task of signalling so. Before I could ask my first question, he warmed to his subject, left hand expressive and waving, right hand motionless, triggered, aimed.

'The form is ancient, of course. You can trace it back to Diophantus in the third century. He really got things rolling with solutions to indeterminate problems. It's good, don't you think, to attempt to solve the indeterminate? The best result, I think, is not to answer the paradox, but to find a way to accommodate it elegantly. Then we can move forward unconfounded and unconstrained.'

'I'm thirsty.'

I might not have spoken. Perhaps I didn't.

'Diophantus wrote a book called *Arithmetica*,' he continued. 'Interesting, actually, but not an indication of divine providence, that hundreds of years after Diophantus another mathematician called Fermat scribbled an equation of his own in the margins of a copy. It became known as Fermat's Last Theorem, and for centuries was supposed to have no solution. Do you know Fermat's Last Theorem, Mr Panther?'

I tried to dry him with a glare, but my eyes failed to obey the command.

'Probably not, I'd imagine. Superstition and folklore are more your line than the precision of numbers, I would think. It doesn't matter. What does matter is that a couple of years ago a solution was found. Fermat's Last Theorem overnight ceased to be one of the great mysteries and took its place alongside the billions of banalities in the world. That's what I like about a godless universe, Mr Panther: we may not be its masters, but nothing can stay hidden forever. Nothing is inexplicable.'

'You finished?'

He stood up and fastidiously adjusted his black suit, stroking out the briefest of rumples. Where last time I had seen him he was wearing a hat, now his pate was uncovered. His hair was perfectly combed, but greying and going bald from the crown. It made him look, for all his puffery, frail and diminished. His expression flashed momentarily offended, then became suffused with the serenity of power. He who holds the weapon is calm; to the victim accords the madness. And to the fool goes the prediction of which will triumph.

'This,' he said, indicating the frame on the wall, 'is the equation for Heisenberg's Uncertainty Principle, which states —'

It was time to stake a territory, especially since I'd already come across the subject in conversations past, and the mists had finally faded from my thoughts. 'That you can have position, or momentum, but never both.'

Porter nodded, half-mocking. 'A crude explanation, perhaps, but serviceable. Well done, Mr Panther, you surprise me, even if you did fail to mention that strictly speaking the equation relates only to observations of subatomic particles. You, however, interpreted it as metaphor, and that's just fine. It's as metaphor that it's very useful. It's the basis of my teaching, you know.' He chuckled, then. 'Tell me, Mr Panther, what's the basis of *your* teaching?'

'Pedagogues suck.'

Anger crossed his face, his patience clearly and suddenly at an end. In five rapid strides he was around the table and upon me. He came from the side, and jabbed the cold barrel of the gun hard into my left cheek. Its perfume of oil filled my nose like frankincense.

'Listen, Panther,' he growled, 'last week I didn't know who the *fuck* you were and I cared even less. Now you're a real big pain in my behind. For reasons known to yourself, you've decided to make my life hell. For reasons of your own pathetic delusions, you've decided to invade my life and that of my students. For reasons of your own mental illness, you've run around making wild allegations, implicating me and my students in a crime as horrible as murder.'

He pressed hard to emphasise his point. His mouth was so close to my head I could feel the spray of his fury moistening my ears.

'*Murder*, you mad shit, *murder*,' he continued. 'How *dare* you? You beat up my student, you tortured him. I thought you killed him, but evidently you didn't. It makes no difference: you still *destroyed* that boy. Now I've got two other students in the lockup — innocent and scared, held on some pettifogging charge designed to make them inform on me — police aiming to get right up my colon if they can find out where I am: homicide detectives, Fraud Squad, too, I hear. No doubt the Tax Department will be following behind. Thanks to you, I'm about to be the party boy at the bottom of a clusterfuck.'

He took a deep breath. The gun barrel was shuddering against me. I said nothing as it slowly came to a halt. He again took a breath.

'What the hell have I ever done to you, Joe Panther? What the hell stupid paranoid psychotic agenda are you working from? Well, you know something? I don't give a shit. This life is over. If I stay here, then tomorrow, the next day, whatever, the police will find me and they'll be crawling all over me and the party's up forever. I had a good, grand operation going here, and I never ever imagined it could all get blown apart by some ragged little loony off the street. But you know what, Joe Panther? It doesn't matter any more. Thanks to you, I'm out of here tonight, way way away, never to be heard from again. It's all over, and I am at peace with fate and *still* in control of my future. There's only one question still to be answered. Actually, two. Is vengeance justified? And should I shoot you?'

The barrel was making my gums hurt, my cheek already rendered numb. My voice sounded like someone else's. Yea, for I am a vessel through which love pours forth. 'Your questions are rhetorical. Like this one: did you kill Gina Compton?'

His reply was an ice-whisper. 'I did not kill Gina.'

'I know.'

'Well, now you can go to your grave knowing it, because I think I *am* going to kill *you*.'

Why must I be so often tempted by these promises unfulfilled? 'You can't,' I replied.

His laugh was stillborn. 'Of course I can. Tomorrow I cease to exist. I become someone else: false name, false address, new city. The police will be looking for Clem Porter for murders suspected and confirmed, for who knows what else, but they won't find him. I've got more than enough money stashed to make it happen.'

'I've seen your accounts. You're laundering a fair wash, but not riches beyond imagining.'

He tutted in my ear. 'You've seen some Transpersonal figures, that's all. You think just that bought this place? I'm fastidious about my laundry, Panther. Casinos, the NASDAQ index, self-improvement courses, online share trading — wherever there's a scam, I've got a piece of it.'

I tried to move my head aside, the better to speak, but he wouldn't let me. I decided it was time to hit this man with the truth, and the madness which must follow. There is no love in the gift of my understanding.

'You misinterpreted me, anyway,' I said. 'You can't kill me. I cannot be killed. I do not die. Just sleep awhile.'

He was silent for a moment, trying to reason out the preposterous. And then he laughed afresh, rich and hearty. The barrel moved fractionally away from my face.

'Of course,' he grinned. 'Silly of me. I forgot for a second. It's true. You think you're Jesus Christ, the undead saviour of the smackheads. Stupid of me not to remember.'

I half-closed my eyes. 'It's not something I like to spread around.'

The barrel jabbed hard back into place. I thought I heard a tooth crack against bone.

'You stupid shit,' he hissed. 'There *is* no god and there never was a Jesus, just lots of people who thought they could repeal the laws of physics. You're just another in a long line of fools, Panther. You're not Jesus. You know who you're like? Who you could be? Yes!' He seemed to be having some kind of epiphany. 'Yes! You're Simon Magus. Brilliant! Of course.'

He pulled the barrel away from my cheek and inserted it instead in my neck, just beneath my jaw, pointing upwards.

'Stand up, Simon Magus,' he sneered. 'Stand up and look around. We're going to play a game.'

With no option but to defer to his will in the matter, I did as I was told. Upright, I experienced a brief vertigo attack. Evidently I had been down and out for a while.

Indicating his wishes only with his chin and eyes, Porter bade me remain on one spot and circle around. I was in a spacious, sunlit room, furnished in expensive, understated good taste. The sliding window, which had been behind me, was tall and wide, revealing the tops of apartment buildings across the street. I could hear the ebb and flow of many vehicles rising up from below. Outside the window was a minuscule balcony, perhaps ten feet wide by three feet deep.

Still keeping the gun aimed at me, Porter edged past and slid open the glass. Immediately the traffic noises built to an industrial-strength hum. The in-rush of air was warm and wet and sluggish.

'You're wondering where you are,' assumed Porter, extending an arm as a host to a guest. 'Come. Look outside. You're at the top end of the city. You're in my apartment, nine storeys up. St Georges Terrace, below, has three lanes of traffic going in either direction and very narrow footpaths. You might commit suicide.'

Cautiously, I leant out of the window, fighting back a resurgence of dizziness. He spoke the truth. At least up until the last bit.

'Hey,' I remarked, 'I can see my house from up here.'

'It's all about choice,' he said, smiling now, content in his power. 'Your choice is this: you can let me shoot you — your body lying around is of no consequence to me, given I'll be gone — or you can step off that balcony and prove to me you're the messiah. Let me watch you, Joe Panther. Let me watch the angels descend and lift you unto heaven.'

I stared back at him, saying nothing. It is a bad move to tempt the Son of God. The prudent shall keep silent, for it is an evil time.

'Or maybe you'll turn out to be another poor Simon,' he taunted, enjoying himself. 'Splat, Joe Panther. Maybe your faith will sustain you on the way down. Maybe you'll be plummeting past the windows of the ground floor, just two feet to go, still thinking to yourself, "Well, nothing has happened so far to make doubt that I'm the living Christ". Do you remember Simon Magus?' Then he laughed and slapped me on the shoulder. 'No, let me guess. You were *there*!'

I wasn't, of course, because Magus never existed. His

story does, though, and that's all that matters. Stories cause far more damage than individuals ever can, by orders of magnitude. I gave him the basics, partly to save myself the grief of listening to him tell it himself, and partly to buy some time to think of an escape.

'Simon Magus,' I began, 'was reputed to be the prime Gnostic leader in Egypt. Paul hated Peter. Peter hated Simon Magus. Paul and Peter teamed up in alliance, the better to hate Simon Magus, who claimed to be the manifestation of God.'

'Ah,' said Porter, 'the terrible fates of the heretics.'

'Heretic, my arse. He was a rival leader of a rival sect. If things had worked out for him, it would have been his image reproduced and worshipped a billion times since then. He got to Rome, Peter and Pauly in hot pursuit, and laid it out before Nero.'

'Good judge of character, that man.'

'Simon conjured up dogs and set them against Peter, who, of course, smote them.'

'How?'

Some questions in theology simply aren't important. 'How do I know? With his trusty smoter, I suppose. Then Simon decided to bugger off, claiming he was going to ascend to heaven.'

'Now we're getting to it.'

And so we were. 'So Nero had a tower built in the Campus Martius. Simon jumps off the top of it and starts flying up to daddy. Then Peter, in my name, commands the angels of Satan to let go of the guy and, whee, thump, there's Gnostic smeared all over the parade ground.'

Porter blinked once, slowly, then languidly indicated the balcony with his gun. 'So have a bit of faith in yourself, Joe Panther. Jump. Do that and if the angels hold you up I swear right now I'll rewrite the Transpersonal Foundation leaflets and chuck old Heisenberg here right down the shit chute. Because, buddy, I call hanging in midair above a main road with no visible means of support a pretty good demonstration of having momentum and position simultaneously.'

No one knew where I was. No one would even think me missing for a couple of days, at least. Perhaps only Yula would be upset when my absence was finally noticed, and even then, given her powers of recovery, not for long. People spend their whole lives waiting for me to arrive, then never notice when I leave.

Except, of course, that I never leave, not in any real sense. It didn't matter whether my eyes closed because of a bullet in my heart, or because the last thing that went through my mind was a six-lane highway. Either way, three days of darkness and absent slumber, and then the intense disappointment of waking, bruised, scabbed but healing, would unveil itself all over again.

Porter seemed to read my mind.

'Oh, you'll die, really, Panther. You can count on it. Of course the angels won't save you. There *are* no angels. Multiple fractures and pulped internal organs from the fall, or a rib cage ripped apart by my bullets. Either way, after that, there'll be an autopsy. They'll remove your brain, they'll crack wide your ribs, slice you open down as far as your little holy willy and pull out all your entrails. If it would make you feel any better, I'll make sure the police or your nominated representative receives a postal order for funds to cover your cremation. Gutless ashes, Panther. There is an end that stays finished.'

I turned away from him, took a step out onto the balcony and looked down. The height perspective made the road seem very narrow, just as the Campus must have looked very small to Simon. Like him, I was not afraid, but that was where the similarity ended. Simon was not afraid because he was deluded. And fictional. I was not afraid because I am the abandoned Son of God, trapped in unwanted immortality.

A bus roared past down below. Then another.

I am. Eyer Asher Eyer. I am the offspring of the divine. I am of His seed and nature, and the laws of gravity do not apply to He who framed them.

But then I thought: perhaps I should jump, just on the off-chance. Perhaps this time it might work. Perhaps there is a limit to infinity and resurrection. Perhaps this time I would die and stay dead. After all, is it right to give up hope after successive disappointment?

Should I exchange my current position for a short burst of momentum? Should I journey hard towards a subatomic heaven where it all, finally, comes to an end? If I could rot, then I would be transformed into myriad molecules and atoms, taken up by the clouds and scattered wide across the globe for all eternity. Little bits of Jesus, bobbing around minutely in the atmospheric gloop. Then I could really get up the Pope's nose.

I looked down again. Then turned back, resting gently against the low barrier.

'Did you write the Transpersonal Foundation leaflets yourself?' I asked.

Porter chuckled, and sat himself in the chair I had vacated, turning it around first so he could face me.

'Of course not. I bought them. They came with the package. The Heisenberg poster, too. It was supposed to be a teaching aid, part of the branding, but I rather preferred it as a piece of interior design. The Transpersonal Foundation is a franchise operation, just like any other. Only instead of selling fast food, it sells slow realisation.'

'The realisation of what?'

'Twofold.' His smile was beatific. 'First, that there is no greater consciousness in the universe than ours, and second, that there is little to be gained by belonging to the Transpersonal Foundation. That's the slow bit.'

'Gina Compton worked it out pretty quickly.'

He shook his head. 'Quite the contrary. Poor Gina worked out that there were potentially very great benefits to being a member. Of course, though, she had the advantage of inside information.'

'Your laundry accounts?'

'In conjunction with the floor safe I put in at Noble Street, yes.'

This was news to me. Somehow I was willing to bet that it would still be news to Hewson, too, no matter how hard a time he had given the boys.

'And what's in this safe?'

Porter was silent a moment, in thought. When he spoke, his tone was calm, even gentle. 'I suppose I can tell you, since you're not going to be around to tell anyone else now. It's probably good for me, isn't it? Confession is supposed to be good for the soul.'

'Shit-house for your lawyer, though.'

He nodded acknowledgement of my wisdom, then continued. 'Ecstasy. Several thousand tabs at any given time, usually. The boys thought they were antibiotics for the poor and sick of Mozambique.'

'And just why would you be asking them to store — I assume you asked them?'

'Asked, told, whatever.'

'Whatever. Why did they think you wanted to store antibiotics for sick Africans in their share-house?'

'Because,' he said, 'I'll show you.'

His aim with the gun was less precise by this time. He had relaxed, imagining himself to be in total control, and just waved it vaguely in my direction as he walked across the room to a sideboard at one end. From inside one of its drawers he withdrew a sheaf of full-colour leaflets and tossed them on the table.

'There,' he said. 'It was perfect. The Transpersonal Foundation franchise includes this international aid plan called, what is it, Life Force. The aim is to help unfortunate Third World people and make them pathetically grateful and indebted. It's the worst kind of cultural imperialism, of course, but an excellent cover.'

I picked up his meaning pretty quickly. I've occupied a few missionary positions myself over the years.

'So you stashed the so-called antibiotics at the house and hid them because ... why? No, let me guess: you told the boys and Gina that the pills were vital life-savers, but not cleared by the Australian regulatory authorities, so they were therefore technically illegal to possess over here — hence the need for secrecy.'

Porter nodded in appreciation. 'These, having not the law, are a law unto themselves. That's Paul, of course. Mate of yours.'

'No he wasn't.'

He shrugged. 'Whatever. Maybe it's a pity we didn't meet in better circumstances, Panther. We think rather similarly. You could have come to work for me.'

I shook my head. 'Gina came to work for you and look where that got her.'

His cheeks coloured. 'I didn't kill her. Neither did I order her killing.'

'But she wasn't fooled by the antibiotics story.'

Fast as mercury, a smile. 'She'd had less of a cloistered life than the others. She twigged pretty quickly that antibiotics don't come with little smiley faces on them. The boys, though, never doubted. For all their materialism they are simple souls. If you tell people persuasively enough what to believe then, hey, they believe it, because it is safer to do that than to work out an alternative line of reasoning. Thus has it ever been. You should try it sometime. You might be rather good at it.'

'Been there, done that,' I retorted, affecting boredom.

I put my hand in my jacket pocket. Instantly his right arm stiffened, gun straight at me, trigger knuckle white. Slowly I pulled my hand back out, holding the Dunhill packet. I winked. He relaxed again, embarrassed by his nervousness. I put a cigarette to my lips, and lit it, never taking my eyes off him. My thought: he's nowhere near as in control as he's trying to project. For all his bullets, he's spooked.

The Lord knows. The Lord knows all your quiet frailties.

'So she tried to shake you down.'

His agreement showed no trace of bitterness, nor triumph. 'Once she started helping out at the office — here, actually — and twigged to the two sets of books, yes. She said she'd go to the papers, the police or whatever.'

'Unless you paid her off.'

He shook his head. 'I called her bluff for a while. I'm not a stupid man, Panther. The tabs arrived monthly at the house inside plastic bags in padded envelopes. The bags and the envelopes were print-free. There was no return address.

The boys — and at first Gina — unpacked the envelopes and stashed the plastic bags by hand into the safe. I always picked up stock from there for distribution when no one was home — you're not the only person who can pick a lock, you know — so there were never any witnesses to, nor records of, my involvement.'

I got it. 'So their prints were all over the stuff. If Gina had dobbed you in, she would have only succeeded in implicating herself and her housemates. Nothing led back to you. She realised that and kept quiet. That's why I'd bet Iain and Adam haven't told the cops anything, either.'

'If you can't save them, involve them. Who is more truly blessed with understanding: the innocent or the culpable? You're a smart man, Panther. Pity you have to die. About time for you to commit suicide, isn't it?'

I looked over my shoulder at the chasm behind me. I felt a sudden, intoxicating desire to fly. Perhaps it was time, after all.

Not, however, before I had finished my Dunhill. Some things remain sacred even at the hour of death.

'So why were you in Gina's flat that night?'

Again, the laugh. 'Talk about poor timing. I had no idea she was dead. Poor sad Nigel's lovelorn efforts to get her back in the fold had manifestly failed, and I realised that enough stock had probably moved since she'd left the house such that her fingerprints were no longer on anything. I felt vulnerable, so I decided to try to find the accounting copies she'd told me she was holding as evidence.'

'In the middle of the night?'

'A good time to burgle, I think you'd agree. I knew it was her birthday. I have all her membership details, remember. Anyway, I figured she would have worked out the timing issue herself as well. I guessed she'd be out celebrating somewhere. And if she wasn't, I figured it best to have the element of surprise.'

'Because you thought she might have been expecting a visit from you.'

He nodded.

Hence the pestle, ready to hand. I smiled sweetly. 'Instead, I was your welcoming committee. And now the copies are in the hands of the Homicide Squad.'

His grimace in return was venomous. 'The very same.' He held the gun before him once more. 'Now jump, cunt.'

I ignored the weapon, but turned to face the air nevertheless. It was decision time. I was not afraid. There was nothing for me to fear save repetition. The gun option might be painful for a while. When I was shot dead by an LA gang-banger who mistook me for a rival, I bled for two hours before silence claimed me. Jumping off the balcony would be quicker, even taking travel time into account.

Where would I awake? Inside a refrigerated compartment at the morgue? Flat on a steel table with a bone-doctor's hand inside me? Or somewhere else again, some silent force having intervened to remove me from the banalities of corpse examination? Perhaps I would wake up back inside the tomb, the rock rolled away. That shock again: the first dull flickerings of thought and light, the dream realisation that the journey long and hard is finally at an end, the flexing of the fingers in anticipation. Then the sudden joyous springing open of the eyes as the mind is flooded with the certainty of meeting my father and claiming my reward in the hereafter. Looking up: seeing only a shadowed curve of rock, some pale lichen, and hearing, somewhere, the irritable squeak of an insomniac bat.

The air cracked and rattled as a courier on a motorcycle accelerated along the road, dodging between cars.

I do not remember my successive awakenings. I must blank them out. They can't be very pleasant.

Hands on the rail, I leant over the edge until I could feel blood gathering in my forehead. Nine storeys. I once read that the human body has its average height and average skull thickness because life is a balancing act. If we were any taller, we'd fall over too often and crack our skulls. If our skulls were any thicker, they'd be too heavy for our bodies and we'd still fall over. Some say that's the elegant beauty of evolution. I say it's my father's sick sense of humour. Either way, was there a method of reckoning whether a nine-storey fall would be sufficient to smash my head apart enough to forestall resurrection?

No angels would come. Of course no angels would come. You'd need private angel insurance for that, and mine was well in arrears. I didn't even have a Medicare card. I hoisted my weight up onto my hands, bringing myself to tiptoe. Then I took a deep breath. I put my feet on the ground again and turned.

Clem Porter was still pointing the gun at me.

'Tell me,' I said, 'how do you reconcile teaching people to take control of their own lives and then selling ecstasy?'

He pealed with laughter. 'Because,' he said, when he could speak again, 'teaching people to take control of their own lives is tautology in action. It's oxymoronic. As a species, we're a bunch of arrogant fucks. And we have to be! It is our arrogance which leads us to imagine ourselves implicit in the universe. We have to imagine that, Panther. It's an inevitable by-product of self-awareness. Without ego, self-awareness would be terrifying. Imagine the fear of knowing yourself alone and unique in creation!'

'I do.'

'Bullshit you do. Your egocentrism is more pathological even than most. My work, Panther, whether motivational or biochemical, is to occupy the ego, to help others develop the necessary defences of conceit and certainty. You might disapprove of my methods, but I hardly think you'd fail to see their usefulness.'

I nodded, as if convinced by his sagacity. And perhaps I was. Perhaps I heard a reflection of me, saw my echo in a balding black-suit dandy with a handgun.

He took a step forward. 'And now, Joe Panther, much as I've enjoyed our chat, the shadows are getting longer against the buildings and evening will fall rather soon. I have many things to do tonight and little time in which to do them. Your manner of death is still your choice, of course, but I'm afraid I'm going to have to pressure you a bit. I'm going to count to ten, and if you're still standing on that balcony when I finish, then I'm going to have to shoot you.'

I nodded once more, silent. I had made my decision and my truth was not for sharing. It is only right that matters of death are, wherever possible, left in the hands of those set to die. Blessed are the dying, because they don't give a fuck any more.

We stared at each other, unblinking.

'Have you ever staged your own disappearance before?'

'One,' he said.

'Fingerprints,' I replied.

'Two.'

'Property lease.'

'Three.'

'Car registration, driver's licence.'

'Four.'

'Franchise documents, tax returns.'

'Five.'

'Accident insurance, fire and theft, home and contents.'

'Six.'

'Scared young men desperate to clear their names.'

'Seven.'

'Cops who know too much.'

'Eight.'

'Fake passports, bank accounts, airport alert lists.'

'Nine.'

'Have you considered the advantages of dying yourself?'

'Ten.'

A moment passed. He blinked.

'Want me to show you how?'

'Come inside.'

Clem Porter forsook his position for momentum, and confounded the observers.

The fire in the building that night was a terrible conflagration. The place reeked of petroleum, and accelerant-aided arson was a natural conclusion for the Fire Brigade and later the cops to draw. So strong and widespread was the blaze that the entire apartment was destroyed. It was all the Fire Brigade could do to save the rest of the property, the evacuation of which only added to the chaos.

The body they found in the dining room was charred beyond recognition, although it was widely assumed to be that of the long-term tenant, Clement Ashley Porter, businessman and professional motivator. Speculation in the immediate wake of the discovery centred predictably on murder or suicide.

I watched the footage on the morning television news, sitting on my single bed, sucking on a much-needed joint and chopping up a line of speed. It had been a sleepless night, one way and another, with little prospect of decent rest foreseeable. I thought of Clem Porter's prophecy: there was much left to do, and little time left to do it in.

It might well be days, though, before anybody willing to speak to a police officer noticed that Dropper was missing.

It hadn't been difficult to lure him into the city on the promise of a free score. He had been greedily and silently calculating the pawn value of Clem Porter's furnishings when I slipped the overloaded fit inside his waiting, open, moist and receptive vein. His eyes had closed in seconds.

At the end of the world: the angels shall come forth, and sever the wicked from among the just, and shall cast them into the furnace of fire.

CHAPTER 19

Laz glared at me like hardened steel and said nothing.

My boots slapped hollow against the floorboards of Sappho's Sisters as I walked the distance from the front door to the battered armchair opposite the one in which she sat. Her posture was slouched and swollen; her demeanour resentful and sullen. She did not smile when I took my seat. She didn't even blink.

We were in the main room of the centre. It looked and felt violated. There was no point trying for privacy in Laz's cramped office. Her tiny sanctuary had been gutted, unspared by the team of uniformed and plain-clothes cops which had descended in the wake of Anita Shadbolt's arrest. Every computer in the building had been impounded on suspicion that somewhere on a Sappho's Sisters hard drive lay further evidence of violent sexual assault, pornography, corroborating evidence in the murders of Berry and Nigel, not to mention any information on suspected racketeer Clem Porter, recently deceased, probable new suspect in the Gina Compton case. All books, files and folders had also been collected, just to be sure.

The activist women had fled, shocked and distressed. The landlord had moved to secure eviction. MURDERS LINKED TO LESBIAN GROUP, the newspaper screamed. Laz sat alone in a temple destroyed, her belly ripe and wide with portent.

'This is all your doing,' she whispered, flat.

I shook my head, lit a cigarette.

'*Don't*!' she snapped.

I dropped it onto the floor and ground it out beneath my boot. It was not an act of consideration, but mercy. It was the least of her troubles, and the most I could help with.

I like to help. I help where I can.

My cooperation seemed to relax her slightly.

'Ayzel didn't want me to come in here today,' she said, just a bit more flesh in her voice. 'She said there wasn't any point. This place is finished, she said. I said she was right.'

'But you came, anyway.'

She looked down at her hands, resting on the fruit of her future. 'I told her I had to say goodbye to an old friend.'

A silence blossomed then, thin and uncertain of itself. She broke it after a few seconds, busily fussing, reaching inside her pocket, pulling out the crumpled cheque.

'Got a figure in mind yet?'

I shook my head.

'You'll just have to trust me, then.'

The intake of my breath was like a martyr seeing his stake for the first time. 'That's not what I mean, Laz.'

She hissed in irritation, and threw the cheque to the ground like a petulant child. 'What *now*, for fuck's sake, Joe? Are you trying to stay around? Is that what all this bullshit is about? You haven't decided to do the it's-my-son-after-all routine and run round claiming paternal rights as if you had some god-given claim on my child, have you?

332

Because if that's what you're up to, pal, then you'd just better change your —'

Whether it was the sight of my head slowly shaking or the glow of the melancholy embers I felt burning behind my eyes which silenced her I don't know. Whatever, something worked.

I stared pointedly at her belly, spoke sombre to its cargo. 'I go the way of all the earth: be thou strong therefore, and show thyself a man.' Then I looked up and into her eyes. 'I don't want your money or your child. Your money is no good.'

And your child may damn the earth, I could have added, but didn't.

Her patience was not without limit. 'Then what the fuck is all this about, Joe? First you tell me that bitch Anita didn't kill Gina. Okay, I accept that. I spoke to one of the investigating officers — an Eileen Chew —'

'Irene. It means peace of God.'

She spoke over the top of me. 'She told me the theory was that Gina's death spurred Anita, who was already barking mad and right on the edge, to kill that child Berry. Obviously whoever killed Gina was supposed to take the blame for that one, too. Only Anita didn't know that Gina had been hotshot because it wasn't in the paper. Then she killed that guy —'

'Nigel.'

'— out of revenge or justice or some such noble crap because he attacked her. Some psychotic excuse to do it all over again, whatever. She was getting her own back or something.'

'That's about the size of it,' I agreed.

'So then you find out that Gina's killer must have been the cult guy.'

'Clem Porter.'

'And he burnt to death. Come on, Joe, don't shit me. A huge fire? Arson? Joe Panther makes hell. It's got you written all over it.'

I acknowledged her conclusions, as far as they went. 'But Clem Porter didn't kill Gina, either. Maybe, eventually, he might have done, because she was getting to be a danger to him, but somebody beat him to it.'

Her eyes turned to slits. She was way past moral judgements, concerned now only with practicalities. 'So why'd you kill him?'

'Because we thus judge, that if one died for all, then were all dead.'

'Blah blah fucking Bible blah,' she whined, mocking. 'What is it you're not telling me about that fire, Joe?'

I shrugged. 'What I'm not telling you.'

'Jesus ...' She was not addressing me.

'But know that Clem Porter did not kill Gina Compton.'

The graze on her cheek flushed momentarily dark with irritation. The effort of levering herself out of her chair further burnished its colour. Her body rocked from side to side as she stomped, puffing slightly, over to the table holding the urn and the instant coffee, pretty much the only office equipment left around.

'So what are you saying?' she demanded, her back towards me, chiming a teaspoon against the rim of a cracked mug. 'The fucking tooth fairy killed my friend? It was all an alien probe gone tragically wrong? Or is it that you just don't fucking know, and all this ...' She paused, sniffed, recovered. 'All this destruction, this waste and violence, all these endings have all been for bloody nothing?'

I have lived through centuries of violence enacted all for bloody nothing. I have spent millennia not fucking knowing.

As I looked at the burdened shoulders of the only person alive who meant anything to me, the friend I was delimiting, I would have given everything to have exchanged the mysteries of my life for the single shred of certainty I held.

I would have thrown in my lot and followed God if God had called. I would have left it all for Him to sort out. But he did not call. My father wasn't there to save me, bathed in gentle light. Perhaps he never had been, not even at the start.

Anyway, I have nothing left to swap for forgiveness. Except maybe Patti Smith's *Horses* album — but there is a limit to sacrifice, even in the hope of salvation.

Laz picked up her mug, then turned to face me. She rested her bulk against the table, which creaked slightly under her weight. She sighed, then took a tentative sip of the brew, recoiling at the heat. She hadn't offered me one. I was glad. Instant coffee always tastes foul, even at the best of times. At that moment, it would have been undrinkable.

She exhaled, long and slow.

'You know, Joe,' she began, not looking at me, 'when I was in detox, about halfway through, when I first thought that maybe, just maybe, it wasn't a pointless exercise, I came to the opinion that life would be fine if I could just give up the junk for good.'

I gave an appropriate grunt.

'Then, at the end of detox, when I really thought I had a chance, I decided that things would be good if I stayed off the junk by getting the hell out of Melbourne.'

Another grunt. She didn't hear it.

'So I did, and things were better. Then I figured things would be better still if I got myself some training, got some skills and a job. Then I figured what I really needed to finally get the junk out of my head was a good stable relationship. It wasn't easy, that, Joe. It wasn't easy to love. It wasn't easy to stay loving. It still isn't, sometimes. And it was bloody really hard to accept that I was loved in return.'

'But you got there.'

'But I got there. I got all of that. I got more than I might ever have dared to hope for. I got things I never knew existed. And then I pushed it and thought, what the hey, life would *really* have turned full circle if I could have a child, if I could bring up a child loved by two people who love each other. So now I'm doing that, too.'

She took a deliberately large gulp from her mug and winced. The pain she inflicted on herself, I guessed, was intentional.

'But you know what, Joe?'

'What?'

'I still feel like a junkie.'

I considered this for a moment. 'Any preference on gender? Gift-wrapped? Home delivery or pick up?'

'Very funny.' She fiddled with her fringe, then walked back to her chair, cradling the coffee. I held the mug for her while she lowered herself, then handed it back. She stared at me for several seconds, not speaking, her face a mask.

Eventually it came. 'This is the last time I'll ever see you, isn't it, Joe Panther?'

I nodded. 'Sad?'

She forced a smile. 'Relieved, more like.'

It sounded like she only half meant it, though. Her ambivalence was warranted, although not perhaps in the way she imagined. This time there would be no chance of us ever meeting up again. At least, as long as she chose to remain in Perth. There is, after all, only so long a messiah can remain in the wilderness.

'You can never forget a junkie's life, can you?' I asked. It sounded lame.

She shook her head, and leant forward, elbows struggling to rest comfortably on her knees.

'You can't afford to,' she said. 'The price of freedom is eternal vigilance. That what the soldiers say, isn't it? Same thing, kind of. It never goes away, and you can never make your peace with it. Once you're out of the life, you have to spend so much time guarding the secret of it. You can't let anybody know, never mention it to a stranger, no matter how drunk or stoned or lonely you get.'

She fell silent then, looking at the floor. I wondered if I was supposed to say something. I was searching for a suitably open-ended inanity when she started again.

'And you've got to be on your guard all the time. There's always something, somewhere, to remind you. I see a fit in the street, I remember. I see a distilled-water bottle, I remember. A razor blade, I remember. Cottonwool. Even a teaspoon'll do it sometimes. Out of nowhere. And you know, Joe, you know what I remember?'

The love I gave you, I thought to myself.

'I remember it as *good*. Isn't that a bastard? I don't remember how it nearly killed me, how I got hep, the things I did to get money, the things I stole, the people I hurt, the friends who just fucking died. I just remember the *rush*. I remember the oblivion and the smoothed-out world without loud noises or sudden movements.'

She shuddered. 'And then the demons start ... Why am I telling you all of this?'

'Because you'll never see me again.'

She accepted the explanation. 'The demons. I find myself thinking: *just a taste*. Just one. Do no harm. Then I scold

337

myself: *no more hitting up, you junkie bitch.* So the demon sings another song: *smoke it* . . . just a couple of grains in a joint, what harm could that do? *Snort it.* Have I been goody-goody drug-free since detox, Joe? Of course not. I've had a line of speed here and there, an E at a dance party, you know, but never . . . never so far . . .'

'Is your strength the strength of stones? I forgive you.'

Her mug was empty. She put it on the floor, scowling. 'I don't need your forgiveness, Joe Panther. I never did.'

'Just Ayzel's.'

Her chest rose, as if she was about to rebuke me for impertinence. Then she sighed once more and relaxed. 'Yes, just Ayzel's. Ayzel's been fantastic. Without her, Joe, I don't think I'd have made it. I really don't. She's been an exception to the rule — that rule about never mentioning your junkie past. I've told her everything: all the bad things I've done, the depths I've been to, all the gory nameless details. I've told her because she wants to listen. She forgives me, Joe. She loves me.'

I crossed my legs and fought back a sudden vicious urge to light a cigarette.

'She cleanses you,' I suggested.

'Meaning?'

'She acts like your confessor. She absolves you of what you think of as your sins, by mining through your deepest pain and combing out the tangles in your history.'

She managed a genuine smile this time. 'You make her sound like a hairdresser.'

'A poor choice of image. Sorry. A priest might be a better comparison.'

'Maybe. She'd maybe like that.'

I gave way, just a bit, pulled a smoke from the packet and

put it in my mouth. I acknowledged her glare, made no move to light.

'Confessors listen well,' I said. 'Priests know more about adultery than adulterers. Vicars know more about theft than thieves.'

'So?'

'And drug counsellors know more about smack than junkies.'

A coldness crept into the room at that point. I could almost see it wrapping itself around Laz, hugging her to its chill, hinting that should it so choose it could squeeze her hard and make her gasp raw for every breath. She seemed to feel something, too, involuntarily folding her arms. She tried to glare at me, but it looked more like confusion.

'Meaning?'

Meaning we were down to the meat of it. It was my turn to stand up, not for any practical reason, but to avoid her eyes, if even for a moment. I walked slowly away from her, and pretended to study a poster tacked to the wall. THE BEST MAN FOR THE JOB IS USUALLY A WOMAN, it said. It didn't help.

'How serious was your affair with Gina Compton?' I asked.

No reply came from behind me. I felt the sharp, uneven fingernail of an incubus scrape up my spine, heard its sarcastic chuckle in my ear, felt its rancid breath against the back of my neck. It made me shiver, just once.

When I turned around, Laz was staring at me. Her pupils looked dilated. Her fingers were intertwined.

'How did you find out?' Her voice sounded like something was slowly crushing her throat.

I made no move to return to my chair. 'You just told me.'

'But ... but you asked. You already thought.'

339

'You did a decade with a needle in your arm, Laz. Compassion needs a reason to survive that. I saw your eyes when you thought I was about to kill the boy Nigel. I saw your eyes when you looked at Anita, when you looked at Nessie. I've seen you regarding that Siobhan woman — she's a police informer, by the way — and when you glance at other people in the pub, in the coffee shop, in the street. At its core, the flame that burns inside you is still ice-blue.'

She tried for a late defence. 'None of which means —'

'You were really upset when Gina went missing. You searched me out, hunted me down. All that stuff about how you were afraid it was a homicidal homophobe was just so much polish. You wanted to do everything you could to make sure as much as possible got done. So you threw me into it as well as the cops, because I can get to places and people they can't. You don't do that for a woman you hardly know.'

I thought she might cry, but her eyes were as dry as a salt lake. 'So I cared about someone. Sue me.'

'Gina Compton was a physical woman. Whether she was insecure or just enjoying her liberation, I don't know, but she put it about a bit.'

Laz made to interrupt. I shook my head, slowly, never taking my eyes off her. Her objection died in the womb of her mouth.

'She slept with Anita Shadbolt at least once.'

Laz grimaced. 'When?'

'Like infidelity is time-dependent. I don't know when. She was having an affair with Irene Chew —'

'The *cop*?'

'Uh-huh. She knew she was a cop, too. Broke it off when she discovered there was more to Clem Porter's business than met the eye. Saw a chance for a big score, I think.'

'She never mentioned anything to me.' Laz realised what she had said, then squeezed her face with her hand, pushing her cheeks and forcing her mouth open, as if rebuking herself. 'I mean ...'

I walked back across the room, closing the space between us. Then I sat down again, and patted her gently on the knee. She pulled her leg away as if I'd burnt it.

'Was it serious, you and her?'

She didn't reply for a moment or two. When she did, she begged the question, her voice full of dread. 'Ayzel will leave me if she finds out.'

'Laz ...'

'Oh fuck, Joe, I got *drunk* one night, okay? And you know I don't really drink any more, so it didn't take much. Ayzel was at a family dinner and I'd said I didn't want to go. We'd had words about it. I love my partner, Joe, but her parents drive me up the wall. It's nothing personal with them — it's just a parent thing, do you understand?'

I signalled that I did.

'Some of us went down to the Court Hotel after closing up here. I got drunk, I got silly, I got *stupid*, yes?'

'But you still got home from Gina's flat before Ayzel got back from her dinner?'

'Uh-huh.'

'You got away with it?'

'*Yes*, Joe. Don't pry.'

I pried. 'So you did it again.'

The breath through her lips made them sound like an outboard motor. 'Maybe I'm not quite as ready to settle down as I keep telling myself. Maybe marriage and motherhood are just ways to avoid going backwards. I don't know. Is the root of belief in intention or action?'

I shrugged. Whatever its genesis, belief is a dangerous concept best avoided.

'It was *fun*, Joe. That's the shame and the pity of it. It was fun. Ayzel's wonderful and fills my life like sunshine, but ... oh hell ... sometimes she can be so *straight*, you know what I mean? She's a pious person, soft and gentle, full of rectitude. Sometimes I wanted to feel like a *whore*, you know? There's some dirt that never washes off your heart. Maybe it never should.'

For what it was worth, I would have forgiven her, but I doubted she needed my absolution.

'So, what? Furtive afternoons? Hurried early evenings?'

She confirmed. 'There's Ayzel, standing patient in a church somewhere, rainbow sash on, quietly demanding communion in a noble, you know, protest. Meanwhile, I've got the thighs of a woman ten years her junior wrapped around my ears. Oh *Jesus*, I'm a slut ...'

She wept for the next quarter hour. I lit my Dunhill and smoked it to the filter. She was in no mind to object. Finally, she made gulping and sniffing noises, wiped her nose on the back of her hand, and looked up at me again. When she spoke, her voice was like a strand of spider web.

'I'd better tell her, hadn't I? Get it over with. Take the chance.'

I kept my face immobile. 'Best you take the key to the flat off your keyring first, perhaps.'

The suggestion both flustered and revivified her. 'Of course,' she said quickly, leaning her body sideways and struggling to get her hand around and down into her pocket. 'Good thinking, Joe. Thanks. No point taking the risk. No point making it worse than it is. Wouldn't be a good idea to ...'

Her voice trailed away. She was holding her keyring in front of her face, fingering each key, looking for the right one. She went through the modest collection three times. At the conclusion of the third, her face was as pale as a virgin martyr drowned.

'Joe,' she said, in a voice subject to collapse.

'Laz.'

'The key's missing.'

'I thought it might be.'

This time, for the first and only time, Laz let me in through the front door of her house. We had walked the short distance from Sappho's Sisters — closed behind us and locked, probably for good — in silence. She declined the offer of my crooked arm to lean on, so I walked beside her, lending amoral support instead.

Ayzel, she explained glumly on the way, was on deadline to complete a big report for the engineering firm which employed her. For the sake of efficiency, she had opted to work from home for the day. When writing she preferred to avoid interruptions.

It was a tactic which on this occasion was doomed to fail.

'Come in,' said Laz, bidding me follow her through the door. 'I'm home!' she called out, affecting a casual tone which her face belied.

She pointed through to the lounge room. 'I'll go and get her from the study.'

As she walked slowly along the passage, her footsteps sounded much heavier than usual. Hers was no longer the tread of a woman weighed down with the bursting vitality of new life, but the defeated trudge of the aristocrat to the tumbrel, or the gnostic brought before the Inquisitor.

I went and sat down in a leather-cracked recliner-rocker. It smelled of stability and firmness and old money. I closed my eyes.

Soon it would be over. Soon I would be gone. Soon would judgement come.

Same as it ever was.

I heard two sets of footsteps enter the room, and opened my eyes again. Laz was leading Ayzel, holding her lover's hand in both of hers. Her face was a kaleidoscope: she kept looking up at Ayzel's eyes, then away, then back, showing adoration, pity, sympathy, concern. Each expression was a variation on the theme of fear.

Ayzel, for her part, towered like a rock upon which to build a church. Even at home, even in casual wear, she came across as noble and dignified. She was perhaps six inches taller than Laz, and would have been much heavier in build, too, were not Laz distended and stretched by her condition. The older woman wore a rather severe dark brown skirt to just below her knees, a white collared shirt buttoned to the neck, and a dark green cardigan. Pinned to the wool was a tiny silver crucifix, an even smaller model of me dangling on arms as thin as filament from the crossbar. She smiled a wary greeting towards me, no more than well-taught politeness dictated.

'Lazarette, dear,' she said softly, but loud enough for me to hear, 'your tramp friend is sitting in my armchair.'

Laz's face flooded with heat and blood, but she controlled herself, just. She patted Ayzel's hand. 'He's got some questions to ask you.' She struggled with the next bit. 'If you love me, then please answer them.'

Ayzel looked confused, and wary. I stood up and indicated silently that she should take her favourite chair. She nodded a curt thanks. As she walked past me she gave my face a good hard stare.

'Have we ever met before, Mr, ah . . . '

'Panther,' reminded Laz.

'Quite. Have we?'

I shook my head.

'Odd,' continued Ayzel, sitting herself with well-learned grace in her chair. 'You look familiar.'

'Perhaps you've seen my father. I'm told there's a resemblance.'

'And who is your father?'

'No one important. Mind if I smoke?'

'Please don't. Lazarette is pregnant, and they make the house smell so.'

I sat on the sofa. Laz struggled down beside me. She stared relentlessly at the carpet, as if it might rise and attack if she let attention waver for even a second.

I decided not to waste time. Torture was never really my style. Not when there was nothing to be gained by it, anyway.

'The night Gina Compton went missing,' I began, addressing Ayzel, 'you and Laz and some of Laz's colleagues from Sappho's Sisters were set to meet her at the Court Hotel, yes?'

Ayzel was sitting with her knees together and her hands resting in her lap, just like a well-bred lady should. Her eyes were as black as winter crows. 'Why is this any of —'

'Please, Ayz.' Laz's voice was soft, like a child's.

The older woman looked at the younger. A gentle smile flicked the corners of her mouth. Then she looked back at me, face set hard. 'Yes, then. And?'

'You didn't meet Laz at the centre. You met her at the pub, a little bit later.'

A curt nod. 'I went straight from work. So?'

'And when Gina was noticed to be late, you phoned her at her flat.'

'Tried to, yes.'

'From the public phone in the Court?'

'Lazarette supplied me with the number. I volunteered because it was my turn to go to the bar anyway.'

I decided it was time to crank things up a bit. 'You already had the number. You never made the call.'

She affected immediate indignation. 'How *dare* you call me a liar! Of *course* I made a call to Gina Compton's number and I'm sure that can be proved. I spoke to the answering machine. No doubt the police have it in their possession.'

I stared at her, right in her eyes. We neither spoke nor blinked. Laz gave out a gentle moan.

'No doubt they do,' I said at last. 'And I've listened to your message on that answering machine.'

She blinked. 'But how did *you* —'

Laz, sounding dead: 'Ayzel, *please* . . .'

Me, killing her: 'You left a message, all right, word perfect. But in silence. There was no music in the background.'

'I don't —'

'If you had phoned from the Court, like you told Laz and the others when you returned with the drinks, then there would have been music on the tape. It's so loud where that phone is you can hardly hear yourself talk.'

'This is ridiculous! What right have you got to —'

Laz began to sob.

'So you phoned sometime beforehand,' I continued. My voice was even. I derived no pleasure from my work. 'You did that to set up an alibi. You knew Gina wasn't in the flat, because she would still have been at Sappho's Sisters that early. You knew she wouldn't turn up at the pub, didn't you?' I switched focus. 'What time did she leave, Laz?'

Her answer made her sound half-asleep, almost as if she was on the nod. ''Bout four, maybe. She went home to change.'

Ayzel's face looked as if she was witnessing massacre. The muscles of her jaw were rigid. She seemed to be trying to say something, but all she managed was a high-pitched whine, like the fearful appeal of a terrified kitten.

Suddenly she pushed herself explosively from her chair. For a moment I thought she was going to attack me, and got ready to head-butt her. Then I thought she was going to attack Laz, so I prepared to kick her. But she did neither. She flung herself to her knees in front of her lover and quietly begged forgiveness.

I was glad she asked Laz, not me. I was all forgiven out.

Laz didn't reply. She shrank back against the sofa, staring at the crown of Ayzel's head. Once she made to reach out and touch it, but hurriedly pulled away her hand at the last moment.

Ayzel lifted her head with painful slowness. She let out a breath which sounded like the fleeing ghost of torment, then turned to me. There was a sort of amused kindness in her eyes, alternating with bedrock despair.

'Now I know where I've met you before, Mr Panther,' she said.

This confused me. To the best of my recollection we had never met before. I had seen her image in the photo on the wall of Laz's office, that's all. Perhaps she had watched as I seeded her lover, all those months ago. Perhaps.

'Tell me,' I said.

The mea culpa commenced.

It came out in a quiet monotone. Not for this woman the pleas and justifications of panic. She faced her destruction with her eyes open and her voice calm. Perhaps she thought her actions justified in the eyes of the Lord. It would have been a waste of time to disabuse her.

It was a tawdry story.

Ayzel had become aware of Laz's infidelity some weeks before, it turned out. She had been told during another get-together at the pub by Siobhan, for whom, it seemed, informing was more a reflex than a matter of conscience. Gina had hardly turned out to be the soul of discretion when it came to bragging about her sexual adventures.

Ayzel had then considered her options. Her first priority, she decided, was to cement still further her relationship with Laz.

'I did it for love of you,' she said.

Laz snorted.

She desperately wanted the child Laz carried, and wanted the pair of them to raise it. Even the most assured among us, however, is prey to terrible doubts. In Ayzel's case, those doubts centred on two matters. First, she feared that because she was older, she might eventually lose her lover to someone young. The affair with Gina Compton seemed to be the realisation of those fears. Second, she had always felt alienated from Laz's past. Their respective lives had been so very different that she had never been able to empathise, much as she had tried. She had hoped that by encouraging Laz to tell her stories she might eventually come to understand. But smack addiction remained forever to her a foreign country, and with that sad realisation came the fear renewed that she would eventually lose the mother of her unborn child to a stranger who understood the language of that land.

She swore that she had really ever only intended to scare the wits out of Gina Compton. She had just wanted her to go away and leave her life alone, that was all.

She had decided to terrify her rival — as she saw her — by using the potent symbol of the barrier she felt to Laz's past: a syringe. Her reasoning, however, hadn't entertained the notion that an empty fit, used correctly, is every bit as frightening as a full one.

'I think that's the dirtiest I've ever felt in my life,' she whispered. 'I remembered what Lazarette had said, about the types of places heroin dealers might be found in, and about how they might whistle, or raise their eyebrows, or whisper 'chasing'. I remembered what to ask for, and not to flash my money about.

'I felt disgusting as I did it. I felt like I had covered myself in a moral filth so dark and viscous and tenacious that a lifetime of prayer would never lift the stain from my soul. I remember looking into those eyes and for a moment feeling that I was consorting with the most evil person in the world.'

'Wickedness proceedeth from the wicked,' I said.

'Samuel 24:13,' she replied, automatically. 'Do you remember me now, Mr Panther? Do you remember what I said as you handed me my purchase?'

I could feel Laz's eyes boring into the side of my face. I remembered nothing. There was still not a glimmer of familiarity in her look, and her story touched no memories.

This did not surprise me. I was probably drunk. Often I forget things. I forget people; I forget faces and places. I would forget myself if I could, believe me.

I didn't doubt her testimony, though. My love is available to the lowest and highest, the newborn and the dying, the high, the mighty, and the crippled in the markets. Whomever so desireth, let them ask and offer up votive, and I shall pour my gifts to their hands.

So Laz had been right that very first meeting when she confessed her fears. It *was* me who killed Gina Compton, after a fashion. I felt no guilt. What is done in my name, who dies by the hands of those who love me, these I cannot know. I will sell my love to the faithful and to strangers alike. Harm may result, but how could I do less? It is not within my power to deny.

'What did you say?' I asked Ayzel.

'I said, "May God forgive us both".'

'He didn't.'

She looked for a moment as if she were about to disagree, but then she looked down at the floor again. 'No,' she whispered, 'He didn't.'

Smack safely stashed and a syringe obtained from a pharmacy, she said, she had waited for an opportunity to put her plan into effect. It came with the arrangements for Gina's birthday. That morning, she had surreptitiously removed the key to the flat from Laz's ring. She had bet that while Laz and colleagues would go straight to the Court from the centre, birthday girl Gina would opt to pop home first and change. She was that kind of girl. Everybody said so.

Ayzel had left her work early, driven to the flat and let herself in. Her plan had been to scare the hell out of Gina by her presence, then scare her even more by waving around the loaded fit and threatening to use it if the younger woman didn't stay well away from Laz.

It was the wait, though, the half hour sitting in the flat with nothing to do but think, that soured the scheme.

'I decided the woman should address herself to God,' she said. 'I thought it might even help her, perhaps open her up to the power of salvation and love in Christ. She was a lost and reckless woman.' She gave a short, bitter laugh. 'I thought that in saving myself I might just be able to save her too, and maybe redeem the sins of violence and jealousy I was committing.'

So the unsuspecting Gina, full of girlish thoughts about a birthday piss-up, had swanned into her flat to be confronted by a tall imposing woman. The intruder had spoken calmly of her relationship with Lazarette Binary, and asked Gina to desist in the adulterous affair she knew she was having.

Gina had played the game wrong, then. Instead of agreeing and acting compliant, in order to encourage the trespasser to leave, she had come on all aggressive, demanding that Ayzel shut her mouth and get out immediately. She'd fuck whoever she wanted to fuck, she had said.

Ayzel had then produced the fit, shouted for a while, and held it under Gina's chin to frighten her. Whether she succeeded or not will never now be known. Ayzel had managed to scare herself, however. Suddenly she saw herself as everything she held herself not to be: violent, dominant, vicious, a brute. And she was struck with shame.

'I said, "Let's both ask the forgiveness of the Lord,"' she recalled. 'I was all fingers and thumbs. I didn't know what to do, what I was doing. I must have still had the syringe to her neck. With my other hand I tried to shove her down to her knees. She tried to stop me. I must have pushed again,

351

even harder. Suddenly her knees bent and she started to sink to the floor. I knelt with her, telling her it was all going to be all right now, that we were both going to be forgiven and shown how to lead lives pure and unblemished. Then I noticed her eyes were bulging out and her breathing was funny. I realised I had driven the syringe right into her, right into an artery or something. I'd pushed the plunger home without realising it. I prayed then, harder than I'd ever prayed before. Gina just kept toppling forwards, onto her knees first, then down, down onto her face.'

Then everything seemed to stop, as if time itself had halted. Ayzel had no idea for long she stayed kneeling and praying.

'But then the prayer just ... went. One moment I was praying, and the next I simply had my eyes shut, talking into a silence in my soul.'

'I know what you mean,' I said, softly.

After that, time sped up again and she became aware that she didn't have much of it to spare. The cold hard logic required for engineering replaced the fuzzy panic of the first-time killer. She found herself operating with a streamlined efficiency which would have appalled her had she witnessed it in someone else.

Gina's body was certainly limp, whether or not the final spark of life had already faded by that point. For a woman the size of Ayzel, it was a comparatively easy matter to gather her up in her arms and carry her down to where she'd parked her car. Then she drove to the heavy haulage depot attached to the engineering works, and let herself in to the hangar-sized vehicle and equipment storage shed. The hunting knife was in one of the staff lockers. She chose it, she said, precisely because it was the sort of huge and awful weapon she would never in a thousand lifetimes contemplate using. She drove it in, then left the body to drain, lying on the grate of a sludge pit.

'Twenty minutes later I arrived at the Court, about when I was expected,' she said. 'I rather impressed myself with how well I covered my fear and guilt that night.'

The usually teetotal Laz once more broke her own habit that night and had a couple of gins. This was partly a result of concern for the welfare of her absent and secret lover. Partly, too, it was because her awkward shape was causing sleepless nights and she damn well wanted to have a decent kip. The strategy worked.

Ayzel looked up at her now, and spoke softly. 'You didn't wake, my sweet, when I snuck out at about 3 am, nor when I returned and got back into bed next to you at 4.30.'

Laz looked revolted. 'You got back into bed and hugged me with hands which had just been touching Gina Compton's dead body.'

Ayzel shook her head, suddenly listless. 'And how often had you got into bed and hugged me with hands that had just been touching her living flesh, sweet?'

'That's not the same.'

'But is it any better?'

I tire of philosophical debate quickly. My work was almost done, two more lives almost destroyed. 'Why did you dump the body in the alley?'

Ayzel turned to look at me as if she'd forgotten there was anybody else in the room. Perhaps she had. She looked like she had to think about the answer.

'Because ... it was easy. It was a place I could back in the car and get her out of the boot without being seen.'

'Was I there?'

She shook her head. 'I was all alone with my conscience.'

Laz reached out in silence and took her hand. She held it not like a lover, but like a palliative care nurse.

'This has been terrible,' mumbled Ayzel. 'What I did was wrong. But I was beginning to think that what was worse still was that I was getting away with it.'

I stood up. 'You have.'

They both looked up at me, faces pulsing with ever changing paradoxical thoughts and emotions.

I laughed a mirthless laugh, then addressed Ayzel directly. 'You think I'm going to dob you in? What's the point of that? Right now the police are ninety per cent sure that Gina Compton was murdered by Clem Porter, himself tragically deceased, possibly by suicide. They have motive, means and opportunity. I doubt they'll look any further. Dead men don't mount defences.'

'Thank you,' she whispered.

'It's not an act of charity,' I replied. 'It's just not my business. Vengeance is not mine. I don't give a fuck about your future, and neither does your god. The only person who has control over you is the one holding your hand.'

Laz snatched her hand away at that, as if it was hot. 'Joe ...' she began.

'Bye, Laz,' I said, not looking at her face. 'One favour.'

'Don't leave town, Joe.'

'One favour.'

'What?'

'Don't call the kid Joshua. It's a bastard of a name to live with.'

Outside, I lit a cigarette and inhaled hard. Six drags and I was down to the filter. I lit another and made the clouds my chariot. I walked upon the wings of the wind.

EPILOGUE

When I got home, nobody was there.

I was glad.

The front window gleamed in the sunlight, the blinds behind it scrubbed white in the blood of the Lamb.

I packed clothes into my backpack, along with a few of the patristic paperbacks, Patti Smith, some smoke, some speed, and a big plastic lunchbox. Everything else I left behind. Casting aside possessions isn't a moral position for me. It's usually a simple necessity.

In a perfect world such actions would be noble sacrifice. But this is not a perfect world, so in my case they were just determined forerunners to as yet unspecified acts of theft.

I left no note. I never do.

Yula arrived just as I was closing the front door for the final time.

'It's all yours now,' I said. 'Supply and distribution. You'll find the names and numbers you need inside. Tell them the lord sent you.'

She looked radiant. Her mobile phone alone looked like it was worth more than everything I'd just abandoned. Or ever owned, come to that.

'Mrs Warburton's taken Nessie to the doctor about her leg,' she said, just in case I cared. 'There's a first time for everything, I guess. I owe you so much.'

'Not any more,' I replied. 'I grabbed the cash you stashed for me beneath the floorboards. Business must be good. From now it's yours completely.'

She blushed and play-punched me on the arm. 'That's not what I mean.'

Her mobile rang. With a brief twitch of irritation she pressed one of its buttons. 'They can leave a message.'

'Customers?'

'Applicants.'

It took a moment to think of a reply to that one. 'Meaning?'

She beamed. 'A recruitment drive, Joe. There's a limit to what Nessie and me can do in a day. We can only travel so far, carry so much. So I've been busy. I'm teaming up teenagers too young to get the dole with oldies left to rot, and sending them out to do business. I give them their own pitch, and they take a percentage of the sale price.'

'Impressive.' I meant it, too.

Yula giggled self-effacingly. 'Everybody wins. It's kind of like *Big Issue*, but not. If any of the teams do well enough, I'll let them buy their own franchise.'

I bowed to her, rehitching my backpack in the process. 'You're going be just fine, Yula.'

She accepted the compliment with modest embarrassment. 'You know, mate, only a few days ago I was a lost and stupid girl, a loser selling my body in the park for peanuts. I didn't have a future, Joe. I couldn't look forward to anything. But now that's all changed. Now — I *never* thought I'd hear myself saying this —

now I have a *goal*, I have a, what do they call it, a driving *ambition*.'

I stepped past her to the gate. 'And what is that ambition, Yula?'

Her smile was like the glory of the lord on the first day of creation. 'To be named in a Royal Commission.'

I laughed, which surprised me.

'Bless you,' I said. Then I walked away.

So here I am, on a bus in the desert.

The seat next to me is empty. All the others are full.

I think of you sometimes. I think of your patient suffering. I think of the anxieties that gnaw at you the moment your head rests against the pillow.

I see the dreams you don't remember, and I know why you don't recall them.

I could tell you, if you want.

I hear the bargains you make when you look at my image.

Best I don't respond, I think. Best for both of us.

My pockets are thick with Yula's cash contribution. I never took the cheque. It would have been pointless in the end. I don't know what Laz chose to do, but if she chose justice over security, the bank account would be cop-frozen by now.

Yet I am not without resources. My deal to facilitate Clem Porter's unnoticed disappearance included the combination to the Noble Street floor safe.

In my big plastic lunchbox I have about ten thousand tabs of ecstasy and a list of all the open air dance parties up the east coast. I'm going to be a hitch-hiking bum of a messiah for a while.

It's not the same as smack, but what the hell. I am famously syncretic. You know that. I adapt.

People still die.

I hear the young. I hear them calling for the light and the peace and the happiness of forgiveness and love.

I hear them.

And I am coming.

And I send them this message from the Lord: Have your money ready.

Where will I be when my son is born into too many secrets, his tiny hands already the cause of too much spilled blood?

Where will I be when the child, like an ulcer, weeps?

I don't know. Away somewhere. Moving mysteriously.

Out of earshot.

Thus has it ever been.

And thus do things reduce.